DAW BOOKS PROUDLY PRESENTS
THE SCIENCE FICTION NOVELS
OF W. MICHAEL GEAR:

The Donovan Series

Outpost

*Abandoned**

The Spider Trilogy

The Warriors of Spider

The Way of Spider

The Web of Spider

The Forbidden Borders Trilogy

Requiem for the Conqueror

Relic of Empire

Countermeasures

★

Starstrike

★

The Artifact

**Available November 2018 from DAW Books*

OUTPOST

DONOVAN: BOOK ONE

W. MICHAEL GEAR

DAW BOOKS, INC.
DONALD A. WOLLHEIM, FOUNDER
375 Hudson Street, New York, NY 10014
ELIZABETH R. WOLLHEIM
SHEILA E. GILBERT
PUBLISHERS
www.dawbooks.com

Jacket art by Steve Stone.

Jacket design by G-Force Design.

Book designed by Fine Design.

DAW Book Collectors No. 1779.

Published by DAW Books, Inc.
375 Hudson Street, New York, NY 10014.

First Printing, February 2018
1 2 3 4 5 6 7 8 9

PRINTED IN THE U.S.A.

TO DONALD A. WOLLHEIM, SHEILA GILBERT,
AND BETSY WOLLHEIM.

IN CELEBRATION OF THE THIRTY YEARS WE'VE
BEEN PUBLISHING TOGETHER.

ACKNOWLEDGMENTS

All novels are team efforts. The proposal for the Donovan series lay in a drawer for two decades. I have to thank my *New York Times*-bestselling wife, Kathleen O'Neal Gear, for her insistence that I take it out, dust it off, and finally submit it to a publisher. The Donovan books might only have my name on the cover, but Kathleen's influence is all over the series. As always, she is my heartbeat, my soul, and the center of my universe.

My thanks, also, to Sheila Gilbert and Betsy Wollheim. As this is written we have just passed the 30th anniversary of the publication of *The Warriors of Spider*, my first DAW novel. And through all those long years we've enjoyed a lasting and wonderful friendship.

Sheila, thanks for the perceptive comments on the *Outpost* manuscript. Here's to the next thirty years. May they be as wonderful.

And, finally, to all the fine folks at DAW who helped bring this book to life. Supper's on me next time we're in the city. Thanks, to you all.

1

A strange mythology has grown about morning; it has sent its roots to twine inextricable rhizomes through the human psyche. Like all mythology, it is mostly falsehood. According to the myth, with the rising of the sun hope is kindled in the human spirit. The body rises refreshed, vigorous. The brain is audacious. Keen again. The profound and dark despair of the predawn soul has been vanquished by those golden bars of light which bathe a reborn world . . . or so the myth would claim.

Morning has another and more pragmatic reputation: the time of attack, of unexpected death intruding rudely and impudently into dawn's domain. In contrast, that ancient reality is all the more gruesome. It is said among observers—at least among those of a sensitive nature—that the horrible irony and tragedy of dying at first light is reflected in the expressions of the newly dead. Only then has the mythology played its final deception.

—Shig Mosadek, Donovan Port Authority, 2153

An exhausted Talina Perez watched the sunrise on Donovan. They still called it sunrise, even if the "sun" was officially named Capella and lay some thirty light-years from Earth. This particular morning began as a brilliant spear of light behind the craggy black silhouette of the Blood Mountains. Donovan rotated in the same direction as Earth, so sunrise was still in the east.

Aching with fatigue and possessed of a pervading sense of futility, Talina would have preferred to be back at Port Authority. She would have awakened this morning, rested and energized from a full night's sleep. Instead she stank of sweat, her feet and legs spotted with dried mud, her overalls filthy and smudged. Her skin stung from thorn punctures that she hadn't been able to avoid in the darkness.

As the first light spilled through the distant gap, she desperately wanted to believe the morning myth, to lower her guard and yawn. Maybe let her mind wander.

Except that she'd seen too many sunrises play across the rictus on a freshly dead man's face.

Donovan did that, destroyed illusion with brutal regularity.

As the dawn brightened, its light softened the angles and contours of the canyon—sifted shadow and form from the darkness.

She crouched on a precarious trail, body tense, the heavy rifle tightly gripped in her slim and tanned fingers. Her dark eyes shifted constantly, desperately searching the shadows. The charge was almost depleted in her thermal scope. Overhead, two of the drones scoured the canyon sides, the hiss of their fans barely audible.

Capella's first rays caressed her face, warming her high cheeks and straight nose as they gave a golden cast to her bronzed skin. They illuminated her ancestral features of Spanish hidalgo mixed with classic Maya. Descended from sun gods and conquistadors, their spirit flashed in her sable eyes as she stalked the wild and rocky trails of another world.

Talina Perez hunted a killer.

She pursed her full lips and brushed back a strand of black hair where it had come loose from her long braid. Hair that adopted a bluish raven tint in the full morning light.

Warm air drifted down the canyon, carrying the odor of dry dirt and the cloying scent of musk bushes. The silence seemed to intensify as Capella's light accented the parched surface of cracked and tumbled stone with pale lavender; high above, it bathed the shredded cirrus clouds in purple and orange streaks where they stretched across the northern sky.

Invertebrates whizzed and chirred in the tangles of brush beneath the sandstone outcrops. To her right the canyon dropped away to a stone-and-sand-choked streambed some twenty meters below.

She swallowed nervously and snugged the rifle butt into her shoulder. Her gaze searched the cap rock above for any irregularity. Then she turned her attention to the narrowing gap where the trail climbed the canyon wall and emptied out onto the flat tableland above. Dotted with aquajade trees and ferngrass, the plain extended to the distant Wind Mountains where they rose some twenty kilometers beyond.

"Where the hell are you?" she whispered.

She tried to still her pounding heart in order to hear even the faintest sound. Changing her focus, she gave careful scrutiny to the ground, looking for scuffed soil, a displaced rock, a broken thorn, or a bruised leaf on one of the plants.

Because of a dead battery in a motion sensor, the quetzal had come undetected in the night, crossed the defensive ditch, unhooked the gate latch, and slipped into town. That was the thing about quetzals, they were intelligent. Learned from their mistakes. This one obviously had previous experience with humans and knew the defenses. After the creature made its kill, it had known how to escape, charging headlong for the uplands. That was another thing about quetzals: for short distances they could run faster than an aircar.

The planet hosted an endless variety of different and deadly beasts. Bems, though solitary and slow, relied on extraordinary camouflage and deadly claws to capture prey. The creature they called the nightmare inhabited the tropical jungle stretches just south of Port Authority. Also a master of camouflage, it mimicked the surrounding vegetation and invoked a special kind of horror: it first impaled and then devoured victims from the inside out. Fortunately nightmares almost exclusively lurked in mundo trees down south. Smaller threats like the slugs, spikes, and semisentient stinging, poisonous, and predatory plants filled out most of the rest of the *known* dangerous flora and fauna.

"Talina? You on the trail?" Allenovich's voice came through her earpiece.

She shifted her rifle, eyes still on the thornbushes as they rotated their branches to expose night-weary leaves to the rising sun. "I'm maybe three hundred meters from the head of the canyon."

"*Still got tracks?"*

Talina filled her lungs, hating the way her heart was hammering at her breastbone. "No. They vanished about fifty meters back."

"*Shit."* A pause. *"You watch your ass."*

"Yeah," she whispered and wished for a drink of water.

"Trish here. I'm on the rim just across the canyon from you, Tal. Iji says the drones are reporting that nothing broke out onto the flat up ahead. It'll take a while to recall them. I'm scanning the canyon with the IR. With the morning sun, that slope you're on is a patchwork of heat signatures. You sure it's there?"

"Yep." She swallowed hard, the rifle up, her pulse racing. "I can almost . . ."

A trickle of dirt broke loose to cascade from above.

Talina dropped to one knee, the rifle lifted for a snap shot as she stared through the optic.

What?

Where?

The buzzing of the invertebrates changed; the chime shifted as if a whole section of them had gone quiet. Odd, that.

A pebble clicked and bounced down through the rocks and into the scrubby thorn brush above. Quetzal? Or just the morning sun expanding the eroded soil?

Damn, I hate this!

Her muscles remained bunched like knotted wire. Something about the invertebrates . . .

"Trish?" she barely whispered. "See anything above me?"

Why the hell couldn't humans have eyes in the backs of their heads?

The morning air had grown heavy, oppressive.

"Can't make out anything definitive, Tal. Be damned careful. We don't want to bury you, too."

"Affirmative on that."

The quetzal had prowled the town, tracks indicating where it had avoided adults—aware of their weapons—and skirted the lighted areas. Sticking to the shadows and back ways, it had made its way to the personal quarters, stopping only long enough to peer into the domes and try the doors.

At Allison Chomko's it had found safe prey, had watched her leave her house on an errand. Then the creature had raised the unlocked latch before entering to make its kill. It had escaped, gone before anyone knew.

A running quetzal made an incredible sight with its flared collar membranes spread for thermal regulation. Its mouth gaped wide to expose serrated jaws, which acted as a sort of ram-air intake. Pushed into three separate lungs, oxygen supercharged the blood. As air was channeled through the body core, it picked up heat and was exhaled, or vented, above the powerful legs and along the tail. All six meters of the animal would turn blaze-white for better radiation. A quetzal running in panic across flat terrain could hit one hundred and sixty kph for short periods of time.

But it came at an incredible cost in energy; and here, in the canyon, it had gone to ground. By now it would have digested the infant girl it had taken from Allison Chomko's cradle. Before it could run again, it had to eat, to replace those depleted resources.

Talina could sense the quetzal's hunger, sense the creature's three shining black eyes as they studied her. As if the gaze were somehow radiant.

The invertebrates began another chime—like a mutual wave of sound that passed from critter to critter. Talina was barely aware as it rolled slowly up from the canyon's mouth.

The fine hair on the nape of her neck rose.

How can a creature that big turn invisible?

But that was the way of so many of Donovan's creatures: masters of camouflage, all of them.

Arguments raged in Inga's tavern. Were quetzals—in their way—as smart as humans? They hunted with uncanny ability, manipulated locks, doors, and tools—but made none of their own. Here, in the canyon, the predator's cunning permeated the very air. A metaphysical odor borne on the currents of the soul.

One small slip, Talina. That's all it takes. Stay crisp—or you'll die here.

Talina took another step, senses at high pitch. People had stepped on quetzals before, oblivious to their presence until that shift of slippery flesh beneath a misplaced foot. For their part, the creatures had learned that a human could be efficiently eliminated by a strike to the head, chest, or neck. All it took was a pistonlike blow from one of their clawed, three-toed feet.

Nerve sweat trickled down Talina's cheek. Capella was a full hand-width above the horizon now, its heat beginning to radiate on the canyon wall. The chirring of the invertebrates swelled, covering any sound—as if the "bugs" were cheering the quetzal on.

Let it go! Just back away!

But she couldn't. This one was too cunning a killer. It would be back. Smarter. Faster. More deadly.

The air pulsed with chime, beating a rhythm that was echoed by the land. Thorncactus reached out with a tentative branch, its spines scratching along her boot's protective leather.

Talina flinched, wheeled, rifle up as she stared at the trail behind her. Empty.

If the thing would just move, the drones would detect it, give her that moment of warning. But for the drones they'd never have tracked the beast this far.

Another swelling of sound rolled up the canyon as the invertebrates song-shared. The chime passed her, heading for the head of the canyon.

Yes! There! A break in the wall of sound—a dead spot of uncharacteristic silence just off to the left—slightly above the trail and not more than ten paces away.

She fixed on it, lowered her cheek to the stock and squinted through the optic. The soil began to flow. A plant seemed to thin, as if reality had turned sideways. A shadow formed in dislodged dirt. Three black eyes emerged from behind mottled, soil-toned lids.

The moment their gazes fixed, they might have shared souls, touched each other's deadly essences.

Talina shot as the quetzal leaped. Explosive-tipped bullets ripped into the rock and brush that surrounded the three eyes that seemed to rise before her.

She reeled back. Lost her footing and hit hard on the uneven stones. Somehow she kept her hold on the rifle, brought it up.

The quetzal's camouflaged colors darkened as the creature landed, bunched, and launched itself.

Talina had a momentary image of its wide mouth, the wickedly serrated teeth. Then it blocked the sky as it hurtled toward her.

She was screaming as she held the trigger back. The rifle thundered as she kicked sideways, flung herself downhill off the trail. The quetzal slammed hard feet into the spot where she'd been, one claw cutting her sleeve.

The world spun as Talina tumbled down the slope, tore through the vegetation, bounced off rocks. She slammed onto a weather-rotten outcrop; sandstone crumbled under her weight. The side of her head hit a rock. Lightning and pain blasted through her skull. Her body bounced, landed on loose scree, slid, and broke through a young aquajade tree.

Suddenly she was weightless, falling. The creek bottom stopped her cold, the impact smacked both breath and sense out of her.

Stunned, vision blurred, she came to. Shocked nerves jangled in her limbs. Synapses overloaded and screamed. She tried to move—and gasped. Pain, like fire, burned through her body.

What the hell? Where am I? What the fuck happened?

Accident.

Yes, I know this feeling.

The distant bang of a rifle bored past the ringing in her ears.

Who's shooting?

Panic caused her to reach out, slap a torn and bleeding hand on a large rock. She was in a canyon bottom.

An image burst into her stumbling brain: *quetzal. Baby killer.*

"Hunting me," she whispered as she reached up to wipe at her eyes—and couldn't, given the long thorns sticking out of her hand.

Dirt and rocks came cascading from somewhere above. A bullet exploded on stone, followed by the crack of a rifle.

Trish!

Talina whimpered as she pulled herself upright and struggled to see through her swimming eyes. Branches snapped above. Pretty clumsy work on the quetzal's part.

Clumsy? Why?

Another bullet popped as it exploded above the cut bank no more than three meters above her.

Talina tried to stand. The numb burning in her leg changed to a white-hot and searing pain that speared through her fumbling brain. She managed to focus on her oddly twisted leg. *Broken!*

The quetzal slipped sideways above her as another of Trish's bullets exploded in the dirt where the creature had been but an instant before. Then it dropped over the edge, feet thudding into the streambed a couple of meters from Talina's boots.

The quetzal gleamed, skin shining, reflecting streaks of black and yellow with the legs mottling into blackened umber on those deadly three-toed feet. Behind the creature's elongated head, the neck expanded; the flaring collar burst into crimson glory.

Talina's hand—heedless of the thorns—slapped for her holstered pistol. To her horror, the holster was empty, the pistol lost during the tumble down the slope.

The quetzal fixed her with its three black and gleaming eyes. The beast wobbled as if hurt. Took a step, then another.

The quetzal uttered an eerie moan as it raised itself sluggishly. Less than a meter separated her from the three vitreous eyes. The creature blasted out a trilling whistle mixed with a hiss of rage. Crystal drops of moisture caught the light in diamond sparkles where they beaded on the razor-ranks of teeth.

"So, you're taking as many with you as you can," Talina told it, dazzled by the glow behind those angry eyes. And in that instant, she could sense the alien intelligence behind that stare.

"Not that I blame you."

The quetzal replied with a clicking down in its iridescent throat, as if in agreement.

Why the hell hadn't Trish taken the final shot? What was keeping . . . Of course, this far down into the narrow-walled canyon, Trish didn't have a shot. Couldn't see the target.

"Sorry, pal." Talina granted the beast a weary smile. Blood was running down the side of her head.

The beast kept wobbling on its feet, mortally wounded. Gaze still fixed on hers, it tilted its head, as though in an effort to understand. It gestured with one of the wickedly clawed forefeet, as if demanding something of her. She could almost feel the bottled emotion as the beast whipped its tongue out between the elongated jaws.

She screamed as it made one final leap.

2

Dirt and rocks exploded under Trish Monagan's heels as she sought to slow her frantic descent down the rocky slope. Each time she leaped she tried to land on the shadowed side of the thorncactus, knowing that the vicious spines would be pointed toward the morning sun. Moving fast like she was, the plants didn't have time to swing their spines in her direction.

Talina was down there with a quetzal, just out of sight over the lip of the drainage. And, damn it, Trish worshipped that woman. She would do anything for Talina.

The moment the beast had leaped down out of sight, Trish had launched herself, calling, "Step! Talina's down!"

"Yeah, I saw. On the way!"

Talina Perez was a living legend. A woman tougher than duraplast tempered with ceramic, a hard-fisted, undaunted, scrapping survivor.

Please, God, tell me she's all right.

What if Trish crested that lip to find Talina halfway down a quetzal's throat? What then?

"Kill the fart-sucking quetzal!" she growled, using her rifle for balance as she skipped sideways and back-heeled down a loose fan of colluvium. She dared to slap the trunk of an aquajade tree to keep upright, then leaped from a crumbling sandstone outcrop. Knees bent to take the impact, she slowed, hopped from boulder to boulder, and, as the ground leveled, charged forward at a run. The tremolo of the invertebrates went silent as she passed. The thorncactus and claw shrubs began keening from broken branches in the wake of her passage.

On trembling legs, Trish dashed up to the lip of the drainage, flipped her auburn hair out of the way, and looked over.

For a couple of heartbeats it didn't register. The quetzal lay curled in the narrow confines of the streambed, its hide glowing all the colors of the rainbow. More actually—but the human eye couldn't see the infrared and ultraviolet.

A broken Talina Perez lay tucked inside the quetzal's protective curve, unmoving and cuddled as if she were a precious infant. Blood covered Tal's face and matted in her hair. Her left leg stuck out at an incongruous angle. Worse, the quetzal's wedge-like head lay against Talina's, its blood mingling with hers, the creature's tongue against Talina's lips. The three eyes seemingly had fixed on Talina's.

"Ah, shit," Trish whispered, her heart suddenly leaden in her breast.

"What's up?" Iji asked through her com system.

"It's Talina!" Trish dropped to her knee and raised her rifle, trying to stabilize it as she panted for breath. Through the optic she studied the quetzal's head, wondering if the thing were still alive. As close as its massive head was to Talina's, she didn't dare use an explosive round.

Pressing the magazine blocking lever, she cycled the bolt and ejected the explosive-tipped round. From her belt, she fished out an armor-piercing cartridge. Slipping it into the chamber, she slapped the bolt home before sighting through the optic.

As the dot fixed on the beast's neck just behind the head, Trish shot, saw the creature's head jerk at the impact.

Dead all right.

"Oh, Tal," she muttered as she stood, made her way to a break in the steep gully side, and slid her way down to the streambed.

She approached, rifle up, her finger hovering over the trigger. A person just didn't take chances with quetzals.

Trish could see the quetzal's torn flesh—the broken bone and shattered cerebral tissue. It still took all of her courage to step over the creature's tail, straddle the thick body, and kick the tongue away from Talina's mouth. Only then did she reach down for Talina's torn hand.

"Talina?"

No response.

Switching her grip to the woman's wrist, a strong pulse beat there.

"She's alive! We need to medevac!"

"We'll have the aircar there in minutes," Stepan replied.

It took all of Trish's strength to pull Talina free of the dead quetzal's coils and ease her over the creature's corpse—especially given Talina's broken leg. Kicking some rocks out of the way, Trish laid her out on the sandy streambed and began checking her vitals. Respiration slow but steady. From her belt pack, Trish took a gauze pad and wiped away as much of the combined blood and gore as she could, then used a quick tie to put pressure on Tal's bleeding head wound.

The sound of rolling rock and cascading sand above made her reach for her rifle. Then Iji appeared on the terrace lip.

"How is she?"

"Unconscious. Took a blow to the head. Broken leg."

"Be right down, Trish."

Iji began working his way down the drainage in search of an easier means of descent.

Trish turned her attention to splinting Talina's leg, finding two rather cumbersome pieces of jadewood and using the last of her quick ties.

She was pulling thorns out of Talina's hand when the woman gasped and blinked her eyes open. For a moment they stared—wide and disoriented. Struggled to focus, and finally fixed. "Trish?"

"Glad to see that you're back with the living. Stepan's called for the aircar. It's picking up the drones. We'll get you out of here."

"But I was . . ." Talina clamped her eyes shut for a moment. "The quetzal and I . . ." She swallowed hard.

"What?" Trish propped her elbows on her knees.

Talina shook her head. "Man, that can't be. It's like I was inside its mind. Seeing myself. Weird. Like it admired me."

"Hey, you took a pretty good knock to the head."

Talina's uneasy gaze fixed on the quetzal. "No. All this happened at the end. Like we were dying together. And then . . . and then I was in its head when it exploded." Talina shivered. "That was really rude, let me tell you."

Trish lifted a skeptical eyebrow. Concussion. Had to be. Raya would know what to do. Probably meant that Talina wasn't getting out of the clinic for a while.

"How we doing?" Iji called as he came trotting up the rocky streambed, his rifle at the ready.

"She's conscious. Broken leg."

"Broken leg?" Talina asked, shifted, only to cry out and stare at her splinted leg. "Shit! There's three weeks in Raya's damn hospital while I chew up Cheng's homemade aspirin like it was candy."

"Who knows? Maybe the supply ship will finally show up with a load of real med."

"Yeah, Trish. Dream on."

The whirr of the aircar descended, dust billowing out as it landed on the terrace flat above. Trish slitted her eyes, bending over Talina to shield her from the deluge of falling grit.

"How we going to get her out of here?" Iji scanned the steep sides of the drainage.

"Rig a pelvic sling," Talina told him. "Clip it to my belt. Tie that off to a rope and attach the rope to the cargo hook on the aircar's bottom. Step lifts me straight out of here. Flies out of the canyon, where he hopefully lowers me *gently* to the ground. I can crawl inside for the trip back."

"That's going to hurt like . . . like . . ."

"Yeah. Um . . . There's probably no words to describe it, huh?" Talina gave him her old evil grin. "Beats spending the rest of my life down here with a rotting quetzal, don't you think? And saves you and Trish the onerous job of packing me out of here on a litter."

"That's my tough lady," Trish said admiringly.

Talina was staring thoughtfully at the quetzal. "Came pretty damn close, didn't you?"

The quetzal's eyes had begun to gray where they peered out of the shattered skull.

From above, Stepan called out, "Talina? You all right?"

"Nothing thirty hours of sleep and a shot of Inga's whiskey won't cure."

A wry humor filled his voice. "Well, if you can survive that stomach rot, you can survive any old quetzal. What happened? Trish lost her touch? Thought she could shoot a fly off a wall at twenty klicks?"

"She tagged it a couple of times. So did I. Just didn't put it down."

Iji was inspecting the quetzal. "I can see eight hits. Might be the bullets going bad. Impact primers deteriorate with age. God knows how old that stuff was *before* The Corporation got their hands on it.

And you know they bought it at bottom dollar. Figure another year in storage, then two years to get it here. And it's been what? Six years since the last supply ship? Hell, yeah. The damn ammo's going bad."

He pulled his long knife from its sheath and waggled the blade for emphasis. "What do you want to bet that if they ever do send another supply ship, there's no ammunition on it?"

"And if there is"—Trish laughed bitterly—"want to bet it won't chamber in our guns?"

Talina—eyes glazed with pain—used the falsetto voice that everyone on Donovan attributed to The Corporation: "Ammunition? What on Earth would you possibly need ammunition for? It's not like you're at war. We cannot process silly, frivolous, and spurious requests. We have shipping limitations. Profit margins. Every kilo of cargo must be absolutely necessary for the long-term success of the Donovan project."

"One more fucking thing we've got to figure out." Trish muttered to herself as she caught the pelvic sling Allenovich tossed down from the aircar. "Now we're going to have to see if we can't suss out how to make our own ammo."

Talina made a pained face, breath catching as if something really hurt, and managed to say, "They can damn well come here and see how long they can last without ammunition." A pause. "Of course there's no guarantee that a quetzal would stoop to eating something as slimy as a Corporation Boardmember." She shot a peculiarly thoughtful look at the dead quetzal. "Quetzals have pride, you know."

Trish studied her as she knotted the rope on the pelvic sling ring. *What the hell are you talking about, Talina? They're fucking beasts!*

"Wonder what the chemistry is for the explosive?" Iji asked himself as he dragged the quetzal's tail straight and began slitting his way up the ventral hide. Rainbows of color spread out like a wake as the knife sliced through the skin.

"Cheng will know." Trish gave the rope a hard tug, ensuring that Stepan had tied it off securely. "The supply ship's six years overdue. Sometimes I forget there's any place in the universe besides Donovan. Like all the talk of Earth, Transluna, and Mars . . . well, they're dreams, you know? Fantasies that never really were."

"Yeah." Iji looked up from where he sliced open the belly, his round face thoughtful beneath his mop of black shaggy hair. "I've heard more than one person say that we're all that's left. That something happened back on Earth. Some disaster. No more ships. Ever. We're it. The last of humankind."

Trish shaded her eyes. Capella's harsh light beat down on the yellow-bedded cap rock above the sloping canyon walls. The scrubby aquajade trees gleamed like turquoise dewdrops, the thorncactus and varieties of what they called sucking scrub were now verdant green as their photosynthesis kicked into high gear. One thing a person couldn't deny about Donovan: It was always colorful.

This was Trish's world. Her parents had arrived with the second ship. She'd been born here nineteen Donovanian years ago, making her first generation. Solar System? It was an abstract. A place she'd never seen.

"You're talking bullshit, Iji." Talina gritted the words through pain-clamped jaws. "Travel's risky. Maybe they finally found out what makes ships fail and disappear. Maybe, until they fix the symmetry inversion, no one will take the chance to space for someplace as far away as Donovan. Lose too many ships and those chickenshit assholes will write off the whole colony—and everyone here—as a bad investment."

Iji used his shoulder to prop up one of the powerful back legs as he slit the hide beneath. He might have been working with a blanket of liquid iridescent color as the tiny scales caught and refracted the light in laser-rich brilliance.

He said, "We're the settlement farthest out. I've read my history as well as my botany texts. The far frontier is the hardest place to hold. The easiest to forget."

"They'll be back," Trish promised. Not because she believed it, but for Talina's sake. The woman's head had dropped onto her chest, eyes clamped shut, breathing labored.

Trish had been six when her geologist father had vanished in the forests to the south. She'd been twelve when a gotcha vine killed her botanist mother. Talina had sort of taken Trish under her wing. Treated her more like a younger sister than an orphan. Saw her through all the shit a teenage girl could get into. Not that there was much to get into in Port Authority. And Trish came from a small circle of friends. A grand total of five who'd been in that initial first generation. Made her a sort of snob. Two boys, two other girls, they'd married, already had kids of their own on the way.

I always was the odd one out.

Iji peeled the hide back, running his knife through the connective tissue and nerve fibers to expose the curious arrangement of gray-blue guts that packed the chest cavity like swollen bladders. Swinging the heavy knife like a sword, Iji chopped through the quetzal's equivalent of ribs—though they weren't bones in the Earthly sense. These were a polymer compound instead of terrestrial calcium and collagen.

The biology on Donovan was fundamentally different from that on Earth, but the colonists used the old terms for the analogous lifeforms and structures. Cutting the slab of tissue free, Iji set it aside, exposing one of the three elongated lungs and the interlaced, kidney-red energy net—a weblike organ that stored oxygen then mixed it with hydrocarbons to provide the chemical energy that enabled a quetzal's tremendous bursts of speed.

"He was used up," Iji noted, pointing his blade at the depleted organ. Whereas Trish had seen the strands so swollen and engorged they almost filled the gut, the strands here were more like fishnet.

With a flourish, Iji sliced out the section, carefully cut out a bulge in the light brown digestive pouch, and lifted it out.

Laying it on the sandy gravel, he hesitated, then slit the organ carefully down its length. Digestive juices dribbled out as he pulled the "stomach" open with the knife tip. A few bits of acid-eroded bone—no longer recognizable as human—were all that remained of Allison Chomko's baby girl. Something, at least, for Allison to bury.

Trish bent down, grunting as she lifted Talina's weight in order to slide the pelvic sling under her hips. Then she drew the strap between the woman's legs. She was buckling the belt when she glanced up. "Talina? You're as white a Corporation lawyer's ass. You look like you're about to . . ."

Talina's eyes flickered as they lost focus; her head lolled loosely forward, and she slumped on the sand.

"Shit!"

"What's wrong?" Stepan called from above.

"Talina's out. Cold. Maybe she's hurt worse than we think." As she spoke, she was tying a loop in the rope. "Step! We're going! Now!"

"What about Iji?"

Looking up from the quetzal, Iji gestured with the knife. "Get her out of here. I've got my weapons along with Talina's rifle and pistol. Just you damn well be back to get me and this hide before dark. Big hide like this? It's worth a fortune."

"But leaving you—"

"Go!" Iji bellowed. "Hell, if luck smiles, I'll have *two* quetzals skinned by the time you get back!"

Trish keyed her throat mic. "Step, I mean it. Talina's not doing well. I've got a loop for my foot, and I can keep a grip on the rope and make sure Tal doesn't fall out of the harness. Now fly our asses out of here! She's not dying on my watch. That's an order."

"Yeah, yeah. But I don't like it." Step called down before he vanished back toward the aircar.

"Iji! You stay damned frosty, you hear me? I'll have Step on his way back for you the moment we're offloaded at hospital."

Iji was grinning, hiding what was obviously worry. No one liked being left alone on Donovan. Especially with a freshly dead quetzal corpse to draw every predator in the countryside down on top of him.

As the aircar spun up, dirt, grit, sand, and small gravel blew out over the gully's edge in a blinding shower.

It took all of Trish's might to get an arm around Talina's shoulder. The slack went out of the rope, almost jerking her loose. Holding on for dear life, she felt herself lift. The loop tightened painfully around her foot as it took her full weight.

"Careful, Step!" she bellowed in the downdraft as she and Talina swung against the rock-filled side of the drainage.

Then they were up, rising, the narrow drainage bottom dropping away as Step sought altitude.

Panting, scared half out of her wits, Trish kept a death grip on the rope—why the hell hadn't she taken time to put on gloves? Her other arm hugged Talina's limp body to her.

The Corporation left us here. Soft-coddled bastards never know what it means to fight. To bury the few bits of bone that remain from your only child. Or your lover.

Heart hammering with fear, she kept her eyes closed, ignoring the pain where the loop cut into her foot and where the rope was eating the skin off the palm of her hand.

3

Images drifted through Talina's imagination. Ill-formed and misty.

Dirt, gritty and clinging, coated her hands as she stood in the open grave. She had insisted that she be the one—along with Stepan—who reached over and got a grip on Mitch's shroud. Stiff and resisting, the canvas fought her as she tried to wrap her fingers around it and get a grip. The way Talina lived it was as fresh as yesterday.

Her gut tightened as she strained, half dragged Mitch's corpse from where it rested at the lip of the grave. He was so cold. Limp. His body sagged as she took his weight and lowered it to the red soil on the bottom of the grave. For a moment she just stood there, his shrouded head between her feet.

Is that all there is? The end of love? The end of life?

Dully, she'd become aware of the voices asking if she were all right.

Hell no.

But some inner strength had caused her to bite off her grief, to reach up and take the offered hand. To help them as they pulled her from the grave. Then she had glanced up at Donovan's memorial at the top of the cemetery. After a second spent staring at the stone monument, Talina stepped over and laid hands on the shovel; she'd driven the blade into the loose dirt. Shoulders working, breath coming in gasps, she'd tossed the rocky soil onto Mitch's corpse.

"I buried my lover. Not like a nice sanitized funeral back home. Here *we* have to shovel the dirt ourselves." Her voice seemed to echo in the curious stillness, and then fade slowly into nothing.

She blinked, coming awake. It took a moment for her vision to clear. Her throat was dry, her body aching. As her focus returned, she stared up at a ceiling. To either side the medical equipment blinked at her in an old and familiar way.

She filled her lungs. Started to exhale a hiss. And caught herself.

Hiss?

What kind of insanity was that?

Talina forced her brain to concentrate. "Hospital. I'm in hospital. What the hell happened this time?"

She ordered her thoughts, remembering the quetzal. How it had attacked, her tumble down the steep slope. Staring into the beast's eyes as if sharing its soul . . .

Did the damn things even *have* souls?

"God, I'm messed up," she whispered to herself, images of burying Mitch once again spinning up from her memory. Was that cold corpse really the same warm man she'd cherished? The lover whose eyes she'd stared into? Laughed with? Who'd held her as she cried? Shared her longings and dreams? That she'd wrapped herself around as he shuddered in orgasm? The man she had tried to press into her very soul?

The man I couldn't save.

It would have been so simple back in Solar System.

She imagined a Boardmember, resplendent in his silk suit. The genuine article, not a synthetic. A smiling man, clean-shaven, with white and perfect teeth. His hands were pale, soft, perfectly manicured, the skin thin and translucent. Without scars or calluses. Perfect health—monitored by the finest physicians—could be seen in his stride, in his perfectly proportioned body with its interactive genetic and metabolic feedback in constant balance. She could see his dissociated smile as Corporate data rolled through his implants, scrolling the abstract mathematics of profit and loss through his brain.

That suit that would have been worth five rifles and eight thousand rounds of ammunition. A day's salary enough to have paid for an electric fence and enough parts to keep it from failing. A week's earnings enough to have supplied the entire perimeter of Port Authority with motion detectors.

In her imagination he gave her a helpless look—eyes impotent and tender—and shrugged slightly. With a wistful smile he lifted his delicate, almost translucent hands, spreading them in apology.

And we have to depend upon the likes of him?

"People are dying here. Dying to make money for you assholes." Her voice rasped, as if from disuse.

It took no effort to remember Mitch's face as they sewed canvas around it. How his slack features disappeared with each stitch.

If I'd only had an ampoule of megacillin I could have saved him.

Dead. For lack of an inexpensive mass-produced antibiotic that no one had deemed worthy of sending to far-off Donovan, despite its continued requisition.

When she looked up through unfocused eyes, the ceiling shimmered in rainbow patterns. A slight ache tightened in the back of her eyeballs. A quetzal ceiling. As if the creature . . . The shimmering faded, and it seemed as though a thousand stars rained from the sky. As though her body were falling through space, weightless and eternal.

What the . . . ?

It hit her that she remembered the stories. The ones her mother had told when she gave lectures on the ancient Maya. About how the shamans of her people could change into spirit beasts. How the souls of animals could possess them. One of her great aunts—who some called a *bruja*—had claimed she could turn herself into a giant snake.

It wasn't coincidence that the first explorers had named the quetzals after the Mayan rainbow-skinned feathered serpent that flew through the night sky and breathed out the spiritual essence of Creation.

Something seemed to move deep inside her, down under her heart and diaphragm. An alien presence that left her frightened and slightly nauseous.

Talina, get a grip on yourself.

A tingle of fear ran through her.

She wondered which of them had actually died that day in the canyon. Talina chuckled dryly. No doubt there were worse forms of madness.

Didn't matter. If a supply ship from Earth didn't arrive, quetzals would wander unhindered through the ruins of Port Authority, perhaps wondering if humans had ever been real, or were just a dream.

4

According to Trish Monagan's bedside clock it was just after three in the morning when Shig's call had roused her from a deep sleep. She had been dreaming of whipped cream, having had a taste of the delicacy when she was a girl. That had been before the last of the cattle had died.

What an odd thing to dream, but the taste had been so clear: thick, sweet, and remarkably rich on the tongue.

She groaned, climbed out of her bed, and pulled on her jumpsuit. Didn't even bother with the light as she belted on her pistol and equipment belt. She stumbled out of her dome and into the night, limping slightly. Her foot still hurt from where the sling had bruised it.

In an effort to clear the cobwebs from her sleep-addled brain, she rolled her shoulders and pressed her palms together with all of her might, stimulating her arm muscles and pectorals.

God, her eyes felt like someone had packed sand into them. She rubbed them with a hard knuckle and yawned as she arrived at the administration dome.

Passing through a section where the light panels were out in the main corridor, she opened the Control Room door and stepped inside.

"Yeah, what's up?"

Shig Mosadek and Yvette Dushane sat with their asses propped on the cluttered work table in the center of the room. "Two Spots" Smith sat in the improvised chair behind the radio. The holo monitors in the work stations to his left were dark.

Only one worked as it was, and that was the one that communicated with the mine office three klicks to the north. Mellie Nagargina—who monitored the mine—wouldn't be in to turn it on until eight in the morning. Unlike Trish and the rest, she was home in bed with her husband and four kids.

Shig turned as she strode in. He stood five foot three, a small man who had a shock of inky hair that sprouted from his round head. The burnt tones of his skin had blackened under the influence of Capella's rays. When he looked at a person the ebony pools of his eyes seemed detached, pensive. His pug nose might have been mashed onto his face as an afterthought. The broad set of his mouth suggested a mild disposition that refused to ruffle. She'd rarely seen his expression change. Not even the time he'd executed Tambuko for rape.

"Ship's coming in." Shig said it so casually, as if it were just another routine matter.

"No shit?" Trish asked, wondering if it could be true.

"Trish, there are times your eloquence leaves me in awe. And yes, a ship's out there at last."

A curious wave of relief washed through her: Joy mixed with apprehension. "'Bout clap-trapping time," Trish said with a sigh. "Where the hell have they been?"

Yvette Dushane sat with the right cheek of her rump planted on the table, her long leg swinging. Though her arms were crossed, she held a cup of steaming tea in her right hand. Given the disheveled look of her thick mane of graying ash-blonde hair, she, too, had just been hauled out of the sack.

She fixed Trish with her hard green eyes. "It's called the *Turalon*. We are waiting out the communications lag. It's still a little more than twenty-five minutes."

"So they're a long way out." Trish fought a yawn. Early in the Donovan colony's thirty-year history, the decision was made to rely on simple, old-fashioned radio for communications. All it took to make one was a coil of copper wire, a speaker, a mic, and a power source. No quantum photon entanglement, computers, lasers, or microwaves. Just figure out the frequency.

That was the thing about survival on Donovan, it was a mishmash of eighteenth and twenty-second century technology.

Shig said, "Thought we'd give you a heads-up. With Talina still in hospital, you're the top cop. Everybody's going to want to celebrate. The tendency is going to be to let things slide. Maybe not pay close attention to their jobs. Especially security. And with Allison's baby, we just had an example of what happens when even the littlest thing like a locked door is overlooked."

Allison was twenty-three, a few years older than Trish. They'd gone to school together. Something about her had always been fragile—as if Allison were just a blonde beauty. The sort to be admired like a fine sculpture rather than depended upon.

"Gotcha," Trish told Shig. And yes, people were going to get a little nutty. She was suddenly feeling her own growing excitement. Sort of like inexplicably getting a new chance at life. Realizing there was a glowing future where dreams might actually come true.

"Where the hell have they been since *Mekong* left?"

"I guess we'll find out when they get here."

Trish ordered her thoughts. "We need to be ready to handle the influx of new people. Figure out where to put them, how to feed them."

"It's not like we don't have the room," Shig noted. "Given the attrition, we have lots of vacant domes in the residential section. But we're going to have to ramp up our food, water, and recycling to be sure we can handle the volume."

"Do the cargo skids even work anymore?" Yvette asked as she fingered her chin, green eyes fixed on the map that covered the wall behind the holo monitors. "We've let so many things fall by the wayside."

"Concentrating on survival does that to you," Trish pointed out with a shake of the index finger. "Let's not forget that while it hasn't really been said, a lot of the people here had more or less come to the conclusion that we were on our own."

Yvette took a deep breath, slitted her eyes, and sipped at her tea.

It was Shig who said, "There's another reason we called you first, Trish. Since Supervisor Clemenceau's death, we've been running things ourselves. Doing it our way. It's pretty much been me, Yvette, and Talina calling the shots. This isn't the same colony The Corporation is expecting to find: fat, ordered, and dutifully following directives in lockstep."

Trish smiled grimly. Donovan wasn't the authoritarian Corporate community it had been when *Mekong* departed six and half years ago.

"Do we even have a *Corporate Operations Manual* around here anymore?"

"Wouldn't matter if we did," Yvette told her coldly. "Trish, your orders are to get Port Authority ready. One way or another, we're going to have an influx of people and cargo. We're granting you whatever authority you need to get the job done while ensuring that no one makes a mistake when it comes to keeping the compound secure."

Yvette's eyes narrowed. "At the same time, we don't know who's on that ship, or what their orders are. It's been over six years. A lot could have changed back home. Perhaps some political or social upheaval. They may not be the people we remember them to be."

"To that point, sure as hell, we are *not* the same obedient rank-and-file Corporate servants they left here." Shig smiled thinly. "Listen, I know that you're young. This is the first time you've been in charge, but trust yourself. Just use your head. Get with Talina, quietly, and consider options in the event that whoever gets off that ship decides they are going to try and force us to be good little employees again."

"What about the awkward little matter of deeds and titles?" Trish arched an eyebrow. "You think maybe The Corporation's going to look slightly askance at that bit of liberty we've taken with their property?"

"I, for one"—Yvette tossed off the last of her tea—"will never be a Corporate slave again." A pause. "How about you, Trish?"

"Hey, I'd just turned thirteen when you guys took Supervisor Clemenceau down. But I remember how Mom and Dad used to scurry around like invertebrates." A cold sensation made her tighten her stomach muscles. "So, Shig? Yvette? If they come down with a show of force, how far are you willing to push this thing?"

She felt a tingle of unease in her guts. Damn! Did they think she was ready to lead a war against The Corporation? She couldn't even get a date!

Shig's enigmatic expression never changed. "As far as we have to."

The tingle in Trish's gut turned to ice. *You have got to be kidding!*

"Let's just hope it doesn't come to that," Yvette said as she crushed her cup between her long fingers.

As if on cue, grim-faced Two Spots—who had been listening—bent back to his radio as the speaker crackled and announced, "*Turalon actual to Port Authority. Please advise the current Supervisor that, subject to Corporate regulation 17-8-2, he is required to immediately submit a detailed report of all colonial activities, production figures, resource utilization, personnel, equipment status, and special needs since the departure of* Freelander *to Supervisor Aguila with your next transmission.*"

Which, of course, was impossible since the last Supervisor was five years dead.

"Wonder what 'since the departure of *Freelander*' means? You think it was a ship?" Two Spots asked.

"I suppose we'll find out when they get closer," Shig replied thoughtfully.

"Shit in a toilet," Trish muttered as Yvette's expression pinched. "How long do we have before they're in orbit?"

"Eight, nine days." Shig arched an eyebrow. "I'd like to keep Talina in hospital for at least another week if possible. We're going to need her as healed as she can be when this all blows up."

"Yeah." Trish wiped at her suddenly sweaty brow. "Meantime, see how much you can learn about who's aboard that air bucket, and what their intentions are."

"And what are you going to do?" Yvette asked.

Already thinking of who had guns, how many rounds of ammunition were left, and how many would stand and fight if it came down to it, Trish felt queasy as she said, "Some of the things we've done? Clemenceau? Title and deeds? There's a good chance The Corporation is going to be pissed off when they find out. So I guess I'll prepare for a war if we have to fight one."

She was nineteen after all. People her age had been fighting wars for most of history, right?

Shit, tell me I'm up for this.

5

The captain's lounge barely measured up to the name. A person could hardly "lounge" in a space that seated six around a small central table. The holographic wall on one side conformed to *Turalon*'s curving hull, while a dispenser in the back provided drinks and limited food.

Max "Cap" Taggart had always considered a summons to the captain's lounge to be an imposition on his absolutely meaningless schedule. As one of the Supervisor's three staff, he was expected to be present. As the man in charge of Corporate security and its detail of twenty marines, he mostly sat through the droning meetings, saying nothing, bored out of his skull. The *only* consolation he got was watching the minutes tick off, realizing he was being paid a small fortune with each flash of the passing seconds.

Cap padded down the command level corridor. Most of the ship was constructed of sialon—a supertough ceramic alloy of silicon, aluminum, oxygen, and nitrogen. He was *tired* of sialon. As he passed the hatch, he glanced in at astrogation. Nandi sat with her head bent forward to allow her to monitor the holographic displays as she interfaced with the ship's guidance.

Their routine sexual liaisons weren't anything serious. She didn't really have much in common with him. Nor did she hesitate to mention that she was in love with an astrogator on *Freelander*—the ship that had undertaken the previous passage to Donovan's World. There just weren't many options for command staff to fulfill their sexual needs—and she'd just come off a bad experience with a transportee.

Cap sighed and continued on his way, passing the engineering hatch and taking a sip of coffee from his zero-g cup. Coffee remained life's single constant—though he wondered if the taste was the same, given the quality of the water now running through the ship's recycling systems.

At the lounge hatch, he knocked on the sialon bulkhead and looked inside.

"Come in, Cap," Board Supervisor Kalico Aguila called. She was seated across from Captain Margo Abibi at the far end of the small table. Information Officer Nancy Fuloni sat to the captain's left, her eyes fixed on a scrolling holo screen projected from the table.

Apparently it was going to be a small meeting, for as he entered, the door swung shut behind him.

Board Supervisor Kalico Aguila met every criterion for a bright, ambitious, rising star. The ultimate Corporate warrior, superbly versed in the cutthroat politics waged by the high and mighty. Word was that Aguila was ruthless when it came to her rivals, coldly competent, and without scruples when it came to advancement. One by one she had destroyed or broken her competition as she rose through the ranks to finally secure a position on Boardmember Taglioni's small staff.

In the halls of power she was both feared and respected, hated for her methods and admired for her successes.

She also fit the definition for the old term "eye candy," definitely nice to look at with her wealth of gleaming black hair, remarkably blue eyes, and sculpted cheeks and nose. It was hard to tell—given the high quality of healthcare for which she qualified—but she looked to be in her late twenties. Kalico favored immaculately tailored clothes that accented her broad shoulders and high breasts, and the taper to her lean waist, sensual hips, and long legs. A body as perfect as programmed genetics could make it.

Unlike Cap, she hadn't been "assigned" to the mission. She'd gambled everything and asked for it. The whispered rumor was that the Board had resisted—thought she was too talented to lose—but that Boardmember Taglioni pushed it through. It had been hinted that Kalico had enthusiastically shared the good Boardmember's bed as a way to seal the deal.

Cap took his chair as Kalico turned back to the report projected above the table. A frown lined her high brow, and her blue eyes were thoughtful as she read. Cap admired the view as she ran supple fingers through her thick black hair. That alone was a sign of status. Most everyone else shipboard had to shave their heads.

Then, just as a man's fantasies began to run away with him, her eyes would fix on him like cutting lasers. An instant later her razor-sharp personality would slice away any semblance of femininity, warmth, or empathy. A reminder that no matter how she looked, Kalico Aguila remained as ruthless as any tiger, and as coldly focused as a cobra.

Ship's Captain Margo Abibi also concentrated on the report; the holographic words and images scrolled with the movement of her light brown eyes. Even sitting there in her chair, she looked the part. A stereotype of a career spacer. No nonsense. Capable, right down to her short fingers with their unpainted nails. That The Corporation had appointed a woman of Abibi's capabilities and record indicated just how seriously they took the Donovan mission.

Cap sat back in the chair, turned his watch up, and watched the display. Ten SDR a day. He watched the seconds tick by. . . . Twenty, thirty, forty . . .

He'd gotten to two hundred and thirty when Kalico said, "I hate to interrupt the amassing of a small fortune, Captain, but I need your attention."

"Yes, Supervisor?" He glanced across the empty seat that separated them.

Kalico leaned back and fingered her implant monitor with her left hand. Her expression communicated a preoccupied tension. She flicked fingers toward the projection. "This is the latest of the fragmentary, disjointed, and ludicrous reports we've been receiving."

Cap shifted, rotating his coffee cup on the desktop. "Fragmentary? Disjointed? What's the Supervisor down there think he's doing?"

"He's dead," Kalico said crisply. "Killed in the 'bush.' Whatever that means." A beat. "Or so they say."

"What the hell? Have they all gone mad down there?"

"You could wonder," Fuloni muttered under her breath.

"It gets worse," Kalico told him. "According to the reports, there's only three hundred and eighty-nine people alive in Port Authority. They think—*think* mind you—that another couple of hundred might be living in the 'bush.'"

"Must be a hell of a big bush."

Abibi was shooting them sidelong glances.

"At least part of the mystery, however, is solved. We're the first ship they've seen since the *Mekong* spaced for Solar System over six years ago."

"*Mekong?* That's the second ship that disappeared, isn't it? After *Nemesis*?"

"Vanished after leaving Donovan for Solar System. But at least it made it this far." She looked uncomfortable as she stared at the display with pinched eyes. "That's *seven*. Seven missing ships in a row! It doesn't make sense. What the *hell* has happened to them? The Board expected the missing ships to be here, in orbit. Perhaps seized by the colonists. Maybe left behind by mutinous crews. But not *vanished*."

"What could have gone wrong?" Abibi wondered. "Anything that failed during inversion should have kicked on the default. Reversed the math, and they should have returned automatically to Solar System. That's the fail-safe."

"Maybe we'll find out when we get dirtside." Kalico massaged her brow.

Cap lowered a skeptical eyebrow. "They've been on their own down there for all that time? Outside of the fact that there's a colony still left, is there any good news?"

"Every sialon shipping crate is full of clay, rare-earth elements, or metals. All stacked and waiting transport." Kalico tapped her fingernails on the tabletop. "Oh, and they have exotics to ship. Locally derived foods, spices, and rare gems. Lots of animal hides." She paused. "*Animal* hides?"

"They refer to some of the indigenous life-forms," Fuloni told her. "I saw a quetzal hide once. Remarkable colors."

"Now there's a moneymaker for the Board."

"What about the political situation?" Cap asked. "You said the Supervisor is dead. What about his deputies? What are we looking at?"

"They seem to be rather vague about that. Questions are answered in terms like 'We think' and 'We're not sure.' As if it's some kind of committee. No one seems to have a title. There are phrases like, 'Talina informs us that the following quarters are ready.' Or 'Shig has heard from Raya that the supplies listed below are exhausted.'"

"There's only three hundred and eighty-nine of them," Fuloni mused. "It's no wonder they use names instead of titles. They all know each other."

Cap took a swig of his coffee and shook his head. "*Xian*'s report was that nearly three thousand people were working the mines, building outlying research bases, surveying, prospecting, cataloging the planet's resources. What happened to them? Disease?"

Kalico flicked her fingers at the report again. "The answer I got was one word: attrition."

"We've only had a colony on Donovan for thirty years. You think it was a social meltdown?" Fuloni asked. "A lack of leadership after the Supervisor died? Maybe they all turned on each other?"

"Might be. We'll know more when we get down there." Kalico turned her intense eyes on Cap. "I want you to get together with your marines, Cap. I know you've been training this entire journey. Be ready for anything. You will function as my personal guard, but I want you and your people learning the ropes. On my command you may have to seize the Port Authority facilities and institute martial law."

"Yes, ma'am." He paused. "But there's something I don't get. You said that it's been six years since they've seen a ship? That the last one was *Mekong*?" He ticked them off on his fingers. "That's *Governor Han Xi, Tableau, Phoenix, Ashanti,* and *Freelander.* They can't have *all* vanished."

Fuloni's expression betrayed a poorly hidden sorrow. "And don't forget *Nemesis* . . . and that *Mekong* never made it home. So apparently they all have."

"We'll get to that problem in its turn. For the moment, our concern is Donovan." Kalico thrust a finger at him like a spear. "Cap, get your people in order. To restore order we may have to kick some ass when we set foot dirtside, and when the shooting's done I want them down instead of us."

His stomach tightened. "Are you sure that—"

"You don't have a reputation for being squeamish when the shooting starts, Captain. I wouldn't think it would be a problem for you."

An image formed in the back of his mind: torn and blasted bodies spiraling in zero g; streamers of blood coalescing into oscillating blobs that floated toward the bulkheads. The staring and sightless eyes and protruding fingers of intestines that leaked from ripped bellies.

Men, women, and the children. All dead.

No, Supervisor. Not a problem.

6

No more than a day out of hospital, Talina Perez felt as weak as a jellyfish—and yes, Donovan had its version of the organism. All of her life she'd presented an image of tough invulnerability. Now she had to stand before the whole of Port Authority—on crutches, no less—when her guts felt like wadded tissue paper.

Not only that, her eyes were playing tricks on her. At odd moments the backs of her eyes would ache, and she'd see a rainbow haze of color at the edges of her vision like a sheen of oil on water. Her muscles would spasm and knot unexpectedly. Hints of odor that she'd never noticed now caught her nose. Her dreams had been off, jumbled with images of color, smells, and the thrill of a chase she could never quite understand.

And there was that weird swelling sensation in her gut just below the heart, as if some foreign body were present.

All of which meant that Talina Perez was in a really pissy mood.

Get it out of your head. You've got a job to do.

She propped herself, stiff-armed, on Inga's bar and used one of the crutches to keep the weight off her healing leg. Raya had explained that the bone was knitting well, but that Talina needed to wear the cast for at least another week. Oh, and don't push it.

That was quetzal crap.

It figured that Shig and Yvette would lay this on her.

For effect she'd worn her sable uniform—or at least what was left of it. The form-fitting garment had begun to look more than a little worse for wear. The elbows and knees had been patched, and the fabric mended here and there, but she'd tried to keep the threadbare look to a minimum. Any other day she'd have worn her quetzal-hide vest, wide-brimmed hat, and chamois shirt and pants.

To her right, Inga Lock braced herself with her left hip against the bar. The big woman had her meaty arms crossed and a stern look on her forty-year-old face. Every trial and tribulation in the woman's long and hard life had left its trace on her broad-boned features. She called her establishment The Bloody Drink, after a particularly harrowing incident that had occurred there many years past. Most folks just called it Inga's Tavern.

Now it functioned as town hall. Probably because Inga served whiskey, beer, and various wines. All made in the stone warehouse immediately behind the dome-covered subterranean tavern. Each time she'd enlarged, it was easier to dig out beneath the dome to increase the room's circumference.

Tonight's meeting consisted of nearly two hundred people, the others still attending to their scheduled duties under Trish's watchful eye.

As if summoned by the thought, the young woman came skipping down the steps from outside. Trish carried a slung rifle over her shoulder and wore a standard brown coverall. From across the room she gave Talina the kind of nod that made her auburn hair bounce—the signal that everyone who wasn't on watch was present.

Talina had sort of adopted Trish after the girl was orphaned. Seen that she stuck out her education. Mentored her through the ups and downs of the teenage years, the heartbreak of Trish's first love, and trauma when one of her classmates died. Somehow, given the bond between them, it wasn't surprising that Trish had taken to security—and done well enough to essentially become Talina's second-in-command. Sometimes she worried about the younger woman's near worship.

"Hey! Attention! I'm calling this to order!" Talina slapped the bar for good measure, and kept slapping it as the room slowly quieted. "And I do mean order! First one of you bastards that crosses me, by God's ugly ass, I'll blow him in two!"

Talina didn't have a commanding voice; she generally talked in a mellow contralto. What she did have was the respect of every man, woman, and child in the place. She might not have outright killed any silly son of a bitch who had the temerity to disrespect her—but she'd have considered maiming him.

In the following silence, she gave the packed room a narrow-eyed glare. "All of you want to know about the ship. It's called the *Turalon*. It inverted symmetry two years ago outside the orbit of Neptune.

Now, here's the thing: Including the *Mekong*, The Corporation has sent seven ships our way, and the *Mekong* never made it back. Every ship since the *Xian* has been lost. That's seven lost ships. *Seven.*"

"What happened to them?" someone called.

"We don't know. Maybe they got lost on the other side? Mechanical failure? Exploded for all we know."

That sobered them.

Soft muttering broke out, people shaking their heads, sharing uneasy glances.

Talina read the character in their faces; trial, self-reliance, and hardship reflected from their sun-leathered features. Keen-eyed and level stares looked back at her, challenging, but willing to hear her out.

All totaled, there were three hundred and eighty-nine of them in and around Port Authority, from old Artie Manfroid who had just turned seventy-two, down to little new-born Macie Han Chow, who hadn't reached a full month.

They wore a mixture of clothing that included bits of hide they'd skinned off the native animals, tanned, and tailored to service. Some still maintained old jumpsuits, mining overalls, and coats from their previous worlds. Over the years, footwear had given way to boots made from durable quetzal hide that shimmered and shot rainbows with each step. Hats of various descriptions—but obvious utility—covered every head. Capella's light could be brutal. Most of the adults carried weapons of one sort or another, a constant reminder that even in the supposed sanctuary of Port Authority, Donovan could strike at any moment. Equipment belts were studded with battered communicators, solar pocket computers, coiled line, carabineers, and the emergency kit that contained fire-starter, a thermal blanket, water purifier, needle, hatchet head, string and thread, along with other necessaries that could mean the difference between life and death.

These are my people.

The thought brought her a sudden pride. An understanding that she couldn't have had without that ship up there in orbit. Now her people waited, heads cocked, expectant of the information she brought.

"You think we got all night?" Tyrell Lawson asked, from the front row. "What's the news?"

"Probably taking their good time about sending a shuttle," someone groused in the back. "Been six years. What's their hurry?"

"They're processing their people," Talina answered. "Shifting cargo. Most of you spaced here. You remember the drill. Ships have to be shut down, inspected. It's not like shucking your coat on the way to Inga's. And after six years and all the missing ships, it's not like they don't want to get it right."

"Damn straight," a man in back called. "Especially if they're taking me back to Transluna."

"Hear, hear," someone else called.

"What the hell does it matter to them?" Toby Montoya asked. "They don't care that we don't have a working hospital. That half the equipment's been cannibalized to keep the rest running. We're just numbers, man. Qubit codes in some computer in Tokyo."

Hofer snorted and looked around. "Hey! We had to wait our turn. You know, like after the stockholders got their vacations to Tahiti taken care of first."

"What about our deeds and titles?" Betty Able demanded. "The Corporation's going to honor them, right?"

"They sure as hell better, or there's gonna be some heads beat in, I'll tell ya!" Step Allenovich bellowed.

"That's *enough*!" Talina slapped the scarred and stained bar. "They lost seven ships. Figure around a hundred crew and another four hundred transportees per ship. That's three thousand five hundred *people*. Not to mention the cost of the ships and cargo. Just gone. Vanished. And no one knows where. Or even how."

She stared around the now silent room. "Supervisor Aguila has made one thing clear: *Turalon* is the last chance The Corporation is going to give us. If it spaces off into inverted symmetry and disappears, there will be no more ships. No more attempts at contacting us."

"So, what are they thinking? Shut the colony down? Pack us up and take us all home?" Stepan Allenovich asked. He stood at the side of the room, back to the wall, arms crossed, one foot propped on a bench. Hard use had polished his equipment belt, and four notches had been carved into his pistol's duralon grip. A gleaming row of crest scales hung in a gaudy necklace over his worn homespun shirt. Step had been an exozoologist once upon a time. A series of articles waited on his desk to be shipped up to *Turalon* for transmission back to Earth.

"Nothing's being shut down." Talina glanced at Trish where the young woman taken up station in the rear of the room, hands clasping her upper arms, the rifle's muzzle sticking up from behind her auburn hair. She looked more like a revolutionary than a suddenly insecure second-in-command of security.

"Now, here's the thing," Talina added. "When they finally land, they're expecting to find a Corporate colony. Remember the old rule book?"

"Fuck that!" Thumbs Exman bellowed. "My contract expired one year, six months, and twenty-seven days ago. I just want to get home. I got family back there. I've got a wife."

"Not so's you'd notice, Thumbs," Betty Able called from across the room. As the madam of Port Authority's best-patronized—and only—brothel, the buxom blonde was one of the community's less prosperous members. Especially given the ratio of women to men these days.

"Yeah, yeah, laugh it up," Thumbs shot back when the guffaws subsided. "Going home? Is that too much to ask? What the hell does The Corporation think we've been doing out here? I busted my ass on their damn geothermal survey. I laid out in the bush for almost two weeks with a thorn in my back 'til Talina finally found me."

"So, Thumbs, why don't you think they'd take you home?" Talina asked. Then she looked around the room. "How many of you have fulfilled your contracts?"

Most the hands in the room went up.

"How many of you want to space back to Transluna and Earth?"

She figured the hand count at around three quarters. Another thirty or so where fidgeting, shifting from side to side in their seats, looking undecided.

"Don't worry. Shig and Yvette will work it out." Talina raised her hands. "The point I'm trying to make is that this Board Supervisor, her name is Kalico Aguila, is landing here tomorrow. When she does, she's going to expect a Corporate colony."

"I'm not cuddling up to kiss her Corporate ass," Toby Montoya said with a snort.

"Hey, you never know," Hofer shot back. "Might be a really nice ass. Me, I'll wait, and then if it looks good, I'll ask her to drop her drawers."

This time Talina used her pistol butt to bang on the bar. "You want me to clear this place?"

"God, no!" Inga almost pleaded. "Tal, they ain't hardly touched the booze I laid in for this."

Talina fought a smile as she pistol-gaveled the crowd back into submission. "I know. We've been running our own show. And yes, I know The Corporation is run by a bunch of worm-gutted, cold-hearted, money-grubbing bastards that we all hate. But we need to work together on this."

"On what?" Step demanded.

Talina took a deep breath. "We've done some pretty amazing things, haven't we? Made it for six years without resupply on a world that will kill us in an instant. Hell, there's a couple hundred of us living out there in the bush. Surviving."

"Yeah, so?"

"So, this is what I want you to consider: Donovan's *ours*!"

The shrill whistles and cheers were deafening as they echoed off the dome overhead.

Talina had to hammer for most of a minute to get silence. "The Corporation doesn't know that. They *can't* know that! Now, do you want to tell me why that might be the case?"

Trish stepped forward, shouting, "Because now that they've figured out we're alive, we need their ships. Need their supplies. Piss them off, and they can choose to just go away. Leave us out here to cope as we can. It sucks toilet water, but for the time being, we *need* them. We've got the clay, the metals and elements, the resources they need. And they've got the ships to carry them back to Solar System. The place that makes the medicines, technology, and materials we need to keep going."

Step raised his hands, the gesture almost imploring. "Talina, what, specifically, are you asking us for?"

She took her time, met their eyes one by one as she looked around the room. Finally, she asked, "No jokes now. How many stupid people are in this room? Give me a count."

She could see the occasional elbow and sidelong nod to friends, who just grinned in return.

"That's what I thought." Talina leaned forward on the bar. "Donovan's killed the stupid ones. So let's be smart, people. *Turalon*'s going to send a report back to The Corporation, along with the information that six years of product is stacked up on our landing field, ready for export."

"Right," Montoya called. "What of it?"

"It's maybe a month that we have to play quetzal and camouflage who and what we are. Just long enough for Supervisor Aguila and her deputies to up-ship, fly out-system, and invert. As long as she sends a glowing report back, we're in fat gravy."

She pointed a finger at Exman. "Assuming you returnees keep your yaps shut about what really goes on here when there isn't a ship up in orbit with a Supervisor on it."

"And then what?" Betty Able asked. "If *Turalon* makes it back, we're on our own for what? Four years?"

"The operative phrase is 'On our own.'" Talina narrowed an eye at her audience. "Not all of us have something to go back to. Me? I can't imagine living anywhere but here, and I want a future for the kids. So we've got to give The Corporation a reason to come back, but at the same time, not make it worth their while to take it over again."

Step Allenovich slowly shook his head. "That's a mighty tricky game to play, Talina."

"Yeah, tell me about it."

7

Beyond the sialon bulkhead an overstressed hydraulic system whined and thumped softly with a sound like boxing gloves hammering a steel post. The man who called himself Dan Wirth blinked awake and opened his gritty eyes to the dim light of the male quarters.

Wasn't his real name. It had been the name of the cowherd. A man met in a Transluna bar, a chance encounter as security was closing in. A desperate last coincidence. Two men who happened to know something about cattle. Turned out that the cowherd—agricultural technician second class—had a Corporate contract that would take him off-world within forty-eight hours.

Three hours later, that Dan Wirth had stared up, eyes glazed with pain. He'd reached out with fingers that shook so badly the blood dripped from them in jiggles. *"Please. Don't . . . Please?"*

They always said please.

Didn't matter who the mark was, rich or poor, the fact that they he or she was being murdered left them as bewildered as the pain and fear. They couldn't grasp the impossibility of it. The desperation with which they clung to hope—that some miracle would save them—it lasted right up to the last instant when their vision faded to black.

"Sorry, pal. I had to get out of that floating tin can."

Left in a blast vent. They'd never find the body.

Dan Wirth—it was such a simple name—lay on his back, enjoying the lax feeling left by sleep. Wonderful sleep. Escape from the ship's suffocating monotony to a place where a person dreamed of blue skies, of fresh air, room to move, and freedom. The strangling existence he lived when awake vanished. Instead of scrubbing decks, cleaning filters, swamping out hydroponic tanks, and seeing the same faces, during his dreams he could walk perfect streets, give other people orders, and all the women he screwed were beautiful, submissive, and compliant.

I live like a rat in a damn small cage.

That hell, however, ended today.

The sounds hadn't changed. The symphony remained the same: The rhythmic humming of pumps; the muted rush of water in the pressure pipes; the soft whisper of the atmosphere plant; or the shuffling passage of people in the corridors. The audience—consisting of his fellow transportees—was renewed. Joyous. Almost giddy with anticipation.

An excitement filled the low voices talking just beyond the duffel storage hatch. Inside the room, even the sounds of men breathing in their sleep seemed lighter, somehow charged.

In the cramped darkness of his bunk, Dan turned his head and glanced at the narrow room. The bunks were a uniform honeycomb of stacked coffin-like recesses molded into the sialon walls. Each was filled with a somnolent body—a man's solitary domain for eight hours before he surrendered it to the second shift. Who in turn surrendered it to the third shift. Who then vacated the bunks for Dan and his companions. Space was at a premium aboard a starship. God, what a shit-sucking way to live.

The bunk-filled walls were like a sort of perverted mixture of universe, womb, and private hell.

Slave ships must have been like this. That's how they treat us. Living cargo. Instead of chains, we have our wrist monitors that determine the extent of our ramblings and actions just as surely as links of iron would.

But then maybe they weren't even human anymore. Maybe they were all a little crazy after the seemingly endless imprisonment within their sialon warren.

How many fistfights, screaming fits, and howling bouts of madness had he increasingly witnessed in the last months? Rico Simpatico had killed himself less than a week ago, his body found in the shower, facedown in a pool of blood. The guy had actually had the balls to slit his own throat. How did a man do that? Keep cutting as he felt the knife slice through his windpipe and esophagus? But he had. The ship's surgeon had proved it by the blood spatter, the prints on the knife, and the way old Rico had sawed at his neck.

I followed my own damned madness.

Nandi would have a little more than two hours of duty before she clocked off. Should he try to see her one last time? Could he look into her eyes and not remember the humiliation she'd caused him? How she'd screamed? The pistol that she'd produced from under her pillow and shoved into his face. How—with fire in her eyes—she'd marched him out into the companionway? He'd stood there naked and trembling with rage as the realization soaked in that she'd really shoot him.

Bitch!

They'd taken his general-access wrist monitor. Replaced it with the restricted-access unit he now wore, allowing him to pass only certain bulkheads. Just like prison back on Earth. He'd hated that. The difference here was that no escape lay just beyond the walls—only empty cold vacuum, or whatever the other side of space really was. He didn't understand asymmetry, or how it all worked.

Crazy. That's what we are. Too many humans packed too tightly, for too long.

Hong Kong had had even less living space per person, but they were stacked up for a thousand stories. People could walk outside, see the sky, purchase a pass to Repulse Bay once a year. Breezes caressed the skin.

I lost control again. Nandi did that to me.

Her outraged eyes burned in the back of his mind.

Memories. Blurred, shattered, and angular pieces of a frantic flight down narrow tunnel-like corridors. People staring as he'd charged past them, naked, cursing. How he'd stormed into this room, dragged the man sleeping in his bunk out, and dropped him shrieking on the floor. How he'd crawled into this warm and comforting womb and burst into sobs of rage.

He never knew who had returned his clothes. He hadn't cared. Had refused to raise his eyes in the mess. Willing his ears closed, he hadn't heard the whispers, the snide comments, or outright mutterings of his fellows.

Only Stryski had made something of it. Stepping into his face and saying, "Been run out of any women's quarters lately?"

They'd had one hell of fight until security gassed them. The next two months had been spent in "solitary."

His father's voice echoed inside his skull. *"You gotta give a little. Learn the rules. Every place runs as a system, and the big guys control the action. You gotta figure what the little guys need and what they'll pay for it. Control that, and you got the world by the balls."*

He'd tried it on the ship the first week out. Turned out the big guys controlled it all. So he'd clammed up. Kept his cards and dice to himself. But what would he find on Donovan?

Come 1200 hours, he'd be lined up to shuttle down.

Nandi would be a memory.

Donovan. The latest narcotic for those who dreamed of easy riches and freedom. Before he slept again, Dan Wirth would be on that world. The very thought was the solvent that washed sleep from his system.

Dan ducked his five-foot-ten frame as he sat up and swung his muscular legs over the edge of his berth. He leaned the back of his head against the cool ceramic that framed O'Leary's bunk above. The place smelled of sweat and humanity—but then a person even got used to a rendering plant's stench after a while. Human, hydroponics, machine, fungus, stale sweat, they'd grown so used to it he wondered if the olfactory senses might be forever blunted.

"Jesus," came the disgusted cry from below. "Damn it, Cowboy, don't you ever wash your damned feet?"

Cowboy. That was Dad's work. Dear old Dad. A nameless, faceless, and frustrated programmer who worked in the Transluna office of personnel and records. Dad had changed the records at the last instant. His message had been succinct. "*They're onto you. Last chance, boy. Like you asked, I've put your new stats into the system. From here on out, you're Dan Wirth. You work with cattle. Be on the shuttle for* Turalon *in five hours, or you're going down for good.*"

Dan grunted to himself and slipped from the bunk, landing with a catlike grace. He flexed his muscles, grinned, and poked his head into Pete Morgan's space. "You want to make something of it?"

In the dark recess of Morgan's bunk, he could see the man shake his head. "Donovan's down there. I got no reason to screw my place in line with a disciplinary action. Especially with you."

"Smart man, and I like smart men."

"Hey," Wan Xi Gow called. "We're trying to sleep here."

"Yeah, you little baby asses sleep." Dan ran a hand over his face as he padded along the sialon deck, half enjoying the chill that ate into the soles of his feet.

He unclipped the flimsy door to his garment locker and reached for the steamed overalls on his shelf. The men's room consisted of toilets, sinks, and showers, all efficiently placed to maximize the small space. The ceramic and plastic fixtures gleamed in malaria-yellow light. Aurobindo Ghosh, the Indian tech engineer, had cobbled up the weird yellow lights after the last of the laser-gas bulbs had died. Somehow The Corporation's supply experts hadn't thought to stock replacements on board.

"Candy-dicked bastards," Dan muttered. "Wonder what else they forgot to stock?"

At the urinal he made his contribution to the hydroponics, then shifted a half step to the sink. He gave the mirror an evil grin. A film covered the glass. Film covered everything in *Turalon*'s sweaty and humid atmosphere. Fucking ceramic gopher hole.

Despite the disinfectants, stains clung to the toilets, urinals, and corners. A dent marred one of the coffin-shaped shower stalls; a gray smudge ran across the ceiling.

"One year, eleven months, and seventeen days," he told his image in the mirror. "Seems like fucking forever."

Nandi would be making final observations in the dome.

He closed his eyes, flexed his hands, and imagined her slim throat crushing under his fingers. Could feel the tensing of the neck muscles, the way the tendons would jerk as she tossed her head about. How the windpipe's stiff cartilage crushed. The voice box always slid up as he squeezed, driving the tongue up into the back of the mouth. In his imagination, he savored that little snap as the hyoid bone broke. The eyes, that was the coolest part—that wide, popping panic as they started out from the sockets.

Paybacks are a bitch, Nandi.

Dan pressed a finger to the water tap, bending over the sink to wash the sleep from his hot face. Nice thing about Gosh's yellow lights, they didn't show the real color of the water. He blanked his mind at the number of times these same molecules had been cycled through human bodies.

He dried and dropped the towel into the steamer. Unrolling the coveralls with a flourish, he stepped into them and sealed the seams. The familiar orange uniform looked worn, the sleeves frayed, elbows shiny from wear. He clipped the collar and stared at the man in the mirror.

In the wake of Nandi's betrayal, he'd taken the hard jobs—anything that punished the body—and spent his free time on the exercise machines. Others had gone soft, but he'd never been in better shape. Especially with the perfectly balanced nutrition they served in the mess. Tasted like shit, but each meal was calculated to provide all the proteins, fats, carbs, fiber, and vitamins the human body needed.

He ran a hand over his close-cropped scalp. "Still not used to looking like a marine," he confessed as he studied his brown, lady-killer eyes. A guy named Terry had given him the faint scar on his chin. Only a slight lump marred the straight line of his nose, legacy of his days in Hong Kong. Tough city, Hong Kong. But there was money to be made. At least until the big guys caught on.

He grinned at himself, half expecting his skull to grin back. With a little imagination he could see it, trace the hollow gaping of the orbits, the emptiness of the nose, see the arch of the cheek bones. In his imagination the image solidified. Haunting. Prophetic.

That's how I'll look someday. A bare skull. Flesh gone. Teeth grinning. The bone stained from long-rotted-away tissue.

For the moment, the gamble had paid off. He'd made it. Once down there, even if they ever discovered who he really was, he could disappear. Vanish again.

Ought to say good-bye to Nandi.

But then he hadn't said good-bye to Cylie. Which was the only reason she was still alive.

"So much for the past." He grunted, thinking back to what Cylie had cost him. The clever cunt had been smart enough to run.

She would have divorced him by now. Gone on to another man—

gullible little slut that she was. Not that she'd ever fix her life. She had needed him to run it for her. And if he knew anything, it was how to run a woman.

At least until Nandi.

How the hell had that gone wrong? How had he misread her so completely that when he put a little pressure on her, she got her back up and told him to fuck off? And when he started to teach her a thing or two, the slit had shoved a gun in his face? Seriously?

"Got to hand it to her, she's got guts."

Which decided him. He stepped out of the lavatory, walked down the cramped sialon tunnel. Regularly spaced light panels illuminated the fiber optic cables, conduit, pipes, and wiring where it snaked its way overhead. The walls were broken by inspection hatches, emergency gear lockers, and doorways set flush with the ship's hull. The familiar closeness pressed in.

He climbed up a tube ladder and found the com cubby empty. Sliding into the seat, he accessed the system. "Astrogation. Nandi, please."

"One moment," the voice told him.

Within seconds her face formed on the holo. Immediately her expression tightened. "What do you want, Dan?"

She sat before the spectrometer, her dark eyes troubled. He'd seen a picture of her before she spaced, and had marveled at her thick and long black hair. Now her close-shaved scalp gleamed in the overhead lights. The angles of her triangular face, high cheeks, and pointed chin made her a beautiful woman. Her uniform looked rumpled, the lieutenant's bars on her shoulders perfectly placed.

"To say I'm sorry. That I lost it that night." He gave her his innocent grin. "Never had a woman put me in my place like that. Wanted to say that there's no hard feelings." *Yeah, right.*

She gave a faint shake of the head. "I don't know what I ever saw in you. I . . . Wait. That's a lie. I knew exactly what you were. Always wanted to try a dangerous man. See if what they said about them was true. Literature is full of them. The cunning rogue brought to heel by a good woman. Learned my lesson right quick."

"Sorry. Must be a relief to make Donovan."

He saw the pinching behind her eyes. She said nothing.

"What's wrong, Nandi?"

She wet her lips, gave a slight shrug. "*Freelander* didn't arrive. Never made it."

He remembered that her fiancée worked as an astrogator on *Freelander.*

"So? They got delayed. Maybe had a problem and had to stop and—"

"Damn you, Cowboy, you never understand, do you?"

"Well, hell, equipment, especially in these ships, with all the computers and number crunching—"

"They were nine months ahead of us. Neptune had them on the monitors when *Freelander* inverted symmetry and went null."

He waited, not sure what that meant.

She sighed. "You may know how to slip along the underbelly of life and run games, Wirth, but don't ever try and pilot a starship. You don't just *stop* in space and fix things. Not in inverted symmetry. You either make it, or you don't."

"Sorry."

"Hey, it happens. Space doesn't come free." She paused, a dead emptiness behind her eyes. "You're a gambler. You know what the *real* figures are? Each time we space we've got an eighty percent chance of making it across the inversion."

"But I thought . . ." He frowned.

"Sure you did. The Corporation lies. You think they'd be able to space if the truth became known? Damn it, Dan, each of these ships is experimental. Each subtly different in design. That's the spinoff that's making The Corporation money."

He kept his expression blank.

"Think about it, Cowboy. This ship's a kilometer and a half long and over two kilometers wide—and we live like rats in a rice can. So cramped that everyone's elbow is shoved up someone else's ass. *Turalon* is all engine and generator with a tiny payload perched on top. The under-the-table figure is that it costs The Corporation fifteen thousand SDRs a kilo to ship past Tau Ceti."

"Then why do it if one out of every five ships is lost?"

She gave him a bitter smile. "It's the money, Dan. Kenji and I, this was our last run. If we both got home we were going to cash out. Buy our own island and grow old in the sun and surf."

She lowered her eyes. "Listen. I'm talking too much. Saying things I'd never say if . . ."

When no more was forthcoming, he said, "Yeah, I know. Like I said, I'm sorry. Go with God."

He cut the connection, thinking, *Shit and shine, doesn't matter what I did back there, they'll never catch me now.*

8

"So, what's the word?" Talina asked as Trish Monagan came striding into the administration dome.

"Did you sleep last night?"

"Hell, no." Talina rubbed her eyes, easing back on her crutches. Her dreams had been filled with bizarre sights and sensations. In one, she'd been flashing across a flat dotted with aquajade trees, a small herd of chamois fleeing before her. The weirdest part had been the sensation of air rushing through her body, the blur of her legs.

So fucking vivid!

She'd jerked awake, quivering and sweating.

Just at the thought, her eyes ached, and the shimmer of color swam at the edges of her vision.

You'd think I had a quetzal inside me.

She glanced down the corridor, seeing Yvette where she supervised the removal of the last of the storage that had been piled in Supervisor Clemenceau's office. It wouldn't look pristine when Kalico Aguila set foot in it, but it at least gave the illusion that Port Authority still respected The Corporation and its people.

Trish arched her back and made a face as she relieved strained muscles. Step Allenovich froze, gaze fixing on the strained fabric that outlined Trish's breasts.

"Hey!" Talina snapped. "Eyes back in your head, or trot your ass off to Betty's and deal with it in a way that's productive for the economy."

Stepan shot her a wink and bowed gallantly to Trish before he carried his box of reports into Shig's office.

Trish sighed. "I guess someone still sees me as a woman. That's something, at least."

"The way you look? I wouldn't think you'd have trouble attracting a man."

"I grew up with two guys and two other girls in my age group.

They're married to each other, having kids. And the slim pickings that are left don't excite me." She glanced upward. "Maybe there's a whole new selection headed my way."

"Count on it, but remember they're soft meat. And they've had two years to pair up in that damn ship."

"Soft meat. Crap. Guess I could go to work for Betty if I want the occasional taste of sex, huh?"

"Trish, you got something I need to know? Or did you plan on discussing your libido all morning?"

"I've got ammo stashed all around the compound. Same with weapons. All of it in personal space. Places where the Skulls won't think to look. Or would get hurt trying. If the Supervisor pulls anything boneheaded, like confiscating weapons, we can be rearmed and ready within an hour." She fished in her pocket. "And here's Raya's list of meds to be forwarded up to the ship."

Talina took it, read down the names. Phenothyazionate? What the hell was that? It was bad enough that Donovan killed people with an insolent regularity. The fact that solid folks like Mitch had died for lack of something as simple as megacillin was like a thorn in the soul. A case of antibiotics didn't mass much, and it would last for years.

Meanwhile, Lee Cheng, their botanical chemist, worked feverishly to come up with local alternatives to terrestrial medicines. He spent his days collecting plants, running them through spectography, FTIR, and every other kind of analysis before hunching over his pestle and mortar much as his ancestors in Beijing had a couple of centuries back. Lack of a sophisticated centrifuge added to his labors, and the scanning electron microscopy unit had ceased to function three years ago. Something inside had burned out, and the guy who knew how to fix it had died when a slug ate its way into his leg.

"Just keep the lid on, huh? The first shuttle's due in a couple of hours. We kowtow to the Supervisor, ritually install her in her office, and bury our asses in processing the soft meat as they come down." She paused. "God, I hope they have coffee."

Talina made a face. "Think about it, they've been locked away in that sky-rolling death trap for two years. Want to bet but that they want to kill each other by now?"

"Maybe we ought to sell them fresh air," Trish suggested. "Half a yuan a breath. Stimulate the economy."

Behind her, the door opened, and Shig leaned out. "Talina, will reality cease if I ask for a moment of your time?"

"Probably. The universe is full of conundrums, Shig." She gave Trish a "carry on" nod and hobbled along on her crutches as Shig led the way into his cramped office. The room didn't measure more than two meters by four. Of the three computers only one remained functional. Last she'd heard someone had pirated the guts out of the broken machines and left the empty consoles. Shig never liked throwing anything away.

Passing his cramped desk, he led her straight through, out the door on the other side, and into the stack yard with its rows of sialon crates piled four high. Each was filled with rare-earth elements, clay from the mine, ore, specimens. The wealth of Donovan—paid for with blood, sweat, and lives—waited for the stars.

At the main gate to the shuttle pad, Shig stopped and gestured around. "You think this will do for check-in? Maybe use a crate for a desk? Bring out a chair? If we leave the big gate closed, use only the smaller man gate, they'll have to come through one at a time. Maybe keep Trish and Step on either side with a rifle to look mean and ensure they don't get out of hand."

Talina glanced up at the partly cloudy sky. "What if it rains?"

"They'll get wet. What about it?"

She gave him a sly grin. "All right. What have we got? Four hundred of them. Fifty per shuttle? It'll take all afternoon, and if we don't get through them, we're gonna have to cancel the last loads."

Talina squinted across the hard-packed landing field, dotted as it was with green-blue weeds. Long time since a shuttle had set down. "We don't want anybody on the other side of the fence after dark. Being eaten within hours of landing could be detrimental to morale."

"If you could process the first couple of shuttles, I'll take over as soon as I can get free of the Supervisor. Or maybe it will be Yvette, depending on who gets along the best with her."

"You don't sound optimistic."

Shig lifted his round shoulders in a weary shrug and slitted his eyes as he stared up at Capella. The slight smile on his broad lips gave his walnut-brown face an almost beatific expression. He sniffed, as if savoring the subtle scents of Donovan: damp soil, musty, tinged by the cardamom-like odor of the plants and the breezes blowing in off the Gulf.

At last he said, "Judging from the supervisor's questions? Her terse demands? I get the impression that she is not impressed with our competence and may wish to make changes in the way Port Authority is administered."

"Might fire us, huh?" Talina leaned forward on her crutches and scuffed the clay with a booted toe. "Be a shame, wouldn't it? Corporation slap. Think I'll miss that couple hundred thousand SDRs they'll withhold? Might put a dent in my lavish lifestyle."

Shig sniffed again, nostrils flaring. "Gonna rain tonight."

"Yep."

"Supervisor Aguila has informed us that she is bringing twenty marines with her. Assuming The Corporation hasn't changed its stripes, I would expect them to have chosen combat veterans on the off chance that the missing ships might be tied to some social upheaval on our end. Perhaps piracy as we commandeered their vessels and crews." He shot her a sloe-eyed look. "Perhaps mutiny?"

"Twenty marines in battle tech could wipe this place flat. We wouldn't stand a chance."

"Nope."

She studied the pale tints in the sky. In little more than an hour the shuttle would descend. There would be questions. Uncomfortable questions. The kind none of them wanted to answer.

The wide expanse of the shuttle field had once been bounded by a perimeter fence—one they had torn down and used to strengthen the town's defenses. Now the pad gave way to what they called "grass," a composite of low-growing native plants that finally surrendered to brushland a couple of kilometers away. As long as a person didn't look too closely, the long thin leaves could almost make you believe you were on Earth. Cheng had concocted a paste from the stems that soothed burns.

"Have to keep someone on this gate at night," Shig reminded. "The soft meat won't understand that if they go out after dark, they're most likely a meal." He paused. "I think you need to consider the possibility that you might be ordered to return on the *Turalon*. Perhaps for reposting at Transluna or one of the colonies."

"Go back? Not a chance, Shig. And they can't make me. My contract was for ten years, and it was up six months ago."

"So what would you do? Couldn't stay in town. Go wild?"

"In a minute. You know that."

"The Corporation made an investment in you. Your contract might be up, but security has a twenty-year enlistment. You don't have the rank to resign. Got to be at least a captain."

She set the crutches to one side and settled herself on a crate, palms on her knees as she stared out across the field. "Sometimes investments go bad, Shig. Sure, I graduated at the top of my class in law enforcement and Corporate security. Almost went military, but jumped at the chance for Donovan because I figured a stint out here would give me a leg up on the competition. Do my time, meet the terms of my contract, and space back to a big cash bonus and a cushy job as head of security on one of the stations. Maybe the nanotech center at Transluna."

"Good position . . . if you could get it. Money, medical, excellent housing, vacation time, and lots of power and status."

As the breeze played with her long black hair, she noticed a loose thread in the patch over her knee. Flipping out her fighting knife she severed it and let it fall to the trampled clay.

"Bet I'd have nice, snazzy new uniforms to wear, too." She grinned up at him as she slipped her knife back in its sheath. "You know what? I lay in bed at night sometimes and think about it. After what we've been through here, Shig? I could almost write my own contract back yonder. But I'm not that same woman anymore. Some administrator in a tailored suit would walk up to me, puffed up with his authority, seek to impress me with his masculinity. First thing, I'd look to see if he had blood under his fingernails. All I'd see is soft meat. That would make it pretty hard to get along with the bosses. I wouldn't fit, couldn't be part of the team."

She sighed. "My guess? I'd be a very unhappy person. So, there it is. I'm a bad investment. I'll take the bush, thank you."

"In the event things deteriorate here, there's a cache of supplies—including ammunition and survival gear—under the white rock at Two Falls Gap. If you need it, it's yours."

"Think you know me pretty well, huh?"

"I remember your arrival. You were young, excited, and so very sure you knew everything. You needed Donovan. The wilderness. A matching of spirits and souls. You came here to sell water by the river."

"Sell *what?* You spouting more of that Hindu crap?"

"Buddhist."

"Shig, you know, most of the time I don't understand a word you're saying."

"It would surprise me if you did. You have a very young soul. Still immature and questing."

"You want to explain that?"

"The soul must experience many lifetimes to learn the lessons it needs to find enlightenment. This is one of your first lives—just as a student needs to take introductory courses and gain a foundation of knowledge before going on to more advanced classes. If you refuse to learn, and fail, you must retake the class. As the soul learns, it integrates, gains an understanding of existence and reality. Passion becomes balanced with wisdom and understanding. Your emotions will become integrated."

"And how many lifetimes does it take?"

"That's up to you."

"When does it end?"

"When you reach Samadhi, illumination."

"Right. And then what?"

"Sublime indifference."

She slapped a knee, laughing. "Got to hand it to you, Shig. You and your Buddhist—"

"What I just explained was Hindu."

"Damn, why do I even bother?"

They turned as Yvette stepped out of Shig's office door and called, "The Supervisor's shuttle has just detached from *Turalon*. Twenty minutes, people."

"Be right there." Shig acknowledged with a wave.

Talina snapped him a salute, adding, "Here's to illumination, boss. Let's give 'em hell."

She watched as Shig walked away; then she collected her crutches and rose to study the bands of high cirrus across Donovan's sky.

As the shuttle came in, its low roar would rise in the distance. Everyone on Donovan would know, including the quetzals. The people who'd taken to the bush, the "Wild Ones," would hear that whistling scream over half the planet. Some had left to escape The Corporation's regulations and laws. Others had just been seduced by Donovan. Then there were those who had gone off to prove themselves. In the days to come each landing would announce the resupply. By ones and twos the Wild Ones would come in to trade and see what was new. Then, restocked with what they could afford, they'd drift out again. Back to their haunts and homesteads.

Some would never return, having fallen prey to quetzals, bems, nightmares, slugs, or any of the growing list of Donovan's deadly flora and fauna. Others got lost, injured, died of exposure, thirst, poisoning, drowning, or any of the myriads of mishaps that could befall a human in the wilds.

Time to check with Trish one last time. As Talina turned, her gaze fixed on the distant line of brush.

The quetzal flared its wide collar in a display of bright crimson, then ran stripes of pearlescent white and orange along its body. Even across the distance, Talina could feel the creature's intent stare, could almost see those three shining eyes.

The uneasy presence inside her stirred, as if awakened. Her lungs filled, throat tightening into a hiss that she consciously stopped short.

"What do you care?" she asked it.

Did she only imagine a whistle of rage?

"God, it's like I'm turning into a quetzal," she chided herself.

When asked about it, the Wild Ones would shrug and say, "Quetzals? I don't know. It's just a thing. Like a truce. We don't bother them, they don't bother us."

Which had never made sense.

She had the unsettling premonition that this was more than just a bump on the head. Maybe it was time to go see Raya, see if . . .

"Talina?" came the call in her earpiece. *"Get your butt in here. We got fifteen minutes."*

"Yeah, I'm coming, Yvette."

She shot one last glance at the quetzal and gave the distant creature a nod.

The Corporation was coming. Some things were more dangerous than quetzals.

9

Cap Taggart—by virtue of rank—got the right-hand seat in the row of three behind the shuttle's pilot and copilot. G-force pressed him into the cushion as the pilot raised the craft's blunt nose and ploughed into Donovan's atmosphere. Remarkably adaptive, the seat had conformed to his combat armor.

Through the window, Cap was able to watch as they curled around the planet. Donovan was a green world, mottled with browns, tans, and grays that gave way to deep blues as the shuttle shot out over the oceans. In so many ways Donovan reminded him of Earth—and in so many ways it was totally alien: oddly configured, the colors slightly off, and the polar caps smaller due to the planet's fifteen-degree inclination. Like Earth, Donovan also had a moon, which, while smaller, orbited closer and at higher relative speed, which drove different tidal and climatic forces.

Unlike Earth, Cap could detect no trace of human beings. The first thing a person noticed while descending to Earth was the agricultural patchwork of fields, the long sinuous Vs of water behind dammed rivers, then the occasional gray-brown patch of city, followed by the linear profusion of power lines and roads. Finally the buildings could be discerned.

On Donovan he saw only wilderness, the patterns of the geology, watersheds, and lakes, all shaded by varying hues of blue-green vegetation.

The untouched nature of the world sent a queasy unease along his spine. Cap had never set foot in a place that wasn't "human." Sure, he'd been to the wilderness areas on Earth. Trained in them. But rescue was just a com call away, his every move monitored by command and control. Down deep he knew that "wilderness" or not, people had been trotting through that very environment for tens of thousands of millennia before he got there.

Donovan was . . . *different*.

The shuttle banked, wings glowing, and the gs increased. Through his window he could see the circular body of water called "the Gulf." It marked Donovan Corporate Port Authority's location. Like a bite out of the continent, the Gulf was an ancient meteor impact; one that had punctured the planet's crust, not only bringing rare-earth elements to the surface, but triggering volcanism that produced a remarkably pure volcanic clay that—when superheated in vacuum—baked into an incredible ceramic that would cut diamond like it was butter.

While the deceptively calm waters of the Gulf filled the east, the western horizon rose in a series of jagged-peaked mountain ranges. Following the curve of the Gulf to the south, however, one found impenetrable jungle. And in the north uplands composed a landscape of ragged chaparral cloaking uplifted sandstone ridges. Beyond that the country consisted of eroded and dissected mesas and buttes. The vegetation then gave way to the steppe, and finally to the distant polar region.

The shuttle shifted attitude and changed pitch as it tightened its approach.

There! Cap could see it now. Just a spot of difference. Tiny against the wilderness. The first thing was the open-pit clay mine, a pale gray crater in the background of aqua. Then its haul road running south. Yes, those were cleared fields by the dimple that slowly formed into a settlement. Settlement? Only thirty years old, Port Authority reminded him of pictures he'd seen of old Iron Age forts. A deep ditch—backed by a tall fence studded with guard towers—surrounded the town on all sides except where the shuttle port stuck out like a stubbed thumb. Occasional breaks were apparently gates in the fortifications.

The place consisted of low domes from the original colony and newer structures built of native stone and wood. He'd seen the pictures and called the architectural style "Donovan primitive." The streets—laid out in a Cartesian grid—remained rutted dirt. Just outside the fence, opposite the shuttle field, he could see a lot where aircars and various vehicles were parked in lines. Between town and the brushland, crops were being grown in addition to those in the big inflated greenhouses in the settlement's rear.

Whatever was going on, this was obviously an ordered society, not a chaotic rabble. Some form of government had survived.

Cap pitched forward as the pilot deftly dropped toward the shuttle port. To Cap's amazement, dust blew out in great clouds as the shuttle settled onto the dirt.

Not concrete. Not sialon. But fucking dirt!

"Jesus," he whispered. "What have we gotten ourselves into?"

"Thank God the atomic accelerators are sealed," the copilot, a trim thirty-year-old woman, muttered.

"Welcome to Donovan," the pilot called over his com. "Please keep your seats for a moment while we shut down."

Where she sat in the middle seat, Kalico Aguila glanced at Cap and suggestively raised her eyebrows. "Well, we're here, Captain. What on Earth do you think we're going to find?"

"Nothing on Earth, that's for sure." He gave her a crooked smile.

The shuttle's whine vanished into silence. "All clear," the pilot called.

"After you, Cap," Kalico told him.

He unbuckled and stood before plucking his helmet from the gear bin and clamping it on his head. Then he slung his weapons and ducked through the hatch into the main cabin. His marines were already suited, waiting on his orders, mirrored helmets turned in his direction.

"All right, people. Tactical deployment. Squad one, take point. You know the drill, children. Let's go."

He watched as Lieutenant Spiro leaped out of her seat, squad one merging behind her. A sense of pride filled him as they undogged the cabin door, dropped the ramp, and filed out in smooth order. Second squad was hot on their heels, followed by third and fourth, and then it was his turn. Clearing the door, he unslung his rifle and trotted down to the ground where his team had a firing perimeter established, weapons up and hot, eyes in all directions.

And . . . nothing.

Cap studied his tactical screens where they projected on his heads-up displays. People were waiting on the other side of the fence, a couple hundred of them, all packed in behind a solid wall of sialon crates. And, yep, they all had weapons.

Even as he watched, three people detached from the crowd and unchained a small "man gate" in the larger main gate in the chain-link and stepped out, walking easily toward his deployment.

Two tall women and a short man, they approached with their hands extended, palms out. Only the young woman—the one with black hair—was armed, a pistol holstered at her hip. As if to soften any threat, a cast on her leg imparted a pronounced limp.

"*Shit!*" Deb Spiro wondered through her battle com. *"What are they wearing?"*

"*Sort of like the circus,"* Sean Finnegan muttered.

"Or freak show," Mark Talbot added.

"Quiet, people," Cap ordered, and started forward.

They did look like a freak show, dressed as they were in worn coveralls with leather patches and iridescent rainbow boots. Only the crippled woman had on anything that passed for a uniform, and Cap hadn't seen that style in years.

Passing through his squad he met the three at the halfway point, rifle at parade rest.

The second woman, older, maybe fifty, her thick blonde hair pulled back in a ponytail, said, "We surrender, soldier. Bit melodramatic for an entry, don't you think?"

"Welcome to Donovan," the short, round-faced fellow of obvious Indian ancestry greeted. "Captain, if you wouldn't mind, could you remove your helmet? The reflection is good enough I can see that I didn't shave this morning."

"Stay frosty, kids," Cap ordered into his com before he shifted his rifle, slung it, and undogged his helmet. Lifting it off his head, he got his initial whiff of Donovan's air. First thing he noticed was the slight scent of spice, and then the fresh tang of soil and moisture. Damn, he'd missed real air.

"Captain Max Taggart, Corporate Security," he introduced. "Forgive the manner of our arrival." He let a cold smile play at his lips.

"We weren't sure what sort of reception we'd receive. And I notice that all of your people are armed."

"I'm Yvette Dushane," the tall blonde said with a slight nod. "This is Shig." A slight hesitation before she added, "Mosadek" as an afterthought.

"Glad to meet you, Captain Taggart," Shig said.

"I'm Talina Perez," the younger black-haired pistol-packer told him. "Port Authority security."

He fixed on her for the first time, taking in the cast and the fact that her uniform was so antiquated and worn it was almost a mockery. The pistol on her hip, however, had the wear-polished look of a familiar tool. Meeting her gaze, he found himself eye-to-eye with some . . . *thing.* A presence. Hard, deadly, almost invincible.

And then it passed, leaving him shaken and uneasy as he gave the woman a nod. Even though her dark eyes were now fully human, nothing about her could be taken for granted. It was a quality she had, unimpressed by his armor, or the troops behind him. As if he weren't shit on her shoe after the things she'd seen. He'd never felt the like.

And worse, she seemed to see right through him.

"Who's in charge here?" Cap asked, flustered and off balance.

"We all are," Shig told him through an inoffensive smile. The man's eyes drifted beyond the troops to the shuttle. "I would assume the Supervisor is with you? Do come. We have her office ready. There is a great deal to do. And no doubt your people would love to set foot on land again."

"Is there a hurry?" Cap asked.

"We'll have to shut down at dusk," Perez told him crisply.

"We have lights," Cap told her.

She hitched a half step closer, and he could see a pink scar still healing on the side of her head. With a finger she pointed past the shuttle. "Not more than ten minutes before you touched down, we had a quetzal just out from that brush. It's there. As I speak. Watching. Wondering. Sniffing the odors of soft meat."

The way she said it sent another shiver through Cap's bones. "Ma'am. Ms. Perez . . . Do you even have a rank? I don't give a damn about any quetzal. If it gets within a half a klick, my people will turn it into charred crisps. My concern is a couple hundred armed civilians just back of that fence."

Talina raised a hand, apparently to stop both Shig and Yvette from interrupting. "You and your people are new here. I get it. I was new once myself. There's a reason we call you 'soft meat.' Nothing derogatory. It's just the way it is."

"Talina?" Shig asked softly.

She lifted her stilling hand higher, hot black gaze never leaving Cap's. "Now, stand your troops down, Captain, and tell the Supervisor that she's welcome to disembark, make her introductions, and join us in the admin building."

"How do I know she'll be safe?"

"Because I give you my word."

He still hesitated, but an instant later, Kalico's voice in his earpiece stated, *"It's all right, Cap. I'm coming. Either that or we look like idiots."*

"Yes, ma'am." To his squad he barked, "Attennn-*shun*!"

Crisp to the point of perfection, they clicked heels together, clapping their weapons to port arms. Heads straight, backs arched, their mirrored visors reflected beams of Capella's harsh light.

Cap never let his attention waver, eyes locked on Perez's as Kalico walked down the ramp. As they were trained, his squad peeled off one by one and formed around her when she walked past. When Kalico stopped before the trio, she used voice amplification to announce, "I am Supervisor Kalico Aguila. I come bearing The Corporation's charter and with the intention of resuming the proper administration of Donovan and its resources. It is with pleasure that I arrive here, and I look forward to working with each and every one of you as we return this colony to order and security. You are right, we have a lot to do, so let us get right to work."

Kalico paused, the wind ruffling her hair in a most unbecoming way. Of course, she wouldn't have thought of the wind, not after two years in the *Turalon*, or her years in Transluna before that.

"Yvette Dushane, Shig Mosadek, Talina Perez." She singled them out one by one. "It is my pleasure to make your acquaintance. If you will lead forward."

Another gust of wind whipped her hair around her face, blinding her and raising havoc with her high collar and the flaring shoulders of her expensive gray suit. It ruined any impression of power and authority Kalico might have hoped to make.

Talina Perez was smiling, something hard and predatory in her eyes.

Cap ground his teeth as the Donovanians turned and led the way. This was madness. They were headed for that fence where a couple hundred armed civilians waited. Any one of them could lift a weapon, shoot Kalico down. There'd be no warning.

As if Perez's word carried that kind of weight.

Only then did Cap see that Kalico's spiked heels were sinking in the weathered clay soil, causing the Supervisor to wobble and fight for balance.

What else hasn't Kalico Aguila anticipated?

10

The light stabbed into Dan Wirth's eyes. Damn! Capella was bright! And he was looking right into it. Judiciously, he stepped off the ramp, stumbling slightly in Donovan's point-nine-five gravity. Not only that, but moving was different. For two years he'd been living in *Turalon*. And for six months before that, on a station. Both maintained g-force by rotation, which meant that a person inherently learned to correct for angular acceleration. It affected everything: balance, how to pour coffee, how to throw something, even how to walk. Directions became spinward and anti-spinward.

"Christ in the mud, Wirth," Stryski grumbled behind him. "It's bad enough we had to wait another day. Would you get out of the fucking way?"

Dan wobbled his way forward, his knees feeling slightly off. But the smell! The air was sweet, like perfume and spice. His nose had suddenly come to life after a long dormancy. And the colors! Everywhere he looked, even the wilted bluish-green plants at his feet.

I've lived for two years without colors.

The notion shocked him. Even in prison there had been colors.

He stopped short where an auburn-haired young woman was calling out, "Form a line! That's it. Next line over here."

Dan took a moment to appreciate her. She must have been just shy of twenty and tanned, green-eyed, with broad, strong-looking shoulders. Nice tits and ass. In his terms, she was the kind of woman who screamed for healthy sex. Right up to the moment she passed close and fixed him with a flinty and dismissively cold gaze.

What was he? Moldy meat?

Not that he could hold the thought. *This was Donovan!* Not Transluna, not Mars, or Io, mind you, but the farthest habitable planet from Earth. An alien world. One where humans didn't need to co-

coon themselves in a safe environment and build a biome. This planet would become the new Eden.

Stryski pushed ahead of him in line, raising his hands to the slightly greener-than-Earth sky. "Yeeeehaaawww! We made it!"

The giddy excitement had found its expression, and they all leaped, shouted, and danced around—if somewhat awkwardly in the new gravity. Dan whirled to the next person in line, hugging her to his breast, grabbing a hand and hop-dancing with Gopi Dava, heedless of the fact that he hated her guts.

"My *blessed* God!" Pete Morgan bellowed at the top of his lungs. "Look at all the wondrously empty space. Empty, I tell you. God, I *love* that word." He bent down and scratched the powdery soil. Cupped it up and held it to his breast as tears streaked down his cheeks.

"How I dreamed of this day," Dava told him as she leaned her face back to the sun, actually looking beautiful for the first time in her life. "I hated that ship . . . and prayed to see the sun again."

"It's not the sun."

"Who the fuck cares?" She giggled like a school girl.

He happened to look up as Nandi walked past in an oddly mincing walk—what he termed spacer's step—as she struggled with the gravity. She didn't look nearly as appealing in the pure light of Donovan's sun. He could see the age in her face, and way the planet's pull tugged at her full breasts.

I'm seeing her out of her element.

Had he been like that on the ship? Was that why the trip was so damned hard? He was a groundhog after all. What the spacers called "a dirtie."

He met Nandi's eyes and nodded, remembering how she'd stood before a monitor and told him, "That's the reason. Out there, Cowboy. Look at it! Forty billion stars . . . and I'm free to fly around them until hell freezes over."

And then she was past him, headed back up the ramp into the shuttle: a space creature returning to her environment.

"All right, Skulls, give me your attention!" a contralto female voice called.

He turned back to the front where a woman stood in the tall fence's pedestrian gate. Wouldn't that be a bastard to have to climb if you were in a hurry?

Then he really fixed on the woman. Maybe five-foot-six, with a really good body barely disguised by a black, form-fitting uniform. Okay, so it looked ten years out of date and was patched like a tramp's. So what? Especially when she had nice, high, and just right jugs, a flat belly, and despite the cast, the sort of thighs a man could dream about having wrapped tightly around his ass.

Who cared that she was on crutches with a cast on her leg?

"I think I'm in love!" Stryski moaned aloud.

"Think again, soft meat," the auburn-haired young woman shot back. "And if you want to get through that gate anytime today, you're gonna shut your yap hole and pay attention, or you can spend the night on *this* side of the fence!"

Dan smiled at Stryski's discomfort. The mechanic wasn't used to be slapped down like a child—and especially not by some green-eyed young slit who was dressed like a homeless derelict.

"I'm Talina Perez," the Latin beauty up front called. "I'm in charge of security here. My word is law. So pay attention. This isn't the Garden of Eden that The Corporation advertises it to be. Once you are processed and in the system, you'll be taken to the cafeteria for an orientation. There you'll be assigned quarters in a dome, and you'll meet your instructor. Your instructor will teach you how keep from ending your short and unhappy days as quetzal shit. Or worse. So, come on, Skulls, let's get a move on."

"Who's she think she is? Some kind of tough bitch?" O'Leary asked.

"Somebody whacked her hard enough to put that leg in a cast." Stryski gave them an evil grin. "Maybe she's into *strenuous* nighttime activity."

"Hey! Soft meat!" The auburn slit was back, face like thinly veiled thunder. "A quetzal broke her leg. Up close and personal. Before I shot it in the head and killed it. You mouth off again"—her hand was white-knuckled on the grip of her pistol—"I'll shoot you myself."

"Yeah, yeah," Stryski said wearily. "My 'pologies to the lady."

"Uh, she doesn't seem to like us," Morgan noted as the auburn-haired young woman stalked away. "What do you think 'Skull' means?"

"Bones, man." Stryski ran a palm over his shaved head to emphasize the rather knobby contours beneath his shining scalp. "So, come on, you heard the lady. Get the line moving!"

"Hey, if all the women look like that Perez and that green-eyed one, I could get to like it here." O'Leary had a dreamy look on his face.

Indu Gautamanandas—hands on her hips—looked back long enough to say, "Keep dreaming, limp dick. You didn't cut such a swath through the women's quarters back on *Turalon*, and you had two years and a captive population."

"Yeah." O'Leary adopted a thoughtful look. "Guess we got a lesson in how The Corporation's policy of preferential lesbian recruitment is working out for them. Would have been nice if they'd added at least a handful of heteros to the manifest this time."

Indu bent her lips in a smile. "A little surgery, O'Leary, a hormone implant to supply a bit more estrogen and progesterone, and you can overcome the mistake of your birth and come into your true flowering. Then you'll know firsthand. And it's not like you've been using your balls and dick for anything but manual dexterity training these last years."

"Fuck you!" O'Leary's complexion had turned a serious shade of red.

"If you'll recall, my refusal is what started us down this path of conversation."

The auburn slit, having overheard, was grinning as she started one of the lines forward.

Behind him, skid loaders rolled up to the shuttle bay, thick pinchers bearing heavy sialon crates.

Dan turned his attention to the surroundings, looking across the slightly-too-blue grass to the distant trees and then off to the north. Atop a low rise was a stone cairn, like a monument. He didn't remember it from the tapes they'd studied, but Port Authority had changed, much of it hidden behind the four-high stack of crates waiting for shipment off world.

"Hey?" he called. "Ma'am? You with the green eyes."

She turned, walking up. "Name's Trish."

"Trish. I'm Dan Wirth." He pointed. "What's that up there? That pile of rocks. Some sort of shrine?"

The humorless smile on her lips twitched slightly. Seeing her up close, she was cute, with a faint sprinkling of freckles on the bridge of her nose—though a deep-set hardness lay behind her green eyes.

"That's the first grave, Skull. The first man to set foot on this planet was named Donovan. Two hours later he was dead. The quetzal only managed to eat half of him before Donovan's crewmates killed it. They dug the rest of him out of the beast's stomach. Didn't want to take the chance of infecting the hydroponics tank with alien pathogens, so they buried him up there. We consider Donovan a sort of historical figure. To date, he's the only person killed on this ball of rock to have a planet named after him."

"But he was killed back in the hills, right?" Dan couldn't help but stare at the lonely monument.

"Sorry, Skull. Donovan stepped out of the survey shuttle to take a leak." She pointed to the top of the supply dome just visible over the line of crates. "Would have been right over there."

Gopi Dava asked, "But quetzals don't come around Port Authority anymore, right? Corporate says they're controlled around the compound."

"Glad to hear it," Trish told her, her gaze shifting reflexively to the distant line of trees. "Maybe the quetzals will get the memo. Either that or the one that took Allison Chomko's baby girl out of its crib last month couldn't read."

Pete Morgan said, "They told us Donovan was perfectly safe. That if a person followed the rules, there was nothing to fear. That there was an electric fence that kept the wildlife out."

"Oh, *that* fence!" Trish chuckled as if to herself. "The one we cut up for wire. See, it took special regulators to keep it hot. And the smart guys back in Tokyo, or wherever, only included one with the fence, figuring no doubt that we could just pick up a spare from supply, right? Maybe write a requisition?"

She paused, a distant look behind her eyes. "I'd love to see their faces when *Turalon* gets back and they read Shig's report." Her expression hardened. "Keep the line moving. We don't have all day."

He watched her as she walked off, thinking, *Nice ass.*

Then he turned his attention to the so-called grass. The pseudo-succulent that cattle could eat—until the arsenic toxicity built up and killed the gut microbes in the rumen. Which begged the question, where were the cattle?

And, fact was, he was going to have to fuck around with the damn cattle for a little while. He'd need the cover until he found the kind of woman he could run, could get established and start his game.

Grazing cattle on Donovan was a tricky business. Mostly they were supposed to eat alfalfa and timothy grass grown special for them. They could supplement with local plants, but had to be monitored, their grazing managed so that they didn't consume too much of any one thing lest it lead to rumen shock. And while most of Donovan's microbiology couldn't stand up to a cow's hostile rumen, a few species could. Those had to be treated before they could take over.

Behind them, lightning flickered in a black cloud that had rolled in from the Gulf. He could feel the coming storm, waiting, saving itself to be whipped into fury.

"Hey, Skull!" Trish cried. "You coming?"

Dan hurried to the gate, offering his papers to Talina Perez where she sat behind a sialon crate and tapped information into a portable solar-powered computer.

"Says you're a cattle production specialist, livestock technician level two?" Perez's voice rose with incredulity. "No shit?"

"I worked in a Corporate farm for a while." She didn't need to know that it was a prison farm—and that he'd hated every minute of it. "It was the only opening for Donovan that hadn't been filled, and I qualified. So, yeah, I'm contracted to take care of the cattle herd."

Perez glanced at Trish, a distasteful amusement in her gleaming dark eyes. "A cowboy?"

Trish broke out in laughter. "Bet he can ride a horse. Assuming we could find one on Donovan."

Perez asked, "What else can you do? Mining? Construction?"

He thought he could drown in Talina Perez's large, dark eyes. She had to be the most beautiful woman he'd ever seen. And at the same time, something in the way she looked at him sent alarm bells ringing down in his guts. That there was a whole lot more to her than just being head of security.

You are warned, Daniel. She could kill you just as easily as looking at you.

"Never done any of those things."

"What *have* you done?"

"Stayed alive."

Talina grunted. "Yeah, well, the last of the cattle died eight years ago, Cowboy." Her fingers were tapping at the keys. "If you had to make your living any other way, how would you do it?"

"I was a pretty good gambler."

"Looks like the odds weren't in your favor when you opted to herd The Corporation's cattle. I'm putting you down for mining. Doesn't take much to dig clay."

"What if I refuse? My contract is for beef production."

"Oh, you can refuse, Cowboy. That's a contract issue. But if you stay it means you're off the payroll. Port Authority is like every other place. Market economy. If you're not on the rolls, you don't eat. Not unless you can pay for it."

"Fuck me," he growled. "What if I don't want to mine?"

"Take that up with the Supervisor. That's her area of responsibility." Perez seemed to be staring into his very soul, seeing him, naked, judging his character. It irritated him.

And the last thing he wanted was to spend another two years stuck down in the rat-warren of *Turalon*'s belly. Let alone end up back at Transluna where questions would be asked about Dan Wirth. All things considered, God was smiling down on him with the same intensity as Capella's warm and slanting sunset rays.

"I'll figure out how to make my own way."

Perez seemed to be hesitating, dissecting him with her eyes, disdainful of the kind of man he was.

And I thought she was beautiful?

"Don't cross me, Cowboy," she said as she handed him his papers. "And don't try anything with the folks here. They don't have a sense of humor when it comes to soft meat."

Lightning flashed followed by a crash of thunder. Storms on Donovan, he thought, could be just as threatening as its women.

The first hard, cold drops were splattering around him as he made his way into the dome for the next stage of his "orientation."

When he glanced back, it was to see Talina Perez's hard eyes watching his every move.

11

"What is it?" Trish asked as the first drops of rain slashed down out of the bruised and storm-tortured sky. Actinic veins of lightning, like great writhing snakes of light, strobed a glowing halo through the twisting clouds. As if knotted by pain, they flickered, contorted, and died, only to be followed by blasts of thunder that shook the ground, each explosive detonation sending its quivering impact through muscle, bone, and blood.

"Something about him." Talina clamped her computer closed against the onslaught. "The cowboy."

Trish ducked her head as the rain hammered down. Running, she led the way to Shig's office door and held it while Talina hobbled in on her crutches. Slamming it shut, Trish shook the water from her now-plastered hair and used her hands to sponge her face. "Damn! That hit with a fury."

Talina was still looking thoughtful as she laid the computer in its place.

"You still worried about the cowboy? Livestock technician, level two? And, I mean, the papers were correct, right? The Corporation actually *sent* him here to take care of cows?"

"You think back in Tokyo they know the herd's been dead for eight years?"

"Nope. It's been so long since I've seen a cow, I can't even remember what a one looks like in the flesh." Trish wrung the water from her sleeves, watched it splatter in starburst patterns on Shig's floor. "That's not what's bothering you."

Talina pulled a rag from her back pocket and wiped her face. "It was something about him. The way he looked at me."

"Hey! Talina! Hello! Every man out there was looking at you—and half of them were peeling your uniform off and fantasizing which position from the *Kama Sutra* they were going to bend you into as they did the ultimate belly bump."

"Then they're using the wrong reference. The *Kama Sutra* is kind of short on variations of the belly bump. Most of the positions are lot more . . . well, anatomically divergent." She shook her head. "No. The guy's a . . ."

"Sneak? Cheat? Reptile? What?" Trish shrugged. "I talked to him. Really cute guy with that soft, brown fuzz of hair and dimple in his chin. He just seemed like another Skull. Maybe a little smarter, but not all that different."

"He's a quetzal," Talina said softly. "Very good with camouflage. You don't realize. Don't see the real him until he drops the illusion. By then, it's too late."

"So? Donovan has a way of revealing who people are in a big hurry."

"So does being locked in the belly of a starship for two years. No, he's good. Me, I'm going to check. See if there was an incident with Wirth on the way here. Something. And I'm betting it was with a woman."

"How's that?"

"Because I'd guess his camouflage works better with women. You saw him, what did you think?"

"Like I said, handsome guy, soft brown eyes, sort of a vulnerable look. Nice hands and ass. Can't tell how he moves until he gets used to being planetside, but he wasn't nearly as wobbly as most of the others. Kind of a cute smile, and just the right amount of muscle. Wasn't a wiseass like so many of the others. Thoughtful, you know? Like when he was asking about Donovan's monument up at the cemetery."

"You picked up on all that? Out of all those men? He's the one who made an impression?"

Trish defensively said, "Well . . . yeah? I mean the rest of them were just soft meat. And yeah, I treated him like he was. That's what you do with Skulls. But, it was sort of . . . well, like he wasn't, you know?"

"Quetzal," Talina said softly. Then she glanced up. "No. Worse.

Quetzals don't prey on their own kind. Trish, you gotta promise me. Don't get close to him. I mean it. This is your warning."

"What warning?"

"I don't want to bury you."

"What in God's name are you talking about?"

"Not really sure . . . but something tells me I'd save everyone a lot of trouble if I just moseyed on over to orientation and shot him."

12

Cap stood at the supervisor's office window, hot coffee in his zero-g cup as he stared out at the fence that separated the admin building from the shuttle field. He'd insisted that coffee be on the second shuttle after learning the beverage hadn't been available on Donovan for years. And, indeed, there had been a rush on it as soon as the first pots were brewed in the cafeteria. And they did mean pots, having no idea what had become of the coffee machine.

Someone said it might have been cannibalized for parts.

"Fucking barbarians," he muttered as he stared out at the flashing lightning and bands of rain that continued to pound the compound. Sheets of water sluiced down the window and—he noticed—leaked in around the edge of the sill to follow a green smear of what looked like fungus down the stained wall.

Like most of Port Authority, the admin dome appeared to be on the verge of falling apart.

Cocking his head, he heard voices raised in the hall outside. It brought a faint smile to his lips. He'd put Lieutenant Spiro in charge of the flood of people who'd mobbed the hallway seeking access to the Supervisor. Most were there to bitch about contract violations, demand redress for some sort of injury, press for word about loved ones back home, request overtime pay, book passage aboard *Turalon*, plead for some special privilege, or what have you; and Deb Spiro was the perfect subordinate to act as interface. The woman had all the imagination and flexibility of a block of granite, was in fact rather brittle when it came to personality. And God help any poor bastards who might serve under her if she were ever promoted.

At the desk, Kalico half grunted, the disgusted sound deep in her throat as she watched the holo screen and read Supervisor Clemenceau's personal log. It had been sealed of course, waiting all this time until Kalico arrived with the Corporate access code.

Finally she slapped a hand to the desk, powered down the display, and straightened. She gave Cap a thoughtful look, face grim. "Un-fucking-believable. Send for Dr. Turnienko."

Cap accessed his com mic, ordering, "Private Finnegan, please escort Dr. Turnienko to the Supervisor's office."

"Firm'tive, Cap. On the way."

"Trouble?" he asked.

Kalico burst into caustic laughter. "Look around! This is a disaster. I've spent the last day reading reports. What few there are. And half the records are on *paper*, for God's sake! And homemade paper at that. Why? Because only a handful of pads still work. Twenty-four aircars are in the inventory, of which *six* remain operative. Of the three excavators only one is still digging. Three of the fifteen ore haulers still run. The others are sitting on blocks. Production at the mines is down to just about zip. Mostly maintenance, because the few miners left are filling out their contracts, and some of the others have been hoping to score big in the event a ship ever came back."

"What about the regional research base stations?"

"Three of the fifteen are still occupied. Strike that. At least as far as Shig and Yvette can tell, they're occupied. Six or seven were abandoned. They think. And there's been no word from the other five that were occupied as of the last contact, which was two years ago."

"And they haven't gone out to check?"

"Cap, they didn't want to risk losing one of the aircars—assuming they could still fly that far. And while they periodically broadcast on the shortwave radio, they're not sure the remaining camps still have electricity, let alone that anyone's alive out there."

"But there's a chance they are?"

Kalico shrugged. "The *only* thing these people have going for them is that terrestrial food plants grow here. Successfully in fact. And the native fauna won't touch them. Not even the invertebrates or microorganisms. Every one of the research bases had their own gardens."

"What about native foods?"

Kalico ran fingers through her black hair. "A botanist by the name of Iji, working with a chemist named Cheng, have determined that a couple of the local plants—if you can call them that—can be eaten.

But only for a meal or two. Until the body begins to suffer from toxicity because of the metals. The rest are either deadly or indigestible. We can eat most of the animals, especially the herbivores. In moderation. Every living organism on Donovan concentrates metals." She paused. "Do you know that they found a mountain of pure palladium just below the equator?"

"You're joking."

She shook her head slowly and stood, walking over to stare out the window at the storm-torn night. "This planet is a gold mine. Literally. Along with just about everything else that can be extracted. That, however, is not my problem."

"What is?"

"Whether to abandon the colony." She rolled her shoulders as if they'd stiffened. "Cap, here's my dilemma: The Corporation has invested nearly ten trillion SDRs in Donovan up to now. They sent me to get answers, and what do I find upon arrival? Seven ships are missing. Just vanished. The colony is in shambles. Three hundred and eighty-nine people are alive—they think—where our last census listed three thousand one hundred and seventy-one. The oldest person alive is a miner in his early seventies. Fifteen percent of the population are children. Barely enough to maintain viability."

She turned dark eyes on his. "Given everything I've told you, what's your analysis of the situation?"

"That mountain of palladium is tempting, except that it's way out here, clear across space from Solar System. But, Supervisor, I think it's too far away, and too uncertain to reach. Especially given the number of ships we've lost just trying to keep this place supplied."

She nodded. "My thought, too." A pause. "And there's another thing: This place is corrosive. I mean that in the social sense. I just finished Supervisor Clemenceau's log. The colony was falling into chaos even before his untimely death. He was almost living in a state of siege. He couldn't even walk across the Port Authority compound without an armed escort. The miners were in open rebellion, having called a strike, and political meetings were being openly held in violation of the Corporate compact. He'd lost control."

"What about his security?"

"Before I get to that, do you know who his main rival for power was?"

"Shig Mosadek?"

"Close. Yvette Dushane. Though Shig is often mentioned, but generally as a sort of easygoing mediator. And then, just as things are coming to a crest, Clemenceau flies south to inspect a promising outcrop of gallium arsenide near the equator. And he dies. Cause of death? You're not going to believe. It's listed as 'nightmare.'"

She arched a provocative eyebrow. "His security officer on that trip was none other than Talina Perez."

"Son of a bitch."

A knock sounded at the door.

"Yes?" Cap called.

Private Finnegan leaned in, announcing, "Dr. Turnienko, Captain. As ordered."

"Send her in."

Raya Turnienko strode into the room on long legs. Cap put her close to six feet, with a slender build, shoulder-length black hair, round Asiatic face, light-brown complexion. Something about her would have screamed Siberian, even if he hadn't reviewed her file. She wore a frayed and stained white lab coat, her hands in the pockets.

She greeted them with a smile. "I'm Raya Turnienko. My pleasure to meet you, Supervisor. You, too, Captain."

And just as quickly she produced a sheaf of papers from a pocket, adding, "Thank you for seeing me so quickly. Here are the requisitions for medical supplies. You'll find the critical list on the top. Hopefully they are in stores, but if we could tap the ship's pharmacy aboard the *Turalon* before the next shuttle, I would really appreciate it."

Kalico had stepped behind the desk, taking the papers. A frown on her forehead, she thumbed through them, expression grim. "I'll see what I can do." Then she glanced up. "But first, I need to have some answers."

"I'll do my best," Turnienko told her, expression flattening to neutral.

"What's the major cause of death on Donovan, Doctor?"

"The wildlife. Immediately after that is heavy metal poisoning. It's not as critical now since we've made major improvements to the water system. Most of that relates to cisterns." She inclined her head to indicate the storm outside. "Infection is number three—though with a resupply of antibiotics, we should be able to just about eliminate that. Next in line come accidents: falls, lacerations, crushings. We still get the occasional suicide and murder when interpersonal violence gets out of hand. Last on the list are natural causes like heart attack."

"What would your professional response be if someone attributed a cause of death to a nightmare?" Kalico asked it casually.

Turnienko hesitated. A flicker of surprise, then it was followed by a hardening of her features. Her voice dropped an octave. "Ah, you're referring to Supervisor Clemenceau. Donovan has no shortage of terrible and horrifying ways to die."

"Wait a minute," Cap interjected. "I have nightmares all the time. Haven't died from one yet."

Turnienko turned her knowing gaze on his, a faint smile on her lips. "What you are really asking is did Talina Perez murder the previous Supervisor?"

"Did she?" Kalico countered.

"Talina doesn't go around randomly killing people. Let alone anyone who doesn't deserve it. There's not that many of us left, and some of us are critical. Take Cheng. If we were to lose him, it could be the final nail in the coffin for Port Authority."

"But not the colony?"

Turnienko had shoved her hands back into her coat pockets, stretching the worn garment as she straightened her arms. "I don't have an answer for you, Supervisor. Some of the Wild Ones are flourishing."

"How?" Cap asked.

"Not sure, exactly. They are making it with their gardens, and through whatever happenstance seem to have brokered some sort of live-and-let-live deal with the quetzals, though the bems, slugs, and sidewinders remain a problem."

"What's a bem?" Kalico asked.

"That's Donovan shorthand for 'bastard evil monster.' We classify it as an animal, though that's an unclear distinction for many species on Donovan. Like all of the predators, it thrives on camouflage, preferring to look like a big rock. Matches the colors and contours of the surrounding stone—right down to the mineral inclusions. Mostly they prey on chamois, which, if you don't know, are one of the local herbivore species. They digest them by engulfing. If you pay attention, you can usually spot a bem, or smell it and avoid it. They're not fast, so they're relatively easy to evade."

"There's no mention of bems in the records," Cap added.

"Your records are eight years old," Turnienko noted dryly.

That was the thing about all of them, Cap noted. They all had that slightly superior arrogance. Treated the Supervisor and him as if they were children.

Kalico had picked up on it as well. "Doctor, give me your neutral, nonpartisan, and professional opinion. Can you do that?"

"Yes, Supervisor."

"Did Talina Perez assassinate Supervisor Clemenceau?"

"I don't have reason to believe Talina lied. She wrote up a report if you'd like to see it. I've got it somewhere in the files."

"I would. Thank you." Kalico steepled her fingers. "Assuming there is no more supply after *Turalon*, what are the chances that human beings can sustain themselves on this planet?"

Turnienko might have been a statue, though her dark brown eyes remained actively fixed on Kalico's. The pause stretched.

Finally, she said, "Long term? Without future supply? Toss a coin, Supervisor. I call it fifty-fifty. And if we make it, we're going to be very different human beings than we started out."

"Thank you for your honesty, Doctor." Kalico tapped the papers she'd been given. "I'll have my cargo load specialist check your request against the inventory and send the rest to the ship's clinic. See what we can come up with. You are dismissed."

At the word dismissed, Turnienko's lips twitched as though amused. Nodding to Kalico, and then to Cap, she turned and left the room.

"Now there's a cheery sort," Kalico stared vacantly at the door. From her pocket, she pulled a token, tossed it into the air, calling, "Heads." She caught it, slapped it on the back of her hand, and said, "It's tails. Donovan's doomed."

"She's lying about Clemenceau," Cap noted, his concerns slightly different from the Supervisor's. "As if this place somehow converts bad dreams to lethality? Was she referring to a sort of self-induced madness? Being stuck in a nightmare and not being able to wake up?"

"More to the point, Cap. The good doctor never denied that Perez killed Clemenceau."

"Yeah, I caught that. I say haul the whole lot of them back to Transluna, charge them with murder, contract violation, sedition, mutiny, theft, and every other charge Corporate Legal can come up with."

"Agreed. There's enough in the records and reports to convict without trial." Kalico stared thoughtfully at the desk. "I'd be within my rights to execute the ringleaders on the spot. But in the meantime, give me solutions. We've got one ship capable of spacing four hundred passengers. *If* there are eight hundred to evacuate from Donovan, how do we get them home on *Turalon*?"

"So, you're pulling the plug?"

"Damn right. But I need to give it a few days, get a better feel for the place and how to keep from having to kill a couple hundred of them when we make the announcement of forced evacuation."

"Any ideas on how to do that?"

"We need to make a statement, set an example. These people have been wild for years. It's time to bring them back under control. And, like wayward children, sometimes it takes a slap across the face to get their attention."

"So, what's the plan?"

"I need you to arrest Yvette Dushane, Shig Mosadek, and Talina Perez on the charge of conspiracy, murder, and theft."

"Those are all death penalty charges."

"Yes." She smiled grimly. "They are."

13

Without a cattle herd to act as camouflage for his actions, Dan had to figure another way to make a living. He just hadn't understood how perfect Port Authority was for his operation. Call it a dream come true. The place was wide open. No laws. No constant monitoring, and people came and went as they pleased. If he could have designed a colony to his own needs and specifications, it would have been Donovan.

The place was ripe for his picking.

The trick to rigging his game was to make it seem probable. Especially in the age of com-chip-brain interface. Any three-finger fool could buy an implant that turned him or her into a mathematical wonder—with all the computational abilities of said genius no more than a thought away.

A fact that had revolutionized gambling to the point it was illegal back in Solar System. No one in Port Authority, it seemed, even cared, let alone ran a game.

Computation of odds coupled with exponentially increased memory had allowed any simpleton to count cards. Instead, Dan relied on sleight of hand to manipulate the odds in his favor. He'd mastered every trick when it came to shuffling and dealing. Three-card monte, faro, and slap-jack were his forte when it came to cards. Craps, chuck-a-luck, crown-and-anchor, and poker dice were his preferred "fixed dice" games. Then there were the mechanical games of roulette and spin the wheel, while lottery pools filled out his repertoire.

He had spent his entire passage aboard *Turalon* biding his time. But for his indiscretion with Nandi, there'd been no hint that he'd been anything but a model passenger. Nothing to suggest that he wasn't the man he pretended to be.

Dan Wirth? The cowboy? A gambler and murderer? Gotta be a mistake. That Dan Wirth never so much as wagered a yuan on the way out.

His special cards and dice, the contacts and electronics, were all safely packed in his duffel. The game boards, craps table, and roulette wheel would have to be locally manufactured. Word was the Skulls could pick their personal effects up at the shuttle port starting tomorrow morning. As soon as he did he'd be in business. For the time being, he would rely on his single deck of cards.

They had all finished their "orientation" with a drill. A blaring siren had sounded and everyone had to drop what they were doing and get to their personal quarters and lock the doors. Supposedly this happened if one of the local predators got into the compound.

Into the compound?

Seriously?

With everyone safely locked away, drones and teams would hunt the creature down while others did a "head check" to ensure folks were where they were supposed to be.

Then two blasts told people the whole thing was over.

Hard to believe it was for real.

From his table in the back, he shuffled his cards as he studied the tavern. The Bloody Drink. What a great name for a place. The room had been dug four or five meters into the ground, the dome stretching high overhead. The floor consisted of carefully fitted stone slabs. A curving bar had been built in the back where an older blonde woman was in the act of writing a charge on a huge wall board. Each time she poured a drink, she'd turn and add the charge to a column behind the appropriate name.

An old meteorological station casing had been made into a keg which dispensed locally brewed beer. The shelving on the back wall displayed various containers ranging from bota bags to plastic gallon jugs, and even a selection of glass bottles all filled with different wines and spirits.

Good. A thriving local brewing and distilling industry made his task that much easier. Alcohol lubricated the entire process. Call it the gambler's best friend. And best of all, there was no Corporate monitoring that limited the number of drinks a patron could consume.

Illumination in the place came from the occasional glow globe and honest-to-god oil lamps—the latter having been made from hand-blown glass complete with impurities, wavering ripples, and bubbles.

The room was packed. People clustered around the chabacho-wood tables. Most were hunched forward on the benches, elbows on the hand-hewn and polished wood. They clutched mugs of beer, or bought shots of whiskey that were consumed with the accompaniment of toasts and cheers.

They jostled elbow-to-elbow, partly as a refuge from the storm, but mostly because everyone had come to inspect the Skulls and hear the news about home. The whole thing resembled a riot on low boil, the locals shouting questions, the Skulls shouting back about politics, explorations, setbacks, disasters, prices, the economy, what was new in movies, games, and sports. Which actors were big, and who was in power.

Way up above it all, the storm roared. Rain drummed on the high dome—bangs of thunder startling and loud.

Pete Morgan caught Dan's eye as he stepped in from outside, dripping rain. Morgan edged his way around the curve of the back wall, dropping onto the bench beside Dan.

"What's wrong?" Dan asked.

Pete spread his hands, water beading on his fingers. "This whole place. I mean . . . uh, it's just not what I thought it would be. Not a damn thing like the orientation they showed us back on Transluna. Some of the buildings look the same, but take a gander at this place. It's the bar. The *only* bar on the whole stinking world. I mean, this is it!"

"So far." Dan shrugged, carefully shuffling his deck of cards. It felt good just to handle them, to reawaken the dexterity in his fingers and wrists. Bottom card? King of hearts. Cut, cut, cut, shuffle, cut. Deal out one, two, three, and yes, there it was, king of hearts. He hadn't lost that special feel.

"Dangerous animals get inside the fence?" Morgan muttered. "So the siren goes off, and we all run to our quarters with this *thing* prowling around? I mean, they were serious! Creatures get inside and *hunt* us?"

"Bet it doesn't happen again. Not with this many people. And there's more of us to keep watch now."

"And did you see that cafeteria?" Morgan moaned. "That's *the* restaurant? I've been a lot of places: Earth, Transluna, a few of the stations. I mean if someone tried to open a ptomaine trap like that, Health Inspection Service would shut them down so fast their asses would still be spinning when they were thrown in the slammer. I swear! I saw a cockroach. With my own eyes."

"Actually, I've seen worse."

"Yeah? Where?"

A jail in Jakarta. What a sewer. "I'll tell you some other time."

Pete started, gaped. "Did you see *that*? That guy Allenovich just spat on the floor! On the floor! What kind of . . . ?" He couldn't finish . . . just shook his head. "Dad told me. Oh man, he said, 'Son, don't be a fool. We've got plenty of work for you here. In the firm. Enough geology to keep you busy for the rest of your life.' Man, he's gonna kill me. Write me out of the will. Especially when *Turalon* gets back and everyone hears what a shithole this place really is."

"Relax. It may not—"

"May not what?" Pete cried. "And what kind of housing have they provided, huh? A dome with four beds and a toilet? The water comes from a barrel in the back. We're supposed to drink *rain* water? People *spit* on the floor? I tell you, Dan, this is a living nightmare."

Pete was studying the backs of his hands, fingers flexed so the veins and tendons stood out. "I graduated at the top of my class at the University of Texas. Now I'm here? Look at them, they're savages. And now every time that siren goes off, we could be eaten by a quetzal?"

"That's why they're all packing. Wonder when we get our guns."

"I never even remember seeing a gun until I came here. Sure, police have them, but even so they only carry disablers when they are out on patrol. I mean, look. Every mother-loving one of them's got a pistol or a rifle at hand. Think they're loaded?"

"Yep."

"And that doesn't bother you?"

Dan shot him a sidelong glance. "Nope. But if it's bothering you, tell the Supervisor you want to break the contract. They'll put you right back in your berth on *Turalon*. In two years, if you don't vanish like all them missing ships, you'll be home."

"And spend the next twenty years of my life working just to repay my penalty to The Corporation."

"So, gut it out. It's only four years, and by then maybe they'll have figured out what's been happening to the ships. You go home with a big check and buy your dad's firm."

Pete shook his head. "It's this place. Did you know that half the houses have dirt floors? Only a couple of buildings have running water for God's sake. It's the twenty-second century, and people are living on dirt floors?"

"Maybe so." Dan cut, smiling as the ace of diamonds came up. "But they're not beholden to The Corporation."

"I'm a petroleum engineer. I was told there was a rotary-bit rig waiting for me out in the backcountry somewhere. A seismic team was supposed to have been on *Freelander* and run a series of vibrasonics on some promising formations west of the mountains. I was hired to interpret the data, supervise the building of a well pad and pit, make hole, log the core, test the cuttings for hydrocarbons, that sort of thing."

"So do it."

"With what? The jugs, computers, and software were on *Freelander*. Along with both of the crawlers for vibra-seising. Sure, I could improvise with explosives, but how do I read them?"

"Guess?"

"Hydrocarbon extraction is a science. Just like keeping your damn cows happy."

"Cows? All dead."

"Why am I surprised?" Pete laughed. "Yeah, well, you see, I got to thinking. Supposedly that rotary-bit drill rig was sent to Donovan on the *Governor Han Xi*."

"Which is lost in space along with all the rest."

Morgan gestured to the locals where they shouted, laughed, and hung on every word the Skulls exhaled. "Those are scientists? Technical experts? Highly educated specialists? You can find better-dressed vagabonds and beggars living in the sewers of Shanghai."

"Another couple of years, maybe you'll look like them. Big hat, hide coat, chamois pants, and a gun on your hip."

"Not on your life."

"Bet me on that? Two thousand yuan says you look just like them in two years."

"Sure."

Dan shook his hand, "You know, I take wagers seriously."

"Oh, yeah?"

To make his point—and to ensure Pete remembered—Dan slipped his little book from his back pocket. He'd been waiting two years for this. With his pen, he wrote, "Pete Morgan: ¥ 2,000. By 2155 he'll be dressed as a local."

"You bet your life on it, Pete."

14

"Excuse me, that's my chair," Talina told the Skull as she shucked the wet slicker off of her shoulders and shook it, much to the Skull's surprise and irritation.

She vaguely remembered that he was some sort of vehicle tech. The guy was big, thick-shouldered and dark-skinned, with a prominent straight nose.

"Your chair?" A hint of challenge lay behind his accented voice. He met her stare for stare.

"I'd move, Skull," Inga told him from behind the bar. "You wouldn't want your unconscious body dragged out of here and left in the rain on your very first night. And recovering from the concussion would be a bitch, let me tell you."

The big man glanced uncertainly at Inga, noted the excited anticipation of the locals who were crowded around, and nodded. "Sorry."

Talina watched him ease into the crowd, still casting unsure glances behind him. "Just a beer, Inga."

"Coming up. How's it look out there? Everybody where they otta be?"

"Yeah. Guards are on their posts and the drones are in the air. I double-checked the gates. All locked up tight. As long as nothing climbs the fence, our soft meat ought to be safe and cozy."

Inga banged Talina's beer mug—one of the very first ever cast at the glassworks down the avenue—onto the bar.

Talina took it, rotated in her tall chair, and braced her elbows on the bar behind her as she studied the throng.

Damn. How many years had it been since the tavern was this packed with people? The roar of them shouting over each other almost hurt her ears. The Skulls stood out, of course, dressed as they were in washed and clean utility coveralls. Not to mention that their shaved heads gleamed in the light. And so many! Had to be close to the entire four hundred of them swarming around maybe a hundred and fifty of her people.

So which one of them is going to start the rumble?

From long experience she knew her troublemakers: Step Allenovich, Tyrell Lawson, surly old Thumbs Exman, and Hofer, of course. But she hadn't a clue about who to keep an eye on when it came to the soft meat.

Speaking of which, where was . . . Oh, yeah. Dan Wirth. In the back, sitting with another Skull and shuffling a deck of cards, of all things. He might have been talking to his friend, but his whole attention was on the room. She saw him shuffle, and fix on Allison Chomko where she sat with Mellie Nagargina and Felicity Strazinsky, who worked as a nurse and seamstress. The women cupped their drinks as they tried to glance surreptitiously at the crowding Skulls. Talking prospects, no doubt; for the moment Mellie and Allison were both single. Donovan tended to be hard on men. A fact that pretty much limited Betty Able's income at the brothel. Suddenly, however, the tables were turned. The ratio of men to women coming in on *Turalon* was three to one.

"Betty ought to be turning handsprings," Talina mused. Might be worth stopping by her establishment before turning in, just to ensure that things were in order.

Yep, Wirth was definitely fixed on Allison, his eyes almost half-lidded, a slight smile on his lips as though in anticipation. Lady-killing fucking asshole with his fuzz of brown hair, those soft, almost vulnerable brown eyes, the full lips, white teeth, and dimpled chin. Talina hated pretty boys—especially the ones who could charm with a shy smile and send a woman's loins tingling with the mere hint of interest.

"Going to keep my eye on you, bucko me boy," Talina promised.

In many ways, Allison was the most beautiful young woman on Donovan: blonde, with delicately formed features and a body that distracted even the most honorable of men. But she'd always been fragile. A sort of china doll. Her husband Rick had been killed when a hauler he'd been working on had rolled backward and crushed him. At the time Allison had barely been two months pregnant. A month ago that child, a mere year old, had been snatched by a quetzal.

Allison blamed herself. Needed time to heal. Talina could sympathize. As long as it had been since she had laid Mitch in his grave, she still hadn't come to grips. Let alone shown interest in seeing another man.

Wait and see.

As if he could sense her, Wirth's gaze shifted, met Talina's. The man's challenge was almost physical, stirring a little flame of rage. The thing in her gut that she'd started calling "her quetzal" coiled tighter. A shiver ran along her spine—a sort of anticipation of combat. Like in the dream where she chased the chamois. Even as she thought about it, rainbows swam at the corners of her vision, and the colors around her shifted in a way that reminded her of an infrared scope.

For the briefest instant, she saw herself walking over, pulling out her pistol, and using it to whip the man half to death.

What the hell is wrong with me?

She gave the guy a half nod, and watched him flick her a three-fingered salute in return, as if in acknowledgement of their mutual dislike.

Returning her attention to the room, she caught sight of Shig as he started down the stairs, the lights gleaming on his black slicker. He stopped halfway, squinted in the direction of her chair, and raised a hand in greeting before diving down into the sea of milling humanity.

Moments later he elbowed his way through the press and studied her through thoughtful brown eyes. "We need to talk."

"Hey!" Talina bellowed. "Give us some room."

The locals around her end of the bar didn't even hesitate, dragging the Skulls with them as they opened a hole around Shig and her.

"Quite the rain out there. Really made a mess of our drill." Shig greeted, shooting a smile at Inga as she shoved his wineglass across the beaten chabacho-wood bar. Like usual, it was only half-full. In all Talina's years she'd never seen Shig drink more than a half glass—and even then he only sipped. Somehow he could make that half glass last him an entire night.

Now he lifted the rim to his lips, barely took a taste, and set it back on the bar.

"Maybe *Turalon* brought the storm?" Talina suggested.

"Oh, you can count on it. What little peace and tranquility we had? Consider the drought of anxiety and worry now to be officially broken." He looked around at the milling Skulls, barely seeming to note the ones watching them curiously from just beyond the protective ring of locals. "The skies have opened, and we are now awash. Flooded, if you will."

"Is all of life a metaphor for you?"

"You dare to suggest that it's not?" Shig lifted an eyebrow, expression sublime.

Talina shook her head, alert eyes on the crowd. Thunder banged, causing the soft meat to shift uneasily and glance, half-panicked, up at the dome overhead. But then, they'd been shrink-wrapped into a ship for two years, and many before that had lived on stations and in cities. For some this was the first thunder they'd ever heard. To them, the novelty of thunder and lightning—especially on an alien world—might have just been one more of Donovan's many miracles.

"I hate nights like this." Talina took a drink of her beer.

"Quetzals will be out," Shig agreed. "Bit early in the year for slugs to be running, but you might want to watch where you put your feet."

"I love an optimist. If that poison Mgumbe cooked up last fall worked, we should have killed most of the ones around the compound. My skin still crawls each time I think of the Han Chow kid."

"Proof that if you don't watch your step, what's way down under your skin can also crawl." A beat. "I take it that everything is operating smoothly and according to plan?"

"I made the rounds. Told everyone on duty to stay extra sharp. So far there's no trouble. For the Skulls it's still all too new, and our folks are trying to make a good impression as they check out the soft meat."

"Raya's unpacking her first crate of supplies. Which prompted me to stroll over here. She casually"—he stressed the word—"mentioned that the Supervisor requested your report on Clemenceau's untimely demise."

Talina's gut slipped and tightened. "Which of course she delivered."

"Raya is as conscientious as anyone on Donovan."

"Well . . . we always knew this day would come. You think it's gonna be trouble?"

"The Buddha taught that all of existence is dukkha, or suffering. We have no other reality. Draw your own conclusions."

"Fuck me, you can be depressing. What's your inscrutable Zen mind tell you she's going to do?"

"You are the one with intensive, top-of-the-line security training, not to mention so many years of hard experience. I am only a humble professor of comparative religion. You tell me." He beamed in triumph as her expression pinched in irritation. He loved doing that to her.

Then, just as she was drawing a breath to explode, he added, "I think the Supervisor is desperately struggling to find a way to proceed on her terrible path."

"What terrible path?"

"She has condemned herself to the relentless pursuit of remarkable and uncompromising success. An undamped inferno of ambition fills her breast, goading her to the point that she has staked her entire future on *Turalon* and Donovan. Risked everything. She has visualized her nirvana: It lies just over the metaphorical horizon. Just there. No more than a decade or so ahead. Only Donovan lies between her consuming ambition and finally slipping herself triumphantly into the Boardroom seat to which she is ultimately dedicated. Donovan is at once her potential opportunity and her potential doom, looming before her as a problem fraught with the high probability that it will destroy her."

"Donovan has a habit of ruining plans."

"Best not to tell her," Shig confided. "She has left no room for error. Compromise is unacceptable. Only through unwavering discipline, ruthlessness, and coldly calculated competence can she succeed. No impediment to her progress can be tolerated."

"Her funeral."

Shig frowned. "How do people get themselves into such predicaments? She has poured herself into a cast-iron straightjacket, her tunnel vision focused only on a distant light. She will miss so much of life as she hurls herself forward, unable to so much as spread her arms and feel the wind of her passage."

"Shit on a shoe, Shig. You sound sorry for her."

"I doubt she's strong enough to burst the crystallizing metal. Let alone free herself. I weep to see such a wasted soul."

Meanwhile the sour sensation in Talina's stomach sucked itself into an uneasy lump. "Getting back to Clemenceau, my guess is that she'll hold an inquest. That would be according to the Corporate book, given that there was no body."

"Expect a summons," Shig agreed. "Nightmare or not, you did admit to shooting him in the head."

She shifted uncomfortably, memories of the pistol in her hand, the almost joy in her heart. After what that scum-sucker had done to people—made Talina party to—she hadn't had so much as a tremor as she stared over the sights and into his horrified face. She could almost feel the gun buck in recoil.

Even as she had shot, the sensation of relief had come flooding through her.

"You could slip away," Shig suggested. "Go now. No one would remark if you left just before daylight. If you stay, try to fight this thing, Supervisor Aguila *will* destroy you."

"It was a nightmare, Shig."

"Clemenceau was a hated man. I am sure that he made copious notes about all of his feelings of frustration and anger when it came to his dealings with you."

"Well, what about Yvette, you, and Mitch? You don't need to be an ambitious Corporate-climbing bitch to find a mutiny in what we did here." She gulped a swallow of beer. "That *is* the term for it, Shig. And that's what my superbly trained in sophisticated security techniques and Corporate law brain tells me. Once Clemenceau and his deputies were out of the way, we took over the fucking colony. Tossed The Corporation's book of law, rules, and regulations into the recycle bin, and ran this place our way."

"She has twenty combat marines. Nothing we could stand against. Yvette considers arrest as probable given that Supervisor Aguila hasn't requested our personal debriefings, input, or advice. The Supervisor's most economical and prudent course of action is to remove us as quickly as possible and confine us to *Turalon*."

"You could slip out, too," she told him with a weary smile. "Same with Yvette. We'd have a better chance with the three of us."

Shig took another tiny sip of his wine. "I cannot survive as a Wild

One, Talina. Nor could Yvette. We don't have your skills or that searing white heat of the soul that makes you great."

"Me? Great?"

"You are our strength. I am the soul. And Yvette? She's the cunning. She and I will fight in our own way, assuming we ever get to Transluna."

"You're sounding remarkably serene about all this."

He shrugged. "I am who I am. Who I was. Even before Donovan refined my understanding of life, death, and karma. Here, dukkha flows around a person as if he is immersed in water."

"Think we ought to move first?" She watched his soft brown eyes for reaction.

"My impression is that she's expecting that." He paused. "Run, Talina. At least for the time being."

She chugged the last of her beer. "Yeah, probably for the best, huh? Damn it, Shig! I hate to run."

"I'll tell the Supervisor I sent you on a scout. Where you gonna be?"

"Rorke Springs. The water there won't kill me."

"Watch your butt out there, Talina. If things become settled here, I'll send you a message."

"Right."

"Now, beat feet."

"Yes, sir."

Talina shrugged on her poncho and headed for the door. Outside the rain continued to pelt down out of the night sky. Shig was right, the quetzals and every other nasty damn thing on Donovan would be out hunting.

She splashed down the muddy avenue into the residential domes, one hand on her pistol. It didn't matter that she was used to the dark sections; the few remaining pools of light were cast by the last of the working street lights. So, which was the more dangerous? Donovan's predators, or the Supervisor?

Nevertheless she arrived at her dome without incident, stepped inside, and flicked on the light.

She had just hung her slicker when she noticed the drying puddles of water on her floor. Her hand tightened on the butt of her pistol when Cap Taggart—dressed in full combat armor—stepped out of her bedroom, rifle up. Another marine popped up from behind her couch, weapon leveled. A third stepped out of her bathroom.

"Go ahead," Taggart urged. "Draw that pistol. You'll save us the time it will take to try you and the effort of executing your ass afterward."

She actually entertained the urge to draw and shoot. A futility, given that they were armored. Nevertheless, she'd have the momentary satisfaction of going down fighting.

Slowly, despite a growing rage, she lifted her hands in surrender.

15

Allison Chomko tilted her head back and gasped, her arms tightening around Dan's back and shoulders. Artfully swiveling his hips he rolled his erection inside her, adding to the intensity of her orgasm.

The feel of her breasts against his chest, her hot panting against his neck, and the viselike way she tightened her legs around his thighs triggered his own response. Driving into her, he arched—as if to penetrate the woman to her center as he sucked air and his loins exploded.

Allison was still moaning when he finally slumped onto her, panting for breath.

"My God, my God," she whispered. "I can't believe it. I just can't."

Dan rolled onto his side, studying the woman's profile. Her pale skin had flushed pink over her cheeks, throat, breasts, and belly. He'd heard of it, but never seen it before.

On this or any other world, Allison Chomko was a find: artfully formed with full and rounded breasts, a narrow waist, and flat belly. Now she lifted a long leg as she used a cloth to stanch the flow of their combined joy.

"Married woman like you? Surely you've been off like this before? How did you ever make your daughter?"

She shifted, her deep-blue eyes almost luminous in the damp sheen of her flushed face. Curls of blonde hair clung to her forehead and cheeks, the rest of it spread out in a golden tangle on her pillow. "My parents were Third Ship. I was six when I came here. Grew up here. There wasn't a whole lot of choice, and the women have always outnumbered the men. Rick was Third Ship, too. He and I, we just kind of grew into each other. I mean, sex was good. But, damn, it was nothing like this."

Her smile exposed white teeth behind her pink lips.

He ran gentle fingertips over her drying skin, tracing patterns over her shoulder, along the line of her clavicle, and down the swell of her breast to circle her pink nipple. With soothing strokes, he teased it erect.

She sighed. "I could get to like this."

He gave her his most reassuring smile. "I've never met a woman like you. So strong, tough, and yet filled with such a compassion and warmth. I wonder if I . . ."

"What? Come on, Dan."

"Well, I was wondering if I had to come across the stars to find a woman that made my dreams come true."

He watched her pupils expand against the blue of her eyes, saw the softening of her lips. He could almost despise the men who'd never cherished her—never encouraged her to discover what a marvelous and giving woman she wanted to be.

Almost.

"That's the kindest thing anyone has ever said to me." Her eyes went suddenly misty, and she looked away, blinking.

"Sorry. Didn't mean to cause you any—"

"No, it's all right." She wiped her eyes, then knotted her fists against her chest. "I mean, you'll get the wrong impression. Rick loved me. He really did. And when he died, it was all I could do to keep one foot ahead of the other. And I knew I had to live for Jessie. Then, when she was taken from me? I guess I thought that was the end."

She took a deep breath, swelling her chest. "When you offered to buy me a drink last night, I just couldn't quite . . . Well, I guess it was your smile. The way you looked at me with such honest appreciation."

He'd read her correctly, all right. A lonely, broken-hearted woman in desperate need of being reminded that she mattered. That a modicum of hope still lay ahead of the current wreckage and pain in her life.

Could he pick them, or what? A smile, the soft-eye look, and she'd melted.

"If I could have one wish," he told her, "do you know what it would be?"

"Wealth and success on Donovan?" she suggested shyly.

"I would shower you with riches. Ensure that you never had to want again, never had to worry about being lonely and forgotten.

How would you like to be one of the most admired and influential women on this entire world?"

"And how are you going to do that? You don't even have a job. They brought you here to take care of cattle, and there's not a cow left."

"There are other ways to make money. Ways that don't involve risk and death and worry. Ways that would see you dressed in fine clothes. That would have others doing your laundry, cleaning, and cooking. Ways that would make you one of the most prosperous women on Donovan." He pointed a finger. "That's not smoke, my dear. I mean it."

For a moment she started to smirk, then her expression changed. "You're serious, aren't you?"

"Allison, I don't joke about things like this. I mean it, and I want you to help me. To share in the dream."

She stared thoughtfully at him. "Do you have some special contract with The Corporation? Know of some ore deposit, or something?"

"No. And let's let others do the hard work, the dangerous work. That sort of thing is risky, as you know so well. Me, I'd prefer the finer things in life. Like hot meals prepared and served. Clean clothes." He winked. "Lazy afternoons making love to the most beautiful woman in all of space. Seeing her smile, holding her hand. That sort of thing."

"And just how are you going to do that?"

"All in good time, Allison. But for right now, I think I've had time to recover. Why don't you lay back and relax? Let me see what I can coax from your body that you never knew you could feel."

He bent over, placing his lips to hers and using them in a caressing kiss that caused her to lace her arms around him.

Beautiful. Sensual. And willing to learn and trust. Allison Chomko couldn't have been more perfect.

16

The few who were out early had stopped, staring with disbelieving eyes as Talina was paraded down the central avenue by a four-man marine guard. The marines might have tied her hands behind her, but they kept their weapons trained on her as if she were still a threat to life and limb.

No sooner had she passed than the morning spectators hurried away. Knowing her people as she did, she had no doubt but that word would be all over town within minutes: Talina's been arrested!

She arched an eyebrow as she was marched up to the tavern door; chairs from the cafeteria were stacked three high on a wagon to the side. The old sign, scrawled in faded red letters, had never been as meaningful to her: THE BLOODY DRINK.

As she was ordered down the stairs inside, it was to see bedlam as marines and Skulls picked up the heavy chabacho-wood tables and hauled them over to be stacked to one side. Chairs were being set out in rows.

"Let me guess," she asked, "this is just the Supervisor's charming way of inviting me out for a drink?"

"Shut up, maggot," the marine—who had *Shintzu* stenciled on her armor—told her. "Head for that door to the right of the bar."

Talina considered her options as she walked across the stained flagstones. Inga's back room was large, filled with shelves, and had a small office in the far corner where the woman kept her accounts. A paved ramp allowed her to roll kegs and palettes of wine and whiskey down from the big double doors that opened to the stone-and-timber distillery and brewery out back.

Once in the room—assuming Talina could get free of the binding straps—was there anything she could use as a weapon? Some way to disable her guards? After that it was up the ramp, out the doors, and no more than a fifty-meter sprint to the west gate. Then another two kilometers to the bush.

As if I'd last a day out there unarmed, without food or water.

One of the marines—Talbot this time—opened the door, then stepped back as she entered. Fuck. More marines. All in armor. All with weapons at port arms.

And there, on a chair in the center of the room, sat Shig, his hands tied behind him, still dressed in yesterday's clothes. Yvette—also bound—slumped in a chair to Shig's right, her ash-blonde hair uncombed. She was wearing a bathrobe and slippers.

"Got you out of bed, did they?" Talina asked as she was led to the third chair. "That's about as rude as you can get."

"I didn't even make it home," Shig told her amiably. "Saved me a long walk in the rain. Thoughtful of them."

"Why the tavern?" Talina wondered as she was shoved into the seat.

"I don't know," Yvette told her. "But given that they were removing the tables, I'm hoping the Supervisor isn't considering shutting it down. Not only will Inga's income suffer, but half the colony will rise in revolt."

At that juncture Captain Taggart and Supervisor Aguila emerged from Inga's back office, where they'd apparently been in conference.

"Oh, the rabble can go back to their dissolute diversions," Supervisor Aguila declared as she walked over to stare down at them. "First things first. I have to deal with the ringleaders and mutineers. That necessitates your removal under circumstances that ensure your people are obedient and compliant. At the time of your convictions there will be an announcement that continuing investigations are underway. We've already had several most informative volunteers who have given us the names of your lieutenants. We'll have them by tonight. After that, anyone who suggests behavior which isn't consistent with the reestablishment of Corporate control will similarly find themselves in most uncomfortable circumstances."

"Got it all figured out, do you?" Talina mused, glancing around at the distribution of the guards. "Why are we here?"

"To be the scapegoats." Yvette didn't wait to be told. "The Supervisor, here, needs a spectacle. She's betting on a psychological bounce.

That the rest will see us taken down, convicted, executed, or hauled up to the ship, and they will be appropriately chastised. The hope is that if we three can be dispatched with such ease, the rest will be tempted to fall in line and not cause any mischief."

Aguila had crossed her arms over the fine black pantsuit she wore. The thing was immaculately tailored and accented in white piping. "Correct. 'Abandon all hope, ye who enter here.' I need order. Compliance. And you are my biggest obstacles to getting it."

"I am curious, Supervisor." Shig spoke in an almost friendly tone. "Upon your arrival, you made the assumption that we would oppose you. To the contrary, we had no agenda based on spite or conflict with you or The Corporation. Why didn't you simply ask for our cooperation?"

Aguila cocked a skeptical eyebrow, blue eyes hardening in her pale face. "Given what you people did to Clemenceau, how you've run this place like a chaotic hive—and in total disregard for Corporate law and regulation—I'm supposed to believe you'd just smile and step aside?"

"Corporate law might be fine for Transluna and the stations back in Solar System"—Yvette's cold green eyes narrowed—"but here it was getting people killed. Clemenceau couldn't see that. The tighter he clenched his fist, the more people he executed for disobedience, the faster the colony began to fray."

"So, you killed him and took over?"

Talina riposted. "You want to know why you've still got a colony here? It's because of us. *We* kept it together. Yeah, sure, we made up our own rules, let people start businesses. Hell, in violation of your precious Corporate law, we even let them wander off into the bush without going out to hunt them down like animals the way Clemenceau did."

Aguila snorted as if irritated. "Then I guess your success is your death warrant, Perez. In your own way, I'd say you've doomed this entire colony." She paused. "Remember that when sentence is served this afternoon."

"And there are no compromises to be made?" Shig asked. "No pleas entertained? No deals to be struck?"

"According to Corporate regulation 17, section 4C, tribunal will consist of myself, Captain Taggart, and First Officer Chan from *Turalon*. I wish you the best of luck with your pleas, Mister Mosadek."

With that she turned and stalked from the room, Captain Taggart close on her heels.

"Well, shit," Talina muttered, a sinking feeling in her gut. "Guess I just played hell, huh?"

"It's not over," Yvette told her. The woman's head was tilted back, and she watched the guards through slitted lids.

"Actually, we're going to trial," Shig said with a serene smile. "I suspect the good Supervisor will go out of her way to demonstrate The Corporation's superior knowledge, power, and invincibility."

"What do you think?" Talina asked, a tingle in her gut. Her vision was going all weird again, her hearing growing acute. Fucking quetzal was screwing with her. "Execution before sunset?"

"Most likely," Yvette said through a slow boil of anger and disgust.

Shig was smiling. "All is duhkka, and the Supervisor will, of course, condemn us based on the facts as she knows them."

"That's depressing." Talina was studying the guards. Would it be a firing squad? Was she looking at the men and women who would blow her body apart?

"It shouldn't be," Shig told her in that infuriating and peace-filled tone of his. "Those who are drowning in the darkness of *tamas* rarely see the inherent error of their ways."

17

Cap had to admire the Supervisor's adroit and swift moves. Her planning had been masterful, the execution flawless, and her sense for the colony's psychology most perceptive. Keep them off balance. Don't give them time to think, let alone organize. Reestablish The Corporation's authority in no uncertain terms.

He had ambushed Talina Perez in her house. Lieutenant Spiro had taken Shig Mosadek on the street as he left the tavern. And Kalico—accompanied by a couple of privates—had roused Yvette Dushane out of her bed. No muss, no fuss, no scene.

The tavern was the only place large enough to hold the trial. And even then, most of the *Turalon*'s transportees were relegated to waiting outside given the lack of available space. The colonists had been processed, one by one, each asked to rack his or her weapon at the door. They'd bitched, moaned, and resisted, but had surrendered their guns with the assurance that they could pick them up again on the way out.

Cap smiled as he looked out at the room with its ranks of seated people. Even now two of his men were wheeling the racked weapons off to the admin dome where they'd be put under lock and key.

The tables had been moved to the back and stacked, extra chairs brought in from the cafeteria. It was still a sight to get used to—people dressed like leather-clad savages with their oversized hats and rainbow-colored boots and coats. Such a collection would have been considered a freak show back on Transluna.

Cap, Kalico, and *Turalon*'s first officer, Zak Chan, sat on elevated chairs behind the bar. The rest of his squad were posted around the tavern perimeter. They stood at attention in their battle armor, helmets off, weapons grounded, and while not obtrusive, the authority they projected couldn't be misinterpreted.

"The natives are restless," Kalico noted as she reviewed her notes.

Cap couldn't ignore the shuffling, the nervous whispering, and downright hostile looks coming from the crowd. The feeling was like the heavy air that preceded a terrible storm.

"It's almost a surreal dream," First Officer Chan observed. He was present as a third, and impartial, official for propriety's sake, if nothing else. Between Cap and Kalico, they had the two votes they needed for conviction.

Lieutenant Spiro entered and stopped at the head of the stairs. Her salute told Cap that everything was attended to outside.

Into his com, he said, "Bring in the prisoners."

The door to Inga Lock's back room opened and Shig Mosadek, Yvette Dushane, and Talina Perez were escorted out by two of *Turalon*'s deck lieutenants. The prisoners were seated on chairs before the bar, facing the tribunal.

Kalico turned on her mic and rose from her seat. "Ladies and gentlemen, I have called you here today for the purpose of a judicial inquest into the charges of mutiny, contract violation, seizure of Corporation property for personal gain, conspiracy, and finally, to address the charge of murder in the death of Supervisor Clemenceau.

"Charged are Shig Mosadek, Yvette Dushane, and Talina Perez."

For a brief instant, the room was silent, shocked.

Then a voice shouted, "That's a crock of fucking chamois shit if I ever heard it!"

At which point the room erupted into bellows and shouts, people rising from their chairs.

"Order! I will have order!" Kalico bellowed over the rising chaos.

Cap gave his signal, and each of his marines lifted his or her weapon, bringing them to ready, safeties off.

Blood and guts! The damned fools weren't going to rush the court, were they? Cap's heart began to hammer as he read the rising anger: people shouting, shaking fists, wild-eyed rage behind their eyes.

Along the wall, his marines shifted uneasily; panic had begun to glitter in their eyes. In a flash, he saw how it was going to unfold. Beemer Station all over. Dead eyes. Floating bodies. Globules of floating blood. Blasted intestines.

His heart might have frozen in his chest.

"Order! I will have Order!" Kalico was screaming, the com thunder-

ing in the room. Contrary to its intent, it seemed to have the same effect as beating the crowd with a whip.

The moment they started forward, or if they so much as threatened a marine, it would take only a single panicked shot that would end in a fusillade. But the marines couldn't get them all. Not in the beginning.

Holy shit. We're all about to die!

He was up, waving his hands, fear like an elixir in his breast. "Wait! Please! *For God's sake!*"

As if that could be heard over the din.

Major Creamer's voice seemed to whisper in his ear.

In that instant a terror—almost an electrical charge—unlike any he'd never known, paralyzed him.

He saw it start. The triggering event. The big man. Step Allenovich. Pulled a pistol from the inside of his coat.

A pistol? How had his people missed it?

Step started forward, two others on his heels. He was raising the pistol, pointing it at the stunned Kalico.

The entire crowd was following in a flood. A mass of enraged humanity, men, women, even the youths and children, their faces expressing the intent of murder.

The subtle knowledge that Cap was about to die flooded through him. He could see it in the crowd, feel it. Stunned and overwhelmed by the certainty of it, he couldn't even reach for his sidearm.

They are going to tear us apart with their bare hands!

And all he could do was accept it.

In that instant Talina Perez shot to her feet. Despite her arms being bound behind her, she hooked her chair with a foot and kicked it into Step Allenovich's path, entangling the man's feet.

And somehow, over the crowd, she bellowed, "*You fucking morons! Stand down! That's an order, God damn you!*"

The crowd paused, and into the sudden silence, Talina cried, "Do you want me to come out there? Kick some ass? This is an inquest, not a pus-fucking riot! Let's hear what they have to say. Now sit your chapped asses back in those seats."

Yvette, also standing, ordered, "You heard Talina. If it's a fair trial, they've got nothing. There isn't a single person in this room guilty of anything. None of us has committed a crime under the Corporate charter. Myself, Shig, Talina, and all of you, we've had to take irregular steps to ensure the survival of this colony during the interim between supply ships. Supervisor Kalico is *required* to follow these procedures and hold an inquest."

Cap, his heart still pounding, wondered why the woman was lying.

"That is correct." Shig Mosadek's voice, somehow soothing, carried through the room. "Supervisor Aguila has ensured us that this will be a *fair* proceeding. A formality to ensure that the Supervisor has followed her proper procedures. As Yvette has assured you. None of us has broken any law. The Supervisor is aware of this, but she must ask the questions for the sake of the record. This is being done in case anyone back on Transluna has any concerns regarding the actions we've all taken to save our colony. The sooner she asks, the sooner Talina, Yvette, and I will be officially acquitted and released."

Cap spared a quick glance at Kalico, taking in the woman's conflicting shock, anger, and mystification. Her face was red, her breathing labored, and the veins in her neck pulsing. But it was her eyes that set him back, glittering in crystalline disbelief. Looking like they might shatter along with the rest of her.

So, now what, Supervisor?

On the floor, Talina Perez added, "You heard Shig. It's a formality. If we need to riot, I'll damned well tell you when to riot. Now put your asses back in those seats, or I'll come out there and put them there for you! *Now!*"

Cap watched in amazement as the mob seemed to defuse, some grinning to their companions as they settled back into their seats. Allenovich and a surprising number of others were shoving pistols and wicked-looking knives back into hidden holsters and scabbards.

For her part, Talina stepped over and used a toe to hook her chair where it lay on its side. Like a soccer player, she kicked it back to its former position, and with a flick of the foot, rocked it back onto its legs. More amazing, she did it despite the cast.

Along the wall, the marines were breathing deeply, no doubt aware how close they'd come to unleashing a storm of blood, death, and blasted bodies they could never have forgiven themselves for. One by one, the rifles were lowered, safeties flicked on, and returned to rest.

Yvette turned, staring Cap, Kalico, and Chan in the eyes. A challenging smile was on her lips, an arched eyebrow adding to the effect, as she said, "Supervisor, will you proceed please?"

It was Talina who added, "We'd like to start with Supervisor Clemenceau's death, if you would."

Kalico shot Cap a terrified glance, her normally ordered countenance in disarray. Only shattered fragments remained of her usual composure, and he'd bet she'd never faced the like of this in her structured Corporate universe back in Solar System.

"Sure." Cap gave Perez a reassuring nod.

If First Officer Chan's face was any indication, he looked as if he were on the verge of throwing up. His hands were shaking as they clasped his zero-g cup in a death grip.

Kalico's voice wavered as she began. "Very well, Security Officer Talina Perez is charged with murder in the death of Supervisor Clemenceau. By her own report, Perez relates that she and the Supervisor had traveled south to an equatorial region by aircar for the purpose of inspecting a potential gallium arsenide deposit. While in the process of taking readings and recording data, Officer Perez and the Supervisor had an argument, is that correct?"

Talina stood, her cast leg thrust forward. "That is correct, Supervisor. We got into it over his method of enforcing policy. I told him flat-out I would *not* continue to act as his assassin."

Cap watched a ripple of unease roll over the room.

"How would you categorize your relationship with the Supervisor?" Kalico asked.

"Not a lick of love lost between us, Supervisor." Talina nodded her head toward the papers on the bar. "If you've got his reports he probably refers to me as insubordinate, outspoken, rebellious, and of surly disposition. More than once he accused me of sabotaging his policies. To best state it for the record, you could say we despised each other."

The room exploded into cheers, applause, and catcalls.

"Order!" Kalico snapped, slapping her trembling hand to the bar.

She might have been pissing into the wind.

Talina turned and shouted, *"Shut up!"*

An almost instant quiet settled on the room.

"Security Officer Perez, at what point in your argument did you stop recording survey data and start back to the aircar?"

"When he told me I was relieved of my position and would be placed under arrest upon return to Port Authority."

Hisses broke out from the audience.

Kalico had recovered enough that acid laced her tone: "Is that when you claim the Supervisor had his nightmare and you shot him?"

"I don't think I'd use the term *had* his nightmare. Rather, the nightmare had him. And, for the record, I warned him beforehand."

"You warned him?"

"I did." Talina paused. "But I think he was more intent on being first back to the aircar where—"

"So, let me get this straight. Supervisor Clemenceau, in the middle of the day, is in the throes of a nightmare, and you shot him." She raised the pages. "In *your* words, 'as an act of mercy.'"

"I imagine anyone in this room would have done the same, Supervisor. Including yourself."

"Why didn't you recover his body?"

"Excuse me?" Perez seemed confused.

"Bring. His. Body. Back. Can I make it any simpler?"

"I *couldn't* retrieve the body. No one, not even your armored marines, could have—"

"Do you have anything else to add?"

"No, ma'am."

Cap tried to gauge the room's response. No one seemed even slightly unsettled by the testimony.

"You may take your seat. The Corporation calls *Turalon*'s ship's physician, Willa Tyler. Please approach and be sworn."

Lieutenant Spiro opened the door to admit Tyler, an older woman in her sixties. The long walk down the central aisle had originally been designed to add dignity and authority to the proceedings. Now Cap wasn't sure that it wasn't more of a death march.

As per plan Willa Tyler stopped before the prisoners, raised her hand, and swore the Corporate oath to relate the facts as she knew them and not to perjure herself.

Kalico asked, "For the record, you are a Corporate-certified physician of nearly forty years of service with all of the approved implants, is that correct?"

"Yes, Supervisor."

"You have heard the testimony, read the report, is that correct?"

"Yes, Supervisor."

"In your professional opinion, is it possible for someone to die from a nightmare?"

"Supervisor, a person might be having a nightmare at the same time they experience a stroke, an embolism, or perhaps a heart attack, but a nightmare during REM sleep, though terrifying, cannot kill you."

At this the crowd burst into incredulous laughter, some guffawing so hard that they slapped themselves on the legs.

"Order!" Kalico snapped. "Restrain yourselves. This is an inquest, not a comedy."

"Could have fooled me!" someone shouted from the rear, which incited yet more laughter.

Talina Perez called, "Hey! Shut your yaps!"

And again the room quieted, though people were choking on their attempts to stifle guffaws.

Cap had to remind himself to keep from gaping like an idiot. What kind of lunatics were these? They reminded him of half-wild animals, and the notion hit him that if they executed the ringleaders, what chance did he and Kalico have to actually control this lot? Was it even possible? Or would they have to have the marines shoot them all?

"Doctor, proceed." Kalico's voice carried a note of uncertainty.

"Well, a nightmare is nothing more than the brain cells responding during the REM cycle of sleep. It functions as a means of expression for the personality that—"

"Excuse me," Yvette interrupted.

"Out of order!" Kalico snapped pointing at the woman.

"Supervisor," Yvette's voice rolled out over the squirming, snickering crowd. "We know that you've just arrived on Donovan. And rather than see you become a laughingstock and figure of ridicule, we'd like to bring this line of questioning to a quick and less painful resolution."

In a voice like deadly ice, Kalico said, "Please do."

Yvette's lips twitched as she studied Ship's Physician Tyler. "A 'nightmare' on Donovan isn't just a disturbing dream during REM sleep—though, believe me, we have those as well. Perhaps more so than ordinary people."

She turned, fixing her green eyes on Kalico. "We didn't know what else to call it. And you can bet your ass, Supervisor, it's your *worst* nightmare. Of all the ways to die on Donovan, nothing else compares with the horror. You'd rather be gutted alive. Slowly. It's a lot the same, you see."

Yvette indicated Perez with a tilt of her head. "Did Talina and Supervisor Clemenceau have their differences? They did. We all did. The man didn't have the *qualities of leadership* to make Donovan a success. He didn't understand the *necessary compromise* that was required as supplies began to run out. Or that *innovation* was required to salvage Port Authority from a meltdown."

Cap ground his teeth, nervous gaze going to the crowd, who were just as good at getting the message as he was.

"If a nightmare had me," Yvette declared, "I'd want a bullet. So would you, Supervisor Aguila. You see, nightmares hide in mundo trees. They blend in. When a person walks beneath, they drop netlike tentacles that once affixed can't be unstuck. They immediately hoist you up into the branches. They start digesting you slowly, painfully, as their barbed tentacles wind ever deeper into your flesh and guts."

She turned to Doctor Tyler. "Ma'am, here on Donovan a nightmare is the local name for an *organism*, as well as a bad dream. Supervisor Clemenceau was already dead, and he knew it. Talina's bullet just saved him the excruciating agony of being digested for days."

Cap swallowed hard. *It's a fucking creature?*

They looked like idiots. And if they voted for conviction . . . ?

"Supervisor." He couldn't bear to look out at the crowd of colonists, didn't want to see the ridicule in their eyes. "Might we reconvene to discuss this?"

Kalico had gone white, her jaw muscles knotted, lips pinched. Something in her shattered expression told Cap that Kalico had never, ever faced anything so far beyond her control. For his part, Chan still looked confused and ill. Doctor Tyler had crossed her arms, an eyebrow cocked as she studied Yvette.

Somehow, Kalico managed to rise. Drawing herself to attention, she said, "I think we have all the facts here. The Corporation will no doubt find that all is in order. Captain Taggart, will you please have the bonds removed from the . . . um, respondents."

The crowd seemed to be teetering on a precipice, this could still go either way. It all depended on what Perez, Mosadek, and Dushane did next.

And if they step out and find their guns missing?

In this throat com, Cap ordered, "Spiro. Change of plans. You had best have that rack of weapons back here faster than spit hits the deck."

"Aye, Cap."

But some people were already started for the door. If they stepped out and those guns weren't there? They'd know they'd been duped, disarmed by a lie.

You better think of something damned fast!

"Ladies and gentlemen!" Cap called as he rose. "We're sorry to have interrupted your morning just so that the Supervisor could meet her responsibilities to The Corporation. As a token of her appreciation, if you will all help us collect these chairs and set out the tables again, the Supervisor would like to stand you all to a drink!"

Step Allenovich, not bothering to fool with the knots, was using a wicked-looking knife to sever Shig's bonds. Cap didn't take the time to wonder just where the blade had come from. Talina was already free, grinning to well-wishers as she rubbed her wrists.

Kalico was giving Cap the kind of stunned look she'd give a madman—or a Donovanian. Leaning close she thumbed off her com asking, "Buy *them* a drink?"

"Do you know how short the hair is on a neutron?"

"Pretty damn short."

"We're that close to a disaster. We're saving our asses, Supervisor.

Look at them." He indicated where the colonists were helping his marines carry chairs. They were laughing, slapping each other on the back. More than the colonists, the marines seemed relieved; no doubt their hearts were still hammering in their chests, and fear sweat had made their underwear clammy.

"What would have happened had Perez not stopped them?"

Cap closed his eyes and exhaled wearily. "Every man, woman, and child would have been shot down in their own blood, Supervisor. Maybe some of the marines would have survived to live with the memory of what they'd done. But not you, me, and the first officer. We'd have gone down in the first wave. We would be bloody corpses right now."

"I just don't get it. I don't . . ." She blinked, bewildered. "How could this have gone so . . . ?"

"Yeah. So let's buy them their drink and make like we didn't just have our undershorts jerked all the way up over our faces, shall we?"

"Could this get any worse?"

"Yep. And the day is still young."

18

Talina had her butt propped on her favorite chair, elbows on the bar as she surveyed the boisterous room. At the gut level her people understood they'd just won a victory—even if they didn't exactly understand the ways, means, or ramifications of it.

As the folks milled around the marines, grinning, passing pleasantries, they weren't paying that much attention to where the Supervisor sat at the other end of the bar, her head bowed close to Captain Taggart's and First Officer Chan's. As Supervisor Aguila talked in a low voice, she kept glancing speculatively at Shig and Yvette, and then at Talina.

Yeah, trying to figure out what to do next now that we bitch-slapped the hell out of them.

Bitch-slapped? She wondered idly what the origins of the words were, and whether it referred to disciplining a female dog or abusing a woman. Whatever. When it came to Supervisor Aguila, Talina figured it fit.

She watched Shig sidle up next to her, his bland face irritatingly smug with that placid look that seemed forever his.

"Dodged the bullet, didn't we?" she said.

"I wondered just how far you were going to let them go before bringing everyone to heel. When dancing with the Devil, one must be careful not to miss a step."

"Figured the Corporate dogs needed a bit of a shock, to be knocked off their balance." She made a face and shook her head. "Didn't figure that they'd just up and hand us an out on Clemenceau. I mean, I didn't even think Skulls could be that stupid. Thought Kalico was supposed to be some hyper-efficient, coldly calculating Corporate hotshot."

"In her world I'm sure she's most formidable. She would not have attained her present position were she not. I suspect she has just been humiliated for the first time in her life. That she hasn't stormed off in a pout indicates a more complex and adaptive personality than I would have suspected."

"We fucked up, Shig. Underestimated them. I mean, I walked in my door and right into an ambush not ten minutes after you warned me."

Shig was staring thoughtfully down the bar where Aguila and Taggart were shaking hands with Chan. A moment later the First Officer took his leave. Then the heads were together again. "If they'd held the hearing in private, we'd be in chains and headed up to the ship, you know that, don't you?"

"Chains?"

"It's a historical reference. Prisoners in the old times were chained. Much more cumbersome than ties."

"Packing the room with our people, you were counting on that, weren't you?"

"You heard the Supervisor. We were supposed to be made an example of. To see us condemned should have disheartened them, deflated any spirit of resistance, fostered the notion that, but for the Supervisor's grace, any one of them could be next."

"They don't know us very well, do they?"

"As of today they are learning."

"Think they took Yvette's hint about brokering a deal?"

"I am always optimistic that even the most benighted of souls lost in *tamas* might be tempted to embrace the quest of a Bodhisattva."

"You know, Shig, there's times when trying to talk to you is like hitting myself in the head with a hammer."

"Ah, self-induced suffering is the ascetic's fastest path to illumination—though given the rajas that dominate your personality, I would suggest simple denial rather than self-mortification."

"What did you just say?"

"That I like you just as you are, Talina. Don't change a thing."

With that, he patted her on the knee, smiled wistfully, and headed off through the crowd on his way to the door.

She shook her head, slapping her right hand to her restored pistol where it rode in her holster. God, it felt good to be back in control.

She was aware when Aguila gave Taggart a nod, straightened, and started toward the door. Four marines detached themselves from the crowd, closing around her in a protective detail. The woman might have been oblivious, although Talina figured that was an act. People watched as she climbed the steps and exited into the afternoon sun.

Talina took another swig of her beer as Captain Taggart bellied up to the bar beside her and leaned forward on his elbows. He seemed to scan the shelving with its various containers. Inga—now reinstalled in her kingdom—walked down, asking, "What'll it be?"

"Beer. Same as the security officer here."

Talina shifted enough to see Inga's suspicious scowl as she walked to the keg and filled an old ceramic mug. Setting it down with a clunk, she asked, "That one go on the Supervisor's account, too?"

"Of course."

"She damn well better be good for it. Don't you Corporate bastards try and stiff me now, or so help me, won't none of you be allowed to set foot in here again."

Before Taggart could reply she was off, heading for a knot of farmers who were back for refills.

"Tough lady," Taggart mused.

"Only if you piss her off."

Taggart kept his gaze focused on the wall. "Thanks for keeping a lid on things."

"No thanks needed." She glanced back over the crowd before fixing on him. He seemed content to let her study his ear and the left side of his head.

"Can we call a truce?" he asked.

"Can we?"

Taggart rocked his mug. The half of his expression Talina could see remained unemotional. "There's no other way to say it: We were idiots. Clemenceau's log entries, the way the reports were written, it looked like you, Shig, and Yvette staged a coup, murdered him, and seized the colony. What were we supposed to think?"

"The same thing you're thinking now: How do we get control of this world back?" Talina paused. "You've still got the marines. In armor, employing tech, and with their weapons, you can flatten this entire compound, blow every last one us away. Or round us up, corral us like cattle, and ship us off world. If *Turalon* makes it back to Transluna, you can hammer us all—one by one—in a courtroom. What's not to love?"

"Assume, just for an instant, that we wouldn't hammer your people in court. Just call bygones bygones. Would your people go? Leave Donovan?"

"Some. From my count, there's one hundred and thirty-six who have their bags packed and are dancing from foot to foot in anticipation of shuttling up to *Turalon*. They can't wait to space for home."

"What about the rest of you?" He still hadn't turned to look at her. He came across as a big, tough, soldier who'd just had his solid sialon foundation turn to sand. A man who was struggling to recover his balance—but didn't have a clue as to how.

"We'll stay. Even if it means your marines evict us from Port Authority en masse. Call us trespassers if you want."

"The entire planet belongs to The Corporation."

"Now, Captain, that's where you, the Supervisor, the Boardmembers, and the whole shit-sucking Corporation are wrong."

"How's that?"

"Donovan belongs to Donovan. Some it kills, some it drives away, and some it takes to its heart and breast. The reason Port Authority is still here for you to claim is because we fought for it. For ourselves." She paused. "The Corporation and our contracts? They were incidental."

"So, what's with these Wild Ones?"

"They belong to Donovan."

"Okay, so we've got the marines and the power of The Corporation. What have you got?"

"I already told you."

"I don't understand."

Talina dropped one hand on his shoulder, the other resting on her pistol butt. "Turn around. Look at me."

Taggart shifted, his hard blue eyes cold on hers.

"That's what we've got, Captain. The fact that you *don't* understand. You came waltzing down here after reading eight-year-old reports and found a self-governing colony . . . a whole world chugging along on its own. A place where The Corporation is irrelevant for the first time in over a hundred years. Man, you didn't even know that a nightmare is a predator. Which, for Donovan, is pretty damn simple. What kind of shit do you think you're going to be wading in when you come face-to-face with the complicated?"

"Talk all you want, you can't beat us."

"Don't need to. Donovan will do it for us."

19

The joke was, "Is Betty Able?" To which the wit replied, "Not only able, but ready, wet, and willing!"

For a price.

Dan sat at a table in the rear of Betty Able's brothel parlor. The room was small by Earthly standards, having only three tables, a couple of couches, and a bar in the back by the door that led to the rooms.

The building itself was of local manufacture, the walls built of hand-squared sandstone blocks, the wooden roof gabled, and a chabacho-wood plank floor underfoot. Refreshments consisted of whiskey, beer, and water. Unlike a similar establishment back in Solar System, neither mind-altering hallucinogens nor stamina-inducing pharmacopeia was offered.

A circumstance Dan would figure out how to change were this his establishment to run.

Unsurprisingly, the room was packed with Skulls—notably the ones who apparently hadn't a chance at getting as lucky with the local women as he had with Allison. And here, Dan had chosen to open his game.

He kept an eye on Betty Able where she dispensed drinks and took reservations for her two girls and the one young man. For the moment, all three were employed productively in the back rooms. And, older, tougher, and harder as she was, Betty could have been turning a trick or two herself but for lack of anyone to run the bar and take the money.

To ensure that he was tolerated, Dan made a habit of buying a round of drinks each time his marks ran low. Across the table sat Jaimie O'Leary, shoulders hunched, eyes squinted at his cards. To the right Fig Paloduro tapped his fingers rhythmically—his tell that he had nothing in his hand. On the left sat Abdul Oman, lips pursed, black brows lowered as he stared first at his cards and then at the pot in the center of the table.

And then there was Stepan Allenovich, the only local in the room. Not more than fifteen minutes ago, he'd emerged from the back, a toothpick protruding from the side of his mouth. Already intoxicated, he had given Betty Able a wink. Buying a beer, he'd pulled up a chair to watch Dan's game, and of course, had finally bought in.

Things were going well for a first night. In the beginning, Dan hadn't been seated for ten minutes before Fig Paloduro walked in the door and peered around nervously. Dan had waved him over, calling, "Fig! Drinks are on me."

Fig, everyone knew, actually had a pretty good stash of cash. No one had made much of it since there wasn't anything on *Turalon* to buy. But Fig had let it be known that he figured on using his stash to smooth his transition into a better life on Donovan, upgrade quarters, outfit himself with knickknacks, and enjoy a higher standard of living as was commensurate with his family's wealth.

"Call," Dan said, laying down his three sevens.

"Shit!" Allenovich cried tossing two pairs of threes and sixes on the table. None of the other hands were any better.

Dan raked in the pot, calling, "Ms. Able, another whiskey for Mr. Paloduro, if you don't mind."

He opened with a yuan as the others tossed in their bets. When she set Fig's drink on the table, the hard-bitten madam lingered long enough to shoot Dan a look full of warning, curiosity, and unease.

He handed her a ten yuan note in return, adding a "keep the change" motion that left no doubt but that he understood. As she palmed the money, she shot a suggestive glance at Allenovich; its meaning was clear: "Watch out for him."

Yeah, right. As if Dan hadn't pegged the big local as the wrong guy to skin right off the bat. The cards seemed to purr as he shuffled and dealt. "Some trial, huh?"

Allenovich shot a cold stare around the table, as if judging his companions' culpability in the proceedings. "Crock of quetzal shit if you ask me. That cold witch of a Supervisor . . . she sure as shit wasn't making no show. Not at the start. Wasn't 'til she saw the shit about to blow that she backed down."

"Heard it was that Perez woman that stopped it," Abdul said.

"Yeah." Allenovich grinned. "If she hadn't kicked that chair in my way, I'd 'ave been up on that bar, face-to-face with that black-haired bitch as I shot her fool head off."

"How'd the marines take it?" O'Leary asked, throwing two in for the draw.

"They was all shook," Allenovich declared. "That Supervisor, too. She's like a whole different woman after Tal stopped the riot. Looked like she just discovered a slug slipping into her foot. That sort of sick, pale, gonna puke look."

"Tal?" Dan asked.

"Short for Talina." Allenovich had a faint smile on his lips as he studied his three sixes and said, "Take two."

Dan dealt him a queen and a jack. Betty Able was watching from the corner of her eye. Time for Dan to show her he wasn't a fool.

"I owe that woman my life." Allenovich pointed a finger for emphasis. "You soft meat, take my advice: Don't mess with Talina. Tal don't take no shit. She's the law here, and she'll kill you as soon as look at you. Not only can she take care of herself, but every man, woman, and child on this rock will back her to their last drop of blood. Same for Shig and Yvette."

"I'll keep that in mind." Not that Dan hadn't already listed her as a threat, but if he had to take her out, it would have to be done judiciously, smartly.

"So," O'Leary asked, "Perez killed Supervisor Clemenceau?"

"Damn straight. Nightmare's a terrible way to die. If it had been the other way, and Tal'd been snatched up? She'd a pleaded with Clemenceau for a bullet. Sorry prick that he was, it would have been just like him to have walked away and left her."

Dan folded, letting the rest play out. "I don't notice a lot of yuan or SDRs floating around. And I don't see a lot of credit transactions through implants. How do folks pay for things?"

"There's ways," Allenovich said softly. "As time goes on, you'll figure it out."

"Tell me about Talina Perez," O'Leary said as he threw his cards in. "She got a man in her life?"

"Had one," Allenovich replied, tossing a long-crumpled ten SDR bill onto the table. "Any of you Skulls up to matching that?"

"Fold," Abdul said with a sigh.

"Sure." Fig shelled out ten. "And I'll raise you ten."

If Dan hadn't slipped in his shuffling, Fig should have two kings, two queens, and the ace of hearts against Allenovich's three tens and a jack kicker.

Allenovich wiggled the toothpick where it rested at the corner of his mouth. The man wanted to bet, ached to. Dan had seen it often enough. Allenovich had just tossed out the last of his cash.

Then, slightly glazed eyes narrowing, he reached in his belt pouch and laid a little gold nugget atop his ten. "I'll see you, and raise you twenty."

Dan kept his composure, but watched the others straighten.

"As time goes on, you'll figure it out." No shit.

Fig actually had a gleam in his eyes as he counted out yuans and SDRs. "See . . . and call."

As Allenovich laid out his three tens, Fig's expression fell. The man was almost salivating as he watched that nugget hauled off the table and back into Allenovich's pocket.

Bill Jones emerged from the back, looking nervous. He gave Betty Able a nod as she told him, "Anything else we can do for you? Maybe a drink?"

"Uh, no."

She was smiling gaily as she said, "Well, you do come back and visit us again."

Jones somehow managed to make his way across the room to the door without meeting anyone else's eyes.

"Mr. O'Leary?" Able called. "If you'd like to follow me back, I believe Angelina's about ready to receive you."

"Guess I gotta go," O'Leary smirked as he stood.

"You ask me," Dan told him, "I'd say your leaving is more about coming than going."

That brought a hard laugh from Allenovich. Fig shot him a slightly disgusted look.

"What about that Supervisor Aguila?" Allenovich asked. "She tight with that marine captain? Looked like they was more than just 'associates' up there at the bar this morning."

It was Fig who said, "Wasn't so much as a word about her bedding down with anyone, man or woman, during the whole trip."

"And you can count out the good Cap Taggart." Dan dealt the cards. "After Nandi and me called it quits, she was slicking her slit with Taggart's dick." He shot Allenovich a placid grin. "It's always rather pleasing to know that you got to something before an officer. Talent before status."

Abdul said, "Too bad she chased you out of her quarters with a pistol."

"No shit?" Allenovich asked as he studied his cards.

"No shit," Abdul told him. "Chased old Dan, here, naked through the ship. Left him heartbroken."

Allenovich paused at that point. "Didn't take you long to get over it, Cowboy. Just so you know, Allison's had a hard time of it. You be damned careful to treat her right."

"Allison's a jewel," Dan replied. "You going to bet that money or talk?"

Allenovich tossed out a yuan for his ante. "So the Supervisor's been without for two whole years? You ask me, God didn't give her that body just to turn it into a museum piece. That kind of equipment isn't meant to be wasted. I might look her up, offer her a reminder of the better things in life."

Dan considered his cards. "Step, my suspicion is that it might be fun to play around with the packaging, but when push came to shove, you'd get the same effect if you fucked a block of ice."

Fig and Abdul were grinning as they took their draws.

Dan checked the time. He had four hours before he wanted to be back at Allison's. At this stage, she needed to be coddled and guided with an expert hand. Not to mention that just through that door and down the hallway, his shipmates were fucking willing bodies. That kind of knowledge built up in a man's subconscious, leading him to memories of Allison as she lay on her back, breasts pooled, one slim leg raised in invitation.

Concentrate.

He chided himself with a smile as he tossed in another two yuan. He'd be home to Allison soon enough. And in the meantime, Step Allenovich had a gold nugget hidden away in his belt pouch.

One way or another, I'm going home with that nugget.

And he'd do it in a way that didn't piss off either Allenovich or Able. Given how things were lining out in his mind, he was going to need both of them. At least for the time being.

20

When a person went to the doctor's, they expected to be poked and prodded, but the way Raya Turnienko was peering into Talina's ear with her otoscope was absolutely annoying. The problem wasn't in her ears.

Although her hearing really had grown more acute.

Raya had just run a cranial functioning magnetic resonance imaging scan of her head and found nothing abnormal. No evidence of damage, nothing out of the ordinary in thought process or brain activity. The only oddity had been unusual activity in the limbic system, visual, olfactory, and language centers.

Talina sat naked to the waist on the examining table, her old uniform unzipped and wadded around her hips. The familiar equipment, lights, and supply cabinets looked old and battered under the failing light panels. Hopefully *Turalon* carried replacements. That or Raya was going to have to fall back on flashlights and lanterns to conduct her exams after sunset.

Raya had checked Talina's blood for heavy metal poisoning. That was protocol on Donovan. Always the prime suspect for any aberration in health. Talina's analysis was only a little high.

"It's weird to describe," Talina added as Raya prodded the glands in her neck. "I call it my quetzal. Which is nuts, right? It's a feeling that there's something inside me. Down here." She tapped her stomach just below her sternum and the V of her ribs. "It feels huge. Scary. Like the stories my mother used to tell about the old-time Maya shamans who had the souls of animal spirits inside them. They could shape-shift, turn themselves into owls, deer, and jaguars. But when they were human, they still had the spirit of the animal inside them."

Raya stepped back and reached for the ultrasound. "We'll find out. Lay back. Lift your arms. Take a deep breath and relax, okay?"

Talina settled onto her back. She clamped her teeth as the woman ran the sensor across her belly. The damn thing was cold and almost tickled.

"What do you see?"

Raya arched an eyebrow. "Oh, it's a quetzal, all right. Flared collar, slashing velociraptor feet, snapping jaws." She couldn't keep her face straight, lips curling into a smile. "Sorry, couldn't help it. I see a perfectly normal liver, large intestine, stomach, and the rest. Kidneys look fine. No sign of inflammation or masses. The diaphragm is normal. No abnormalities around the lower lobes of the lungs."

She ran the sensor between Talina's breasts and watched the screen. "Nothing around or beneath the heart. Beat looks normal, no sign of an abscess or mass. I wish all my patients looked as fit as you do."

As Talina sat up, Raya replaced her sensor and turned. "Tal, I don't think it's anything physical. But listen to me: You're lucky to be alive. First, you took a hell of a bump to the head. Second, you were badly injured. You're still recovering from the physical trauma. But third—and perhaps most important—that thing came within a whisker of killing you in a horrible way. That kind of traumatic stress changes a person. I'd be surprised if you weren't having nightmares."

"Not nightmares. It's like I'm running down chamois. Hunting. Seeing it like a quetzal would. I mean, I *live* it."

"The things you think you are seeing, the colors, the sharpening and changing of images? We call those flashbacks. And they're normal."

Talina took a deep breath. "But people with flashbacks, they relive past events, right? I should be back in that canyon, falling or fighting. What's going on with my vision? It's like seeing through a night scope. Like overlaying infrared and ultraviolet over an everyday vision, and the backs of my eyes have been aching like crazy."

"All I can detect is a swelling behind the retina and along the optic nerve. Maybe as a result of the bump you took. Best I can do without going in and taking a tissue sample." She reached for a pill bottle, shook it. "Look. Real aspirin. Take two, morning, noon, and night. But listen, I'm not finding any decrease in your vision. If anything, it's sharper than it should be."

"You're not helping, Raya."

The woman crossed her arms, head cocked. The hum of the refrigeration unit and the overhead lights were the only sound. "Tal, there's no creature in your stomach."

Talina raised helpless hands. "It's *my* body, right? There's something in here with me. I get this rush at the notion of a fight. And it's . . . it's *alien*. Like the thing is seeing, hearing, tasting, and smelling through me."

"Upsetting, huh?"

"God, Raya, it's like waking in the middle of the night when you can't sleep. Like knowing you have cancer—knowing its growing inside you. Then comes the feeling of despair and the knowledge that it's only a matter of time. And all you can do is lay there, and stare at the darkness, and feel the *thing* inside you."

Raya nodded. "You're in luck. *Turalon* showed up. I've got some meds that will allow you to sleep. Change the dopamine levels so that you can—"

"I don't need an antipsychotic." Talina snapped, then grinned in apology. "Not yet, anyway. Not that we aren't all a little crazy on Donovan. I can't take a chance on dulling my wits. Not now. Not with Aguila and Taggart scheming and plotting."

Raya smiled at something she didn't share with Talina. "All right. Listen. You're lucid, with excellent cognition. For the time being, I'm sticking with my call that what you are experiencing is a reaction to trauma. You have a Mayan cultural predisposition to internalize a spirit as a means of coping. Hey, my ancestors aren't that many generations removed from soul-flying shamans either."

"So?"

"So, you tell me that you can still control your quetzal, right?"

"Yeah, I can shut the irritating little son of a bitch off when I concentrate. It's only when I'm not thinking that I want to hiss or attack someone." Talina slitted a challenging eye.

Raya didn't go for the bait. "Sarcasm aside, how about when it gets to the point that you can't control it? That's when we'll worry."

"You sure about that?" Talina shrugged into her uniform sleeves and sealed the fasteners.

Raya tossed the aspirin to Talina, saying, "No abnormalities showed up on the scans except some accelerated brain activity and inflammation. Your lymph nodes are swollen. White blood cells and C-reactive proteins slightly elevated. Probably an allergic reaction. No tumors, no growths, no quetzal. I think that having that reassurance is going to make your life a whole lot better. Now, take your aspirin three times a day, and if things get worse, come see me."

"All right, Raya. But if I start changing colors, I'm gonna come kick your ass like it's never been kicked before."

"I think I can take the risk. Now, get out of here."

21

"I want you to know, *I hate this fucking planet!*" Kalico's expression left no doubt of her sincerity. She stood before the window in her office, blue eyes glittering as though on the point of tears. Knotted so tight the knuckles stood out white, her fists shook impotently before her.

Cap watched Kalico turn, stalk across to her desk, and drop into the chair. Propping her elbows, she ran nervous fingers through her thick wealth of black hair. "Damn them! I've never been so scared, so frustrated." She swallowed hard. "So *fucking* humiliated! Not only did we come within a whisker of dying, they made us look like *fools*!"

She lifted her head, fixing him with a fiery blue stare. "Nobody does that to me!" She shivered in rage. *"Nobody!"*

Cap knew better than to interrupt.

"As God is my witness, I will *break* them!" She slammed a fist on her desk. "Who the fuck do these people think they are? Don't they know who I am? *Nobody treats me this way!*"

Her eyes narrowed to slits. "I'm tempted to nuke this entire fucking hive. Burn it off the face of this foul piece of shit of a planet."

She fixed her heated gaze on him. "If you ordered it, your people would carry it out, wouldn't they? I mean, kill them all?"

"Yes, ma'am." He struggled to keep his expression blank, but inside, his gut was churning.

Worse, he could see her considering it. A woman who'd never lost at anything. He could only imagine the psychic trauma she was feeling. Enough to murder a whole planet? Shit, it was Major Creamer all over again.

What the hell are you doing, Max? he asked himself. *Who are you serving here?*

He took a deep breath, forced himself to relax, adopt a nonchalant posture.

"Supervisor, I've been giving this a lot of thought." Cap—trying to appear casual—chewed on the callus padding his right thumb. "Perez's got a point. You've seen the inventories. They were out of everything before *Turalon* arrived. Most of the equipment—crawlers, aircars, excavators, generators, you name it—was being cannibalized for parts. They were making their own meds, experimenting with pharmaceuticals, evolving their own form of agriculture. Battling to keep the damn wildlife out of their houses, for God's sake!"

"So, what's your point?" She flipped her raven hair back, giving him a narrow-eyed look that threatened death and dismemberment.

Careful, Cap.

"Something that Perez said. That they didn't have to offer us a truce, didn't have to lift a finger. That in the end, Donovan would beat us."

"And you believe that?"

"Ma'am, until we can figure out what happened to all those ships, this is a dead end. You know it as well as I do."

"So?" The word was like a lash.

He carefully said, "We don't evacuate the colony. Instead we load up every crate of resource down here, take the one hundred and thirty-six returnees, and wave good-bye."

"Just leave?"

"Yep. Sayonara."

She considered, an eyebrow slightly lifted. "Raya Turnienko said survival here was fifty-fifty. So, what if they make it? We come back fifty years from now and there's a thriving colony here? A world *they* claim as their own?"

"What of it?" Cap spread his hands. "The Corporation lands with a couple companies of marines, our tech, updated materiel, and builds a colony on the other side of the planet. This dump isn't sitting on the only outcrop of minable clay and rare metals. We can ignore the Donovanians. They'll be little better than Iron-Age farmers by that point in time."

"Just leave them to their fates?" she mused, and he watched the rage and insanity dial back a notch or two. "I like that. God fucking damn, I do."

Cap filled in the part she wouldn't commit to words. "Supervisor, you go home, write your report, and declare Donovan to be economically unfeasible until such time as the mystery of the missing ships is solved. You know the politics; most of the Board was for abandoning Donovan. *Turalon* was the last shot at salvaging the project.

"And God alone knows if they'll ever figure out what happened to those seven ships. Maybe it's something changed in the astrogation? Some fluctuation in inverted space that we don't understand? Or it's a flaw in the design of the ships?"

She shot him a wary glance. "Doesn't answer why all the ships up to *Xian* made it, why the next seven didn't, and we did. Assuming we can even make it back. *Mekong* sure as hell didn't. Now, that's a nice thought, isn't it? We're leaving these bastards here to die, but the moment we invert symmetry, it could be us who disappear forever."

"Your call, Supervisor."

Frown lines deepened on her brow as she thought. "How long until *Turalon*'s loaded and we can space?"

"The last of the download should be finished tomorrow. They've been shuffling freight around the cargo bays, filling space as soon as they empty it. The shuttles should have the last load up and sealed in three days. Maybe four."

She rose again, stepped back to the window. "As much as I'd like to just wash my hands of this damned place, we have legal responsibilities. If I'm going to abandon Donovan, I have to offer this load of transportees and those who've served out their contract the chance to return with us."

"Do we have the space aboard ship?"

She shrugged. "I don't know. If everyone we brought wants to go back in addition to the hundred and thirty Donovanians, that's five hundred and thirty some. Get with Chan and see what he says. Maybe we can make additional space in the pressurized cargo deck. Most of the cargo, the clay, the metals can ship in vacuum."

She added, "Oh, and get an idea of the Port Authority food stocks. Figure out how much we can requisition, and if there's a way of preserving it."

Cap inspected his dentally manicured thumb. By God, he'd dodged the bullet. "Anything else?"

"Yes. Try and have your people do this as inconspicuously as possible. The less the triumvirate knows, the better."

"Triumvirate?"

"It's an old Latin term for a three-man ruling council. As in Perez, Mosadek, and Dushane."

"I get your point."

"Good, because I'm still wavering about what to do with them. Would it be kinder to just execute them, or leave them alive to watch their friends and hopes die one after another?"

22

"What do you think is going on?" Shig asked as he leaned up next to Talina and gripped the chain-link fence with his fingers.

They stood at the shuttle port perimeter, mere spectators as the first loads of dried vegetables were loaded onto one of the shuttle cargo decks.

The day was mostly sunny, the temperature balmy; the breeze blowing in from the Gulf was thick with dew. Damp enough to turn even Talina's straight black hair slightly frizzy.

"They're outfitting the *Turalon*. Paying in SDRs," Talina told him. "Buying anything edible. Leaves and stems from things like carrots are being purchased at top dollar. Even the cactus pulp, if you can believe it."

"The stuff we grind up for mucilage? That we put it in the water system because it absorbs metals and particulate matter? What do they need an organic water purifier for on *Turalon*?"

"Think back, Shig. Three years ago when the big storm took out an entire crop."

"Okay, so we cooked the cactus pads in stew. I called it slimy shit. Tasted okay, but nobody wanted to eat it after we got through the thin times. Reminded people of starving."

"Survival food," Talina said thoughtfully.

Terrestrial cactus was one of the first plants to grow on Donovan; in addition to its benefits in water filtration and cleansing, the tunas, or fruits, and the blossoms were still collected and used for sweets.

She pointed. "Fifty sialon crates filled with clay. Still sitting. What do you want to bet? Aguila's cutting and running."

"You think she's going to write off the colony?" Shig had a dreamy look on his face.

"At the last minute, the good Supervisor is going to announce that any transportee who wishes to renegotiate their contract and ship for home can do so." Talina guessed. "Probably based on some excuse like the fact that their jobs no longer exist."

"She can't take us all."

"Nope. Not enough room on that boat." Talina pointed. "You see that stack of tarped equipment? It's grapples and such. For tying down cargo. Just about the amount you'd need to tie down those fifty crates of clay they aren't in any hurry to load."

"Which means? Come on, Talina. I'm not a space guy."

"That's where they're getting the room for our one hundred and thirty-six returnees. They're making living space in the pressurized hold. Socking in extra food. Probably freeze-drying it in vacuum and packing it in hopes that they can extend the hydroponics."

"What about water?"

"That they can make with hydrogen and oxygen from the tanks."

"What are we going to do about it?" Shig, for once, had a pinched look on his normally bland face.

"What can we?" Talina disentangled her fingers from the fence. "More to the point, Shig, what do we want to do about it? How many of us want to go back? To what?"

"But to be abandoned here? To know that after *Turalon* leaves, there won't be another? No more resupply? That will have an effect. It's one thing to muddle along, wondering where in hell they are and when they're coming. Another to face the fact that we're on our own here. Forever."

"I'm not going back." She shot him a glance. "You?"

Shig smiled wearily, as if amused at himself. "Too many people back there. Not enough quetzals. And what would I do? Go back to teaching? I fear that even the brightest of students couldn't synthesize the lessons I would try to impart. The totality of experience from which they come—let alone the culture in which they live—has nothing in common with what I've experienced here."

"No shit." Talina turned. "But we need to get the word out. Our folks need a chance to make that decision on their own."

"And if the Supervisor declares that she has no more room?"

Talina gave him a grim smile. "Well, Shig, she's a rational sort. Capable of weighing evidence and balancing the pros and cons of an argument. All I have to do is get close enough to shove the muzzle of my pistol into her ear. Once I explain the situation, I'm sure she'll be most judicious in her reply. Especially knowing that if our people don't get a chance to choose, she's not going back on that ship either."

23

The image of his father's penis filled Dan Wirth's mind as he lay staring up at Allison's bedroom ceiling. That that particular memory—so long forgotten—should pop into his head now, left him suddenly uneasy. He'd been what? Four? Maybe five?

His father had been laying on the bed, naked and masturbating when Dan entered the room. Not that little Dan had understood. Father had stopped, stared at him with those clever and hard eyes.

"Climb up here, boy. Take it in your hands." Father's voice seemed to echo inside Dan's skull.

He remembered climbing onto the bed, staring at how proudly that erection rose from the soft cushion of dark pubic hair. He'd been fascinated by the swollen pink glans, curious about the thick veins that ran like worms down the sides.

"I mean it. Take it."

Dan had been surprised by how warm it was, wood-hard under the delicate skin.

"*Squeeze it, boy.*"

His father had sighed, closed his eyes and leaned his head back, before saying, *"Now, put it in your mouth . . ."*

"Do you *really* have to go off to your game?" Allison interrupted the memory, voice petulant.

The image in Dan's head popped, leaving him feeling frustrated and disgusted. Fucking dumb kid that he'd been. He'd been what? Twelve before he'd gotten wise enough to sneak in during the middle of the night and lay a chef's knife across his father's throat. And when the old man had blinked awake, he'd whispered, "You ever make me suck your cock again, you'll wake up in blood."

That was the moment he'd become a man. Figured out who he was—and how the world really worked.

"Dan? Baby?" Allison lay beside him, head back on the pillow, her blonde hair spread like a halo. The sheet was twisted around her hips and right thigh. Her left arm was draped across her brow, and she stared up at the bedroom ceiling with glassy eyes, her pupils large and black against blue irises.

The drug was commonly called Eros, and in some circles it was considered the triumph of twenty-first-century pharmaceuticals. In small doses it not only altered the limbic system—numbing fear, fight, and flight, and enhancing libido—but it intensified the physical sensations of erotic stimulation and orgasm by a factor of two.

Outlawed as addictive for more than a century, it was nevertheless the staple of a thriving underground industry back in Solar System. Dan had thoughtfully obtained a half pint that he'd disguised in a cognac bottle and had sealed in his duffel.

She glanced at his erection, asked, "Thinking of me again?"

"Nope." He gave her a sardonic grin. "Thinking about my father. How thoroughly the sick son of a bitch used me. But then, given what I could do to him in return? Just by a mere accusation? I *own* that poor bastard."

"What did he do to you?"

"Nothing." As if he'd ever tell another living soul. "But for him manipulating the personnel data, there's no way I'd have ever scored a berth on *Turalon*." Or a new identity. And God alone knew how close Corporate security had been to catching him before he stepped into Dan Wirth's manure-stained boots.

As he rolled off the bed, he shot Allison a shy smile. "As much as I hate to, I've got a game."

She sighed, the action almost theatrical. "How'd you do that? You won almost two thousand yuan? Just playing cards in that place?"

"More than that, actually. Betty gets ten percent." He dressed, irritated that the crotch of his overalls cramped his erection. What the hell? Thinking of the old man should have left him as limp as yesterday's laundry.

"Can't you play cards somewhere else?"

"I'll start an occasional game at the Tavern, but for the moment, I need to scout the lay of the land. Figure out where I can work a deal to get a private room."

"Why don't you buy a place?"

"Buy a place?" He tried to keep the derision out of his voice. "Ah, perhaps wander into the administration dome, knock on the Supervisor's door, and inquire, 'Would The Corporation *sell* me a dome to use as a casino?'"

She gave him the pinched-lip look that she did when he said something stupid. "No, I mean buy a place from whomever owns it. Pay them money for their deed."

"I don't understand."

"Listen, Clemenceau was dead. It had been years since a ship had shown up. There were getting to be fewer and fewer of us. We didn't know if The Corporation was ever coming back. So we all got a piece of Port Authority. Surveyed it out. Drew up deeds to property and titles to pieces of equipment." She made a dismissive gesture. "We're just keeping quiet about it until we find out what's going to happen. Word is Shig, Yvette, and Tal are going to see how the Supervisor comes down on the idea."

Deeds? Titles? These fools thought they *owned* property? "She'll never go for it."

"Whispers are that she's thinking about abandoning the colony. Evacuating everyone who doesn't want to stay."

"*Turalon* can't carry them all. She's not big enough."

Allison gave a flip of the head. "Then the title question is moot, isn't it? What's left is ours to do with as we want."

"Assuming we can stay alive without supply." If they could, a vacuum would be left in the wake of The Corporation's withdrawal. He could end up a very big fish in a very small and possibly shrinking pond. Assuming he didn't mind getting his hands a little dirty in the process.

Blood—he'd learned by the time he was sixteen—washed off with soap and water.

What matter? It wasn't like there was anything to go back to in Solar System. While the odds were that they'd never find the real Dan Wirth's body, if he went back his time would be measured in hours rather than days. The first required medical exam as he was deboarding *Turalon* would turn up a discrepancy in the DNA, and maybe even blood type. Once that was put into the system for clarification, it would all come undone.

He'd already sucked his father dry of any benefit the old man might have left. And for all Dan knew, in the meantime since *Turalon* shipped, Corporate security might have stumbled onto the old man's record tampering.

Better to be a king in Port Authority than an executed corpse tossed headlong into a hydroponics vat back on Transluna.

"It all depends on what the Supervisor decides?" That notion intrigued him. "Have you heard anything about that?"

"Mellie Nagargina works in the control room. She hasn't heard anything straight out, but there's rumors that they aren't shuttling all the crates up to *Turalon*. And you've heard how they're buying up all the produce."

He had indeed. Via several of the farmers who patronized Betty Able's establishment, Corporate SDRs had been flowing into his pockets.

She added, "None of the ships ever bought so much produce before, Dan. Not like this."

"Trying to balance additional mouths against the output of the hydroponics," he guessed. "I worked there. *Turalon* was barely able to feed the crew and four hundred of us as it was. Makes you wonder if that's what happened to the other ships. Something broke and they starved to death."

Another reason he wasn't going back.

"So what do you think?" She was studying him as if he were a divine oracle. Damn, he loved it when a woman looked at him with adoring eyes like that. Reminded him of Cylie before she went all apeshit on him.

"So, Betty *owns* her joint?"

"Well, she's got title. Assuming Aguila either honors it, or doesn't stay on Donovan with her marines to enforce any damn order she gives."

Dan chuckled as he pulled on his boots. Life had indeed just become a great deal more interesting.

"Do me a favor, dearest love. While I'm at work, spend a little more time around Millie. See what else she hears."

"Dan, Millie will know it's coming from me if you start spreading it around."

"Anything but! Allison, this is for us. And only us. You can't tell Felicity or Trish."

Her brow lined slightly. "I won't. It's like something's changed. They don't say it outright, but since you moved in, they're different. Like they don't trust me anymore."

Of course not. They can see the changes, Allison my love. You're not the woman you used to be.

He took one last moment to revel in the lines of her body, and to savor the beauty she was.

Perfect. Just perfect.

He was still smiling as he walked out her door and headed toward the game.

24

What the hell was it about that woman? Cap—despite all of his better judgment—couldn't help but be intrigued by Talina Perez.

He perched off to the side of the Supervisor's office, his back to the wall, butt resting on the corner of a crate. In the three chairs facing Kalico's desk sat Yvette Dushane, Shig Mosadek, and Talina Perez.

Through the window at his shoulder he could see the latest shuttle loading bales of carrots, peas, and potatoes, much of it still a month or so shy of ripe. Didn't matter. It was digestible, if not at the pinnacle of taste. Vacuum dried, it might not be an epicurean repast, but it would augment the hydroponics.

Survival fare for the masses. Thank God I'm an officer.

He turned his attention back to Talina Perez—a much preferable diversion to thinking about the long and tedious passage back to Solar System.

Assuming they even made it back. A possibility that was gnawing ever deeper into his subconscious. *Mekong* had vanished without a trace. Not knowing the fate of the missing ships—not even having a clue as to why, let alone where they'd disappeared to—loosened the heebee jeebees to slip along his bones.

Better to concentrate on Perez.

Cap had thought her to be an attractive woman from the first moment he'd laid eyes on her: The planes of her face, those large dark eyes, the delicate nose, and the fall of ink-black hair imparted an exotic beauty that had only been accented by her healing scar and the cast on her leg. Tough, pretty, and wounded—with some dangerous quality that he couldn't quite describe.

But what had really sealed it for him was the way she'd shut down that riot at the trial. Nipped it in the bud with a bellowed command. That image of her kicking the chair into Allenovich's way, the fiery stance she'd taken, kept replaying in his mind. By God in heaven, she'd looked magnificent as she faced them down.

Had he really been ready to execute her like a common criminal?

Stop it! You're spacing out of here within the week.

When he went, so, too, went any chance of getting to know who and what Talina Perez really was.

Exotic? Hell yes! There were times she had an almost alien quality, as if some other intelligence was staring back at him through those haunting dark eyes.

The perfect woman? His skeptical thoughts lingered on that.

"Thank you for seeing us, Supervisor," Yvette Dushane began. "We know your time is precious, so we won't take much of it."

"That would be appreciated. What can I do for you?" Kalico's voice carried ice.

Talina bluntly stated: "How about, just this once, honesty?"

Cap watched Kalico stiffen. "I assure you, I have—"

"Yes, yes," Yvette waved it away, her slender hand flicking as if at a fly. "So how about you just tell us straight: How many people can *Turalon* actually carry? We've figured out that you are abandoning Donovan. We're used to running the figures on production, and you're leaving valuable cargo behind in order to pack additional food. That suggests more people than the hydroponics can support."

Shig added, "Which means you find yourself in the unenviable position, under contract, of having to return all of your transportees as well as those who have fulfilled their contract and request transportation home. No doubt it would be easier and preferable to leave them all behind and maximize profit from the minerals, but lawsuits brought by the outraged families over contract violation and abandonment would not only damage The Corporation's reputation, they'd cost more in the long run."

Talina then added, "Nor can you ignore the one hundred and thirty-six Donovanians who have requested return. The transportees would ultimately report that you'd left them behind."

"So, you're stuck taking them all," Yvette finished as she crossed her arms.

"What is your point?" Kalico barely managed to keep her voice civil.

Yvette cocked her head, smiling. "Talina's been conducting an unofficial poll. She's been asking, 'If it came down to it, would you go back if *Turalon* was the last ship to Earth?' Looks like you've only got another fifteen or so takers."

"The rest want to stay?" Kalico leaned forward.

"Even more would, with some incentive." Yvette held her stare.

"Such as?"

"You know that in The Corporation's absence, we granted deeds to individuals for property. We didn't do that lightly, but as contracts ran out, and no ship appeared in the sky, we had to find a way to keep people motivated. With a deed in hand, people started businesses, farms, mines, you name it."

"You had no authority. It's *still* Corporate property."

Yvette shrugged. "You want to keep from having a run on the ship when it finally gets out that you're leaving for good? That there will be no more ships. Ever?"

Shig was giving her that inoffensive look of understanding. "That means that essentially you are violating all the contracts . . . even for those who haven't finished their terms of engagement." He paused. "That will have to be dealt with when you return to Transluna. Someone will say, 'What about the people you left behind?'"

"We can solve that problem for you, Supervisor," Yvette continued. "All you have to do is validate their deeds and claims. Once you do, you call it 'negotiated compensation.' Your hands are clean. The Corporation owes them nothing. You have no legal liability."

"And they'd sign such an agreement?" Cap asked in disbelief. "The Corporation is their only way of ever getting off this rock."

Talina shot him a sidelong look. "Hey, Skull, what have they got to look forward to back there? Sure, there's family and friends. But even with the bonus, they still face the rest of their lives in a high-rise, or a cubicle on a station, or a piddling job packed in with a bunch of soft meat who've never scrambled. They know they're going to be paying rent for the rest of their lives. The Corporation owns *everything* back there."

Cap almost smiled at the challenge in her dark-eyed stare.

Kalico responded, "They *all* came here as Corporate contractees. Doesn't matter that their contracts have run out, they're living on Corporate property. Using Corporate equipment and dwellings. By the strictest terms of the law, they're Corporate wards who—by virtue of their presence on and utilization of Corporate property—have placed themselves under my control. This whole rock of a planet is Corporate property. Why should I give up so much as a square inch of it?"

"I suppose it's outside of your intellectual paradigm"—Shig arched expressive brows—"but let me try to explain. Inga's tavern? That's *hers*. To run as she pleases. Were she to go back to Mars, she could probably contract with The Corporation to administer a tavern for a specified period, pending renewal based on satisfactory profit and efficiency. However, her inventory, prices, hours of operation, and profit would be dictated by Corporate algorithms."

Kalico coldly stated, "The algorithms ensure that everything is fair, and all people are treated equally. The system is efficient. Goods are ordered in proportion to their anticipated demand at a given point of sale. There is no waste, shortages are rare. And when they occur, goods are fairly rationed. Prices are controlled and balanced to income and demand. There are no surprises, no errors. It's safe, serves the common good."

"Safe?" Talina said the word with such distaste that Cap squirmed.

"And sterile," Yvette added softly. "No risk. No freedom."

Kalico began twiddling her stylus between her thumb and fingers. "Your definition of freedom smacks of chaos and confusion. Why would anyone want to trade Donovan for home? People die here. There's no future beyond deprivation and uncertainty."

"As you see it." Yvette arched a mocking eyebrow. "Just assume we're all crazy here and don't have the sense to understand what bliss we're turning down back in Solar System. You've still got a problem: too many people to jam into the last ship headed home. We've got a solution: as Supervisor, you can validate our deeds. Sign over The Corporation's interest in Port Authority. Why not? You're leaving. Which means that it's ours in the end no matter what you decide."

"And what do we get out of this?" Cap demanded. "Like you say, once we space, anyone left behind can do with Port Authority as they wish."

Talina gave him a knowing look. "If Supervisor Aguila agrees to this? It makes a statement. A symbolic one. We're betting that once word gets out, *Turalon* will head back with empty berths, and you can pack all that space that would have been filled with unprofitable people with valuable metals and gems instead."

Kalico glanced uncertainly at Cap. "Would anyone actually agree to this? Stay behind just to call a square of Donovan's dirt their own?"

Cap took a deep breath. *Would they?*

Shig laced his fingers together. "One of the things we've learned to do here during the time before *Turalon* finally showed up is to take risks. For many of us, well, I'm not sure we'd fit in back in Solar System after what we've lived here. We'd probably be in trouble all the time. Life lived in the sterile control of the algorithms? Letting them determine what is best for us? The very idea is demeaning."

"And they certainly won't like our manner of dress," Yvette added. "Seriously, Supervisor, we're offering you a way out. A solution to the Donovan problem. Our people will go for the chance to own their own houses and businesses. Opportunity to trade as they will and make a profit? They'll bet that against the odds that they'll never see a ship from Earth again."

"You're telling me you can sell this?" Kalico asked skeptically.

"Damn straight!" Talina said.

"What's straight? I don't understand."

A crooked smile bent Talina's lips. "It's an old figure of speech, Supervisor. It means *of course* we can sell it."

Yvette then added, "What if we can sweeten the deal, make it even more profitable for you?"

"And that would be?"

Yvette gave Kalico a conspiratorial grin, reached into a pants pocket, and tossed what looked like a lime-sized chunk of frosted pink glass onto the desk.

Kalico picked the translucent stone up, held it up to the light. "What's this?"

"An uncut diamond." Yvette seemed to stifle a yawn. "Sure, they can manufacture something similar back in Solar System." She reached back into her pocket, tossing a walnut-sized gold nugget after the diamond. "That they *can't* manufacture."

"Where did these come from?"

"An undisclosed location. See, here's the thing: Goodies like that? They're in no short supply. Prior to the first of *Turalon*'s shuttles landing, most of the gems and precious nuggets vanished from circulation. Too easy to confiscate, right? They are, however, staples of what you would call the underground economy here. They could be yours."

Kalico had picked up the heavy gold nugget, juggling it as if to determine its weight and value.

"You're leaving," Yvette continued. "Abandoning all of the supplies and equipment that isn't deemed absolutely necessary."

"What if you didn't have to write it off as a loss?" Shig asked amiably. "You agree to our deal, we'll insist that our people *purchase* all of the supplies you're leaving behind. Auction to the highest bidder if you'd prefer. Or we can just go around and collect gold, platinum, gems, and the like—you should see some of the emeralds—and dump them in a crate for transshipment. Your choice."

Kalico stared fixedly at the diamond. "They'd give it all up?"

"Like we said." Yvette gave a bored shrug. "There's more where those came from. Here's the thing: Currently they are contraband, property of The Corporation, and as such, will remain hidden. We call it plunder. With a stroke of your pen, plunder becomes legitimate wealth, and can be traded. Get the idea?"

"Have to figure a rough exchange rate." Talina's gaze remained fixed on Aguila. "A given number of SDRs per karat or ounce, pending the grade of a gem."

Kalico took a deep breath. "Captain? Any thoughts?"

Maybe it was Talina's almost arrogant confidence, or the fact that for some odd reason, he'd come to trust her. And—what the hell—it wasn't like The Corporation was ever coming back.

"Supervisor, what have we got to lose? If these people can actually talk Donovanians into staying? With that extra cargo space, we've got a hell of a lot more profit to show if we make it home."

Still Kalico hesitated—and well she might. It would be an

unprecedented decision. The sort upon which her future might one day hang.

Yvette slipped a hand inside her quetzal-hide coat, withdrawing a sheaf of papers. "In hopes that you might be amenable, we've drawn up a preliminary agreement. As soon as we have a deal, we'll make the announcement and start the celebration."

Shig grinned slyly, "And Supervisor, it will be the sort of celebration you've never seen back on Earth or in one of the domes."

"Why doesn't that surprise me?" Kalico arched a skeptical eyebrow, a curiously amused smile on her lips as she took the papers and began to scan them.

Talina's deadly expression sent a shiver down Cap's back as she said, "At this stage of the game, nothing on Donovan should come as a surprise, Supervisor. And just between you and me? Take the deal. It beats the alternatives."

And with that, Talina Perez rose, nodded, and barely limped as she strode from the room.

25

"Take the deal. It beats the alternatives?" Kalico asked as she and Cap sat at what they'd come to call their "end" of the bar. Marines occupied chairs in a loose circle around them, trying to look nonchalant.

"Was that a threat?" she wondered.

"Supervisor, I don't think Talina Perez minces words. She's been too deep in the shit for too long to bow to the finer graces of diplomatic language."

"How far do you think she'd go?"

"We were going to stand her against a wall and shoot her, remember? That doesn't exactly inspire loyalty, trust, and fond feelings."

Which bothered him deep down. Too many things were bothering him. Like what kind of meaningless hell the rest of his life was going to be.

"Sounds like you admire her, Cap."

"Can we go off the record, Supervisor?"

She laughed, actually sounding amused, and for once her eyes sparkled. "God, yes! I'm at the end of my wits, Max. What the fuck do I do? You and I both know that we can't load everybody into *Turalon* and make it home. Just taking the ones we're contractually obligated to transport is going to stretch life support to the last millimeter. And that's not taking into consideration what the psychological effects *another* two years of cramped deprivation might precipitate among the transportees, let alone these wild-assed hooligan Donovanians."

"Assuming we even make it back." He gave words to the worry that consumed them all.

Her gaze seemed to clarify—and for the first time he could see the fear in her eyes. "That scares me more than you could know."

"Oh, believe me, I know."

She almost jerked. "You've seen? Have I let it show?"

"You've come across as a rock. Solid. Without a hint of hesitation."

"Well, thank God for that." Her eyes seemed to lose focus. "When I took this job, I knew the risks, but damn it, I really seriously figured we'd find those ships here. On this side. That every last one of them disappeared?" She exhaled in a half shudder.

"I know you've had Captain Abibi and her people working on it. Do they have any ideas?"

"Not a clue. The physicists aren't even sure what happens when a ship inverts symmetry. Everything is in the hands of the computers. Qubit computation manipulates more data than the postulated number of atoms in the multiverse. Some call it the 'mind of God.' Then throw probability into the equation, and maybe it turns out that making it through—following the math—is nothing more than a random chance."

She gave him a searching look. "You want to trust your life to that?"

"Sixteen out of twenty ships made it before *Nemesis* vanished. And of the four that didn't, that was early in the game when the route was still being tested. *Kleggan, Impala, Vixen,* and *Uhuru* were mostly survey vessels. Small, with deep space crews."

"You trying to reassure me?" Her lips quirked in a way that formed dimples at the sides of her mouth.

"Hell, I don't know, Kalico. I'm torn myself. And it's not just the *Mekong.*"

"How so?"

"We still off the record?"

"God, yes."

"Out there. Beyond the fence. You can feel it, can't you? It's like the planet calls to you. I mean, what's *out* there? Things no human has ever seen. That wasn't an act when Yvette tossed that diamond onto your desk. She meant it when she said that there was no shortage of wealth on Donovan."

"We can manufacture any size diamond you want back home."

"Oh, come on. You know the definition of perceived value. You get that big pink diamond faceted, hang it around your neck, and walk into a Board meeting? Everyone in that room is going to say, 'Holy shit! She's wearing a Donovan diamond.'"

She gave him a grunting nod. "If we take the triumvirate's deal—and if it wasn't just flapping lips—we'll make one hell of a dent in the precious gem and metal markets."

"No, we won't." He leveled his beer mug at her. "The algorithms will cause The Corporation to absorb the windfall and ration it out over time so as not to shock the market. Sure, the Board will read the report. You'll get a nice asterisk in your professional file, maybe a couple of points toward promotion. And over the next ten years or so all those gems will dribble into the market."

"Halfway pisses you off, doesn't it?"

"You've been here too long, Supervisor. You're starting to sound local."

That brought another burst of laughter. She was almost allowing herself to be human. Then her gaze cooled again. "What's the right choice, Max? I mean, shit, say we take their deal, sign the colony over, pack the ship full of wealth, and we actually do arrive alive. We unload a bloody fortune from *Turalon*'s holds, and I stumble into the Board and announce, 'I just abandoned the colony, but before I did I signed every Corporate asset on that rock over to the colonists.'"

"You could say 'Screw it' and stay here as Supervisor. Send *Turalon* back loaded with treasure and anyone who wants to go home. Gamble the ship makes it, and that it's enough wealth to entice the Board to send another ship. By then we've got even more gold and jewels and ceramic clay. Play it right, you've got your own empire here."

He watched the fleeting thoughts behind her normally controlled face. Seeing her like this, he realized that she could actually be as attractive as her physical appearance implied. For a moment her expression of vulnerability hinted that there really was a human being in there.

"My God, you're starting to sound local, too," she countered. "But try this on: I'm pretty sure I can justify abandoning the colony."

She gestured out toward the west. "You're right. There's a whole planet out there. I can walk into the Board and tell them, 'Port Authority is a write-off. More trouble than it's worth, so I signed it over. Ladies and gentlemen, the decision as to whether we go back to Donovan is in your hands. Evaluate the potential wealth against the costs and losses. If you do decide to go back, I am offering the following plan, which, if considered and adopted, will allow us to do this thing right.'"

"Assuming we survive the trip home."

She took a deep breath, lifted her small glass of whiskey and downed a swallow. She made a face as the stuff burned down her throat. "What do you think the odds are, Max?"

"No idea. If we just so much as had a clue as to why those ships disappeared . . ."

"I'm going to take their deal."

"You're sure?"

"For one thing, it buys us time. For another, I'm hoping their boast wasn't just wind, and they can indeed cut the number of people we have to transport. It will vastly increase our profits—especially if we charge not only for the supplies we're leaving behind, but for their property as well. Which gives me cover with the Board: I didn't just give Port Authority away; I *sold* it for whatever salvage I could. And finally, it changes our relationship with the locals. We're no longer the big bad Corporation." A pause. "And hell, once we're gone, it's theirs anyway."

"Then why are you still looking so worried?"

"Because now—and this is way off the record, Max—I have to see if I can find the courage to ride up to *Turalon* and order her to space for home."

"You as scared as I am?"

"As they say on Donovan, damn straight." She couldn't hide the terror that lurked behind her crystalline-blue eyes.

26

So, the deed was done. The Supervisor had agreed to recognize both deeds and titles.

Dan Wirth considered the sudden change in the community as he strolled down the avenue. The Donovanians were ecstatic. The mood in the town had changed in an instant. Like a switch being thrown, people had gone from circumspect and suspicious to outright friendly and open. Worry had given way to smiles, affable nods of the head, and genuine relief.

The new energy even extended to the somber and uncertain transportees, most of whom were still in a state of shock as they struggled to come to grips with the reality of Port Authority and their sudden reversals of fortune. That, Dan figured, wouldn't last. After all, the Donovanians owned everything now. The transportees, they had nothing but shattered hopes and expectations.

Dan smiled at the remarkable change in his own situation. He'd come here knowing that Donovan was his end of the line. A place from which there was no escape. Better that than the rather grim alternatives he'd left behind in Solar System. Corporate law enforcement had been closing in on him after Cylie spilled her fucking guts.

If he closed his eyes, he could imagine the hot thrill he would have enjoyed as he cut her throat. Something about the blood jetting from her severed arteries, splashing hot, steaming, and sticky on his hands as the knife sliced through her neck.

He wondered if she understood just what a lucky cunt she was, let alone the lengths to which her betrayal had led him.

To date he had assumed the identity of three different men. Changing identities in the Corporate universe was illegal, expensive, complicated, and full of risk. The right people had to be paid to change or expunge records, and a small but highly sophisticated black market existed to serve people like him.

The first time he'd needed a new identity—at the age of seventeen—he'd stumbled into the perfect solution: a friend of his father's in the office of records and personnel management wanted his young wife to disappear.

Dan had already killed a kid who'd screwed him on a deal to sell some stolen goods, so he thought he was prepared. Punishing someone was just a payback. Killing Asha Tan was different. Harder. He'd had to look into her eyes, hear her squealing behind the gag and, damnit, she'd been a pretty young woman. Twenty-six. With a killer body. He'd sobbed like a baby as he tied that plastic sack around her head, watched it puff and deflate as she sucked for breath on the inevitable path to suffocation.

After that, murder had never been hard. Unlike changing his identity in a universe where a person's life was controlled, monitored, and orchestrated by The Corporation. Not impossible. Just expensive to buy off the right people. After his first new identity change, he'd needed a CRISPR-IV kit to change his DNA. After his second, he needed a CRISPR-VII kit to add just enough genes to fool the identi-scan.

After Cylie turned him in, he didn't have time for a third. Instead Dan Wirth had crossed his path—and left him the perfect one-way ticket to a new life.

Boarding *Turalon,* he'd carefully handed over one of Dan Wirth's pulled hairs. He'd watched as the follicle was inserted in the reader, and Dan's DNA came up as a match. Thanks to his pedophilic father's help, his photo had been inserted and Dan Wirth's deleted in the Corporate OPM database.

And now he was here, walking the shitty streets of Port Authority. End of the line . . . and a dream come true the moment the Supervisor validated the deeds and titles. Call it a fucking miracle. These people *owned* their own property. To do with as they saw fit. Which meant that Dan Wirth had been dropped into an environment—however small—that brimmed with opportunity.

No watchful Corporation hung like the sword of Damocles above his head. Here, a man of his skills was only hobbled by his own imagination and dreams.

And did he ever have dreams. But first he needed a lair, a base of operations. Someplace that gave him respectability.

He considered the central avenue he walked down. Both sides of the street were lined with buildings. Some were domes from the original construction of Port Authority, while others had been built out of native materials. Take the big warehouse there on the corner. That belonged to Thumbs Exman. And the location was perfect, just a block north of the tavern on the main thoroughfare and two blocks from the residential section.

Dan considered the building. Sturdy, the walls had been constructed of sandstone blocks. The roof was an arched affair, and looked to be in good shape.

In the front, a large garage door filled most of the wall, and a smaller door was cleverly set in the building's corner. Walking down the length, windows in the rear indicated offices to either side of the back door. If a man wanted to start his own operation, Dan could think of no better location.

Returning to the front, he tried the door, found it open, and stepped inside the spacious room. The floor was duraplast, but high windows gave the room light. Walking to the back, the door to the hallway was open. Beyond it on the left were two rooms, on the right one large office.

Back in the main room, he imagined the tables, where he'd put the bar. And, yes, a cashier's cage in the back next to the rear door to the hall. Perfect.

A melodious tone rose on the still air, and Dan stopped. Cocked his head. Listened. Another musical trilling, a harmonic song . . . no, call it a chiming, rose to join the first. Then a third added its melody to create a symphonic sound that was both alien and beautiful. Like no music Dan had ever heard.

What the hell?

He traced the sound to where a shaft of sunlight from one of the high windows glowed in an irregular square on the duraplast floor.

Three creatures, each about the size of an almond, clustered together. Rounded shells, like hulls, shimmered in metallic greenish-blue. The effect was dazzling, reminding him of peacock feathers in sunlight. The music—like nothing he'd ever heard—enchanted him, brought a smile to his lips.

Bending down to stare, Dan realized it was the shells, vibrating so fast they shimmered laserlike in the light, that made the warbling harmonic.

"They're like bugs," he whispered, awed by the rising and falling music the little creatures made. "Fucking bugs. Who'd have thought?"

He straightened, glanced around at the big, empty warehouse. Yes, this was the place. Too damned good a place for bugs. No matter how pretty they sang.

He started for the door. Hesitated, then returned just long enough to mash each of the little bug-shaped creatures under his shoe. The shells crunching audibly beneath his sole felt rewarding.

27

Rising on a shower of crackling yellow sparks, the rocket soared into the night sky accompanied by oohing ahs from the crowd. At the height of its ascent, the rocket exploded in a lacery of yellow, red, and blue across the black night sky. The hollow boom followed a half second later.

People applauded.

Talina grinned, glancing out past the buildings to the perimeter fence and beyond. *Wonder what the quetzals think of all this?*

In answer something uncomfortable stirred inside her—as if irritated and amused at the same time. The beast Raya insisted didn't exist.

For that matter, she wondered what Supervisor Aguila and her shippies from *Turalon* thought. No doubt this night's reverie was like nothing they'd experienced this side of a historical VR-holo.

The soft meat, on the other hand, stood rapt in the amber light cast by the celebratory bonfires. Flames crackled and rose in reddish-orange tongues from the aquajade and chabacho logs. The stuff didn't exactly burn like terrestrial wood, but was close enough to serve the purpose. And around them, the Skulls openly gaped, pointing, sucking in great breaths of amazement.

Talina stood with feet braced, her right hand on her pistol butt. Screams of delight and whistles accompanied each of Cheng's rockets as they shot into the night sky. Flasks, bottles, and jugs were being passed from hand to hand. Laughter filled the night.

"Live it for all it's worth, buckos!" Talina shouted, raising her left fist high and shaking it. Because the day after *Turalon* spaced, the reality would begin to sink in.

"So those are fireworks?" a voice announced as a man emerged from the night.

She gave Cap Taggart a sidelong appraisal. "The very thing."

Another rocket rode a fountain of sparks and fire as it sailed high over Port Authority. It burst in green and blue streaks, then the report followed in a loud clap.

"Impressive," Cap admitted. "Never thought I'd see such a thing."

"Stick around, Skull. We'll show you some real amazements."

"Can we get past this 'Skull' thing, Security Officer Perez? I get it that there's a lot I don't know about Donovan. But I'm willing to bet you never led a company of marines in a firefight either."

"I'll consider it, Captain."

She was acutely aware as he took a position beside her, muscular arms crossed on his chest. Head up, he watched the dark wreath of smoke drift eastward across the brilliant frosting of stars.

He said, "All this just for the signing? The Supervisor merely scribbled a signature on a piece of paper."

"Uh huh, and everyone who could get to a monitor watched her do it." She sidestepped as a group of little boys burst out of the darkness and charged through the forest of adult legs. "You've got to understand. With that stroke of the pen, these people *own* their own lives now. It's freedom. The future. All they've got is title to a bit of ground, a dome, and the two feet they stand on. Anything else is what they make it."

He scratched the side of his jaw. "But, Talina, there's no certainty. Anything could go wrong. Who's there to save them if it does?"

She winced. His use of her name was oddly inappropriate. A sort of invasion. "They'll save themselves." She paused before hostilely adding, "*Max*."

He stiffened, seemed to swell, then let it go with a laugh. "Okay, I deserved that."

"Yeah, you did. And just after I'd decided to refrain from calling you Skull."

She watched the last rocket shoot into the sky, a big thing that whistled as it thundered up and up. It burst in a flowering of white light. Seconds later the detonation hit her like slap. Additional stars of color burst out of the trailing sparks like colorful sparkles. The subsequent crackle carried down as the displays danced in the blackness.

"Wow," Taggart whispered.

For a moment the crowd was silent, then burst out in applause and whoops of joy. As if on cue, Inga's band began to play where they'd been placed on an elevated stage. As spectators clapped in time to the music, others grabbed arms, dancing to the tune, feet flying, arms extended, and bodies whirling.

"Unfuckingbelievable," Taggart said softly.

"Yeah. God help us poor lost souls, huh?"

He turned, expression almost puzzled in the glow of the firelight. "Could I buy you a drink? Just sit and talk to you like one human being to another?"

"What in fuck for?"

He shrugged his confusion and finally said, "Maybe it's because we'll ship out, and I'll never see this place again. Maybe I just want a chance to know what makes you so . . . damned *capable.*"

"Why, thank you." A beat. "I think."

"I've been hung out a couple of times. Knew that I was going to die. Been in some pretty deep shit. You've got something that makes you different, that's all."

"Yeah," she told him pointedly. "I've got a quetzal inside me."

He didn't scoff, but honestly said, "I can believe that. And I don't even know what a quetzal is."

She hesitated, mocking herself for a fool.

"All right, Captain, you can buy me a beer at the stand over yonder, and we'll park our butts on that broken aircar so I can keep an eye on folks. Might need to bust up a fight or two before the night's out."

He went for the beer while she climbed up on her perch, careful of her tender leg. Then she propped hands on knees to keep watch on the crowd. Behind the band, the perimeter lights were burning, illuminating the farmland beyond the fence with a sea of light she hadn't seen in years. Thank God the right bulbs had been in the supplies. And in their light, the surveillance drones were flying, crisscrossing the fields looking for predators.

Taggart was back bearing two big duraplast mugs of beer. He handed them up, then jumped up to a seat beside her. "I can't believe it. She asked for an SDR. Refused a Corporate charge. And all I had was a ten note."

"Welcome to our brave new world."

Talina had no more said it than Toby Montoya appeared out of the dark asking, "Tal? Is it true that we can use our plunder? We won't get in trouble?"

"It's true. Corporation signed it over. Can't call it plunder anymore. You found it or traded for it, it's yours."

"Halleluiah!" And he went stumbling off, obviously deep in his cups.

"Plunder?"

"Toby's been sitting on a cache of nuggets and rubies for a couple of years now. His biggest concern was how in the name of hell he was going to smuggle them back to Solar System. Didn't matter that we kept telling him that even if he got them past customs, he'd never find a legitimate buyer. And if he did, it would be the kind of black market person who'd kill him as soon as look at him."

"That's a fact." Taggart paused. "You could go back, you know. Woman with your skills, you could pretty much write your own contract."

She took a swig of Inga's beer. Made a face. This batch was a bit green and yeasty yet. "I'll stay."

"Seriously, it might be years before someone mounts a mission to come see what became of the 'lost colony of Donovan.' I know how thin things were getting before *Turalon*'s arrival. They're going to get a hell of a lot worse."

She pointed out past the floodlights to the west. "There are people living out there. Some of them for close to ten years now. It's a tough haul and a chancy thing that takes a special knowledge and skill. They've somehow come to an agreement with Donovan. Something I didn't have even a glimmer about until I killed that quetzal."

"What keeps the predators and metals from killing them?"

"Most of their water comes from rain, and what doesn't they purify with cactus mucilage. Grow their own food. Claim they've made a deal with the quetzals. A sort of live and let live."

"Deal how?"

"It's something they can't explain. I sort of know without knowing. That make any sense?"

"No. But it's Donovan," he told her wryly.

For a time they just sat, watching the people dance, listening to the music as the band made their magic with two violins, a bass, drums, a couple of guitars, and a trumpet.

"I want to go out there," he told her unexpectedly. "It's as if I'm being called. That there's something out there for me. The closest I can come is to say that when I leave Donovan, it will be like I'm going with an empty place inside me that will never be complete."

She studied him from the corner of her eye. Was this the same Captain Taggart who'd ambushed her in her house and looked forward to shooting her?

"So . . . go. You're a bloody damn captain. Commandeer an aircar and pick a direction. But if you want to come back, take me, Trish, Step, or one of the others with you. And pay fucking close attention to everything you're told, or you'll stay on Donovan. Most likely as a pile of quetzal or bem shit."

"Yes, ma'am." A pause. "Even if I could, I don't think Kalico would give me permission."

"Yeah, I keep forgetting that chain of command problem you Skulls have."

"Got another question."

"Yep."

"Was asking Kalico to validate the titles and deeds your idea?"

"Shig and Yvette talked me into it."

"You were going to take a blunter course of action, weren't you?"

She cocked her head, eyes slitted. "What makes you think that?"

"'Cause it's what I would have done." Firelight flickered on his pale and angular face. "Maybe if I'd had a Shig Mosadek to council me and my unruly ways, I might not have ended up here on what's most likely a suicide run."

"That leads me to believe they don't have a clue about what happened to those missing ships. *Turalon* made it this far. What makes you think it won't make it back?"

"Captain Abibi and her officers are worried sick. And there's the fate of the *Mekong* hanging like a deadweight over our heads." He paused. "So what would you people do if *Turalon*'s crew mutinied, refused to space, and landed down here demanding asylum?"

"We'd welcome them with open arms, survey out a garden plot for them, and, as of today, hand them title to their property."

"I'd best not let that get around the ship."

Talina shrugged. "We're not going to broadcast it, so don't lose sleep over it. Our interests here are best served if *Turalon* makes it back to Solar System all packed up with clay, gold, platinum, gallium arsenide, concentrated lanthanides, scandium, yttrium, and all those gemstones. Your Supervisor might want to write us off, but eventually someone will be back."

"You sure?"

She shrugged and took another swig of beer. "If not it doesn't make much difference how pure our mineral deposits are. They'll think it's more cost-effective to crunch up a couple hundred thousand asteroids and ship poor quality ore up from the Martian and lunar mines than build and send a ship with the attendant risk to life and limb."

"And what will you people do out here?"

"We'll live, Captain." She waved her mug toward the crowd. "We'll sing and dance and suffer and die, but we'll make lives here. Which is what existence is all about, isn't it?"

"I've got family back there. Even had a girl once." He sounded like he was trying to convince himself. "But, if I get the chance, will you take me out there? Beyond the fence and the fields?"

"I might hold a grudge against someone who was going to stand me against a wall and blow my guts apart."

She saw his crooked smile, the amusement in his eyes as they sparkled in the firelight. "I'll take that chance. My guess is Clemenceau deserved what he got—and no matter what our history is—will you promise to bring me back?"

"A person can't make that kind of promise on Donovan, but I'll give it my best shot. Assuming you're not a stupid idiot."

"I can live with that."

"You better hope . . . Ah, shit." She saw the first thrown punch. Yep. Exman and a Skull. "I gotta see to that. You have a nice night, Captain." She hopped down, calling over her shoulder, "And thanks for the beer!"

So, Taggart wanted to see something of Donovan, huh? Maybe he wasn't as odious as she thought.

That, or he had motives she could only guess at. In either case, she'd trust him no further than she would a hungry bem.

28

The celebrants who packed into Betty Able's crowded parlor tried to shout over each other as they swilled drinks and laughed; it actually hurt Dan's ears. Worse, he kept getting jostled by men stumbling into his chair, knocking him with elbows.

All of which both delighted and annoyed the ever-loving hell out of him.

This was *the* game. The one he'd been waiting for.

The Supervisor had signed the proclamation granting title and deed to all properties duly filed upon and recorded in the administration building records. "Plunder" now belonged to the individual who found it. The wealth of Donovan was free for the taking.

Alcohol had been flowing along with something called "mash," a viscous pressing from a local plant called blue nasty. Whatever that was. To date Dan hadn't bothered to partake, although he'd obtained a fingertip-sized container for Allison.

She'd absently told him that she hadn't tried it since she was in her teens, and that it had cost her two days and a severe whipping by her father.

Dosing her hadn't even been a challenge. "We'll do it together," he'd told her. "Just imagine sex while doing this stuff."

All it took was a dab the size of a match head, which he'd easily palmed while pretending to take it.

The way Allison had writhed and cried out as she clamped herself around him had made him wonder if maybe he hadn't made a mistake—or if perhaps mash, mixed with Eros, was a combination to be explored for use at Betty Able's.

He'd left her exhausted, half-asleep on the bed, her dreamy eyes unfocused as she uttered whimpering sounds of delight and smiled at the nothingness floating above her.

Dan had dressed and hurried here, to the game, having baited

Thumbs Exman for two days in a row. Now he studied the mark where he sat across the table. Thumbs wasn't a handsome man to start with—a recent fistfight had left him with a swelling bruise on his cheek. Donovan had taken what God had given Exman and made it worse, coarsening his features. The man's hands were callused, the nails brittle, and he wore a poorly tailored chamois shirt, canvas britches, and shimmering quetzal-hide boots.

Exman kept blinking at his cards, wincing every time the loud laughter hit a crescendo and flinching when his chair was banged.

Igor Stryski and Jaime O'Leary sat to either side, unaware that they were acting as shills. As needed, Dan threw them a hand, keeping them in the game, knowing just how to reward their weaknesses.

Exman—some sort of mineral surveyor, prospector, or whatever the hell he was—couldn't have been a more accommodating mark. The man considered himself smarter, harder, and tougher than any man in the room. He kept bragging about all the things he was going to do when he got back to Solar System.

"Yep"—Exman shot a wink at O'Leary—"it's just two years of rest and relaxation aboard *Turalon*. And then there's the bonus. I didn't just quit, you know. Lots of them did. Not me. I figured The Corporation would be fair. Worked nigh onto two and half years after my contract expired."

"That why the big three gave you that warehouse on the avenue?" Dan asked mildly. "Big sucker. Lot of space."

"Yeah. Used to be the toolshed for the portable core drills. Last of them stopped working and died three years ago." He tossed a small ruby onto the pile of nuggets and gems.

The amount of wealth that had appeared as if from thin air could be called flat-out amazing. No doubt it had set the Supervisor back on her heels as well, wondering—as she now no doubt was—if declaring private property rights had been such a good idea.

Dan raised, tossing in a packet of yuan. "That's a thousand."

"Fold," O'Leary said, followed immediately by Stryski.

"How's your courage, Wally?" Dan asked.

"Wally? Who's Wally?" Exman asked.

"You just look like a Wally to me." Dan leaned forward. "Are you in? Or is your vaunted talent just bullshit?"

Thumbs blinked, fighting the whiskey haze in his head as he studied his cards. Then he squinted at the pot; gold, yuans and SDRs, and clustered gems that sparkled red, green, pink, and topaz. Most of it was his: he'd been losing slowly but surely.

"How much is that?"

Dan leaned forward, narrowing his eyes. "I figure I'm in about forty thousand. You're a couple of thousand short." He glanced at Stryski. "You agree, Igor?"

"Yeah, I guess. I mean damn, I never seen that much before."

"Me neither," O'Leary agreed.

"You in . . . or out?" Dan annunciated the words slowly, almost like a verbal lash.

"I got the cards," Thumbs protested. "That's my stash! All I got."

"What about the deed?" Dan asked, slumping back in his chair. "You've got the cards, right? You win this hand, you go back to Transluna close to forty thousand richer. And that's Donovan figuring. Translate that into the home economy, you're looking at a couple hundred thousand yuan—no telling what the exchange rate to SDRs will be—just in the gems alone by the time they hit the streets."

Exman studied his cards again, blinked, and took a breath before wiping at his perspiring face. "I don't know . . ."

"Fine." Dan reached out and cupped his hand around the pile.

"*Wait!*" Exman swallowed. "Fuck. What am I doing? I got the cards!" He leaned back, unsnapped his belt pouch, and fished around. He produced a duralon sheet, carefully lettered, and tossed it onto the table.

Dan took only long enough to flip the sheet open, read the script, and say, "Call."

With a silly grin, Thumbs spread out his cards one by one, as if to prolong and build the climax. "Full house. Jacks over fours." Giggling to himself, he grabbed his glass of whiskey and sucked down a swallow. "Been nice playing with you, Cowboy."

"It pains me," Dan told him evenly, reaching out with his left hand

and grabbing Exman's wrist as he reached for the pot. Tightening his grip he carefully laid out his cards. "Spade flush, Queen high."

For a long moment, Exman stared as if trying to comprehend. "That can't be."

"Read 'em and see," Dan told him. "But I'm not here to break a poor bastard like you." And so saying, he shoved part of the pile back. "That's about thirty thousand, which will set you up just fine when you get home. But do find the right guys when you go to fence it. Those Corporate pieces of shit will figure a way of taking it if you don't. Bunch of fucking thieves if you ask me."

As if absently, Dan scooped what remained of the pot into a sack he unfolded from inside his shirt.

Thumbs was still staring through a whiskey-laced gaze. "Thirty thousand?" he whispered, wavering gaze on the remaining pile of yuans and the few gems and nuggets.

"Look here," Dan told him as he stood and walked around the table. "How about I buy you a girl? The rumor is that you have a real attraction to that Angelina. It'll be a long two years to get home to that wife of yours. That's an eternity to lay in that cramped bunk short-stroking that half-hung cock of yours. What say I set you up for the whole night. You can knock off a piece again in the morning."

"That's not even a *quarter*!" Thumbs protested, his voice slurring.

"Guys, how about we call the game for tonight? I'll take Thumbs, here, and get him tucked in with Angelina. Maybe get his flute played if he can't get it up for more strenuous action."

With that, Dan pulled Thumbs to his feet with one hand, using the other to pack the man's belt pouch with what remained on the table.

"Fucking thieves," Thumbs kept repeating under his breath.

Steering the staggering Thumbs through the crowd, luck was again with Dan. Betty was arguing with a young man at her bar.

Dan opened the door and shoved Thumbs into the hallway.

"No. You took my fucking money," the man slurred. "Tha'ss cheating me. Som' bitch."

Thumbs careened off the wall as Dan urged him forward. As he passed the famous Angelina's door, he could hear a female voice crying, "Yes! Yes! Oh, God!"

"Must have got religion," he whispered into Thumb's ear.

And then they were out the back, into the night. The sound of music and laughter came from over in the direction of the tavern.

"You . . . piece of . . ." Thumbs bent forward. His body convulsed. Vomit shot out in a hollow spray.

"Oh, yeah," Dan said, voice low next to Exman's ear. "Your new best friend."

Then he got a grip on the man's collar and headed him out toward the fence.

To himself, he said, "Allison, my sweet, looks like we're finally in business."

29

Kalico stepped off the ramp and onto the shuttle bay deck, oddly dismayed that she was back aboard *Turalon*. Something about the ship felt stifling; the air—though processed and several times purified since she'd shuttled down—had a heavy and stale quality. The ceramic corridor beneath her feet was polished now, almost every inch of the ship having been cleaned and scoured.

What Abibi's crew had accomplished was little short of a miracle. *Turalon* almost looked new. As *Mekong* had no doubt looked before she spaced from Donovan.

With Astrogation Officer Nandi in the lead, Kalico followed the familiar ship's corridors to the officer's deck and passed a machine that whirred as it polished the walls. Here she could smell a chemical freshness that, while not unpleasant, left a tang in her nose.

Two years of this. If we make it at all.

Turalon sent a shiver through her.

Am I walking through my tomb?

It was as if the walls knew some secret she didn't. As if the hull was slightly out of sync with time.

"Idiocy," she murmured under her breath and nodded to Nandi as the astrogator stopped at the captain's hatch and saluted.

"Thank you, Nandi."

"Ma'am."

Stepping inside, the hatch swung shut behind her and she found herself in the captain's lounge with its curving holographic wall, the table, and heads-up displays.

Captain Abibi sat in her traditional spot at the head of her table, First Officer Chan at her right. Both looked oddly worried as they stood and saluted.

To Kalico's eyes, their uniforms looked cleaner, starched, and pressed. The room didn't have quite the dingy appearance—though it felt even more restrictive after her time down-planet.

"Captain, good to see you. You, too, First Officer. I assume there's a reason you wanted me personally. Is there some problem with the manifest? Our program to free up the space for returnees has had an unusual rate of success."

"No, Supervisor," Abibi told her, tension in her eyes. "We're all relived that we're only looking at two hundred and sixty-six returnees. It's like a bloody damn miracle."

"I wouldn't have thought it possible," Chan agreed, running a finger around his collar as if it was too tight. "Having been down in that dump, the notion that you could get any of them to stay except at gunpoint is more than unbelievable."

Kalico slapped a hand to the table as she sat. "Apparently, my friends, this what the lure of gold, jewels, and blind greed can lead people to commit themselves to. Even the newcomers."

She smiled thinly. "Couple the chance for wealth with the worry generated by the missing ships and it's a whole new calculus. I've been appraised of odds makers down there. Based on their probability figuring, we're getting less than one in five odds that we'll make it home."

At the mention, both Abibi and Chan seemed to blanch. They shot each other worried looks.

"Could I have a cup of coffee?" Kalico asked, more to alleviate their sudden discomfort than her own.

Chan stepped to the dispenser where he filled a zero-g cup for her. She thanked him and waited as he reseated himself.

"All right, what's the problem? From your expressions, it's something dire. So, let me ask: You do think we can make it home, right?"

In that moment she felt half-starved for air, heart juddering in her breast. *Come on. Tell me you've solved it!*

Abibi spread her hands wide. "We don't know, Supervisor. Our people can't find anything wrong with the ship's systems, the generator, hull integrity, you name it. Systems are green. *Turalon* is as fit as when she finished her first shakedown."

"And even if the system were not sealed, we're not about to go mucking with the computers or the programming. They're way beyond our abilities." Chan added, as if grateful to change the subject. "We think we have one of the best crews to ever space, but those kinds of equations and code are so specialized that they're tamper-proof for a reason."

"Sealed?" Kalico glanced back and forth between them.

Abibi lifted an eyebrow. "You understand about qubit N-dimensional computing, don't you? Ultimately our navigation on the other side—once symmetry is inverted—is essentially a fractally derived probability statistic. A mathematical function generated during the time that we're 'outside' of our universe. Essentially we 'navigate' by probability. When that probability occurs, the ship ceases to generate the inversion field and symmetry resumes."

Chan added, "If everything has worked correctly, we're in a different part of space. The return 'trip,' if you'd call it that, is accomplished by the ship's generators again inverting space, and the mathematics are essentially run backward."

"Theoretically," Abibi amended. "As best we can understand what the computers are doing."

Kalico rubbed her jaw. "Okay, so maybe having somebody trying to tinker with the system might be a bad idea. I get that. But if this is all just running the math backward, if you don't end up in the right place, you should be able to backtrack, right?"

"Theoretically," Abibi told her dryly. "At least, that's how it's worked on the ships that have made it home." Her smile was humorless. "We don't have any idea about what went wrong on the ships that have disappeared. Something about a lack of data."

"But we should be in a pretty good position; just invert symmetry, run the math backward, and we're home?"

"We should be." Abibi's voice was soft.

"Then, how soon can we space?"

"Space?" Abibi said through an exhale, "At your order, ma'am. *Turalon* is ready to go as soon as the transportees are aboard." She paused, jaws knotting, and then added, "Assuming you want to give that order given what we've discovered."

Kalico's heart began to skip at the gravity in the woman's voice. "And what might that be?"

Abibi swallowed hard as Kalico took a swig of the coffee. Miracle of miracles, it even tasted good for once.

"We've had a ping on the long-range scanners," Abibi told her. "It's *Freelander.* She's in-system, headed for a Donovan orbit."

Kalico's stomach did a flip. "Then why the dour looks? That's good news, isn't it? Another ship heard from. She's not lost!"

"Good news?" Abibi shot another of those half-panicked looks at Chan. "We don't know what it means yet, ma'am. But she's coming in on automatic, and though we've been hailing her, all we get is the ID and locator beacon."

"So?"

"So no one is answering our hail, ma'am."

"I don't understand."

"Neither do we. She spaced from Solar System seven months before we did. If she ran the same math we did, she should have arrived at Donovan roughly the same amount of time in advance of us as she left Solar System, give or take a little relativity before and after inverting symmetry."

"Theoretically," Chan amended.

"So, could she have stopped somewhere along the way?"

"It doesn't work that way. The programs and code are sealed, remember? And if for some reason the field generation failed, and the ship regained symmetry, she's default programmed to run the math backward and take her home. It's a fail-safe to keep her from getting lost. To ensure the recovery of the ship, and to allow the engineers to figure out what went wrong so that it doesn't happen again."

"I see."

"As soon as we determined that they were only responding on automatic, we sent an access code that would trigger a data dump. We've been receiving it for the last fifteen minutes or so. Rather than just shout this out, it was my decision to bring you up here and brief you as the data came in."

Kalico struggled to understand what it all meant. When ships inverted symmetry no one really knew where they "went." If it was even a "place." Some theorized it was into another universe or "bubble" in the foamlike multiverse, others insisted it was "outside" of even that.

But at least *Freelander* wasn't lost. That was a huge relief. So it was possible some of the other missing ships would be showing up. A whisper of hope lightened her soul.

"Maybe their hyperlink entangled communications system has a glitch in it."

"Maybe," Chan told her. "But we've defaulted to radio. Donovan still communicates by old fashioned radio waves. It's an easy technology to create and maintain. Just like when we arrived in-system, we broadcast on what's called standard frequency. Unlike laser and microwave burst systems, any three-thumbed idiot can cobble together a radio with a power source, a coil of copper wire, a speaker, and an antenna to broadcast and receive. It's just a matter of finding the right frequency."

"Then I guess we'll just have to wait until they match orbit." Kalico took another swig of her coffee. "How long will that be?"

"Another couple of weeks, Supervisor," Abibi told her. "They were farther out, clear on the other side of Donovan's orbit around Capella."

"Then we're definitely on hold until we know what's caused their delay."

And it changed the entire dynamic for Donovan. Another shipload of supplies and equipment were inbound, along with additional transportees with contracts hot in hand. Most of them for jobs that no longer existed.

And another ship to space additional clay, metals, and gems. The Corporation's losses were no longer looking so exorbitant. Her position vis-à-vis the Board had just taken a huge leap forward.

Even as she was considering her rapidly changing fortunes, a chime sounded, and the hatch opened to admit Information Officer Fuloni. The no-nonsense redhead looked even more dour, were that possible. At sight of Kalico, she pulled herself to attention and saluted, then turned worried brown eyes on Abibi.

"What have we got, Nancy?" Abibi asked.

"We're only a fraction into the download, ma'am. It's huge. But right off the top we received the captain's log. It's grim, ma'am. We'll be able to fill in the blanks as the data comes in, but essentially, and crazy as it sounds, they're all dead."

"Dead?" Abibi came out of her chair. "Of what?"

Fuloni grimaced and swallowed hard, as if something were stuck in her throat. A look resembling panic lay behind her disbelieving eyes. "The records are clear. Statements from the captain's and first officer's log." She winced. "They murdered the transportees. All of them. And, ma'am, according to the ship's records . . . that happened more than *one hundred and twenty years ago.*"

30

Talina slung her gear into the aircar, the pack thumping onto the deck plate. Next she racked her rifle beside the control panel and, out of habit, lifted the hatch to ensure the emergency supplies and medical kit were not only present, but that they had been replenished after their last usage, which had been her treatment after the quetzal attack.

"Yeah," she said as the beast resettled itself inside her. "That was your doing."

She'd have sworn the quetzal that coiled in her chest grinned in appreciation.

And just what the hell is this, anyway? Some uniquely twisted form of insanity?

Or maybe she wasn't crazy to believe she had an alien beast living inside her. Donovan was full of physical parasites like slugs that would burrow into a person's body. Why not a psychological parasite, too?

"Hey, Security Officer!"

She slammed the hatch closed, then turned to see Cap Taggart striding across the trampled landing field. Behind him the fence gleamed in the sunlight where it separated the town from the harsher reality in which she stood.

The marine was grinning from under a campaign hat, wearing military fatigues with bulging pockets, an overstuffed field pack over his left shoulder, and a pistol, flashlight, and four magazines on his web gear. A slung rifle hung over his right shoulder.

"You got a problem?"

"Got a reprieve," he told her with a grin, his blue eyes almost gleaming. "Supervisor's up on the *Turalon*. Some kind of ship's business. We're delayed for a couple of weeks."

She studied his outfit. "So, let me guess. You wanted to dress up like a soldier to remind yourself you really do still have balls?"

"Took a shower this morning so no reminder's necessary. Everything was hanging right where it belongs." Then he laughed, as if at himself. "You're going out. Some sort of emergency call on the radio."

"How'd you know that?"

"Two Spots can be bribed. Turns out he had a weakness for a duralon bowie knife I picked up in Selsus Station. Not a lot of duralon knives on Donovan."

She took a deep breath, crossed her arms, and considered. "Look, it's not that I don't understand. And it's a pretty easy gig. Just ride out, collect Madison Briggs, and bring her back to hospital. She's due to give birth in a week or so, and Raya wants her in. The thing is, I'm not sure I like you enough that I'd want to spend a couple of hours of enforced company."

He rocked his jaw, narrowed an eye, and nodded. "Fair enough, Security Officer Perez. But you should know that Step Allenovich had something come up. Some kind of problem with a missing person. He said I could cover for him."

"You're soft meat, Captain. And what was it that bothered me about you? Let's see if I can remember. Oh, yeah! You were going to kill me, Shig, and Yvette."

He tilted his head. "It's a hard world, S.O. Let me think. Wait, it's coming to me. As I recall, the last guy on The Corporation's payroll that you went out with? I think it was established that you put a bullet in his brain. Me, I was following orders in the investigation of a mutiny. But we learn, don't we? Maybe there's reasons for both of our actions."

He pinned her with hard eyes. "I'm willing to beg, trade, or buy a trip out there. Now, you can be a bitch and bust my balls, or let me come along for the ride. Your call."

Something about his earnest, level gaze caused her to nod. "Call me a fool. Stow your gear. But it's just out and back. Chaco and Madison Briggs have a farm about two hundred and eighty klicks out. Kind of a cool place. They built a cliff house in a vertical canyon wall. Easily defensible. Rain water that runs down the cliff collects in a cistern. They've got a nice garden patch on the cap rock above. This is their fourth kid coming."

He slung his pack onto the deck, clambered over the gunwale, and racked his rifle—a sleek military automatic with a forty-round magazine.

Talina shook her head. "I'm probably going to regret this."

"Yeah, S.O., that's kind of how life works, isn't it?"

"You always so cheery?" She took the control wheel with one hand while she pushed the throttle forward with the other. The fans spun up, blowing dust from beneath the vehicle.

As the car rose, she spun it around, gaining altitude as she headed out toward the southwest. Leaving the last of the fields behind, they crossed over the brush.

"There you go, Taggart." She indicated the blue-green maze of vegetation. "That's the bush. Wild, free, and dangerous."

He was staring over the side, a thoughtful interest reflected in his expression. "I have to admire them. People like these Briggs folks that you're talking about. How do they do it? Living out there all alone? I mean, it's just them, right? Who do they ever see? Or are there other Wild Ones close by?"

"Just them. They get into town every six months or so. We'll get a call that they have a load of trade, and would we be willing to send an aircar to pick them up."

"What kind of trade?"

At her reluctance, he added, "Oh, come on. Kalico has effectively signed the whole damn world over to you guys. I could give a fig. But I really want to know. For me. What do they trade?"

"Gold mostly. They're sitting on a pretty impressive vein. Chaco built a water-powered mill down in the canyon bottom to crush the ore. Madison tans chamois hides, does some sewing."

"Do the kids go to school?"

"Not in the traditional sense. They're being taught to read, do math, chemistry, and geology. But the big lessons are in how to stay alive. Can't remember how old the kids are. But the boys can survive on Donovan with only a knife and rope. On this world, that's like genius."

Taggart didn't respond but only nodded.

She studied him from the corner of her eye as they wound up one of the canyons in the Blood Mountains and broke out on the flats above the sandstone cap rock. Ahead of them, the higher Wind Mountains rose like a row of jutting teeth—as if they'd been formed to saw at the very sky.

"Those are the Winds up ahead." She pointed as they skimmed over aquajade and chabacho trees that turned their branches, as if following the aircar as it passed. "They form sort of a semicircle around Port Authority and the bay. About a million years ago one big honking asteroid slammed into Donovan where the bay sits today. Fractured the surface like a bullet does glass. The Winds are part of the deep crust that was thrust up. Absolutely loaded with threads of rare-earth elements, gold, lead, platinum, copper, you name it. And, of course, the volcanism that resulted is what spewed all that clay that's so valuable back home."

"They use it for making qubit computer matrix," Taggart told her. "That and superhard temperature-resistant ceramics."

Yeah, Skull, as the people who mine it, we really do know what it's used for.

She bit off a grin as they swooped over a herd of chamois that exploded in all directions like a sunburst beneath them.

"Chamois!" Taggart cried in delight. "They're beautiful! And my God, are they fast or what? Almost outrunning us."

He was staring down at the ones they overtook as they darted between the trees.

"They have to be able to outrun predators. The quetzal is faster, but a chamois is more maneuverable. The things have three-hundred-and-sixty-degree vision. At the last instant before a quetzal grabs them, they jink right or left. Quetzals can't change course as quickly."

"How do you ever catch them?"

She arched an eyebrow. "When it comes to bagging chamois, a bullet is faster than even a quetzal. And people like Chaco and Madison? They trap them. Doesn't matter how fast a critter is when it's in a trap."

She pulled the wheel back, gaining elevation as they passed over fractured and uplifted beds of sandstone and shot into Mainway Canyon.

"This is the best route through the mountains," she told Taggart.

"This canyon leads to Best Pass. Aptly, if not exotically, named, it's the easiest and safest way west through the Winds."

He was fixed on the almost vitreous walls of rock that rose to either side. Pinkish red gave way to black swirls and large veins of white that were intersected by greens, blues, and blood red.

"The colors are different metal-bearing minerals," she told him. "Black is manganese and molybdenum mixed with nickel and lead. Greens are the copper-heavy ores, and the reds are iron."

Around them the tall peaks towered, tufts of cloud streaming from their tops.

"Damn rugged country," Taggart noted as he inspected the jagged rock, sheer walls, and shadow-black depths below them.

"No one has crossed these on foot yet, that's for sure."

"Whoever finally does, that's going to be one tough bastard," he amended as Talina piloted them through the narrow V of the pass. The winds were always bad in here.

After passing through, they started descending in calmer air and followed a canyon created by the fracturing of great uplifted blocks of bedrock.

"You're literally traveling up through time," she told him. "We're still in deep crustal rock here, but keep your eyes open. Up ahead you'll see a band of orange sandstone. That's two-billion-year-old ocean bottom. Then each superimposed layer we pass marks a different geological epoch up to the present when we break out onto open ground."

"Do you ever get used to that smell?"

"What smell?"

"That kind of perfume? Sort of like cardamom and anise."

"I guess you do, because I stopped smelling it years ago. But yeah, it's there when I sniff for it. It's the vegetation, the musk bush, thorncactus, aquajade, blue nasty, and gotcha vine."

"Nightmares, biteya bush, cutthroat flower, gotcha vine, you gotta love the names." He shot her a smile. "And yes, S.O., I get it. I'm soft meat and don't have the smarts of a ten-year-old with a knife and a rope."

"Keep that attitude and you might make it a whole year on Donovan."

"Odds makers are giving *Turalon* less than a one in five chance of making it back to Solar System." He stared pensively at the passing levels of sandstone, dolomite, and shales. "I owe you for this, S.O. I really wanted to see something of Donovan before heading back."

"You are welcome, Captain." She found herself oddly touched by the earnest tone in his voice. "Why'd you volunteer for this trip in the first place?"

"I could tell you it was the excitement of seeing a far-off world."

"But that would be a lie, right?"

"Yeah." A grim smile played at his lips, as if he were arguing with himself. "I was *assigned*. That's the euphemism for being punished." He hesitated. "My commanding officer prior to this trip, the good Major Creamer, sent us out to knock a bunch of asteroid miners back into line. They'd 'requisitioned' some pretty expensive Corporate property. Sounds familiar, huh?"

Having just "requisitioned" an entire planet, she didn't think it was her duty to comment.

"Problem was, good ol' Major Creamer, unknown to me, told the miscreants at Beemer Station they could hand over the collector and all the ore, or twenty hours later, Corporate security was going to hit them with a full squad."

She watched the corners of his eyes tighten before he said, "Being so warned, they used that time to set demolition charges in several of the asteroids along our most likely route of approach. It wasn't explosions that did the damage, mind you, but the mass of debris it blew into our path."

"How many did you lose?"

"Twenty-two. Good people." He frowned at the layers of gray-white shale they were now passing. "Changes you when people you care about, and under your command, die in your arms. What was left of us weren't in the mood for what you'd call negotiation when we breached their little station a couple of hours later."

He studied her from the corner of his eye, then admitted: "The image of blasted bodies in freefall lives with you. Sort of clings to the soul. Especially the leaking corpses of the children."

"And good ol' Major Creamer?"

"I didn't so much as lay a finger on him, let alone beat the ever-loving shit out of him like he deserved. It wasn't just my people, but what we did to those miners. None of it had to happen. We could have just arrived unannounced, taken our stuff, arrested the ringleaders, and it would have been over. Problem was, he just couldn't take constructive criticism, especially when I gave it to him in front of a Boardmember."

"Thought they taught you guys better than that."

He grinned sheepishly. "You know, you people scared the shit out of me that day we had you on trial. I thought it was going to happen all over again, but this time it was going to be me that was carried out feet first along with the rest of you."

"Did I ever tell you that you and the Supervisor are assholes?"

"Nope. But no one's around, so this would be a very good time if you absolutely had to get it off your chest."

"You and the Supervisor are assholes. Wouldn't want to leave any doubt in your mind should you ever have the slightest question."

He was grinning, that sparkle back in his eyes as they broke out into the flats; the river flowed below them as it snaked through a thick forest of chabacho trees. Scarlet fliers burst from the blue-green foliage, their crimson wings glittering, rudder-like tails flipping behind them.

"Is everything colorful here?"

"You bet. And just about as deadly."

"This place kind of grows on you, doesn't it?"

"What are you going to go back to, Captain?"

"Money. A pile of it. Every second I'm gone, the SDRs just pile up."

"And then what? You gonna retire?"

"I'm only thirty. Maybe go into personal security. Bodyguard for one of the Boardmembers."

"Spend the rest of your life standing behind his shoulder? Doing advances at his mistress's house?"

"Or boyfriend's."

"Wow! I can see how that would attract a man like you. How your every waking hour will be filled with excitement and satisfaction. Almost makes me wish I was you."

He winced. "Do you think you could get a little more disgust in your voice? Maybe slur the words a little, or nasalize, or something?"

"Might be that I could. Now that you mention it."

The warning buzzer went off, the charge light flashing on the dash. "Shit!"

"What's that?"

"Power failure. Battery's shorted internally and overheating. Got to put down."

She cranked the wheel, hearing the strain in the rotors, heading out away from the thick forest around the river. Ahead lay nothing but an unbroken field of trees.

Damn it, Tal! How much time have we got?

She could see hilly uplands no more than a couple of kilometers to the south. Not that they had a chance of making it that far. "Look for a hole in the trees, Captain. We've only got seconds of flight left."

"Got it. There!"

She saw it the same time he did. Veered right.

Come on! Come on! Keep us aloft! Just a little while longer!

She corkscrewed down into the opening, dropping into shade, feeling a growing heat through the deck.

"Get your gear, Taggart. When we touch down, bail!"

"Copy."

The rotors failed a couple of meters shy of the ground. They dropped like a rock, slammed into a bulge of root. The car tilted, slid sideways and crashed into the root mat at a steep angle.

Talina was thrown against the gunwale. Pain shot through her hip as she cart wheeled over the side and flipped onto her shoulder in the soft lacery of intertwined roots. She had a vague image of Taggart tumbling into another of the roots, his pack bouncing beside him.

For a moment, she just lay there, trying to gather her wits. Then the pain came blasting up from her hip. "Fuck me!" she gasped, forcing herself to sit up.

The down side of the aircar had sliced through the roots and was embedded in the loose organic soil. The rest of the craft slanted at a thirty degree angle, but was falling as the damaged root tried to squirm away from the insult.

"Cap? You all right?" she asked through gritted teeth.

"I think. Yeah." He winced. "What the hell went wrong?"

"Old equipment pushed past its recommended service life. But we should have had some warning. Like it wouldn't take a charge. Or wasn't holding one. Listen, we've got to get away from here."

She forced herself up on her good leg. The one that was still healing from being broken. Gingerly, she moved her right leg. Hip and femur seemed intact, but damn she was going to have a bruise.

She watched him clamber to his feet, shaking his head. A blue-green streak on his cheek marked the spot where it had banged into the unforgiving root.

Talina hopped over, pulled her rifle from the rack, and snagged her pack where the gunwale had stopped it. Slinging the gun, she pulled Taggart's rifle free and tossed it to him.

"Wouldn't it be better to stay by the aircar? Wait for rescue?"

She pointed. "See the way these roots are moving?"

"Well, yeah, but—"

"The trees are trying to figure out what just happened. When they do, they're going to engulf the vehicle. And us, too, if we're in the vicinity."

He stared in thinly veiled disbelief at the slowly twisting roots. "No shit? They're alive?"

"Skulls," she whispered in despair. And now she was stuck with one. The kindest thing would be to turn and blow his brains out with a pistol shot.

She reached for the emergency kit hatch, only to see smoke streaming from beneath the lid. She cursed as the hot metal burned her fingers. As she backed away, the seat cushions browned and burst into flame.

"Got to get out of here," she called.

Each step was excruciating as she led the way to a low gap in the already writhing root mass. As she looked back over her shoulder, it was to see the aircar glowing red as the battery melted. The roots were recoiling from the heat, squirming away, leaving the disabled craft to burn and smolder on the disturbed ground. Overhead the branches were turning, exposing their leaves to the energy they could absorb from the rising heat.

"What next?" Taggart asked.

"High ground two klicks south." She took a breath. "Stop too long and the roots will get us. It's that high ground or nothing. Assuming we live long enough to get there."

"And what are the chances of that?"

"Does the term 'fucking grim' mean anything to you?"

31

The sound of tapping hammers and whining drills filled the air as Trish stepped inside Thumbs Exman's old core-drill warehouse. The place had the cardamom and cinnamon smell of sawdust. Four men were working on chabacho-wood tables; another was fitting what looked like a wheel to a vertical spindle that rose out of a long-defunct centrifuge.

In the back she could see the subject of her inquiry. Dan Wirth sat at a raised desk, Allison perched at his side as they stared at an oversized ledger book. It took Trish a moment to recognize the volume as a bound core log. The sort used for recording cuttings when, for whatever reason, a computer wasn't an option.

She strode past the four guys working on one of the tables and wondered what the hell it was. Big, oval shaped, it was more like an oversized, straight-sided bathtub, and one of the guys was pressing some sort of scrounged padding around the oval circumference.

She stopped before the elevated desk, announcing, "Hey, Allison, how's it going?"

The blonde looked up and smiled, her eyes brightening as she said, "Hey, yourself, Trish. Can you believe? We're going into business."

Dan Wirth studied Trish through emotionless and uncaring brown eyes, as if she were some sort of nonentity.

"Really glad to hear that, Al." Trish looked around. "Thumbs rent the place to you?"

"Purchased," Wirth said with a curious formality. "After a fashion."

"I heard you won it in a poker game." Trish arched an eyebrow.

Wirth glanced sidelong at Allison. "And if you heard that, why ask if I was renting?"

Trish glanced around, taking in the space. "You don't happen to know where Thumbs is, do you?"

"Haven't seen him since the other night," Wirth replied mildly.

"Quite the party. The man was a little wobbly. Something about the whiskey he drank. There seemed to be a lot of whiskey that night. Or maybe it was because someone smacked him in the head. He had a most colorful bruise on his cheek."

He glanced sidelong, as if gauging Allison's response, before adding, "Among other things. Like I said, quite the party."

Allison glanced away somewhat unsurely, her fist knotting.

What the hell was that all about? Allison wasn't the same person Trish had known in school. She'd always been the beauty, the girl everyone instinctively protected. Where she'd been brittle, like walking glass, she was now somehow detached, sort of dreamy. Trish had overheard Felicity say, "You know, the woman's finally discovering what it's all about. From the way she talks, that Dan Wirth doesn't have a flesh-and-blood dick. Allison would have you believe it's a stick of dynamite. She almost glows just talking about it."

Trish wondered what a man with a stick of dynamite for a dick might have been like. Her own experimentations hadn't come anywhere close.

"I talked to O'Leary and Igor Stryski." Trish propped her hand on her pistol. "They said that the last they saw, you were taking Thumbs into the back at Betty's."

"Alli, my love, would you excuse me for a moment? I don't want to bore you with all this, and I'll bet Officer Monagan has never seen a craps table."

"Sure, beloved," Allison told him, leaning forward to peck him on the cheek before he stepped down from the high desk. As he did, she shot Trish a shy smile, her blue eyes seeming unnaturally bright, a blush on her pale cheeks.

Looks more like drugs than love.

"Can we talk in confidence?" Wirth asked, voice barely above a whisper as he led her away. His entire demeanor had changed. Back was the boyish rogue, the soft-brown-eyed, dimple-chinned devil.

"That's the general idea," she told him, remembering Talina's warning about the guy.

"Hey, fellas, take a break," he said as he approached what Trish now knew was a craps table. She'd heard of them over the years, but this was new to Donovan. Corporate wouldn't have allowed it.

The men grinned, then filed for the door.

"You ever played craps?" He had stopped at one end of the table, having produced a pair of dice, God knew from where.

"Never have."

"Give it a try. Just toss them down yonder."

She took them, shook them, and sent them rattling down the table.

"A six! You're a natural, Trish."

She took a deep breath. "Imagine that. Look. I got a problem. No one has seen Thumbs. Word is you were the last one with him, and you turn up allegedly having 'bought' his warehouse."

Wirth was already fishing in his belt pouch, fingers producing a duralon document. "Here's the deed. That's his signature down there. The smudged thing. Uh . . . he wasn't exactly a model of grace. Damn near puked on the deed."

"And he just signed it over? Just like that?"

"No, Officer, it wasn't 'just like that.' Listen, you talked to O'Leary and Stryski, right? Then they told you I won that last hand. He and I had bet everything."

"That's what they said."

"And did they tell you I gave back about thirty thousand in yuan, gold, and jewels?" He retrieved the dice, casting them to bounce down the table. A seven.

She watched him, looking for any clue as to his veracity.

"Yeah," he continued, "we were all drunk. I wouldn't have bet my whole stash if I hadn't been. But I wasn't drunk enough to take every last yuan the guy had. Thumbs might have some issues with his personality . . . Okay, the guy's a dick. But he shouldn't be taken and humiliated either."

"Nice of you to think that way."

"I don't need to be a hard-ass, and I want people to know that I play fair. Call it good for business." He waved around.

"So, where's Thumbs?" She watched him like a nightmare might watch a hapless chamois.

"I don't have a clue."

"Tell me what happened when you and Thumbs went through Betty's door."

"Well, I, uh, took Thumbs back to Angelina's room."

"To do what?"

He lifted a mocking brow. "Use your imagination, Officer. I didn't want Thumbs to have any hard feelings about losing that hand. And everyone knows he has a thing for Angelina."

"She doesn't remember that."

"Well . . . what does she remember?"

"You, the next morning."

He winced slightly. "Then ask Thumbs."

She arched a pissed-looking eyebrow.

Wirth took a deep breath. "What the fuck? Why does this happen to me? Right when I'm finally getting everything to . . ." He gestured futility. "Shit! All right! We got to her room. Angelina had just finished with a client and was headed out to troll for business. Like just the right timing, you know?"

"Actually, I don't."

"So we're in the room, and I'm asking Angelina how much she'd take to spend the whole night with Thumbs. Sort of a sendoff for the guy to remember for the next two years cramped up in *Turalon*. That's when Thumbs turns green, says, 'I gotta puke. I'll be right back,' and bolts out the door."

"Did he come back?"

"I don't know," he almost whispered, tossing the dice again. "Maybe."

"Maybe?"

"Well . . . Angelina and I would have been busy."

"So, you spent the entire night with her?"

He cast a guilty glance at Allison. "I know how it sounds, but I was drunk. And maybe a little pissed off."

"At whom?"

"Allison." He bent down staring into her eyes. "I know you got a job to do. But being a cop—if you're a real cop—you know that there's times people tell you things. Stuff they don't want bandied around."

"Then I guess you're gonna have to take that risk."

"Like I said, quite the party. One of Allison's friends shared a hit of mash with her earlier in the evening. She was out like a light. Sort of grinning and staring at nothing. Wouldn't even talk. Some celebration, huh? So I went out to see what was happening, been running a game at Betty's for some time now. Never. Ever. Tried out the 'other' merchandise. Betty will back me up on that."

"And?" She gave him a hard-eyed look.

"And what? Angelina was a bit intoxicated herself. Thumbs was out puking in the back. Next thing I know, she's got my fly open, and she's got a mouthful. And then . . . Well, one thing leads to another."

He paused, looking guiltily at Allison. "Next thing I know, I wake up, and it's morning. I panic. Bust ass back to Allison's and find her still whacked out. So I crawl in bed, and she wakes up a couple of hours later."

Trish studied him, looking for any kind of a tell, seeing only guilt as he glanced hollowly at Allison.

"And you never saw Thumbs again?"

"No. But as drunk as he was, the guy's probably still hungover somewhere." A pause. "Uh, you know he was in a fight. Maybe you might want to ask whoever hit him if there was bad blood? Like, perhaps they took it up again?"

"Already did. Fig Paloduro was in Maya's hospital getting his broken nose reset."

"Then I'm betting Thumbs will show up after he dries out."

Trish took a deep breath. "All right. But let me know if you remember anything."

"Check with Angelina."

"I already did." *And she said all she remembers is some of the greatest sex she ever had*. "Have a good day, Skull. And as long as you didn't bullshit me, Ali doesn't need to know."

"Yeah, thanks!" he seemed genuinely relieved. "Want to try another toss of the dice? You might be one of those really lucky ones."

"Another time."

She stepped outside, tilted her head up to Capella's light, and took a deep breath. Something about the guy just sent a queer little spasm down her spine.

"Trish?" her implant inquired.

"What's up, Two Spots?"

"Just had a call in from one of the farmers out in A plot. Says he's got what's left of a body. Chased a swarm of invertebrates off of it. Says the ident in the equipment belt is Thumbs Exman's."

32

Panting for breath, Talina glanced down at the compass she'd clipped to her cuff. There. Just off to the right. That was the way. She stared at the gloomy and dark passage that lay between the myriad of tree trunks. Little more than a low spot in the jumbled roots, it looked like the easiest way forward.

At first sight, the maze of interlocked roots might have been an impenetrable barrier. Dark-green and waxy, the roots merged into thick boles—giant columns that thrust up into the dim and hazy air. But there were ways around, over, and through them.

Overhead the branches wove together in an infinite tapestry as they supported the weight of succulent leaves high above the forest floor. A tangle so thick it blotted out the light, leaving the shadowed forest floor in a dim twilight.

The thrill had started down in her gut. A curious sensation of challenge and excitement. With it came a strange taste in her mouth reminiscent of bitter mint. The blood in her veins had charged . . . but without her consent. She'd experienced the sensation before, when given drugs during medical procedures that had caused areas of her body to respond as if autonomously.

Was it just that Taggart had brought it to her attention, or did her nose filter more of the forest scents? The medley of delicate sweet and spicy odors played through her as she sniffed. And there, coming from the dark passage, came a slightly more acrid scent.

Don't go there.

Tal stopped. Swallowed her oddly peppermint saliva.

What's happening to me?

She tried to shake it off. Couldn't. The roots had started to twist toward her and Cap.

Go, Tal! She told herself. *Figure it out later.*

She turned away from the easy-looking path through the roots.

"S.O.?" Cap Taggart asked cautiously from behind her. He kept sidestepping and glancing down uncertainly as the roots under his feet squirmed.

"This way," she said, climbing over the root mass. "But hurry."

She leaped, wincing at the pain her in hip, scrambled to the top of another waxy root, and spun around to give Taggart a hand as he sought to follow. The guy was lighter on his feet than she'd imagined as he hauled himself up beside her.

The root had already begun to move as they dropped down the other side. Rifle in hand, Talina ducked through a low arch and scurried forward. Glanced back as Taggart cleared the already constricting passage. Beneath her feet, the smaller roots shifted as her weight bore down on them.

That acrid smell back there. As if she knew it.

"Come on, Tal," she told herself as she glanced at the compass. She needed to veer more to the right. "Got to keep moving."

"Looked better off to the right back there," Taggart said suggestively.

"Something wasn't right."

"Not right how?" he asked as they clambered over a bunched root that looked like a broken arm.

"Can't tell you."

Her vision had taken on that odd quality in the half light. Streaks of glowing green reflected in the ultraviolet, and she caught a faint thermal image of something alive as it scurried away in the shadows.

Impossible. I should be half-blind down here.

She felt the quetzal stretching and flexing inside her.

Was that it?

She gave an irritated shake of the head, hitching her bruised hip upward as she straddled a root, nearly fell into a hole, and caught herself.

"Got to move fast, Cap," she called over her shoulder as she leaped athletically from root to root over the gap. "And don't miss your step. Fall down there and you're dead."

She reached an exposed outcrop of rock and turned as Cap, rifle held for balance, leaped, root by root, across the shifting footing to land beside her.

"Son of a fucking bitch," he gasped, and wiped his sweat-damp face. "I've never been this freaked and scared in my whole life. When does this shit end?"

She glanced down at her compass, sniffed at the breeze, and picked out a hint of unscented air from the right. "Got to be close."

She looked back the way they'd come, watched the roots writhe in the gloom. Reflexively, she glanced down at the cracked shale upon which they stood. Rhizomes along the margins of the rock were feeling their way, somehow sensing them. Maybe it was the vibrations? Odors from their feet or clothing? Who knew?

Move. Follow the air.

She didn't question, just hefted her rifle, adjusted her pack, and despite the trembling in her exhausted legs, forced herself to pound off across the matted layer of blue, green, and brown roots. The way was uphill now, growing steeper as she went. The roots thinner here, almost threadlike—unlike back where the thick roots drove down into deep soil.

Not that that lessened the danger. Thin rhizomatic roots didn't have the mass and weren't as deeply anchored; they could move faster and latch hold.

"Don't stop, Cap," she shouted over her shoulder. "And for God's sake, don't trip or stumble."

He was panting behind her, the sound of his boots hammering on the ground as the climb sapped his energy. The guy might have been muscular, but he'd been exercising in a ship's gym, not scrambling up hills. He just didn't have the wind.

She shut off the pain in her hip, let a surge of panic act as an anesthetic. Ducking and dodging through the thinning trees, the climb grew steeper. Vines—indicative of forest margins—now laced their way up the slim trunks of the aquajade trees that began to appear among the thicker chabacho boles. More light pierced the canopy overhead.

The thing inside made her duck right, as if it controlled her movements. As she did, Talina recognized a gotcha vine obscured by the shadows.

"Jink right, Cap! Right!"

He did. The barbed tendrils barely grazed his fatigues, catching just enough of the fabric to almost trip him. But he caught himself, hammering his way forward on dogged feet.

"What the hell?" he said through hard gasps.

"Gotcha vine."

She turned her attention to the climb, lungs now laboring as she forced herself up the slope, finding more and more patches of bedrock. Some part of her brain had surrendered to the quetzal—as though an unbidden force were plotting her way through the trees. Each time, at the last instant, she stepped right, or perhaps left—the action completely involuntary—only to realize she'd avoided brown caps, sucking scrub, or chokeya.

"Follow in my footsteps, Cap," she called back. "Don't fuck it up."

God, was he going to make it? The guy was stumbling with fatigue, pushing himself on by sheer force of will.

As they broke out of the trees Cap tripped, sprawled hard, breath exploding as he hit the ground with a thud.

"Cap?" she called, turning.

He was open-mouthed, face glowing in her thermal vision, sweat-streaked, eyes almost glazed. Still game, he was almost to his feet when the sidewinder unleashed itself from beneath a sucking shrub off to his right.

Changing color from mottled green to iridescent turquoise, to purple, to brilliant crimson, the four-meter-long creature was as thick as a fire hose, rubbery. Without feet—and true to its name—it whipped sideways, planted a curled section of body, and propelled itself across the ground with uncanny speed.

Like a lash, it slapped one end of its length around Cap's shin. As it flexed to whip the rest of itself around his other leg, Talina jerked her rifle around, shot from the hip.

The report echoed off through the trees as the explosive bullet hit low and blew sharp fragments of shale through the sidewinder's muscular body.

It was enough to disrupt and shock the beast.

Talina shouldered the rifle, took aim, and blew the thing in two before it could recover.

"Cap, come on!" she shouted as the sucking shrub reached out. The branches were already feeling their way along the sidewinder's side, fluttering at the wounds.

"But this thing's—"

"What's left will fall off. Can't stop yet." And with that she turned, sprinting up the hill.

A glance over her shoulder showed Cap hurrying along, slinging wide the leg with the portion of sidewinder. The beast's bodily fluids leaked out and it grew limp. On his next step, it fell free.

Then they were out under a clear sky, stumbling and gasping, lungs heaving as she led the way past thorncactus and scrawny aquajade trees. She climbed the last bit of rocky slope at a walk.

Picking a spot where resistant sandstone overhung the gray shale, she finally unslung her pack and rifle and dropped into the shallow alcove.

"Fuck me," she whispered through air-starved lungs. "If I never have to do that again, I'll call this life a success."

"What the hell . . ." Cap threw himself down beside her, sweat trickling down his face, lungs pumping like bellows. "I mean, that *thing* . . ."

"Sidewinder," she told him between breaths. "Wraps around you. As long as you can get to a knife, you can cut it into pieces and get free. Or shoot it apart if you can get a hand on a pistol before it wraps you up."

"So it wasn't going to kill me before you could have got it off?"

"Nope." She wiped the sweat from her face. "But, by the time I did, the roots would have had you."

"What kind of world is this?" he cried, leaning his head back to gulp air into his frantic lungs.

She reached for her pack, pulling out her water bottle and sucking down swallows between deep breaths. "Screw me, but that was a close one."

"Thought we were dead." He actually burst out laughing, almost wheezing between breaths. "Haven't pushed myself that hard since boot camp. Damn, I'm out of shape."

She sat up, taking stock of their location. From this elevation she could trace their route through the forest by the line of writhing trees stirred up by their passage. The chime was all around them, intensifying at their presence.

"What's that sound?" he asked.

"Invertebrates."

"They dangerous?"

"Not in these parts. But we've barely sampled the rest of the planet."

"Charming."

"Welcome to Donovan. Glad you came along?"

He gave her a crooked grin. "I'm starting to like you, Security Officer Perez. And the longer you keep me alive, the more I'm going to like you."

She took another swig of water and capped her bottle. "Call me Tal, Captain." Stowing it in her pack, she added, "You've earned it."

Climbing to her feet, she winced at the pain in her hip. Fingered two cartridges from her belt magazine and slipped them into the rifle to top it up. From the shadow cast by the hill, it had to be close onto sunset. Any direction she looked, her vista consisted of nothing but an unbroken wall of forest all the way back to the Wind Mountains where the high peaks glowed orange in the sunset.

"So now what?" Cap asked, levering himself to his feet.

She pointed to the scattering of dead aquajade trees along the rocky slope. "Cut wood. Build a fire. We're going to need the heat, light, and defense. Not to mention a signal fire if we live long enough."

"Yes, ma'am." He gave her a sober look, having mostly caught his breath. "How did you do it back there? It was like you had a second sense. A couple of times, I could see you hesitate, then you'd jerk out of the way as something reached out for you. Like that gotcha vine. What was that?"

"Really unpleasant. It won't kill you. Doesn't like the taste of human. But once the hooks are sunk into your skin they have to be dug out one by one."

He made a face. "There's a locator beacon on the aircar, right?"

"There is, but even if it didn't burn up and it's transmitting on emergency power, it's buried in a huge mass of roots by now. Doubt it can broadcast through that kind of cover."

"A party is coming to look for us, aren't they?"

"Yeah, but probably not until morning. We don't fly at night."

"Why's that?"

She cocked an eyebrow as she gave him a wry look. "What if you go down? You want to try what we just did in the dark, Captain?"

He pursed his lips, gave her a pensive look, and said, "I've got a pocket saw in my pack. How about I go cut us some wood?"

"Stay on the bedrock, Cap. Don't get close to rock outcrops, especially if they smell funny. Sort of like vinegar. And don't hesitate to use your rifle."

He was squinting at her. "Seriously, how'd you do it? It was like you could sense the danger."

"Got a quetzal inside me, Cap."

The feel of the creature as it curled inside her was almost reassuring. But that was false security. From the angle of the setting sun, night was coming. It would be a long and dangerous one.

33

Kalico Aguila sat in the Captain's lounge and rubbed her tired brow. In the air before her, a section of *Freelander*'s log glowed, frozen where she had paused it.

Around her, the ship hummed, as if mocking her sense of despair.

Volunteering for this assignment had been a long shot—a gamble that she'd calculated would pay off. She'd expected to find some sort of operation gone rogue, perhaps a Supervisor with his own private army who'd hijacked the missing ships. A world shanghaied for someone's personal gain, but still operating along Corporate lines.

What made *Turalon* different from its predecessors was that none of the other ships had carried a Board-grade Supervisor, least of all one with the discretionary powers she'd been given. Kalico had the authorization to take whatever measures were necessary to regain control of the situation.

She'd fantasized that she would drop in with her marines, retake possession of the colony, and ship home as a hero. Right into a Boardmember's position, and on a hot track toward the Chairman's seat.

Instead she had chaos. A nightmare.

Nightmare? She *hated* that term. Never, in all of her life, had she been so humiliated.

Or frightened.

Or played for a fool.

Damn it, she'd lived her entire life at the center of Corporate power. She'd mastered the game, learned the subtle give and take of alliances, power plays, and how to destroy an adversary. Her subtle sense had recognized those who would be successful, and she'd made herself indispensable to them. Each assignment had been a springboard for advancement. Nor had she hesitated to cut a competitor's throat if he or she stood in Kalico's way. Her brilliance manifested in the way she brokered her power, exerted it for the greatest gain and leverage.

Her climb had elevated her all the way to Boardmember Taglioni's small staff. He had used her just as ruthlessly as she'd used him. Right up to the point that she'd managed to land the Donovan assignment. Salvage Donovan, and she'd eclipse Taglioni. Actually be able to use him and his influence to unseat one of the other Boardmembers . . .

Had this not all gone so wrong.

"So, what are you going to do now, Kalico?" she asked herself. The *Freelander* log glowed eerily in the dim light.

Kalico shook her head, wanting with all of her soul to disbelieve what she'd been reading.

I bet everything on Donovan. Prostituted my body and sold my soul.

Could this get any worse?

The hatch hissed as Captain Abibi stepped in, read Kalico's expression in a glance, and uncharacteristically seated herself in the chair closest to the door. "It reads like horror fiction, doesn't it?"

Kalico blinked her gritty and tired eyes, waved at the log entry. "They laid it out so rationally. Every step of their decision-making process. They knew they were in trouble. Realized that they were lost. That they didn't have the resources to keep everyone alive, that the hydroponics would fail under the load. Starvation was inevitable."

Abibi watched her, expression flat, eyes emotionless. "They euthanized the transportees. Five hundred men and women."

Kalico clenched her fists. "Euthanized. Nice word, huh? They would have died anyway, right? The hydroponics couldn't have supported that many people for that long."

"That is correct."

"It's the unemotional, almost mechanical way they talk about it. Just another routine ship's operation. Murder the transportees, freeze-dry them, and slowly add them to the hydroponics system as the organic molecules upon which it depends decayed into nonproductive elements." Kalico made a face. "Talk about a macabre form of cannibalism."

"Ma'am, hydroponics—boiled down to their basics—has been a form of cannibalism since the first ships went into space. It's just that with *Freelander* we have a whole new scale of selection and implementation."

"My God, Captain, you sound as numb and passionless as Captain Orten."

"Orten did what he thought was best for his ship and crew." Abibi cocked her head, gaze hard. "So, get over the emotional indignation, Supervisor. Put yourself in Orten's place: Things are falling apart. The transportees are turning violent, going slowly mad, and realizing they're trapped in *Freelander* for the rest of their lives. There is no rescue. No hope. It's only a matter of time before everyone on the ship turns on each other. It's already a flying coffin. A mass grave. Everyone is going to die. One way or another." A pause. "What would *you* do, Supervisor?"

"I . . ." But no words came.

Abibi didn't relent. "If you order us to space, how do you know *Turalon* won't find herself in a similar predicament? It's no longer just an academic question. Who gets to live the longest in hopes that some miracle saves them? Especially now that we know *Freelander* eventually arrived where she was supposed to. It just took one hundred and twenty-nine years."

Kalico felt her heart begin to race.

Abibi didn't relent. "If we space for Solar System . . . and it goes wrong? You might have to make that decision, Supervisor. Sitting right here. In this room. In that chair. You are The Corporation. The final arbiter of who lives . . . and who dies."

"All right. I'll save the ship and crew for the longest," she snapped. "There, does that help? Feel better, Captain? You and your people just made it."

Abibi stared at her, her light brown eyes oddly intense.

Kalico thrust out a finger. "But first, we're going to wait until *Freelander* is in orbit. Then we're going to scour her from one end to the other and see if there's anything that leads us to some understanding of what went wrong. A way of ever keeping this from happening again."

Abibi seemed nonplussed. "I knew Jem Orten. Smart man. Outstanding captain. His crew was among the best, too. You've seen the logs. They spent the rest of their lives trying to solve the problem. What makes you think you can when they couldn't?"

Kalico had no answer. Instead she slapped a hand to the long-distance telemetry controls. The holographic display shifted, showing a background of a thousand stars with a yellow pip to mark *Freelander*'s position. She was still too far out to see, even for *Turalon*'s advanced optics.

For the first time in Kalico's life, she found herself adrift; she had no clue as to what her next step would be. Or even if she would ever dare to leave Donovan. It was a new and frightening calculus.

34

Fire popped as Cap lay back on the uncomfortable shale. Talina Perez had warned him about lying on dirt, about the kinds of creatures that could come crawling out of it. Especially slugs, though they preferred wet or even damp soil.

He studied Talina where she sat on a sandstone boulder. The fire played a dancing game, bathing her smooth cheeks, the thrust of her nose, and her fine forehead in flickers of yellow. The woman's ink-black hair seemed to absorb the light, as if drawing from the source of the illumination.

Max Taggart had to admit, he'd never imagined that a woman like this one existed in the whole of the universe.

And to think that but for a turn of chance—and my own ignorance and stupidity—I might have shot her dead.

God, there were times he wondered if the universe didn't continually play him for a fool.

"What if there had been no hills?" he asked. "No stony outcrops to run to?"

Talina gave him a sidelong glance, a faint smile on her lips. "Got to climb. The roots will kill you, but the branches are safe. At least with regard to the tree. There are other creatures up there that will get you. Not much study has been done on the forest or what lives in the branches. Then there's gotcha vine, you're screwed vine, chokeya, and cutthroat flower that live up there. Got to keep your eyes open."

"Where do you get these names?"

"What else would you call them?"

"And you people *choose* to stay here instead of space with *Turalon*?" He tried to make sense of it, to come to grips with the reality of the place. Death seemed to hang like a film in the very air.

"You talking odds, Cap? Or quality of life? If it's odds, I gotta tell you, the ships haven't been doing so well lately. We'd have to figure the numbers, but thousands are missing and presumed dead in all those vanished ships. Sure, *Turalon* made it this far, but if *Mekong* is any indication, you've got no guarantee you're making it home again. And if you don't? How you going to die? Slow starvation in a failing ship? Or does it just happen all at once? With a big bang. And you're gone. Floating in whatever reality those ships invert to."

She gave him a ribald wink. "Me, Cap? I'll take my chances here."

He nodded, took a deep breath of the scented air. The burning aquajade wood had a resinous essence, an odor somewhat mindful of hickory, cinnamon, and mesquite all mixed together.

"All right," he admitted. "The idea of spacing back on that ship scares the shit out of me. Not that I liked it all that much on the way out, either. Two years is a long time to be confined in a warren like that."

"What if it turned out to be the rest of your life? Like it popped back into space somewhere in the flat middle of nothing. Hundreds of light-years from the nearest star system. Generators failed. Just *Turalon* all alone in the middle of the empty cold and black."

"You trying to make a point, or just be damned depressing?"

She laughed. "I'm just saying that living is a dangerous business. But look up there. A hundred billion stars, the Milky Way glowing white and luminous as you've never seen it from Solar System. Those black patches are concentrations of dark matter, the patterns and constellations all different. I know where you came from, what you came from. I'll take my chances here."

He stared out at the dark forest, heard a low and melodic hooting, almost a song coming from the trees. "What if no one comes looking for us? What if we're on our own here, Talina? We're surrounded by forest. What's next?"

She pointed. "That river we were following? It's over there to the north. Might take us two days of hard traveling, humping butt over the roots until we're exhausted. Then we rope up into the branches, rest, and go arboreal. We'll need to make scaffolding to sleep on at night. Periodically drop to the ground and hump butt some more when the branches don't go our way."

"And when we're at the river?"

"Chabacho trees have pods about midway up. I haven't seen it done, but I've heard tell that split in half they make a kind of canoe. Might be another three or four days' float west to the mouth of the Briggs River. We should find their homestead another couple of days' walk north in one of the tributary canyons."

"Just like that?" He thought he sounded trite.

She arched a slim eyebrow in return. "Pretty much. If something doesn't eat us on the way."

Cap threw his head back and laughed. "And we thought we were going to intimidate you with a handful of marines?"

"You don't know how close you and the Supervisor came to dying that day."

"You saved everyone's ass."

"I wasn't any hero. I had the damnedest urge to let Step and the crowd kill you all. But it would have been stupid. On Donovan, stupidity is a death sentence."

"Is that why you killed Clemenceau?"

"Now, that man was anything but stupid." Fine lines appeared in her brow as she frowned. "He wanted me on that survey trip. There was a reason it was only the two of us. I wasn't supposed to make it back. After he'd taken his sample that day, he took the lead on the way back to the aircar. A gesture meant to reassure me that he trusted me to have his back. And damn him, he knew me. Knew I wouldn't back-shoot him."

She was shaking her head, eyes fixed on the distance.

"Was there really a nightmare?" Cap realized the answer was important to him.

"Oh, yes." She smiled. "I even warned him. Said: 'Supervisor, you might not want to take the straight route back. Too many mundo trees that way.'"

Her expression hardened. "See, whereas he knew I wouldn't shoot him in the back, I knew that he'd disregard any advice I gave, figuring it was a trick to put him at a disadvantage. Of course he took the direct route under the mundo trees. He was happy enough to have me lag behind, too. He wanted to get to the aircar first . . . and to that pistol. The one he'd taped to the bulkhead inside the door while I was out securing our landing spot when we first got there."

"So you knew there was a nightmare?"

"Too many bones on the ground. He was a town guy. Couldn't read the signs."

"Isn't that cold, Tal? Letting him walk into a mess like that?"

"Cold, Cap? As cold as stepping into an aircar door, tearing a pistol loose from tape, and shooting your security officer in the face before flying back to Port Authority to report that something in the bush got her?"

Again the slight shrug of her shoulders. "As it was, I looked him right in the eyes when I shot him. I might have hated him, but I couldn't leave him to that kind of fate."

"Shit on a shoe, how did it get that poisonous?"

"He was losing control. The Corporation was light-years away. Donovan was subverting people, seducing them away from the rules and regulations. Instead of adapting to the new conditions, his solution was to clamp down. Tighten his authority. Punish any infraction." She paused wistfully. "I *killed* people on his orders."

She smiled grimly and tossed another piece of wood into the fire. "I went along at first, green as I was, indoctrinated by my years of Corporate training. He used me, and when I finally realized I'd killed the wrong people, that was the final straw."

"What you just told me, that's a death sentence, you know. Doesn't matter that you were acquitted. That's new evidence. A confession to a Corporate officer."

"What are you going to do about it, Captain? Take me prisoner?" She offered her wrists as if for manacles.

He thought back to their flight through the forest. Had it been him, alone, he'd have died within minutes at the aircar, milling about stupidly as the roots closed in. And even if he'd had the sense to run, how far would he have made it? A hundred meters? Two hundred? Images of the gotcha vine, the sidewinder, and all the other dangers she hadn't named came back to haunt him.

He rubbed his tired eyes. "Stupidity is a death sentence on Donovan. Those are your words. I'm tired of being stupid. Tired of being a Corporate stooge. Raya Turnienko told Kalico and me that you'd never killed a man who didn't deserve it." He paused. "How do you tell the difference?"

"Raya lied. On Clemenceau's orders I killed two men who just wanted to go home. I'd like to think that after that, I never killed anyone who didn't deserve it." Talina took a deep breath, and he tried not to notice how it emphasized her figure. Silly man, he'd never be worthy of a woman like this.

"I learned that the measure of human life on Donovan is relatively simple: Are you purposefully going out of your way to get other people killed? Are you working toward the detriment of society? If the answer is yes, that puts you in a pretty shady area on the plus or minus category."

"The greatest good for the greatest number. Talina, you could be a Corporate algorithm."

"It's a little more nuanced out here." She glanced his way. "What about you? Still looking forward to that fat-padded life as a Corporate bodyguard?"

Was he? He stared out at the night, smelled the perfumed breeze. The chime was waxing and waning, the hooting down in the trees almost a symphony. The unfamiliar constellations, the swirls of stars, and the black patches of dark in their midst smacked of the exotic. Terror and beauty, what an odd reconciliation of opposites.

"I don't know what I want." It stunned him that he'd just told himself the truth. "One thing's for sure: I don't want to set foot in that ship and space back for Earth. The idea of inverting space and just vanishing? That scares the ever-loving hell out of me." He met her eyes. "Does that make me less of a man?"

She was thoughtful as she shook her head. "In my book, it makes you more of one."

"Well, if fear is your measure of masculinity"—he waved a hand toward the forest—"I had my heart in my throat for that entire run. So, consider me twice the man you thought I was."

"You'll do, Cap. Yes, I think you will." She nodded to herself. "You've just taken the first step toward becoming a fully realized human being."

"Why, thank you, Security Officer, I appreciate that." He tried to keep the venom out of his voice.

"It's because it's unfamiliar," she seemed almost to be talking to herself. "You can learn it, Cap. Not everyone has the knack for it, but you do. That's assuming . . ."

"Yes? Assuming?"

When she looked at him again, her eyes had gone black, alien, and cold. Even her voice seemed to change as she said, "Assuming you can stay alive long enough."

35

Trish had buried herself in the investigation over Thumbs Exman's death. Enough of the corpse remained that Raya determined that Thumbs had been thumped on the back of the head and then strangled. Manually.

That kind of murder didn't happen in Port Authority. Killings came in the form of gunshots and stab wounds when interpersonal violence broke out. The creed of "fair fight" had developed over the years. Even Clemenceau had endorsed it as a means of "disposing" of potential troublemakers. The notion of dishonorably sneaking up behind someone and smacking them in the head just had a noxious loathsomeness about it.

Which meant it had to be a recently arrived transportee. One without apparent scruples.

Dan Wirth. Had to be.

Trish had thrown herself, full-tilt, into trying to prove it. And failed. She'd gone to question the bastard after hearing Raya's report; he'd given her a mystified look, offered his hands for her inspection, and even suggested that she take scrapings from under the fingernails.

"Hey, Officer," he'd told her, "I'm just as anxious as you are to find who did this. After all, I was the last guy seen with him. I don't want that shadow cast on my door. All I want is to run an honest business."

She'd even gone to the extent of secreting sensors beneath her uniform to monitor the guy.

Now she stood in Raya's examining room, watching the instruments as Raya reviewed her interview with Wirth.

"I'm seeing nothing in the recordings, Trish. No sweats, no dilation of the pupils. Not even a trace of galvanic skin response, increased respiration, or accelerated heartbeat." Raya stood back, a frown on her face. "What about his expressions? I mean, you were there. Surely you must have had a sense for when he was lying."

"I didn't get a single tell," Trish told her. "Talina taught me what to look for. Usually it's the eyes and eyebrows, a wrinkling of the forehead. Subconsciously a liar wants to emphasize the lie. The subtlest of communication. Make a statement of 'I really didn't do it.' But I got nothing. If anything, the guy was too calm."

"From the readings I'm seeing here, he might have been discussing the color of mud while drinking a cup of morning coffee."

"That's just it, Raya. When you're interrogating a person about something as incriminating as murder, essentially attacking them, you should get some kind of reaction. Hey, if I came in here and started questioning you, you'd be surprised, then alarmed, and finally defensive. Especially if you knew you hadn't done it."

"Well, the instruments didn't record so much as a skip of his heart."

Trish fingered her chin as she stared thoughtfully at the monitor.

"So what kind of human being doesn't even show a change of brain waves when he's lying about killing someone?"

"One kind," Turnienko told her. "A stone-cold psychopath."

"But why did he do it?" Trish parked her butt on a counter, arms crossed. "The guy won the title in a card game. It was all fair. Thumbs was in the game of his own free will."

"All fair?" Turnienko arched an eyebrow. "You sure?"

"Two of the Skulls, Stryski and O'Leary, were in the game. They said it was just luck of the draw. They said that Wirth even gave about thirty thousand back. That he went out of his way to make sure Thumbs had enough left to make him a rich man back in Solar System. Talked to Step. He says the guy plays a straight game."

"And of course, the thirty thousand wasn't found on the body, right?"

"How'd you guess?"

Raya Turnienko smiled. "Admirably orchestrated. Perfectly performed. I'm glad that Dan Wirth is your problem, Trish. But be careful. Very, very, careful. He's not just a psychopath, but a damned brilliant one. Especially if he managed to get past the Corporate psych screening. I don't want to come in some morning and find you on the table where Thumbs is lying."

Trish glanced at the wall separating Turnienko's exam room from the morgue. Thumbs was just waiting for one of Pamlico Jones' overwhelmed crew on the shuttle landing field to get time enough to run the backhoe up to the cemetery and dig a hole. Then Thumbs would be hauled out on the cart and buried.

As Trish considered this, boots came thudding down the hallway, and Step Allenovich leaned in, his face grim. "Trish?"

"Yeah."

"Two Spots just ran me down. Tal's overdue."

"Overdue from what?"

Raya Turnienko said, "She went out to pick up Madison Briggs. She's got a baby coming in the next couple of weeks. Given the complications she had last time, I wanted her here for observation. Tal was supposed to pick her up a couple of days ago."

Trish felt a cold rush in her spine. "A couple of days?"

Step took a deep breath, jaw muscles tensing in his craggy face. "Two Spots didn't get any distress call. First he knew that something was wrong was when Chaco called just now asking when Tal was supposed to pick Madison up. He thought it was today."

"Tal would have called if something had gone wrong."

"Yeah. You'd think." Step gestured. "She's not the kind to go off lollygagging. Oh, and Two Spots says she took that marine, Taggart, with her."

The cold chill of premonition grew. "Cap Taggart? The bastard that arrested her? That was going to put her against a wall and shoot her?"

"The very same."

"Get your rifle and a survival pack, Step. We've got to find her. One of the aircars charged?"

"Yeah, the blue one should be."

But Trish was already pushing past him, headed for the weapons locker.

36

"See it?" Talina asked. She stood frozen on the dim forest floor, her rifle at the ready. Overhead the maze of branches rose into an interlaced roof that blocked most of the light. She'd been ready to step over one of the waxy green roots when the quetzal hissed inside her.

Cap, similarly frozen, stood just behind her left shoulder. She could smell him, his odor sour with sweat. As was her own. Too many days in the same clothes.

Overhead the forest symphony had dropped to a low musical hum; invertebrates kept fluttering through the still and muggy air. Her nose caught the subtle odors of decay; perspiration beaded on her skin. The twilight shadows and dim light just added to the creepy sensations of danger.

Cap swallowed hard. "Yeah," he whispered. "Cutthroat flower. Right?"

"Yep. And to its right. There, in the darkness under that root?"

"Sidewinder?"

"Very good."

"Guess we're going back the other way?"

"Guess we are."

She sensed him as he backed slowly away, retracing his steps around the thick tangle of roots clustered at the base of a huge chabacho tree. The massive trunk had to be five meters in diameter.

Step by step, she backed beyond of any possible reach from the sidewinder.

As he let her pass, Cap asked, "I suppose cutthroat flower isn't named for its colors, since I didn't see any."

"Oh, it's colorful enough. It's just not blooming right now. It won't, in fact. Not until it grabs something with its tendrils to slice open and drink. And even then, the word 'flower' doesn't really describe the reproductive process. It's just a visual signal that the plant has enough food to reproduce. Cheng and Iji aren't really sure how that happens yet."

"You don't seem to know a whole lot."

"Cap, it's a huge planet. Humans have only been here for a little over thirty years, and most of that was spent building and mining. There's so much we don't know. Haven't had time to study."

She led the way around the roots, felt the quetzal's hesitation inside her. Peering into the shadowy depths, she just knew: *Trouble that way.*

Looking back through the gloom, she could see where a young chabacho had toppled sideways, the ground around it buckled and slanting.

"We're headed up, Cap. Time to take to the branches for a while."

As she started up the loose incline where the roots fought to hold the soil, Cap asked, "What causes a tree to fall like this?"

"Mind you, we don't know for sure, but Iji thinks the trees gang up on other trees in some form of alliance."

Cap gave a dismissive shake of the head. "Do you know how weird that sounds?"

"Do you remember what world you're on?"

He grinned in macabre amusement.

She slung her rifle and scrambled on all fours up a webbing of roots, feeling them squirm as she did so. Not a place to either slip or linger. Beneath her gaped a dark emptiness where the root ball had been pulled out of the ground. The fact that none of the smaller roots sought to loosen themselves suggested the tree was holding for dear life onto what dirt it still could.

Talina clambered up onto a knotted twist and reached back to give Cap a hand. "Look how the tree's holding on. And here, on the other side, the roots are wrapped around the next tree's."

"Yeah, like they're fighting." Cap paused, considering the spectacle. "Alliances between trees, huh? How do they communicate?"

"No idea, Cap."

She glanced up the slanting trunk, seeing where the branches had interwoven with those of its neighbors. "Danged if it doesn't look like the tree doesn't have a choke hold on older ones. It's like it grabbed hold as it started to fall, and it's not letting go."

"Wonder what it did to piss off its neighbors."

"Something. Think about it while we climb." She felt her way up the inclined trunk. Thank God that somewhere deep in her ancestral past her ancestors had been arboreal apes.

As she made her way into the branches, it was to find them wound into the thick lower branches of the surrounding trees. Instead of the round branches common to terrestrial species, life on Donovan had taken a different structural approach, with a triangular cross section and interior bracing.

"Why's that?" Cap had asked the first night when they'd climbed into the trees.

"Triangle's the strongest geometric shape," she'd told him as they constructed their platform in the fork of a branch. "That's why they're used in bridges and load-bearing construction."

They'd been learning a lot about the forest. For one thing, it seemed that as long as no one crashed a burning aircar into them, the roots seemed a lot less aggressive, really only reacting if they provoked them through hard stomping or rapid travel. But moving slowly, watching where a person put his or her feet, caused a minimum of reaction.

No threat, her quetzal sense insisted.

The creature's presence no longer disturbed her as it once had. Maybe there was too much of her *bruja* aunt in her genes. Talina understood that her quetzal was smelling through her nose—that its instincts were melding into hers. The how and why of it still eluded her.

Nor did she fully trust the creature. It had, after all, sneaked into Port Authority and eaten Allison Chomko's baby.

A sense of disappointment coupled with frustration rose inside her. Call it a feeling that hinted that eating the baby hadn't been worth it.

Whatever that meant.

No mind.

"Yeah, right. Whatever," Talina almost growled as she led the way across a mat of interwoven branches. Hands out for balance, she crossed onto a thicker branch jutting out from one of the older trees. Glancing at her wrist, she checked her compass. Still on course.

"You talking to yourself, or did I do something to piss you off?" Cap asked from behind her.

"Talking to the quetzal." She took a moment to study the way ahead where an interlacing of thick branches offered several paths forward. The important thing was to look first, really study how they wove their way across other branches. Many were twisted, making them impassible as the flat tops bent away until they presented a sharp angle no one could cross.

"You and your quetzal."

"Yeah. Sure, I can see better. Even into the IR and UV. And I can smell, almost sense trouble. I get thoughts. Like it's communicating. At the same time, I know it's not friendly. Like it's waiting for something."

"So will you tell me when I should start being concerned?"

"How about when my skin starts turning colors?" She figured the grin she gave him was more like a rictus.

He chuckled, taking time to unscrew his water bottle and take a swig. It wasn't safe by any means, but they had an unlimited supply. She had shown him how to drill into the aquajade tree's veins to tap one of the water-bearing arteries. She'd worry about the amount and kind of heavy metals it contained when, and if, they ever got back to Port Authority.

Off to the left a tree clinger chattered and leaped away on long back legs. Since taking to the trees they had seen a host of new and unknown creatures. In addition to the tree clingers, were several different species of what Cap had called "squirrels," though they had no similarity to the earthly rodents. Scarlet fliers were in evidence but tended toward the higher branches. Then came something they had tagged as live vines, which only looked plantlike; the things were definitely animals. Other creatures had only been glimpsed for a second before fleeing, defying any kind of name at this early stage.

Talina checked her compass, picked a route, and started forward. So much for "follow the yellow brick road." This was more like a turquoise ribbon in midair. The thick branches like this one were nearly a meter wide across the flat and didn't so much as jiggle as she and Cap trotted along. Not that she didn't have an eerie sense of the heights—of what a fall meant if she should misstep. It was a long way down, bouncing from branch to branch the entire way.

"How you doing, Cap?"

"Heart in my throat, Tal. I'd rather be working in vacuum in free-fall. Gravity's a scary thing."

She grinned to herself, wondering just when Cap Taggart had managed to work his way into her very narrow and highly select circle of acceptable companions. The guy was solid, no bullshit, and smart enough to know his limitations.

She carefully climbed over a cross branch and picked another branch leading the direction she wanted to go. Invertebrates skittered this way and that, fleeing at her approach. As they did, the chime changed, deepening in tone.

The first thick stalk of vine lay just ahead, proof that they were nearing a break in the forest. She passed it, noting that it was lumpy enough, with protrusions in the bark, that climbing up or down wasn't out of the question.

She hadn't made fifty meters before the number of vines began to increase. "River's close," she told him, scanning the shaded surroundings for an appropriate chabacho pod.

Just as she saw one where it sprouted from a smooth-barked trunk, the chime changed, a subtle alto harmony growing in background.

Fear. Like a fist to the gut, it stunned her with its intensity. She froze, heart battering in her chest. That quetzal sense inside locked her muscles. Surrendering to impulse, she dropped onto the branch.

"Cap? Lie down. Don't move." She struggled for breath, smelling the forest's slight tang. A bizarre shimmering of color crossed her vision; then it clarified with an intensity she'd never experienced before.

"What's up?" Cap asked as he dropped to his belly behind her.

"Don't know." Chin propped, she scanned as widely as she could.

They appeared as a flicker of movement at the edge of Talina's vision. Darting and gliding shapes, bits of light green and semitranslucent shadows. As they flew into full view she could see that they came as a flock. Tens of them swooping and darting among the branches. They weren't very big, none larger than the common raven back on

Earth—but instead of black they each radiated a full spectrum of colors, the intensity and pattern of which made them particularly hard to track.

"What the . . . ?" Cap whispered.

Immediately the lead flier flipped its colorful wings, changing course. Wings? Four of them. Two on each side, fore and aft, and crap, did they ever make the creature agile in the air. They flew like nothing Talina had ever seen, literally turning back on their tracks, jinking sideways as if batted.

Cap was smart enough to go mum as the first of the flock darted in to hover overhead.

Careful. The word formed in her thoughts.

Talina narrowed her eyes. The things had to be damned dangerous.

She sensed the quetzal's terror.

It probably wasn't an eternity—maybe only ten or fifteen seconds as the beasts collected, hovered, and stared down at Talina and Cap where they lay prone and exposed on the branch. One flapped down to eye level, and Talina stared into its three-eyed face. In response, the flier burst into vivid colors—blues, golden hues, yellows and black. She'd never seen anything so vivid, so intense, all radiating as it spread wicked jaws filled with rows of bladelike teeth.

The tension was broken by a shriek as a tree clinger on a nearby branch lost its nerve and leaped away.

One second the flock was hovering just above, the next the creatures were gone like a shot. Talina forgot herself, lifted her head and watched the chase. The tree clinger catapulted itself from branch to branch, the horde of fliers hotly in pursuit.

"Holy shit," Cap whispered from behind, "would you look at that?"

Talina wouldn't have believed that animals could move that fast, the tree clinger ricocheting from branch to branch in a blur. Despite that, the flock of predators couldn't have been a fraction of a second behind.

She craned her neck to watch as they dropped down through the branches. And there the tree clinger found salvation; it bounced off what looked like a green lump at the axial branch of a chabacho limb.

The lump reacted, shifted, colors splashing, before it betrayed itself as a young quetzal. As the tree clinger propelled itself away, the quetzal hissed, mouth open at the violation. It snapped up the closest of the fliers, crushing it in tooth-filled jaws.

Just as fast, the rest of the fliers were all over it, slashing with the hooklike blades at the tips of their omnicolor wings. The quetzal screamed.

Talina went rigid.

Cap asked, "What's wrong?"

"Didn't you hear that?"

"Hear what?"

"That scream."

"Tal, all I hear is the forest and those things chittering as they mob that . . . well, whatever it is."

Talina watched in fascinated horror as the fliers mobbed the young quetzal. Bite, strike, and flail as it might, the quetzal was simply overwhelmed.

"They're eating their way into that, uh . . ." Cap's voice rasped hoarsely.

"It's a quetzal, Cap. Couple of years old."

"That's a quetzal? A terrible and feared quetzal? And those things are killing it?"

"Yeah. Holy shit, huh?" Talina's heart was pounding. Crap. She'd been face-to-face with one of the things.

"What do you call those flying things?"

"Never seen them before, Cap. They're new."

"Thought quetzals were the dominant predators on Donovan."

"So did we," she answered. And who knew that quetzals could climb trees?

Go, the voice inside her whispered. She didn't need the sense of urgency to spur her onward.

Talina climbed shakily to her feet, muscles unsteady with fear as she crouched low and scuttled for the thick tangle of vines up ahead.

"They just mobbed that thing," Cap kept repeating behind her. "If they'd have come for us? I mean, how can a person defend themselves against those *things*?"

"Why didn't they attack us?" she asked the quetzal.

Didn't know.

"Didn't know what? What we were?"

The thing played with her emotions, filling her with a sense of disgusted amusement, and something unbidden insisted, *They will learn.*

"Shit," was all she could say in response.

They needed a pod, a big one, and some way to cut it in half and get it down to the river. As she looked around for one, a terrible fear was eating away down in her belly. For the first time, she was deeply, truly frightened, and so, too, was the quetzal lurking down in her soul.

37

For three days now, Trish and Step had piloted the aircar westward from Port Authority. Each morning at dawn they were in the air. Trish insisted. Step had been willing in the beginning. But he'd worried that she pushed the batteries to the limit, refusing to let them return until dusk. At the end of the second day, he'd told her, "One more day, Trish. That's all."

Six days! That's how long Talina and the marine had been missing. The growing sense of despair in Trish's gut was like a yawning wound.

And it wasn't like she and Step hadn't looked. They had crisscrossed the route Tal would have taken up Mainway Canyon, searched the crags and depths for wreckage, and then through Best Pass and down the Grand River to the Briggs homestead.

At the wheel, she'd avoided the forest where it spread over the wide plain until last. Mostly because if Tal had gone down in it, chances were good that she was dead.

"Trish?" Step said as they worked a series of transects across the forest south of the river.

"Yeah." She was leaning out, looking down at the green mass of leaves that rose in mounded lumps. It gave the forest top a soft, almost inviting look. Hard to believe that in places, the ground lay another three hundred feet below.

"If she went down here, you know there'd be nothing to see. By now the branches would have mended, healed any damage her aircar would have caused."

"Maybe."

"You're not thinking, girl." Step resettled his muscular body, binoculars hanging from one hand as he stared over the side. "I really hate this. Now is not the time for us to have a battery problem."

"It's Talina. You know, just as well as I do, that if it was the other way around, she'd be looking."

Step shot her an evaluative glance. "Yeah, I know. But that's forest down there. Not even Talina . . ."

He stopped when she raised a threatening hand. Out of habit, she noted that they were down to twenty-seven percent in the battery. Worse, the sun was slanting in the west. How long did they have?

"She's pretty special, I'll agree," Step told her. "And you've done the best you could. But Trish, the last thing Tal would want was anyone losing their lives on her account."

"I know."

"Not that much light left." Step indicated the west.

"When Dad died, Tal pretty much took me under her wing. Damn it, Step. Sometimes you owe people more than you can tell them. Me? But for Talina, who the hell knows. I might be turning tricks at Betty's just to keep my belly full. Looking back, I wasn't in any better position than Angelina was."

He leaned out, using the binoculars to scan a hole in the tree cover. "Angelina was always out for a good time. You had that serious streak. Talina knew. We all did. And once you started following her around, she'd have cracked your skull if you hadn't lived up to your potential."

"I always wanted to be like her."

Dryly, Step said, "Yeah? Well, you've got a real good start on it. Now, are we going back before our battery fizzles and we drop down into the darkness and die?"

Trish, reflexively checked the battery again. Twenty-five percent.

"So," she mused, "let's say you were following the river. And bang, the battery starts to fry." She straightened, staring out across the canopy, noting the distant outcrops slightly to the west. Yes, that's what she'd do.

"Hang on, Step." Trish pulled them into a turn, lining out for the knobs.

"Uh, that's enough, Trish." He took a position beside her, checking the battery. "We're at twenty-five percent. It's late. We'll be racing darkness as it is to get back."

"Gotta check something."

"Trish," Step snapped. "Did you hear me?"

"Yeah, Step. Loud and clear." She gave him a sour look. "All right, damn it. She's probably dead. I get that. Let me check this one last thing, okay? Then we'll head for home, and I'll carve her tombstone. But let me do this."

He gave her his flinty look, then it collapsed into a smile. "You really are a lot like her, you know? If it was anyone but you . . ."

"Yeah, you'd smack me, grab the wheel, and head us home."

"You know I always give you more leeway than the others."

"Not that it's doing you any good. I know how you look at me. Sorry. You're not my type. Not to mention how much older you are. If I want a man, I want him to be a one-woman-at-a-time sort who isn't in hock to a murdering psychopath."

"I call it the raw idealism of youth."

"I call it self-preservation." She paused. "How much are you in hock to Wirth?"

"Actually, I'm not." Step's eyes narrowed as he fixed on the rocky outcrops sticking up from the forest. "Barely. I caught on in time. He's damned good. I think he's got an implant. Something that allows him to rig the games so that he can win or lose as much as he wants, when he wants. I may like taking a chance just as much as the next guy, but I'm not playing a rigged game."

"Tal said he was a human quetzal. You got proof he's rigging the games?"

"Nope. You'd have to have one hell of a statistical program and monitor his games for a period of time, and even in the end it would tell you that his winnings were just improbable, but not impossible."

"So why do you hang out there?"

"Maybe because you won't marry me and fill my evenings with meaning." He gave her a wink and lecherous smile that told her he was kidding. "But seriously, Trish. I know, just like everyone else does, that he killed Thumbs. So, here's the deal: I'm letting you risk my life to check these outcrops. In return, you save yours by backing off Dan Wirth."

"Back off?"

"Yeah. He killed Thumbs in a way we're not going to be able to prove. What worries me is that you're going to keep pushing, and eventually we'll find your dead body lying out in some field." His lips twitched. "That would break all of our hearts."

"Let him get away with it?"

"For now." Step shrugged as they neared the first of the sandstone anticlines. "Wait for the right time. No one, no matter how smart, is perfect forever. It's Donovan."

"You know what Tal would do."

"She'd walk in and shoot his ass. You're not Tal. And he might shoot you first. He's got a pistol wired under his desk. Trust me. Dan Wirth likes to control the odds. Now, have we got a deal? Or do I reach over and muscle you out of the way and do the smart thing, which is head for home?"

He could outwrestle her for the wheel. She'd have no recourse but to shoot him if she wanted to make an issue out of it. And, damn it, miscreant whoring drunk that he was, he was still Step. She might not approve of the way he lived his life, but he'd always been there for her, for the people of Port Authority. And yes, for Talina, as well. His had been the shoulder Talina had cried on when they buried Mitch.

"All right. I'll back off Wirth."

"Assuming we can still make it back before running out of battery, I'll call that a victory."

She was watching the charge level as they rounded the first of the buttes. At twenty percent, she'd have to call it. Step had been right. Tal wouldn't want her going down in a place like this. Not with Step along, too.

That sense of futility tightened in her gut. The moment she rolled the wheel and headed them back toward Best Pass it would be like a declaration.

I'm sorry, Tal. So very sorry.

She curled them around the second of the outcrops, searching vainly for a waving human being on the slope, or atop the angular sandstone. Nothing but bare rock, shale, and a scattering of aquajade trees on the lower slopes greeted her quest.

Trish swallowed hard, her heart lead-heavy. She'd tightened her grip on the wheel. The battery meter had just dropped to twenty percent. Time to go.

"Holy shit," Step cried, pointing.

Trish still didn't see it. "What?"

"Look! There!" Step was almost bouncing, the aircar rocking under his weight.

Then Trish saw the cold smear of ash that indicated a fire. And just below it, laid out in brown sandstone blocks atop the gray layers of shale, she made out the words: GONE TO BRIGGS.

38

It couldn't have been working better. Dan Wirth smiled down from his elevated chair at the men and women filling his gambling den. He'd called it "The Jewel" and proclaimed that fact through the big sign he'd had painted and hung out front.

Not only that, but people were flocking to his place. The Jewel was a novelty and a welcome relief from the usual haunts of the cafeteria and the tavern. Not only was it the new diversion, but it appealed. Especially on Donovan where life was a gamble each and every day. These people were used to taking risks, and it wasn't as if they had a lot to lose. For the hardcore locals, it wasn't life-ending if they got cleaned out at the tables. Gold? Emeralds? Diamonds? There were more of those for the taking. It just meant outfitting and spending another half year out in the bush, drilling away in the mines, or prospecting for a new strike.

For the truly down-and-out, losing it all meant that no matter how far they might fall, The Corporation still owed them a trip back to Solar System and a healthy bonus for filling out their contracts when they arrived back at Transluna.

Assuming, that is, that they wanted to consign their sorry asses to the *Turalon* and take the uncomfortably long odds that they'd actually arrive back home.

Even with that depressing probability, a new sense of hope was in the air. Word was that *Freelander* had finally arrived. Supervisor Aguila might have wanted to keep it under wraps, but it turned out that keeping a secret—even under orders—wasn't as easy as it was back in Solar System. Donovan wasn't The Corporation.

Everyone knew that something had gone terribly awry with *Freelander*, though just what hadn't made its way through the net of censorship and down to the gossip channels yet. All anyone knew was that she was in-system, headed for orbit, and that something was very, very wrong.

Dan nodded as Betty Able stepped in the door, glanced around, and made her way to his elevated perch in the rear. Dan touched his forehead in salute and said, "My office in the back. It's a better place to talk."

As he stepped down from his chair to follow, speculation about *Freelander* was the major topic of conversation at each of the tables. It was either that, or what terrible fate had befallen Talina Perez and Cap Taggart out in the bush.

He'd despised Taggart not only because he was Corporate law, but because the marine had hopped right into Nandi's bed. No doubt the bitch had told Taggart all the gory details. As to Talina Perez, it was something about her—that sense that of all the people on Donovan she was the one he needed to fear the most.

Under his breath he whispered, "May you both be rotting quetzal shit in the forest."

People nodded warily. They understood. Trish Monagan's investigation had come to nothing. Thumbs Exman's ghost might have walked with him, a constant reminder that Dan Wirth was never to be taken for granted.

Allison—decked out in a revealing silver outfit that emphasized her breasts—sat on the stool behind the window in the cashier's cage, exchanging chips for gold and gems. He liked it that she dressed to emphasize her sexuality. Liked it even more when other men stared enviously at her, knowing all the while that she was filling Dan Wirth's bed and not their own.

To his surprise, she'd taken to the role of cashier, apparently dazzled by her sudden status as one of the most wealthy and influential of Donovan's citizens.

Just off the hallway, his small office was outfitted not only with a desk, table, and chairs, but also a safe that he'd had bolted to the floor for chips and money.

Betty Able seated herself across from his desk. Like so many others, she had taken to walking over to try her luck at his tables. At the moment she owed the Jewel nineteen thousand two hundred and fifty SDRs. A number Dan had allowed to slowly accrue as he skillfully manipulated her favorite game of monte.

"What do you hear, Betty?" he asked as he stepped into his private warren, closed the door behind them for privacy, and poured a glass of brandy. This was the first of a new stock Inga had distilled from a better-than-average grape harvest.

"*Freelander* is the talk of the whole town."

"Anything new?" He seated himself opposite the madam as he took the woman's measure. She appeared to have the slightly glassy eyes left behind after a good dose of mash.

"Speculation runs the gamut from plague, to mutiny, to mechanical failure, rampant insanity, famine, radiation poisoning, and even alien contact in some universe where *Freelander* had been waylaid, boarded, and then managed to escape."

"Aliens, huh?" He shrugged. "What do you want to bet they got bounced back into Solar System by a glitch? That it reset itself, and the ship immediately inverted again?"

"Could be," Betty agreed, glanced around. "You've done well for yourself, Dan." Her voice dropped. "Wouldn't have believed it."

"Donovan's just a world of opportunity."

"For the right kind." Her gaze cooled. "What do you have the tables set to pay out?"

"A little under thirty-five percent for the house. Odds differ depending on the game." He pointed to the cameras he'd acquired to peer down at his customers. Since the validation of the deeds and titles, everything was for sale in Port Authority. "I've got a couple of statistical programs monitoring the action to keep tabs. I want people to know they're getting a fair shake."

Her clever eyes didn't match her disarming smile. "But you could change that, couldn't you?"

"Betty, let me be frank. I want to give my clientele whatever they want. If they come in here looking to relax over a drink, that's what I want to provide them. If they want to come in and try their luck, have a good chance to walk out with a little something extra, why that's fine, too. If they think they can buck the tiger on two-hundred-to-one long odds like Spin the Wheel, or betting black twenty-two on the roulette table, I'm all for letting them try."

"So what did you want to see me for?" She leaned back as he

reached over for a second glass, set it before her, and poured it half-full of brandy.

"I have two rooms across the hall."

"Used to be Thumbs' personal storage."

"Those are the ones."

"Why do I care?" She lifted the brandy, sipped, and nodded.

"I want Angelina in one of those rooms."

Betty seemed to freeze, as if her heart had skipped. "And just how do you think Allison is going to react to that?"

Fool, Dan thought. *You don't think I've got my own house under control?*

It hadn't been as hard as he'd thought to convince Allison that it was in the Jewel's interest to offer sexual services. She'd made a face at the mention, but her resistance softened as Dan laid out the potential financial returns.

"It won't be like at Betty's," he'd told Allison in his most reasonable voice. "Not whores, but more like courtesans."

"How's that?" Allison had crossed her arms, but the frown on her brow indicated curiosity about a life with which she'd had no contact.

Dan had given her his conspiratorial wink. "Consider the floor, darling. All filled with potential marks, but the games are new, sometimes intimidating. Gambling has been illegal for years. Vigorously prosecuted by The Corporation back home, and essentially unheard of here. Now, what if a mark had a guide, someone with whom he'd been intimate, who could steer him through the complexities of the game? Someone who, if he wins, could take him into the back to share his good luck?"

"You have someone in mind to be this guide?" She'd arched an eyebrow.

"Angelina. You've heard of her?"

"Grew up with her. She was a couple of years younger than me. Her father died when she was young. It was her mother who urged her to go to Betty's, make money on what she was giving away for free anyway."

"She's a smart woman," Dan had said. "Talked to her a couple of times when she was between tricks and I had my game at Betty's. Said she'd like a higher standard of living. Wants more opportunity than she's currently got."

"How much opportunity?" Allison had arched a suspicious eyebrow.

"That would depend on how well she can learn the games, and her dexterity when it came to separating the mark from his plunder. If she made us another hundred thousand a year, how much compensation do you think that would be worth?"

Allison had immediately sharpened. "You think Angelina could make us that much?"

"More probably." He'd watched Allison's suspicion and resistance crumble.

Now it was Betty's turn to fall. Dan told her, "Oh, believe me. Allison's definitely on board. It's not like I'm going into competition with your house. Just the opposite, in fact. I'm willing to hand out tokens to your place as part of the winnings."

"Oh? Just out of the goodness of your heart?"

He gave her a bland smile. "Goodness has nothing to do with it. For a percentage, of course. It's a win-win for both of us. You get a john fresh from the tables with money in his pocket and a token for, say, a free hand job. No telling how many would want to up that to the full treatment."

She might have been granite. "But I'm down my best-earning girl. The ones the regulars want to patronize. Who do I put in her room?"

"Who do you want?"

"Kalico Aguila?"

"Wouldn't that be a fantastic turn of events? This whole town would hand over their fortunes to literally fuck The Corporation. Some just to see if she's as good looking naked as they think she is. Wonder what it would take to get her?"

She blinked, taken aback by his reply.

He waved it away. "We can fantasize, can't we? Getting back to the point, I've got three women who'd be glad to step into Angelina's place."

"Who?"

"Manzanita Hamilton, Miko Ituro, and Solange Flossey. In fact all three ladies are rather desperate at the moment to make income."

"Manzanita I know. These other two must have come on *Turalon.* Why would Manzanita, with her own dome and a sack full of plunder, want to make a living on her back? She's never been a prude, but I wouldn't call her loose, either."

"She no longer has a dome or plunder." Dan sipped his brandy, letting his satisfaction show. "In fact, she's rather desperate to keep her dome. Told me she'd do anything to get title back and not have to move out into the street."

"She lost at your tables, huh?"

"Miko and Solange, it seems, have a similar failing, especially when it comes to covering their markers. Sure, they could both opt to ship out on *Turalon*, but there's no telling when she's going to space. And, well, neither lady is willing to cross me. In fact, both seem rather anxious to remain in my good graces."

He made a face. "They keep bringing up poor old Thumbs Exman. Wish they wouldn't. I liked Thumbs. Considered him a friend. And to think, unlike people who owe me money, Thumbs wasn't under a single obligation."

He paused, tightened an eye. "Too bad that his killer's still on the loose. Never know when he might strike again. Who he'd choose, or why."

As he'd spoken, Betty Able had stiffened, realization crystallizing behind her eyes.

Dan smiled. "That's the thing about people. Most are willing to make things right. Just give them a chance. I'll send all three gals over to your place. You can interview them, make your own decision. Take one, two, or all three if you want. I can have a construction crew there within a day or two if you decide to add extra rooms out back."

A frost might have settled on Betty's soul given the anxiety in her expression. "I'll have you paid back soon as I can, Dan. Hope you know that."

"Hey! Drink your brandy, Betty. I know that you're good for it. In fact, that's why I called you over. We've done pretty well together. I'd like to buy in. Partnership. I figure your place is worth about forty thousand yuan, maybe ten grand in SDRs."

Betty's racing heart could be seen where the artery pulsed in her neck. She was thinking hard, putting it all in perspective. She owed him. Didn't dare try and stiff him, knowing full well that she could end up just as dead as Thumbs Exman. Dan had to admire her, she was struggling mightily to maintain her sense of optimism as she frantically searched for a way out.

"Forty thousand?" she asked dryly, eyes gone vacant.

Dan sipped his brandy. "What do you say I call your debt even, and throw in another couple thousand yuan? That will give me just over fifty percent ownership. You'll still be in charge over there, run things the way you always have. The difference is, I've got your back financially. Or when it comes to any labor problems, or other difficulties. And, like I said earlier, we can augment both businesses. I send winners over to your place with a token, you hand out free chips to any johns your people turn. They can come here and try their luck on the house."

"What if I decide . . . ?" She couldn't finish. Couldn't utter the words that might seal her death.

"Oh, please don't, Betty. Not in a place like Port Authority where a simple mistake could be . . . well, permanent."

"You've talked to Angelina about this?"

"Of course. She's as keen for an opportunity as anyone."

Betty swallowed hard, closed her eyes, and nodded. "I'll have Angelina pack her things. As to the papers . . ." Again she couldn't manage to utter the words.

"Oh, don't bother your head about them." Dan reached over for the sheaf of papers on his desk. "I've already drawn them up. All you need to do is sign, and I'll have Yvette Dushane register them."

She finally raised her pained eyes to his. "Why are you doing this? What do you want?"

"What do *I* want?" He chuckled happily. "Just a seat at the big table, Betty. And, by God, I will *have it.*"

39

Lightning flashed. Seconds later thunder hammered the room, shaking the walls of the administration dome. Trish glanced at the window as heavy rain slashed down out of the darkened sky to sheet across the glass.

She prayed it was raining on Talina. Making her absolutely miserable. If it were, that meant Tal was still alive to be inconvenienced.

At his desk, Shig's expression communicated disgust as he shuffled the papers and handed them over to Yvette Dushane.

"Nothing we can do about it," he said. "It's all legal. The guy bought into Betty's business."

Trish raised her arms helplessly. "There's more to it. I swear. When I talked to Betty, there was this hesitation, almost fear. I mean, she's always been a hard woman, tougher than quetzal leather, but she was holding back. Insisted that it was her decision to accept Wirth's offer. Insisted that, as a partner, he was backing her expansion by paying for the new rooms in back."

"Betty was barely hanging on as it was," Yvette mused. "*Turalon*'s arrival changed all that by altering the sex ratio. Could be that they're betting *Freelander* is going to bring in that much more business."

"Maybe," Shig said with a weary shrug. "Whatever is wrong with *Freelander* is serious. Were it not, Supervisor Aguila would be advising us on how many transportees to expect, shuttle schedules, priority down-shipments, available manpower, and all the rest."

"She hasn't asked for the marines to ship up." Yvette rubbed her nose as she scanned the papers registering Dan Wirth's majority ownership in Betty Able's building and business. "That means whatever is wrong, it's not going to require enforcement."

"The only communication we've had about *Freelander* is ambiguous." Shig thoughtfully laced his fingers together. "Nothing about personnel, which suggests to me that either the ship is abandoned, or . . ."

"Or they're all dead." Trish put her worst fears into words. Of course, she was thinking of Talina and Taggart. The notion that her best friend's bones were moldering out there in that huge expanse of forest haunted her in the wee hours of the night. As did the guilt that Trish had somehow failed her friend. That she'd not searched hard enough.

All the more reason for her to hate that despicable Dan Wirth. He'd distracted her from paying attention to Talina's plight. If he hadn't murdered Exman when he did, she'd have been on it. Realized immediately that Talina was overdue. She'd have found that outcrop before Talina was forced to leave it in search of water and food.

No one can walk across kilometers of thick forest, Talina. What got into you?

To top it all off, Wirth had gotten away with the murder.

"I should just shoot the son of a bitch."

Shig and Yvette both raised their eyes, startled by the violence in Trish's voice. She added, "Talina tagged him that day at the shuttle port. Said right then that shooting Wirth would probably save us all a lot of heartache."

"That could come back to haunt us somewhere down the line," Shig noted absently. "Though it does have its appeal."

"Talina said he was a quetzal, camouflaged by his easygoing nature and boyish charm." Trish crossed her arms as lightning strobed outside the window.

"He's got title to half a dozen properties around Port Authority," Yvette noted. "At the moment he's our largest landholder. All of it came through my office, duly filed, with both parties having signed."

"He won it. Gambling. Didn't earn it the hard way. Our people had no clue. No idea how gambling worked. It was totally new. Something fun and exciting. Right up to the moment they couldn't pay. Worse, some of them still haven't wised up."

"Going to outlaw gambling, are we?" Shig had that absolutely aggravating placid expression on his face.

"No one is forcing anyone to enter the Jewel." Yvette walked over and filed Betty Able's papers in the title drawer.

"One of those domes Wirth owns is Manzanita Hamilton's, isn't it?" Trish asked.

"It is." Yvette didn't even have to check the records.

"She's one of Wirth's new whores at Betty's. When I tried to ask her about it, she told me to go away. That it was her business. Her decision. And the whole time she wouldn't meet my eyes. You ask me, this whole thing stinks."

"What would you have us do?" Yvette asked. "Tell people they have to get our approval to sell or trade property? Pass an ordinance banning gambling? Or prostitution? Or just unilaterally banish Dan Wirth? Do you know how that would play over the long run? Protecting Donovanians from themselves would make us a laughing stock."

"It's an old problem," Shig said softly. "One that's haunted human society from the beginning. Who makes the decisions governing the behavior of others? Where is the balance between individual freedom and the normative behavior of the society? Back in Solar System, The Corporation dictates everything, right down to the style of underwear a person wears. We, on the other hand, tossed out the Corporate book after Clemenceau's demise and ran full-tilt into the camp of ultimate libertarianism: do as you will, take responsibility for yourself, as long as you only harm yourself. It's unwritten, but it has become our creed."

"The man's a predator," Trish insisted.

"And a very adept one at that," Shig agreed. "So what would you condemn him for? Misleading the gullible? Preying on the willing? The only actionable offense he may have committed was the murder and robbery of Thumbs Exman, but as you continually note, you have no proof that he was the perpetrator."

"Is it that easy for you?" Trish demanded.

"No." Shig sighed and ran fingers through his mop of disheveled hair. "Nor has it ever been for anyone. While it is inevitable that we will start down the path of protecting the people from themselves, I'm not willing to begin that process quite yet."

"Why not?" Yvette asked.

"Because I am not ready to begin instituting the hypocrisy of governance." Shig smiled absently. "Ultimately government and hypocrisy become synonymous. The assumption spreads that government best knows what is good for its people, when ultimately it does not. And the inevitability of one set of permissive rules for the governors, and another set of much stricter rules for the governed, just sticks in my throat like a rotten fruit."

"So, just let him get away with it?" Trish asked as thunder banged outside the dome.

"I'm with Trish," Yvette snapped.

"Question." Shig raised his eyebrows. "Who gave us the authority to eliminate this man?"

"Well, we're . . ." Yvette frowned. "What did the Supervisor call us? The triumvirate?"

"That was you, me, and Talina," Shig objected. "Not you, me, and Trish. And, if we get right down to it, whoever invested us with the authority to run Port Authority, let alone, Donovan? I recall no election, not even a popular acclamation. Nor do I remember seizing control by force of arms. Governance was never granted us by any writ from The Corporation transferring authority to you, me, and Talina. Parse it down, and the only authority invested in any of us is by the lack of objection from anyone else, including, oddly enough, even the Supervisor."

"Does this have a point?" Trish asked.

"Only if you come from the academic camp that studies the concept of social contract and the philosophy of government." Shig lifted his hands helplessly.

"Can you say that in language I can understand?" Trish shook her head.

"*Ipso facto*." Yvette winked at her. "We're here because we're here."

Shig added, "But just because we're here and have accepted the responsibility, my suspicion is that the people wouldn't consent to Trish killing Dan Wirth just because we suspect him of murdering Thumbs. Nor would they condone killing him for successfully obtaining property through his games of chance. If anything, most I've talked to—while they don't trust him—actually rather admire his spunk and initiative. Newcomer that he is, they nevertheless consider him a sort of Donovanian success story."

"God, I'm going to puke," Trish whispered. "I wish Talina were here. She'd just shoot him and ask, 'What the hell are you going to do about it?'"

"That's Talina," Shig agreed with a laugh. "And only Talina. Fascinating, isn't it?"

"How's that?" Yvette asked.

"Talina is judged by a separate criterion, set apart by a suprapopular ethical standard in which her actions are automatically assumed to be for the common good."

"Ever since Clemenceau she's never killed anyone who didn't need killing," Yvette agreed. "God, I wish she were here."

"Yeah," Trish agreed. "But come on, people. Let's face reality. No one has ever walked out of the forest alive."

"I know." Yvette pulled at her chin. "Meanwhile, leave Wirth alone, Trish. It's bad enough that we've lost Talina. Don't want to lose you, too."

"People keep telling me that."

Outside thunder crashed as if the sky were rent.

40

Chopping down the pod was one thing. Getting it through the thick vegetation to the ground was another. Splitting it in two with knives had been a challenge of still greater difficulty. Then had come the task of cutting out the little seedlings inside—though the term wasn't quite right. No one had seen a true seed produced by a plant on Donovan. Instead "seedlings" grew in pods as tiny replicas of the parent plant. When they had matured enough to be viable, the pods opened and the seedlings dropped out. Landing on the ground, they first sought nutrition with their roots, and once nourished, began moving slowly and surely in search of the perfect spot to send down roots. Plants often moved kilometers over their lifespan.

"Makes you wish for a machete, doesn't it?" Cap had asked as he wiped sweat from his brow.

"I'll put that on the requisition list before *Turalon* spaces for home. Might actually get one in the next fifty years or so."

Nevertheless they had finally cut, sawed, hacked, and chopped a hole through the thick wall of vines that allowed them access to the water.

Only at that juncture did Talina discover that quetzals were afraid of water. "Can't swim, huh?" she'd asked the beast residing within her.

"Hell, are you kidding?" Cap had shot back. "I can swim fine, thanks."

"Talking to the quetzal," she told him. "It won't . . . I mean . . . The thing's just . . . It's not going to let me get on the water."

Cap glanced down at the half pod—a canoe-shaped vegetable husk about four meters in length. Then he chewed his lips as he inspected the passage they'd cut down to the sandy beach. Beyond it, the river ran placid in the midday light, surface sucking and swirling. The "canoe" lay half in, half on the bank. Behind them, the vegetation was closing in on their hole.

When Cap glanced back, his eyes widened. "Holy shit, Tal. Look! Mobbers!"

As she turned, expecting to see the flying, multicolored monsters, Cap whipped his coat around her head and shoulders, and she was plucked, kicking and screaming, from the ground.

Arms pinioned, she felt herself lifted, spun around, and set down in the confines of the canoe. The man's strength wasn't up for debate. His grip on her was like a vise.

"Hold still!" he bellowed. "You tip us over, and that quetzal is going to get more water than it ever bargained on."

"Stop it!" she hissed to the beast inside. "You'll kill us all!"

Inside, the quetzal curled itself into a tight ball, literally trembling in the darkness. A numbing fear ran though her in waves, sending the shakes down her arms. Tears formed behind her eyes, the dark wrapping of the coat around her like a suffocating barrier to sanity.

She felt the canoe bobbing, rocking from side to side. "Holy shit, we're on the water."

"Yep." Cap's grip slacked off. "Just hold still."

Down inside, the quetzal gave off a peculiar whistling shriek. Its panic paralyzed her; she almost cried out in terror.

"Serves you right," Talina told it as she somehow managed to pull Cap's jacket off of her head with trembling hands. It smelled of sweat and man: acrid, but not all that unpleasant. She kept her balance, raising herself to stare out at the smooth surface. Half of her wanted to cower down into the narrow craft's bottom.

She made a face and forced the impulse down. By dint of will she sat up, placing her hands on the gunwales.

"You. Don't. Own. Me," she told the quetzal through gritted teeth. Inside the beast continued to shriek in terror.

The tree line ran right to the water, whatever hole they'd emerged from now vanished.

Cap was grinning, which accented the dimple in his chin, his blue eyes alight with the success of his audacious move. "Of course I don't own you."

"I was talking to the damned quetzal." She shook her head. "God, it's like having a separate part of me inside. One I can't quite control."

"So, what's it doing now?"

"It's terrified. Sort of like something shivering in fear halfway between my heart and my stomach." She made a face. "Damn, does that sound fucked up, or what?"

She took a deep breath, willing the beast inside her to be still. For once, it actually complied.

"Don't ask me," Cap said, picking up one of the dried branches they'd collected for paddles. With a couple of strokes he sent them headlong into the current, turning them downriver. "Funny world you've got here, Tal."

"Yeah, well I've got the stinking beast under control, but don't tip us over. If it goes berserk and panics, I'm not sure I can keep it together."

"You mean it's like alive? You're saying it's like that creature in that ancient movie? The one that eats its way out of your chest?"

"No. More like the quetzal's essence. Like I'm sharing its thoughts."

He was silent for a time after that. Then he chuckled. "You're a hell of a woman, Tal. I'll say that for you."

"Not so bad a man yourself, Cap. Glad I didn't have to kill you back at Port Authority."

"Makes two of us." A pause. "So, tell me. Now that we're out of the forest, away from the mobbers, sidewinders, and all those other crawly things, is the worst of it past?"

She shrugged, still fighting to keep the quetzal quiet. "Haven't a clue, Cap. No one's ever floated this river in a pod before. No telling what sort of nasty beasties live down in the depths here."

She pointed at the swelling and roiling surface. "My guess is that if we just float along for the most part, we'll look just like another piece of drifting log. Like that chunk of aquajade bobbing over there."

He immediately changed the way he was paddling. Rather than driving them forcefully ahead, he carefully pulled the paddle back. Then he let it drag until they started to lose steerage before taking another easy stroke.

"Where'd you learn to canoe?"

"Grew up in a place called Minnesota back on Earth. Lots of lakes and streams. My father was a fisherman in his leisure time. Took me with him. Probably what steered me toward the military instead of Corporate law like he wanted." He paused. "You?"

"I grew up in a Mexican state called Chiapas until I was ten. From the time I was little, Mama told me to find something better. That I was worth more. She was a Mayan archaeologist, led tours through the ruins. I could have followed in her footsteps. That, or I was going to end up married, have my allotment of children chosen based on my DNA and his, and I could have grown corn for the rest of my life."

"How'd you get out?"

"Had an uncle who'd been trained in the military. Chiapas has always had a culture of resistance. Goes clear back to when my ancestors fought the Spanish. He taught me enough of the basics so that I showed promise on the aptitude tests. Security came naturally since I grew up helping to protect the archaeological sites from looting."

"Ever married?"

"Nope." She hesitated. "Would have married Mitch, though."

"What happened?"

"Dead of an infection." She saw the dirt again as it cascaded down into the grave to cover his wrapped face.

"Sorry."

"You?" She tilted her head back, scenting the river, trying to know its smells and soul. The quetzal quailed inside her.

"Yep. Didn't work. Military," he said as if it explained it all. "Career comes first. Postings change. Relationships come and go. Then I had that bad experience at Beemer Station. Civilians dead. Creamer skated. And I got assigned to *Turalon*."

"What are you going to do if we make it back alive?"

Another silence, and then he said, "Been thinking about that, Tal. If we make it back? There's a woman I'd like to spend some time with. See if I could get to know her." He smacked his lips. "Might be tough, though. She's sort of out of reach."

"Who? The Supervisor?"

"Kalico? Hardly. No, this one's a security officer at Port Authority. We've got a past, her and me. I thought for a while I was going to have to shoot her. Then she saved my life a couple hundred times, and I saved her a few times, myself."

"Me?" she asked, almost laughing at the absurdity of it.

"Yeah, you," he said, still keeping the sincerity in his voice. "Which is probably a surprise to us both, and I'm not sure how it happened."

Talina kept a hand to her knotted stomach as she swiveled to look him in the eyes. "What could you possibly see in me?"

"Courage, skill, self-control, remarkable accomplishments, a sense of duty, the respect of just about everyone on this planet, and one of the few women I've ever met who leaves me in complete awe. I'd like nothing better than just to look at you. At your hair, stare at those dark eyes, marvel at the tones in your skin." A beat. "And you do have a quetzal inside you. I'm not sure, but that might end up being sexy as hell."

"You don't want my kind of trouble. I'm not good at relationships."

"Like I said, she's a bit out of my reach." He laughed softly. "Problem is, I look around and wonder what man on this whole terrifying planet can stand toe-to-toe with her. Look her in the eyes as an equal. My bet is that she intimidates the hell out every male on this ball of rock."

"You'd be surprised, Cap. There are men, Wild Ones, who I don't intimidate in the slightest."

"Yeah? Well, the only thing I've got going for me is that those guys—the ones you really respect—they all started as soft meat once upon a time. Sort of like me. Now, I'm a little behind the curve here, but I'm catching up. Compared to the guy who crawled into that aircar, I've come a hell of a long way. Watched everything you've done, studied at staying alive harder than I've ever studied anything."

She considered that. Fact was, he'd been damned near perfect. Now that he brought it up, she had to admit, she couldn't have conceived of a better traveling companion. And somewhere in that time, she *had* begun to look at him as a companion. But as a lover?

"I have problems with men and relationships, Cap. I don't know what they want from me."

"What was it about Mitch?"

"He and I just fit together. Kind of like he was part of me that had always been missing. Said it was the same for him. Hard to explain, but we shared thoughts . . . just fit."

"Gotcha." He stroked them forward again. "See, that's the thing causing me to lose sleep at night. A big part of me doesn't want this trip to end. Not that I enjoy having the ever-loving shit scared out of me every half hour or so, but I spend the other twenty-nine minutes totally, thoroughly, and absolutely enjoying your company."

"You're a sick and twisted man, Cap."

"So, just for the record, Tal, how am I doing? Do I have any redeeming factors that might make me tolerable enough that you'd consider spending time with me in other circumstances than this?"

"Honestly, Cap, my friends are few and damned far between. There's Trish, Shig, Yvette, Cheng, Iji, Inga . . ." She let him hang for a couple of seconds. " . . . and you."

"Okay," he said slowly. "I can live with that."

"But you understand, you're a new part of the equation." She swiveled her head to look him in the eyes. "I've got a lot of history with the others."

He gave her a knowing smile. "Sure you do. Course, think back for the last week or so. Seems we've been making our own history right along. Provided we live through it, we're gonna be making a heap more before we're out of this." Again the dimple-accenting smile. "Or else I'm just an optimist at heart."

She turned forward again. "You are that, Cap. But what happens if we get back? You thought that through? You're going to be Kalico's marine captain. The Corporation's hired gun. Kalico might give you orders to arrest me, maybe even shoot me in the back. How are you going to balance this newfound attraction against your duty?"

"All right," he admitted, "that part's got me a little perplexed."

She turned her attention to the shoreline, watching the wall of trees pass as the current carried them. She was getting the hang of the canoe, how to move without making it pitch wildly.

"You know," he said softly, "we don't have to go back."

But down in her heart she knew they did. Supervisor Aguila wasn't done with her, Shig, and Yvette. That woman wasn't about to forgive and forget.

She shot an uneasy look up at the sky. *Turalon* was still up there. Cap might be enamored of her, but what happened when it really came down to the knife's edge? Which way would it cut?

41

Freelander floated no more than a kilometer away. Bathed in *Turalon*'s floodlights, she stood out against the background of a billion stars that looked like a smear of smoke over the velvet black of space. The two thick rings that composed the crew and cargo sections were still counter-rotating. Like awkward donuts, they perched atop the bulky gray sphere containing the reactor and inversion generators.

The way the retractable pods containing the nuclear motors were deployed for propulsion brought bug legs to mind, and attitude thrusters maintained the great ship's position vis-à-vis *Turalon*. This was all remotely piloted through Nandi's com in astrogation.

Kalico leaned forward, studying the ship through the windows as her shuttle approached. *Freelander*'s massive hull looked pristine. No scorch marks, not a sign of impacts, decompression, or mishap.

"See anything wrong?" she asked Abibi, who sat in the pilot's seat.

"Not on the surface," Abibi told her. "She was the biggest of the Donovan carriers. *Turalon* is half her size. As to why they built her so big, well, Supervisor, you'd know more about that than I would."

"At the time she was conceived and approved, she was to be the first of a series of large deep-space haulers. The vessel that would finally make Donovan profitable and stem the hemorrhage of cash and resources The Corporation was pouring into the project. Keep in mind, back when we started construction on her, no one had any idea how bad the situation was."

Abibi said nothing as she slowed her approach. *Freelander* had grown to fill the view. Now Abibi began a slow circle of the big vessel. As they rounded the far side, Kalico could still see nothing wrong.

"One of the shuttles is missing," Chan noted from the passenger seat. "That bay there, coming into view. That doesn't make any sense. Where would they have gone?"

"Wasn't in the log," Kalico replied as she followed the first officer's pointing finger to the empty docking bay just below the zero-g spindle.

"Well," Abibi noted as she changed her approach, "that solves one problem. That's where we'll dock. Assuming the locks and hatches are still functional."

"Why wouldn't they be?" First Officer Chan asked. "There's no sign of damage."

Kalico could see the tension in his shoulders.

"A shuttle is missing?" Abibi mused. "If they'd disembarked in the Donovan system, we'd be reading their signal. If they'd disembarked back in Solar System, it would have been in the logs. Shit on a shoe, I don't like this."

Kalico nodded to herself as she stared at the looming hull where the shuttle bay lay so eerily empty. People didn't just leave a ship when it was in inverted symmetry. No one ever had. According to the physicists, there was no "place," no "space," to go to. Despite the decades of hypotheses testing and experimentation, all the potential theories had collapsed. How could theorists even postulate a universe where mathematics—at least as humans conceived them—didn't exist?

Over the years, probes had been sent past the inversion. Countless probes. Of all kinds and designs. Once they passed beyond the inversion horizon, they vanished. Tethers had been tried. When they were reeled back, they ended in a smooth molecular surface where the tether had breached the field.

"And we're sure they didn't pop into regular space somewhere along the way?" Willa Tyler, the ship's physician, asked from her seat behind Kalico's.

"If they had popped into regular space, as you so quaintly put it, the logs would have mentioned it. They do it automatically, recording everything for subsequent analysis."

"Then why didn't we have a record of any shuttle leaving *Freelander*?" Tyler persisted.

Abibi's expression didn't change as she maneuvered into the shuttle bay. "Lots of gaps in the records, Willa. It's like a mix of chaos and insanity to read them."

Kalico fixed on the hull just beyond the window as Abibi eased the shuttle into the bay and set it down atop the locking lugs.

She felt the familiar bump through her seat, heard the thump and clank as the latches secured the shuttle into *Freelander*'s bay. The lights began to flicker at the hatch, changing from red, to yellow, to green.

"*Freelander*'s lock is functional," Chan noted as he powered down the systems. "But it's using the shuttle's power to cycle the system." He glanced uneasily at Abibi. "It's dead on the other side."

Abibi was sucking on her lips. A nervous trait she'd rarely exhibited over the entire two years of *Turalon*'s spacing to Donovan.

Kalico rubbed her forehead. "No telling what's on the other side of that hatch. We're going in suited. Combat and hazard protocol."

She raised her voice. "Lieutenant Spiro? Prepare your squad and proceed at will."

"Yes, ma'am," Spiro called from the back. She bellowed, "All right, children. By the book. Helmets on, weapons hot, safeties on. Condition Three."

God, Kalico missed Cap Taggart. What had the damned idiot been thinking? Ride out into the bush? With Talina Perez? A woman Kalico still planned to execute? Who'd admitted to killing a Supervisor? The damned fool had lost his mind.

And apparently his life.

I'd kill him myself if Donovan or Perez hadn't beaten me to it.

Kalico stood, watching as the marines fastened their helmets, formed up at the hatch, and unslung their weapons. Spiro in the lead, they cycled the hatch, passing through, squad after squad.

"*We're in!*" Spiro's voice came through the com. "*Power's off. Corridor's dark. Temperature's about twenty below centigrade. Air's good, but really high in CO_2. Ma'am, we're getting nothing on battle tech. No life signs.*"

A pause.

"Reconnaissance drones are deployed. Proceeding to secure the corridor."

Kalico turned to the side monitors, leaning over Abibi's shoulder to watch as the system displayed the marines' battle com images. She saw a dark lobby area with seats along the walls, bits of what appeared to be trash on the floor. Frost glittered in the marines' suit lights as they shone on the surfaces.

On separate monitors, the armed drones flew down the hallway, past open hatches, their sensors reading no life-forms.

"Let's go, people." Spiro led the way past the shuttle bay doors and into what looked like a standard ship's corridor. The helmet-mounted cams cast cones of white down the black length.

"*Fucking spooky,*" one of the marines muttered.

"*Cut the chatter, Finnegan.*" Tension filled Spiro's voice.

At the first intersection, Spiro's squad carefully used their tech to peer around the corners, finding nothing but dark, cold, and empty hallways.

This would have been the transportees' section of the ship, set up as a big dormitory. The part of the ship the crew had vented to suffocate the transportees. What Kalico was looking at was the scene of mass murder. It sent a shiver down her back.

"Ma'am?" Spiro asked. "*Request permission to continue deployment of additional recon tech.*"

"Proceed, Lieutenant," Kalico said into her mic.

In the light of the head cams, the marines set one of their equipment cases on the deck, unlatched it, and triggered the systems. A swarm of smaller unarmed drones lifted from the case, separated into groups, and vanished into the dark halls branching out from the intersection.

As Spiro issued orders, the marines split into threes, heading off down the hallways in pursuit.

"Nothing to do but wait now," Abibi said.

Kalico crossed her arms, watching the various holo projections as the marines started their search of the ship. It was just plain eerie to see the honeycomb stacks of bunks, empty, black, and yawning. The mess room, plates still on the tables, desiccated food still visible. The bathrooms with bits of clothing strewn around, toilets in a line, shower stalls shadowed and cold.

"We're at the main corridor. Officer's country on the other side. Got a shut hatch here," Private Miso reported; her helmet cam displayed a closed decompression hatch. She plugged her power relay into the socket, the hatch monitors springing to life. *"Got atmosphere on the other side. Opening now."*

In the holo, the hatch groaned and lifted. A puff of air frosted as different air pressures equalized. Stepping through, Miso palmed the lights, and to Kalico's surprise, the corridor illuminated.

"*Still got high CO_2. Temp's up to thirty-two degrees C.*" Talbot's voice reported.

"Continue on to the command deck," Spiro ordered.

"Yes, ma'am," Miso replied, showing her four companions as she turned in their direction.

"They shut themselves away from the rest of the ship," Abibi said. "Kept the core warm. Probably to conserve resources."

"Or there were too many ghosts on the other side," Chan muttered.

"There's no such thing as ghosts," Tyler chided from behind.

Miso's team trotted down the hall, the sialon walls looking oddly brown, streaked, sometimes splotched. At astrogation they were stopped by another closed hatch. The bypass didn't work.

"Uh, Lieutenant? This has been welded shut."

"Well . . . burn it." Lieutenant Spiro's voice replied.

On the holo, Spiro's squad had reached the officer's deck and another closed hatch. This, too, they opened, only to encounter a partially lit corridor.

"Looks like they left the lights on here, but they're on their last legs." Spiro stepped through the hatch, slowing as she looked around. *"Holy shit. Ma'am? You seeing this?"*

Kalico triggered her mic. "What is that, Lieutenant?"

Spiro leaned forward, her helmet cam playing across the walls. *"It's writing, ma'am. Screw me in vacuum. Look at this!"*

The wall was depicted in perfect clarity, but what was that? Curling, looping, lines over lines, all scrawled in black, as a sort of design that . . . It was writing! Thousands upon thousands of lines of script. Every square inch of wall was covered with it. From the ceiling down to the floor, across the floor, and up the other side. The scrawled lines were written atop one another, hundreds or more. Often to the point of being illegible.

From the look of the corridor, the writing extended all the way down the hall. Spiro and her team were muttering under their breaths as they walked along, cameras on the writing-covered walls. It seemed endless.

"How many hours would that have taken?" Abibi wondered. "Thousands? A lifetime?"

Kalico asked, "Lieutenant? Check your biodetectors."

The image shifted as Lieutenant Spiro lifted her belt pack and thumbed the boxy detector. Images flashed across the holo. "*Looks good, ma'am. Nothing lethal reading on this end.*"

"What do you think, Doctor?" she asked Tyler who was monitoring the display.

"I see the signature for molds, fungus, lots of the usual spores. Heavy concentrations of organic molecules. Skin cells, HEBs, which are human endogenous bacteria. It's also reading dormant viral elements, occasional pollen from the hydroponics, bits of microscopic endemic arthropods." Tyler was checking her own readouts which were channeled through *Turalon*'s computers for analysis. "Jesus, it's as if the ship's never been cleaned. I mean, the thing's filthy!"

"Malevolent organisms?" Abibi asked.

"No sign, Captain. Whatever happened, it wasn't pathogenic."

"I'm going in," Kalico decided.

"Supervisor?" Abibi asked uncertainly.

"I need to know. If it was disease, the biodetectors would have cued on it. The drones are most of the way through the ship now. If there's anything, they'll find it." She made her way back past the seats in the main cabin to the lockers.

It took her only moments to slip into the hazard suit, seal it, check the oxygen, and secure her helmet.

At the shuttle hatch, she hesitated.

Whatever is over there, it's going to change my life forever. Kalico? You sure you want to go through with this?

She palmed the hatch and passed into the cold. Flipping on her suit lights, she took a deep breath and stepped into the dead ship.

42

Fire crackled and spit sparks at the roof of their little shelter as rain pattered down. Lightning flashed, illuminating the gravel bar upon which they'd made their camp. The pod canoe was pulled up high, tied with a length of cord. Behind them, rain in the leaves made a hissing and spattering as it fell on the endless forest.

They had made camp early, choosing a gravel bar a couple of hundred meters up from the confluence of the Briggs River where what looked like basalt cliffs rose above the marshy floodplain.

As a precaution against slugs, they had made sure the pool behind the gravel bar lay on impermeable bedrock. They'd both bathed and washed their clothes in the clear water, and Talina had been able to relax as Cap foraged for wood. She'd laid her head back and let Capella's warm rays dry her long black hair. After days in the forest, she realized what a relief clear sky and bright sun could be. At least until the clouds had moved in.

And she'd had time to really think about Taggart. No matter what the suspicious side of her insisted, she really had come to like the guy. She respected people who had the sense to learn what they didn't know, and he'd been an apt student. She needed no more proof than the fact that he was still alive. More than that, they were both alive. Had it not been for Cap, she'd have never made it off the beach when the quetzal froze her nerves.

Nor was she sure she could have kept from capsizing the canoe in the beginning. That, too, had been Cap's expertise.

So, what was this attraction? She'd slipped more than her share of curious glances at his muscular body as he bathed, liking his lines, the ripples on his hard belly, the power in his shoulders and arms. Long white scars on his left hip and thigh piqued her interest, and she'd covertly admired his muscular buttocks.

At the same time, the looks he'd shot her way had built a tingle down in her loins. Not only was his interest palpable, but he'd fought to keep from gawking as she scrubbed herself. She knew the difference when a man watched her with appreciation rather than lust. And that just added more kindling to the fire she wasn't sure she wanted to damp.

Supper had consisted of a crest who had appeared at the edge of the trees to stare at them. The beast had no doubt never seen a human before, and displayed its amazement by erecting every glittering scale on its body.

"Edible?" Cap had asked.

"Very," she'd replied.

Cap's movements had been fluid as he reached down, pulled his knife, and with a flip of his arm, impaled the crest dead center in the chest. She'd never seen a knife thrown faster or better.

"Why waste a bullet?" he'd asked. Then glanced around. "Besides, the report would ruin the peace and beauty, don't you think?"

She'd laughed at that, remembering the way his eyes had almost shone. Recalled the movements of his hands as she showed him the proper way to gut the animal and drain its fluids to minimize the heavy metals. How those strong hands had handled the knife, the sure way they worked, how he didn't mind the blood and juices. Competent hands.

What was it about a man's hands? How the tendons flexed, and the skin formed to the bones? Hands, eyes, muscular butt, and hard belly. So, Cap was a finely made package.

While they cooked the crest, the clouds had built, rolling in from the east.

She showed him how to cut broad vine leaves and weave them into a mat. He cut the stalks and sections of vine to lash them together. As the first drops of rain fell, they were sitting shoulder to shoulder, grease running down their fingers as they laughed and chewed tender crest meat from the creature's polymer bones.

The fire popped again, spitting more sparks. Talina watched the flickers of flame. "If we do make it back, there's a real good chance that *Turalon* will have spaced. You'll be left behind."

He smiled at that, firelight dancing on the lines of his face. "Just the thought of it is almost too good to be true. That solves a whole host of potential problems."

"There may never be another ship, Max. You're here. Probably for the rest of your life. You're never going back. Your family, your friends. All those ties and memories. They're gone."

"I think I've made my choice." He took a deep breath, laid his arm across her back.

She didn't stiffen, didn't reach to remove it.

"I can't promise you anything."

"I know." He grinned, as if amused at himself. "I'm not asking it of you."

"The Corporation—"

"Sent me here as punishment. My vaunted career? Call it mediocre, Tal. I made captain by luck. By being in the right place at the right time. I was always just good enough, but never above average. If I had been, they would have overlooked it when I confronted Major Creamer. It was an excuse. A chance to get me out of the way. So, send me off to Donovan. With my record, they think if I have to kill a bunch of civilians, I'll do it. If I don't come back, they've washed their hands of me. If I make it home, they hand me a big check and a suggestion that I go into private security."

"Since the aircar went down you haven't struck me as mediocre."

He frowned at the fire. "Would it make sense if I said that I found something here? You were talking about how you and Mitch just seemed to fit together? It's like part of me was missing until I set foot on Donovan. A part of me sort of kicked into place that had never been there before."

"I can accept that." The warmth of his arm over her shoulder actually soothed her. It had happened so slowly, she didn't realize when she'd melted against his side. Down inside the quetzal seemed to be waiting, curious.

Lightning flashed and reflected silver off the rain-stippled river.

"The other day in the canoe, you asked what I'd do if Kalico ordered me to arrest you or the rest."

"Uh huh."

"I guess I'd take a squad. Katsuro, Dina, Paco, and Finnegan. The ones who really trust my orders without thinking them through. I'd have to round you all up, load you on an aircar, and make sure you were deposited somewhere where you couldn't be found until *Turalon* spaced. Then I'd have to vanish myself. Maybe see if Step Allenovich couldn't smuggle me out of Port Authority and off to wherever I'd hidden you."

"They could order your execution just for saying that, you know."

He smiled out at the rain. "Like I said, a piece of me clicked into place. Look around, Tal. We're camping where no human has ever set foot. Sure, there's danger, and I might die tomorrow morning. If I do, I'm whole. Complete in a way I've never been. Never known I could be." He paused. "And there's you."

"Me?"

He turned to stare into her eyes. Miniature flames from the fire reflected in his large, dark pupils. "I never want to leave your side. I'd give my life for a single evening with you. Just to hear your voice. To watch your smile and the dream in your eyes."

She swallowed hard, her heart beginning to pound.

"Understand?" he asked.

She nodded, wondering when she'd grown short of breath.

"How'd you get those scars on your hip?"

"Wounded. Firefight with rebels and insurgents in China. How'd you get that line of scars along your right thigh?"

"Gotcha vine. They don't infect right off, but it was over two weeks before I could get back to Raya's to have them cut out."

"Talina Perez, I'd cross a thousand galaxies just to sit here and share your company."

Every nerve in her body was singing.

Do I want to do this?

But she did. The old fire had been lit, the flame warming her core. She reached up, pulling his lips to hers as he curled her around onto his chest.

Then she was tugging his jacket and shirt away, running her hands over his chest and shoulders. He peeled away the top of her coveralls, hands tracing down her shoulders to her breasts.

She shifted onto her back as he pulled the last of her clothing away. Lightning outlined his muscular body, haloing it with silver as she wrapped her legs around his hips and exalted in the almost forgotten sensations of man and sex.

43

A couple of hours after entering *Freelander*, Kalico Aguila wasn't sure what she believed. She stood behind Miso's team as they worked with a molecular cutter to open the door to astrogation and what would have been termed "the bridge" in earlier centuries.

They weren't the first to try. The heavy duraplast and steel was dented, pock-marked, as if someone had hammered at it with a battering ram.

The marines now stood around as Private Paco Anderssoni worked the cutting tool around the thick door's margins.

"Weird place," the marine who had "Abu Sassi" emblazoned on the back of his armor said softly. "Man, I keep thinking I'm seeing things in the corner of my eye. Like flitting, you know? Sort of like creatures that are there . . . and then aren't."

"It's space jitters," Spiro told him. "But I gotta tell you, after that corridor? All that writing? I mean, who does that? Just covers wall after wall with script? In places it was so thick you'd think it was paint."

Private Michegan said, "I could make some of it out. Over and over, it read, 'I am vacuum. A cloud of emptiness.' It just went on and on."

"Wonder what they used for ink?" Kalico asked, half-unnerved as she glanced back down the dim corridor with its flickering lights and filth-covered walls. She, too, had caught glimpses of something, or things, that flickered at the edges of her vision.

Nerves. Had to be. Her stomach had yanked itself into a knotted ball.

"We're through," Anderssoni announced and dragged his torch out of the way. "Back! Everybody!"

The heavy hatch tilted out, slowly accelerated, and slammed down onto the sialon deck with a bang that shook the corridor. Ten billion dust motes rose to float through their suit lights.

Kalico stepped into the doorway and shone her light around. "Holy shit," she muttered. "Get some light in here, people."

As the marines filed in behind her, she could barely understand what she was seeing. A bed was shoved up against the astrogation console. The now-dead holo displays were almost hidden behind sialon storage chests stacked six high. The captain's chair and first officer's station were piled with personal items, clothing, and a stack of antique books. Five-gallon water jugs stood in a line atop the plotting table, and a peculiar apparatus of tubing, condensers, and filters rested on a platform to one side. What looked like a small, cobbled-together hydroponics unit took up space before the sensor array. Long-dead stalks of desiccated vegetation hung over the sides.

Kalico's heart skipped. What she'd thought at first glance to be wadded and discarded rags on the floor was a uniform. She swallowed hard as she realized that the clutter inside was bones; what resembled a smashed pot was a skull. And there, behind the first skeletonized remains, lay a second. It took a moment for her to synthesize what she was seeing. The skulls. Both were damaged, the backs shattered, shards of bone spread as if burst from the inside out. A thick film of what had to be long human hair covered the floor.

"Fuck me," Private Garcia whispered.

Spiro stepped forward, shining her light down. She knelt, picking up a pistol from where it lay beside the closest skeleton. "Firetron. It's a personal sidearm. Not military or security issue. Expensive. Shoots a twelve-millimeter explosive bullet." She checked the magazine. "Still loaded, but two rounds missing."

"This was a fight?" Kalico asked. "Murder?"

The broken skulls, their jaws slightly agape in what could have been silent laughter, mocked her.

Spiro glanced around, peering at the room's contents. "Welder's right there by the door. Sealed it from the inside. Whoever welded the hatch shut is still in here." She waved at the bodies. "My guess, ma'am? This first one's the shooter. Popped that second one in the head . . . and then shot himself."

Kalico felt herself sway as though something invisible was passing through her. The sensation sent a tickle through her bones and nerves.

Concentrate, damn it.

She forced herself to fix on the bones, discolored as they were and dark with age. Stains could be seen where the bodies had leaked juices onto the sialon floor as they had decomposed.

At that moment, Dr. Tyler stepped in, stopped short, and gaped at the scene.

"Willa?" Kalico almost gagged given the images playing through her imagination. "What can you tell me about these, uh, bones?"

Dr. Tyler pushed through the surrounding knot of marines and bent down. Using her light, she peered at the shattered skulls, then picked up the facial piece. The jaw fell free. She turned the shattered skull over to study the hard palate and teeth.

Replacing it, she moved on to the next, again studying the skull.

To Kalico's eyes, the second pile of bones was smaller in stature, the bones lighter and thinner.

Dr. Tyler sighed. "The male skeleton at your feet is probably Jem Ortner. Not only is he in a captain's uniform, but the age and stature are right. The second body is probably his first officer, Tyne Sakihara. I'll know when I run the DNA."

"Murder?"

Tyler stood, staring down at the bodies. "My first call is suicide, ma'am. From the damage to the teeth and bones, the pistol barrel was in each victim's mouth when the gun went off."

"How long since this happened?" Kalico asked.

Tyler knelt again, using a probe to lift the worn-looking uniform jacket over the rib area. "See the white stuff inside around the bones? How the ribs have all sort of folded down so neatly? The white stuff is what we call corpse wax, body fat that can't be completely digested by bacteria. The hair spread behind the skulls is still black. Without any sign of gray. My guess—and again, I'll need to test the remains to be sure—is that they've been dead for decades."

"They were only six months ahead of us," Kalico whispered.

The marines were looking stunned, staring anxiously at each other, shifting nervously.

"That might be," Tyler said, standing again. "But I've spent my life in ships, Supervisor. This thing's almost a derelict. Those bodies have laid there a long, long time."

Tyler turned, pointed at the tube-and-filter apparatus with a gloved finger. "My take? That distillation unit? It's to process water from urine. The jury-rigged hydroponics? That was for food. This was their last stand. They sealed themselves in, hoping to outlast whatever had gone wrong. When it became clear that they'd reached the end, pop and pop, they checked out."

Kalico tried to imagine. Shook her head. Couldn't.

On the floor, the shadowed eye sockets in Jem Ortner's exploded skull stared at her with an intensity that unnerved her. As if the grisly thing could see the empty hollow that had grown inside her.

She knotted a fist. *My God, what sort of insanity is this?*

"Supervisor? Lieutenant?" a half-panicked voice called through the com. *"You better get down here. Crew mess. I mean . . . Well, you just aren't going to believe this."*

44

Kalico led the way into the crew's mess hall. Unlike the Spartan utility in the transportees' section—they were just cargo after all—attention had been paid to the crew's mess. The hall was large, the only two-story room in the ship, elegantly designed, with pleasing lines that carried the gaze upward to the second story with its balcony seating above. The center of the high ceiling was dominated by a crystalline dome that contained the holo projectors for the entertainment system.

Now the tables and chairs were missing, the room dark, sepulchral and alien. And in the center?

Kalico stopped short, trying to make sense of the free-standing structure in the middle of the room: an isolated dome-like thing rising to a point. Maybe two meters across and two and a half tall at the pinnacle. Call it knobby in construction, sticklike with thin gaps everywhere, as though cobbled together with irregular pieces, all fitted in an artistically unsettling design. Kind of a poorly woven knitting. The supporting level was made of sticklike supports—all slightly bowed—that resembled a warped picket fence. Then irregular triangular pieces had been placed in a ring, or decorative outer band. Above them rose another level of columns—thin supports topped with more of the triangular pieces. What looked like slender curving laths had been tastefully interwoven in chevron patterns over the vertical, thin pieces. Then came a higher band of bean-shaped elements ending in small triangular perforations. Globular shapes dominated the next level, and so on.

The entire exterior had been decorated, a brocade of patterns affixed to the surface. Flower motifs had been created from small, round pieces with petals sprouting three protrusions. And then, looking closer, she could see the patterns of starburst, chevrons, curlicues, zigzags, and other designs where tiny pieces had been affixed to the outside, the effect reminiscent of rococo.

"What the hell?" she whispered.

"It's like some kind of shrine," Lieutenant Spiro muttered.

"And look," Shintzu, one of the marines who'd found the room, pointed. "In the doorway. There's a body."

Kalico nerved herself and walked across the dark floor. No, not dark. Just covered with more of the eerie writing. At the front of the structure, she bent down, staring at the desiccated corpse. Mostly skeletonized, the jaw sagged; straggly white hair still clung to shards of dried scalp that had peeled up from the skull. In other places yellowed bone could be seen.

The hideous thing wore a threadbare and patched set of coveralls that had once been yellow. It slumped against a box set just inside the structure door, but seemingly had become disjointed along the vertebrae and collapsed into a heap, the skull lolling to one side.

"What the hell is this, ma'am?" Spiro asked. "I mean, you ever heard of anything like this? Seen it before? Maybe some weird religion from one of the stations or something?"

Kalico shook her head, backing away, feeling oddly unclean—as if even her soul had taken on a smutty taint. The room seemed to pulse around her, evil, menacing. Down in her gut, the nerve that triggered her to throw up was tingling.

There's no such thing as ghosts.

Close as she was, she fixed her gaze on the side of the entryway. Really got a close look at the vertical supporting pieces that held up the wall's lower tier.

She blinked, knowing that shape, the two knuckles at the bottom, the slightly bent shaft, and the canted neck that ended in a ball.

"God in heaven," she whispered.

Powered by adrenaline, she scuttled back, almost bowling over the marine behind her. In horror, she stared at the building. Shrine. Whatever it was. The corpse in the doorway, broken as it was, leered crookedly at the shadowed room.

"It's bones," she whispered. "The whole fucking thing. The building, the decorations. It's built of human bones."

And at that moment, she saw movement inside the shadowed depths. Realized it was a person. The image seemed to waver, fade into translucence, and then solidify again.

Dressed in colorful quetzal hide, and wearing a Donovanian hat, the figure ducked through the low doorway. For the barest heartbeat, they were face-to-face. The rugged clothing faded into translucence again, and Kalico could see the scars crisscrossing the woman's whip-thin body. Even as she stared, crystalline blue eyes met hers, a familiar smile bent the woman's lips, and she said, "If you go back, you'll die."

Kalico gasped, raised a hand, and staggered back.

Blinked.

"Did you see that?" she asked.

"See what?" Lieutenant Spiro asked.

"That woman?"

"The dead one? The skeleton? That's a woman?"

"No." Kalico struggled to fill her lungs. In that instant, something inside her snapped. Like a keening scream in her mind. "Nothing. It was nothing."

But it hadn't been. Imfuckingpossible. That ghostly image that had emerged from the tomb of bones? The familiar eyes and smile? She knew that woman. All but the inexplicable scars.

That was me.

45

The body hung awkwardly, head cocked to the side at an unnatural angle; the rope wire cut deeply into the neck tissue. The woman's eyes were wide, blank, and popped out of the face. Her tongue—a dark shade of purple—protruded from her mouth as if to fling a final insult at the universe that had betrayed her. Her shoulders, in contrast, sagged wearily. She barely swung in the breeze that blew through the open door; it fingered her thin fabric dress. A puddle of urine was drying on the floor beneath her feet.

"Ah, shit," Trish whispered as she took in the sight.

"I couldn't do anything," one of the women said, her voice strained with emotion, pleading. "I climbed up on the chair. But I couldn't undo the wire. I couldn't save her."

"What's your name?"

"I'm Gopi Dava. One of her roommates."

"Nothing you could have done," Trish told her, glancing back at the other women who clustered at the door behind her, unwilling to set foot in the room. "See how the head's hanging? Neck's broke. And that thin-gauge wire? It's cut clear through to the ligaments. That's all that's holding her together."

Behind her, she heard someone gag, then run. A faint sound of vomiting followed.

The room was sparsely furnished with a couple of utilitarian chairs, a table with a holo box, some pictures of a family on the wall: smiling people dressed in fine, shining clothes of a style Trish had never seen. A door led to the bunks in the back room.

"What's her name?" Trish asked.

"Indu Gautamanandas. She's a hydraulics specialist sent to service the Semex 81-B roto mill."

"What's a Semex 81-B roto mill? Never heard of it." Trish winced as another drop of urine spattered onto the floor.

"It's a machine to crush ore. As far as Indu could determine, that model of roto mill was on *Ashanti*. *Turalon* is carrying spare parts that Indu was supposed to install and service." Dava swallowed hard, ran a nervous hand over her short black hair.

"Did she give any clue that she was despondent? Any hint that she might do this?"

Dava glanced nervously at the door where her other two roommates waited in terrified silence. "We're all . . . I mean, no. Not any more than the rest of us. We're specialists. They promised us jobs. Things we're trained for. We were told we would have quarters, a clean dormitory. But here we are. Living in a dome with a plastic floor. She was assigned to the cafeteria! Scrubbing tables. Sterilizing plates and eating utensils. Me, I'm a university-trained polymer chemist. I'm supposed to have a lab here. Instead I am tending plants for a farmer beyond the fence."

Dava's voice broke, tears streaming down her face. "Maybe Indu's the lucky one. She's out of this hell."

"Then leave," Trish cried. "You know the contract. If The Corporation can't fulfill its obligations, you've got a free ride home."

"You tell us that?" one of the women at the door said harshly. "Space on *Turalon*? Take a chance on vanishing in space? To what fate? Wind up dead, like the rumors say happened to the people on *Freelander?* You call that a *choice*?"

Trish bit her lip, attention on the gruesome corpse. "Beats ending up like this."

"Does it?" Another of the women—Trish vaguely remembered her name was Sian Whay—almost spat the words. "Locked up in that rats' warren of a ship? Living with the constant fear that you're going to just vanish? Maybe suffocate slowly like they say happened on *Freelander*? And the worst part is that your family never knows." She gestured to the photos on the wall.

Trish bit off a retort. What did they expect? That life was without its risks? She gritted her teeth, reached into her utility belt for her multitool, and climbed up on the chair.

As she opened her cutters and fastened the jaws on the wire, she said, "Some of you come catch her when I cut her loose."

The women stood frozen, eyes wide, faces pale.

"Did you hear?" Trish asked. "Catch her when I cut her loose."

"Not me," Dava said, backing away from the door.

"Me either," Whay said. "That's not my responsibility. I'm not medical."

"Catch her?" the other woman at the door said weakly. "As in, you mean, touch her? Dead like she is?"

Trish hesitated, cutters on the wire. "It's just a dead person. Meat and bone. What's the matter? Haven't you ever seen a dead person before?"

They were all shaking their heads, eyes wide.

"Oh, for the love of pus." Trish clipped the wire, Gautamanandas' body dropped to the floor in a loose-limbed series of thumps.

The women screamed, hands to faces, mouths open.

Trish reholstered her multitool. "Trust me, she didn't feel a thing."

Another of the women turned, bent double, and threw up.

Trish stared up at the loop of wire left on the dome strut. Considered untying it; then decided to leave it in place as a reminder to the others.

She jumped down, grabbed Gautamanandas' arms, and pulled her out straight; the woman's head came flopping along, held on only by the ligaments.

"God, you people are heartless and cold," Dava whispered through tears. "She was my friend."

"This is Donovan. Chances are that you'll bury a lot of friends. Or that they're going to bury you. Assuming you're lucky enough to be a corpse instead of a pile of quetzal shit."

Something had changed in Gopi Dava's eyes—a half-panicked resolve forming there. "We're not going to live like this."

"How are you going to live?" Trish asked absently as she hauled the corpse around and pointed it at the door.

"Take matters into our own hands, that's what."

"Uh huh, thinking of taking over Port Authority? Some folks here might object to that. And that snotty Supervisor Aguila has her marines. Which—as that maggot Dan Wirth would say—is the ultimate trump card in the deck." She looked up from where she gripped the dead woman's clothing. "Any of you going to help me with her?"

She met stares laced with hatred and disgust.

"All right then, move please." She gave the corpse a tug, sliding it across the floor, smearing urine in the process.

Gautamanandas bumped and flopped her way across the threshold and out onto the dirt, the women scattering from her path.

Trish straightened and thumbed her mic. "Two Spots? Got a body. Dome sixty-four. Female. Name of Indu Gautamanandas. Send the hearse if you will."

"Roger that. I'll send word to old man Han Chow. Um, I was just about to give you a call. Inga's. Two Skulls got into it. Some sort of dispute. Someone pulled a knife. One guy's on the floor. You want to check into it?"

"Sure. On my way." She straightened. "Wagon's on the way to pick her up. As her friends, you want to follow along? Help with the burial? Maybe say a few words?"

The women, wordless, just stared at her as if she were some sort of loathsome monster.

"All right, fine. Look, I've got to go break up a fight between Skulls." She turned, trotting toward Inga's.

God, what was wrong with the soft meat? They were killing themselves faster than Donovan could.

And it's going to be trouble in the end.

She remembered Dava's words: "Take matters into our own hands."

46

Talina and Cap gave up on the canoe at the first rapids. It had been hard enough paddling upriver along the Briggs River's eddies and currents; they'd had to struggle to keep out of the river's main thread.

Talina squinted against the mist as pounding plumes of water hammered down onto the rocks. Something about the streaming water reminded her of muscles that flexed and strained, only to surrender to a white froth of sound and spray.

"Quite a sight, wouldn't you say?" Cap shouted into her ear. "But looking at these cliffs, it'll be hell to portage."

"What's a portage?" she'd shouted back above the river's roar.

"Carry the canoe up those cliffs. And what's upstream? More rapids?"

She shifted uneasily, trying to remember. Truth was, she'd only flown over this country. Mostly she had watched the gauges, ever cognizant of the charge in her batteries.

"Can't tell you."

"How far to Briggs'?"

"Maybe a day. Maybe more." She gave him a shrug.

"Go on foot?"

"Might be the best bet."

Much to the quetzal's relief, they clambered up a tenuous trail in the canyon wall to the top of the basalt.

"What made the flat like this?" Cap asked as they crested the top.

"Volcanic. Lots of volcanism rippling out from the impact zone that created the Gulf and the Wind Mountains."

He propped hands on his hips, pack resting high on his shoulders. Sweat had already begun to glisten on his face and neck. "Now I know why you all wear those big hats."

He'd lost his campaign hat that first day in the scramble through the forest.

"Should have kept the hide off that crest and made you one," she told him with a grin. "Made me one at the same time."

"Next critter we kill, we'll do that. What do I watch for besides a handy crest popping its head out of the brush?"

"See how the trees are smaller, more widely spaced and growing where fractures and low spots have allowed soil to accumulate?" she told him. "This is a lot better country for bems, brown caps, and skewers. Keep your eyes open, and if you smell vinegar, tell me. Immediately. And steer as wide as you can from any large rocks."

He looked around. "All I see are large rocks."

"Yeah, there's always something, isn't there?"

"That's Donovan for you."

"You're learning, Max."

He followed as she led off along the rim overlooking the river. Following behind, it took all of his self-control to pay attention to his surroundings and not the sway of her hips. Not to imagine the soft curves that lay just under that worn fabric. How it felt to slip his fingertips along the gentle swell of her . . .

"Got trouble here," Talina said as she stopped and he almost ran into her.

A dark chasm split the ash-gray bedrock. Peering down, its depths were inky with shadow.

"Have to go around."

She was working her lips, squinting up at the sun and then north in the direction of the Briggs homestead. "Wonder how many more of these we've got between us and Briggs'?"

"Not much choice, huh?" He gestured to the west. "If we can find a narrow gap, we can bridge it. Lots of trees to use."

She raised an eyebrow. "You don't sound like you're in any kind of hurry."

"I'm not." Anything but. "Gives more time for *Turalon* to vanish into the hereafter. More time that I don't have to share your company with others."

"It's those others who drive me." She lifted her water bottle from its holder and drank. "Cap, they think I'm dead. Donovan doesn't give much hope for miracles."

"Yeah, I know. How about we get to Briggs' and you call in and tell them that everything's all right, and then after Madison has her baby, they can send an aircar after us in a couple of months or so?"

"You're truly smitten, aren't you?"

"Not a single regret, girl." He gestured for her to proceed, then, forcing himself to pay attention, asked, "What about you?"

"Still working through it. God, Max. The last thing I would have expected was . . . well, a relationship of any kind. I'd shut it out of my reality. I'm caught between that giddy hormone rush and wondering what happens when we get back. I mean, what then? If *Turalon*'s still in orbit, you can bet the Supervisor's going to want you back. So how does that work? And if the ship's gone, then what? Where do you go? What do you do? Do I move you into my place? And even so, we're going to be under a damn microscope. Every eye in town is going to be on us."

"Work it out when we get there."

"What I'm saying is that everything's going to be different when we get back. I . . . well, I'll need time to sort it all out."

He nodded futilely at her back. "My guess? Your people are going to be swarming over you, asking questions you don't want to answer. Like, what you're doing sleeping with the man who was going to execute you? And what you see in a soft meat outsider, even if he is a marine? Mine—if they're still there—are going to be doing the same to me."

"One day at a time?"

"Works for me. There. We can bridge that." He stepped over, studying the narrowing in the chasm. Here it wasn't more than four meters across.

"You know how?"

"Hey, woman, I'm more than just a giddy hormonal rush. Let me get my saw out and I'll show you how to build a bridge." *And, by all the powers in the universe, help me bridge all the shit that's going to lay between Tal and me when we get back to Port Authority.*

Even as he thought it, the long boom of a shuttle entering atmosphere came rolling down from the heavens.

"Sounds like *Turalon*'s still here."

Cap took a deep breath. "Yeah, it does."

And that was just the first of the sonic booms they heard as they bridged the gap and headed north. This wasn't just *Turalon*. It sounded more like the days just after the ship had arrived, like cargo being ferried.

"That's a lot of shuttle traffic. I think our world's just changed," Talina said, shading her eyes as she stared up at a vapor trail high overhead.

"Yeah." He wiped a hand over his sweaty brow. "But how?"

47

Kalico sat in an overplush chair in the astrogation dome and cradled a cup of coffee in her hands. The steam rose in slender fingers to tease her with its aroma. She had pulled her legs up under her, the posture almost defensive. She'd sat like this when she was a girl. Done so during those times when Father had done or said something to humiliate her, or Mother was on one of her binges.

I goddamned saw myself step out of that temple of bones.

Kalico thought she'd outgrown the need to sit thus. But at the sight of that apparition, the woman who had been Kalico Aguila had shattered. Had left *Freelander* shivering and almost stumbling.

In the hours since, Kalico hadn't gotten her old self back. Now here she was. Sitting with her legs tucked beneath her, staring across the narrow distance to where *Freelander* gleamed whitely against the inky void of space.

"If you go back, you'll die." The words had been so clear.

And none of the others present had seen so much as a flicker.

She hadn't been able to sleep since returning to *Turalon*. Nightmares had plagued her to the point that Kalico had turned to Dr. Tyler for a soporific. Still the images haunted her.

She closed her eyes, the distant ship's image ghostlike against her lids.

A hollow desperation sent a tickle through her guts. Power, a seat on the Board, the wealth and status, all were slipping away. She was a Corporate creature, adept at the acquisition and manipulation of power. No one was better at the brutal inside politics of the Corporate Board. Played right, she could be the Chairperson. The most powerful woman in Solar System.

What the hell has happened to me?

Since she had landed at Donovan, her foundation had begun to crack and sunder. Seeing her phantom self emerging from that temple of bones? It had turned everything to shifting sand.

"Who am I?" she whispered.

She'd be dead before she'd be dressed in quetzal hide. The scars? Her subconscious was trying to tell her something. That's all. The fucking ghost was an illusion. Had to be. Some fantasy conjured from stress and lack of sleep.

Then why the hell was she on the verge of tears?

"Supervisor?" Captain Abibi's voice asked softly from the hatch.

Kalico sighed and swallowed her bitter despair, forced herself to slip her legs out from under her and sit forward. To project that old air of competence. Fucking lie that it was. "Come in, Captain. Have a seat."

Abibi—looking rather grim herself—seated herself, laced her hands together, and stared distastefully through the transparency at *Freelander.* "More of the pieces are starting to fit together."

"The minds of the insane usually cleave to some sort of pattern." Kalico ground her teeth to keep control. Who said she was seeing ghosts? Then added, "And what happened over there? That's madness, Captain."

"Was it?" Abibi asked. "My people have most of the systems functioning again. The *Freelander* crew cut out the ship's brain. Actually took cutting torches to the ship's AI. What kind of nuts is that? But we've recovered some of the personal logs. They knew they were lost. That something had gone wrong, and they were going to spend the rest of their lives in that ship."

"So they went insane? Killed the transportees? Orten and Sakihara weld themselves into astrogation, and then kill themselves?"

"They were hoping the ship would eventually do what it did. That whatever dimension, universe, or flux they were in wasn't eternal. Supervisor, for all the effects relativity has in our own universe, who knows how it functions in others?"

Abibi frowned across space at *Freelander.* "It's long been postulated that each time a ship inverts symmetry, it slips into another universe, but not necessarily the same universe each time. The multiverse is postulated to be infinite."

"I've also heard that some theorists hypothesize that each inversion of symmetry creates a universe."

"Could be." Abibi gestured to *Freelander.* "But wherever *that ship* went, Orten was right. The mathematics worked, the statistical projections were correct, and when the generators ceased inverting, she ended up right where she was supposed to."

"But not *when* she was supposed to," Kalico reminded. "She was months late getting back to our universe. And she spent more than a century in some other dimension."

Abibi stared uneasily through the transparency. "It was a death cult. Tyler's showing a curious streak to her personality. She's fascinated. Been reading the logs, studying that script they wrote all over the corridors and mess floor. Me, I figure it was the guilt. They knew they were spending their lives in the same ship where they'd killed and vacuum-frozen five hundred and some people."

"That would spook me, too, I suppose."

"Remember, they were feeding the corpses one by one into the hydroponics as the chemistry broke down. Living off the dead. And each time they did, they recovered the bones. It started as a means of showing respect. Over the years, it grew. Became ritualized."

"And the building of bones?" The image replayed of Kalico's alter self ducking out of that door.

"The temple of life, they called it." Abibi frowned. "Tyler says they went there to commune with the dead. And then, when the crew started to die, they were tossed into the hydroponics, too. Their bones were added to the temple. Tyler says they used all the bones. Skulls, leg and arm bones, those were wired together for the structural elements. Vertebrae, phalanges, scapulas, ribs, and such for the decorations on the outside. All intricately constructed with safety wire."

"Madness."

"Perhaps." Abibi shrugged. "Tyler says that she's found examples all through human history. Lots of people make ossuaries, and some, like Catholicism's Capuchin order, actually made constructions out of their dead similar to *Freelander*'s."

"Jesus."

"Correct. Salvation. At least in the case of the Capuchins."

Across the distance, *Freelander* looked deceptively pacific, its exterior bathed in Capella's light. Only on the inside, with its temple of bones and scrawled lunacy, did the horror become manifest.

"Has anyone solved the mystery of the missing shuttle?"

"We have. Schism among the crew. A small group decided they were going to chance leaving. Fly through the inversion. In their minds, they figured that instant death was better than living out hopeless lives in *Freelander.* On the other hand, it was a step into the unknown. For all they knew, they might come out the other side, or pop back into our universe."

"And what if they did?" Kalico asked. "Popped back into interstellar space? Somewhere light-years between planets? Instead of the rest of their lives in *Freelander,* they're locked in a tiny little shuttle."

"Well, that's hope for you, ma'am. Sometimes it's better to do something—even if it's potentially disastrous—than wait around faced with boring certainty."

"I detect a grim humor in your voice, Captain."

"You've got the grim part right, ma'am." Abibi's gaze had narrowed.

"What about the cargo?"

"We've started shipping it dirtside. My load specialists are still checking, but most of the machinery and spare parts seem to have made it. The *Freelander* crew raided the food stores, of course."

"Continue shipping it down, Captain."

Abibi hesitated, the corners of her mouth twitching.

"Yes, Captain?"

"About *Freelander*. Ma'am, my crew say they're starting to see things. Some are saying that they hear voices. One woman even saw herself walk past in one of the corridors. I had Willa check her into hospital for a scan. They're afraid that what happened to *Freelander* is going to happen to *Turalon.*" Abibi paused. "It's just a few, but it's going to spread the longer they work in that derelict."

The words sent a tremor through Kalico's soul. "And your point?"

"They don't want to end up like *Freelander*'s crew. Trapped for the rest of their lives on the other side. Only to pop out as long-dead corpses. There's a great big planet down below that's full of wealth and opportunity. That's a mighty tempting draw. My point is that if you want to space for Solar System, you might want to go now. As soon as possible. Before the crew has time to think about it."

Kalico didn't mean to sound sharp when she said, "Discipline is your problem, Captain."

"It is. And I can maintain it . . . up to a point." Abibi worked her jaws, before continuing. "Some damned idiot accessed the historical files. You ever hear of a ship called the *Bounty*?"

"No. A Corporate vessel? If so, she wasn't important enough to come to my attention."

"English. Old sailing ship. She was exploring the Pacific Ocean. Had a rather nasty captain by the name of Bligh. When she made land at a delightful tropical island, the crew mutinied. And that's where they stayed."

"Donovan isn't a delightful tropical island."

"No, ma'am. But it beats knowing that your bones are going to be wired in as structural elements in some macabre temple in the crew's mess."

48

Talina panted, every muscle straining, as she and Cap levered the thin chabacho trunk over and watched it fall with a crash on top of three of its previous mates. They were all young trees, slim. More poles than logs.

This was the last length added to yet another bridge they were building to span one of the innumerable cracks in the basalt. Tal took another swig from her water bottle and wiped the perspiration from her forehead before it could drip into her eyes.

The sting of it ate into her blistered and cracked hands. They'd taken turns sawing with Cap's handheld chainsaw. All told it took a couple of hours each time they had to bridge a gap—and sometimes more. First the narrowest span had to be located. Then the right-sized trees felled and stripped before they were dragged to the crevasse. Muscling them up, getting them to fall just right was more luck than art.

As she paused to drink, she took a moment to glance around at the turquoise leaves of the aquajades and the more emerald chabachos. Puffy white clouds were building in the east over the Gulf, indicating that they'd have another chance for rain in the afternoon. Hot as the day was, and as sweaty as they were, it would be a welcome relief.

The chime seemed to agree as the sound of the invertebrates rose and fell in tremolo.

"When have I ever worked this hard?" she wondered, rolling her shoulders and feeling the hot looseness that would settle into a stiff pain by morning. Since that night when they'd first made love, she and Cap had made a habit of waking to a coital tryst to start the day. It more than made up for the stiff muscles.

Cap stood with his hands propped on his waist, head back as he stared at the scarlet fliers that passed overhead. "This was survival training. Never thought I'd really have to use these kind of skills."

"Yeah, comes in real handy when you're breaching a station, I'll bet."

"Not in the slightest, Tal. Here. Give me a hand. Let's see if we can scoot these ends closer together. It'll be springy, but I think I can make it across."

She let Cap take the lead. He minced his way across the four logs they'd laid over the drop, reached the other side, and turned. It took but a moment for him to snug the ends of the poles together and lash them. His face lit with a grin, as though to encourage her as she started to pick her way over the tricky footing.

The breeze at her back, she had no warning. No chance to smell the threat. All she saw was a flash of color with her alien-enhanced eyes.

The skewer shot up from behind one of the tumbled basalt boulders; its stalk-mounted eyes fixed on Cap's back. The beast's whiplike arms shot out. Even as Tal screamed a warning, the thing had jabbed its long black thorn into Cap's upper left arm. The skewer's arms slapped onto his body and sank their spines into his jacket to deny any escape.

Danger forgotten, she charged across the bridge. Dragging Cap to the side, she pulled her pistol and shot the skewer through its globular body. The thing convulsed, tightening its stalklike arms, and contorted as it pulled Cap over backward on top of itself.

Cap was screaming his agony and fear as he tried to buck away, the skewer holding him tightly across its wounded body as the mouthpieces bit into his fatigues.

Tal vaulted the angular chunk of basalt, dropped to a knee on one side, and shot the thing three more times through the body. It shivered, trembled, and slowly relaxed as its fluids leaked out through the bullet holes.

"Oh, God!" Cap bellowed, his mouth working like a beached fish's.

Seeing the skewer was no more threat, Talina holstered the pistol and carefully peeled the beast's arms from the fabric of Cap's coat. Just because the thing was dead didn't mean the hooked bristles were any less dangerous. As she worked, the slender spike pulled painfully sideways in the tissue of Cap's upper arm.

Cap bit off the scream, face working. His jaw muscles bunched and twitched as he clamped his eyes against the pain.

Easing him down, Talina used her knife to sever the thorn from its tentacle. She grimaced as she extracted it. Cap screamed. Talina inspected the hard black length and tossed it away in disgust. From her pack, she pulled a field dressing and managed to stanch the worst of the bleeding.

"What was that thing?" Cap asked, sweat already popping from his forehead and cheeks.

"What we call a skewer. Normally they're not this big."

"Is it poisonous?"

"Nope. Not to humans." She gritted her teeth, images of Mitch dying of bacteremia welling from the depths. "The danger's from your own bacteria. What it dragged off your jacket and skin and left in the wound."

He blinked, eyes wavering as if on the verge of passing out. He kept gasping for air. "By God, Tal. That really fucking hurts. I mean . . . really."

She took a worried breath, saying, "Just sit for a minute, Cap. Take your time. Get your wits back."

He blinked again, lips working.

She stood, kicked the dead skewer—just because—and climbed up on the rock. Looking north, she shaded her eyes, desperate to see some sign of the Briggs place. Perhaps smoke. Or maybe a rooftop. All that met her gaze were the humped tops of the trees, and in the distance, an irregular bluff that might be the location of the Briggs homestead. Or might not.

"Tal?" Cap asked, his breathing almost normal. "What next?"

She pasted a smile on her face to hide the sudden terror that was eating at her soul.

"It's not far now," she lied. "Just a little way to go."

"Give me another five minutes," he told her bluffly. "Just another five. Then I'll be ready to go."

Talina ground her teeth and hopped down from the rock.

She couldn't let him see the desperation she was feeling.

49

Trish stood beside the ramp extended from one of the grounded shuttles. Its crew worked to disgorge cargo as the skid loaders carried crate after crate to stack along the fence.

That night, after the woman's suicide, when she'd arrived at Inga's, it was to find a dead Skull, his bloody guts leaking out of a slashed stomach.

"Fair fight," Inga had said, pointing to where the killer—four sheets drunk—swayed as he was held by several of his fellows. "They both started yelling that they were going to kill each other. First it was shoving, then they both pulled their knives."

"What was it about?" Trish asked, turning to the men holding the killer. Winner. Whatever.

"Fulon and Cates, here, got into it over a shirt. They're rooming together. Used to be best friends."

"How does an argument over a shirt end up in a cutting?"

"Iss Fulon's fault," Cates slurred in his own defense. "Bastard. Talked me into signing onto this shit-sucking death trap." The man hung his head, sniffing as tears ran down his face. "Nothing left. Nothing but death and this damn rock of a planet."

"You gonna arrest him?" one of the men had asked. "Fulon's dead."

"They both wanted to fight, right? Neither one pushed the other into it? Both were willing?" At their nods, she said, "Fair fight. No law against that."

"But he killed Fulon!"

"Who had a knife in his hand, right? And Fulon was trying to kill Cates."

The men had blinked stupidly, even Cates, crying as he was and with snot running down his upper lip.

"The cart's busy for the moment," she'd said to Inga. "Soon as old Han Chow drops the suicide off, I'll have him swing by. Meantime, you men carry Fulon here out to the street, will you?" She paused. "Oh, and you, Cates. Drunk or sober, you're cleaning the blood and guts off Inga's floor, you hear?"

To the others she added, "The rest of you, you make sure it's spotless when he's done."

They'd looked at her like she was crazy. What the fuck was the matter with the damned Skulls, anyway? Self-defense was a simple concept.

But then she'd never lived in Solar System. Things were different there.

She plugged her ears as a second shuttle set down several hundred meters to the north. Eyes squinted, Trish turned away from the blast of carbonized clay and dust and waited while the thrusters were spun down.

When hearing approached something like normal, she asked the load master standing by the ramp, "How many more are coming?"

The young man wore standard coveralls with the name Bateman on the left breast. His complexion was spacer-pale, his skull neatly shaved. The guy—perhaps in his late twenties—squinted hazel eyes at the newly arrived shuttle and waved. "We're working double shifts. Using our shuttles and the one's we've reconditioned on *Freelander.* The captain's ordered us to get *Freelander's* hold cleared."

She tried to understand the look in his hazel eyes, half-panicked and haunted, like a man on the edge.

Before the newly landed shuttle could completely spool down, he said, "You're Trish Monagan, right? The security head?"

"Yeah."

"Manny Bateman." He worked his lips, as if desperate to say something, hands clenching at his sides.

"Spit it out, load specialist. I could give a bem's ass what's cooking on those ships up there. Something's wrong with *Freelander.* We all know. The crew's dead, right?"

He glanced uncertainly at the shuttle hold where a skid loader was backing slowly down the ramp with a crate in its grapples.

"You got a place we can talk? Maybe that tavern we've all heard so much about?" A pleading lay behind his eyes.

"Sure."

"Off the record?"

"Sure."

Manny turned, the noise level having almost dropped to bearable. "Sun Ho! When you get that cargo stacked I want the main compressor pulled and checked. I think the seal's about to go."

The fellow on the loader turned in his seat, expression confused. "The main compressor? Nothing's wrong with the—"

"You heard that whine, right? Like the seal's about to go?" Manny raised his hands, as if in futility. He carefully said, "Should take about an hour to pull and check. Right? About an hour. Have Shandy alert control that we've got a simple mechanical delay."

"Oh, right," Sun Ho agreed, catching on. "About an hour." The man swallowed hard and fixed nervous eyes on Trish, as if wondering what her role was in the deception. "We got it covered here."

Manny turned, licked his lips. "Let's go check out this tavern."

She led the way through the man gate in the fence, shooting wary glances at the load specialist. Even as they approached the admin door, a lieutenant stepped out, *Turalon*'s patch visible on her shoulder.

Manny stopped short, throwing up a hand in salute.

"What's wrong, Manny? Why are you on this side of the gate?" The woman looked harried herself, tension in the set of her mouth. Eyes hard.

Trish, sensing Manny's near panic, said, "He fell off a crate working a load. Hurt his other shoulder. I'm Trish Monagan. Head of security. I'm taking him to hospital to have Raya x-ray it. Probably just bruised, but figured that since they're pulling a whatzit to inspect a seal, it wouldn't hurt to have him checked out."

The lieutenant raised an eyebrow, nodded, and said, "He's your charge. Just get him back before there's a delay. We're on a tight schedule."

"Come on, Skull," Trish told Manny, who was now holding his left shoulder at an angle, as if in pain. "This way."

She led him through the dome, out into the street, and down the block to Inga's. As they descended the steps inside the dome, she said, "Your lieutenant didn't look any too happy either. Something's really wrong up there. What's up? And why did you want to talk to me?"

She walked by the place Fulon had been knifed, satisfied to see the stones so spotless they were a shade lighter than the stained paving around them.

Trish pulled up Tal's old stool, acutely aware that it felt like a betrayal. The grief knot tightened under her tongue as she beckoned to Inga for two beers.

Manny leaned forward on the bar, staring around the insides of the big dome, at the tables, chairs, and benches, and the big board in the back where Inga kept her accounts. "Okay, you know *Freelander's* crew was dead. But this rest, if they ever hear it came from me? Officer, they'll flush me out an airlock and let me die." He emphasized the words "Do. You. Understand?"

"Yeah. I get it. We're not exactly cozy or trusting of The Corporation. I give you my word as a Donovanian. Now, what gives?"

"*Freelander* got caught in some kind of time relativity well on the other side. They didn't just die of old age, Officer Monagan. I mean, they did, and they didn't. They . . . They went nuts. I *saw* the temple they made of bones in the crew's mess. The writing on the walls. The filth."

Trish watched the man shiver as he clasped his hands around the beer. "We're all weirded out. Sure, everyone knows the stories about being marooned aboard ship. Spending eternity drifting out in the black. But they killed the transportees. Five hundred people. Saved their corpses for the hydroponics. And then they made a death cult out of it."

"Seriously?"

"Yeah. And the officers are doing everything in their power to keep it quiet." Manny paused. "I'm not afraid of death, Officer. I'll take the risks. But the Donovan run is jinxed. If we space out of here, *Turalon* isn't making it back to Solar System. It's a doomed ship on a doomed run. We all know it."

Trish sipped her beer, that eerie sense of premonition pulling her strings. "So what do you want from me?"

"What if a bunch of us wanted to stay? Try our fortunes on Donovan? How would you people feel about that?"

"Glad to have you. But what about your captain? Or her Supervisor with her squad of marines? They might have other ideas about you guys making a breach of contract."

Manny's wince was almost painful. "So, you'd follow their orders? Bring us back?"

"Look, Manny, here's how it lines out for us: It's a gray area. We're on our own here. Most of us don't work for The Corporation. We don't take their orders anymore. But that lady up there still has those marines to enforce her will. If it comes down to the knife's edge, we're not going to take a stand on your behalf."

She watched the man's face drop in defeat.

"On the other hand," she told him, "if you and your mates should happen to walk off the landing port and disappear? Maybe take one of the aircars we hear is being downloaded? Maybe vanish into the bush? We sure as hell wouldn't stop you, let alone hunt you down."

"Disappear into the bush?" He didn't seem to get it.

"There are research stations, um, like settlements. Places that we've had to abandon because we didn't have the people to keep them running. The facilities are pretty basic, but with your technical experience, you could fix them up. Lie low until *Turalon* spaces. Hell, if it turns out you liked it out there, we'll give you title to it."

"What's that?"

"Means we'll give you ownership. You and your people can have it as your private property. No orders. No directives. You'd have to farm, operate the mining facilities, but you'd be welcome to come sell your surplus food and trade any of the metals or gems you mine."

"Officer, we don't know the first thing about farming or mining."

"Then figure it out. Find out what you can do." She took another swig of beer. "At least you'd be out under a sky, with the sun, fresh air, and a chance. But, Manny, you've got to understand: This is Donovan. It will try to kill you."

He didn't seem to taste the beer as he drank, eyes fixed on infinity.

She added, "Maybe it's a shitty choice, but it's the best we can do. Float it around among your people. If you decide to choose Donovan, we'll have somebody ready to show you the way out to the closest station, give you a crash course on what to do, and how to stay alive."

"And then what?"

"Freedom's a terrible thing, Manny. It means that the rest is up to you."

He pursed his lips, nodded, and winced as the sound of another shuttle could be heard building in the west as it came in for a landing.

50

Two days. That's what it had taken Cap and Talina to make it to the bluff she'd seen back where the skewer had attacked them. Only to find another bluff in the distance. And when they made that, another. Talina hadn't told Cap that any might have been Briggs' place. It would have been too disheartening when he discovered she was wrong.

As she climbed the rocky incline toward yet another rise, she swallowed dryly against the desperate thirst that tormented her. She'd allocated all of her water to Cap in a desperate attempt to keep him hydrated. The hope had been that they'd reach Briggs', but it was increasingly apparent that she would have to take the time to drill into an aquajade and tap a vein. That, or take the time to climb down to the river.

It didn't help matters that she could hear the river roaring down in the canyon just off to her right. Nor did Capella; it shot its merciless hot yellow glare down to bake her as she followed the irregular trail.

The chime seemed to mock her.

When Talina looked back at Cap, his face dripped sweat, and his blue eyes had taken on a glassy sheen. His left arm rested in the sling she'd made from his jacket. Nevertheless, he still clung to his rifle, and his jaw was set in determination.

She continued to slow her pace to match his as his energy flagged.

Around her, the aquajade trees had mostly replaced chabacho. Ferngrass, claw shrub, and sucking scrub now filled in the understory. Down in the canyon the Briggs River could be heard as it tumbled over rocks. Looking back, she could see how far they'd climbed from the lowlands.

"How you doing, Cap?" she asked, trying to keep the worry from her voice.

"One foot after the other, Tal," he said doggedly. "You just lead on."

She nodded, chewed on her lips, and turned wary eyes back to the trail, such as it was. Over the years chamois, bushbok, and little herds of fastbreak had beaten a path over the angular basalt that paralleled the river. While traveling on rock lessened the danger of slugs, it added to Cap's misery as he fought fever and struggled over the uneven footing.

The man's arm had swollen, turned red and angry. From the heat in his brow, Tal figured he was running a fever of forty or so.

"Come on, Cap. Just a little way to go," she told him. And then, as if in answer to a prayer, she gazed upon the stump: an aquajade, cut off flush with a saw. She grinned, pointing. "One of the Briggs family cut that. We're close, Cap."

"Let's beat feet, Tal," he whispered dryly. "I got a little left in me. Don't want to let it run out before I get there."

Even as he said it, his eyes rolled back in his head. He swayed, and his knees buckled. The rifle clattered from nerveless fingers. She barely managed to ease his collapse as he wilted to the ground.

"Damn it!" She knelt by his side, fishing for her water bottle. Managed to splash some on his face, lifted it to his hot lips.

Cap drank, coughed, his focus returning. "Wha' happened?"

"You passed out." She looked around at the surrounding trees, the ferngrass waving in the easterly breeze. The chime had a soft tone, dispersed, as though lazy in the burning midday sun.

"I can do it," Cap rasped dryly. "Help me up."

She slung her rifle, and then his. Pulling his good arm over her shoulder, she flexed her legs. Together they staggered up, almost toppled. Cap managed to catch himself, and wearily, they started forward.

Talina could feel his weakness and gritted her teeth. *This is not happening to me again. I won't let it.*

How far to the Briggs'? An hour at this pace? Maybe more?

If she could get Cap there, to the radio, she could send in a call.

Glancing up, the sun was right at zenith. If they hurried, if it wasn't far, she still might have a chance that Trish or Step could fly out before dark with some of the new antibiotic.

If it wasn't until morning, well, it would be what it would be.

The distant boom of a shuttle let her know that *Turalon* was still in orbit—a great big ship with a well-stocked medical facility fully capable of whipping an infected arm back into health.

Come on, Max. Hang in there.

A half hour later, she was panting, sweating, staggering under Cap's weight as she fought to keep her feet. Cap had started mumbling to himself, tripping over his own feet.

And then they were down, landing in a heap of loose limbs and clattering rifles.

Cap rolled onto his side, sucking air through his mouth, eyes half-lidded.

Talina sat up, shifted where she'd landed on the rifles, and pulled them free.

The path here was well used, showing wheel ruts where wood had been hauled. The ferngrass was beaten down in places. Lots of sign of human activity. Just over there was a curious wooden frame, weathered now, but built for some purpose.

Capella might have been trying to bake them given the way it beat down.

"Max?" she said through gasps. "I'm going to leave you for a bit. Help is just up ahead. I'll be back with Chaco and some of the kids. You've got to stay here, understand? Wait for me. Don't try to go anywhere."

He blinked.

She slapped him to get his attention. "Did you hear what I said?"

"Yeah. Gone for help."

"You stay right here. That's an order. I'll be back as soon as I can."

"Yes, ma'am," he told her hollowly, eyes rubbery in his head.

"Here's your rifle. It's on safety. We'll call when we're close, so don't shoot us."

He chuckled softly.

She stood, shouldering her rifle. "Gonna leave you with something, Max. Gonna leave you knowing that I'm not going to let you die. You gotta believe me."

"Gotcha, Tal." He grinned up at her. "Damn, you're a hell of a woman. Better'n I deserve."

"Goes both ways, Max. Now, you stay put. Be right back."

With his good hand, he flipped a salute. As he did, she could see the yellow caking of pus where it leaked from the bound wound and permeated the binding.

Then she turned, took a deep breath, and started forward at a weary trot. The days of travel had taken their toll. While they'd eaten along the way, much of the food they scavenged hadn't been nutritious, and the rations short. Not all of the proteins and fats in Donovan's wildlife were digestible in the human gut. At least not without supplemental enzymes to break them down. Cheng was still working on that.

She was tired. Stumbling.

Mistakes happened when a person was in that condition.

She'd proceeded for maybe ten minutes.

The only warning was the quetzal inside her, hissing an alert.

She barely managed to stop, clawing for her rifle as the rocks seemed to erupt, rising, spreading.

Freeze!

She stopped short, paralyzed as a quetzal arose from the trail before her and flared its collar in a brilliant scarlet and emerald blaze of color. The three eyes fixed on hers, the mouth wide as it shrilled a whistling challenge.

Unthinking, Talina lowered herself, heart pounding. The beast inside took control, locking her muscles, hissing and swelling in her gut.

Towering over her, the quetzal cocked its head, the three eyes fixed on hers. Rocking on its powerful back legs, it craned its head down to her level, the serrated jaws agape, inches from hers as it peered into her eyes.

Talina struggled to draw breath. The beast inside her squirmed.

And in that instant, she realized she couldn't move. Couldn't breathe. The only sensation was fear and her heart pounding panic and terror through her chest.

She would have screamed, would have thrown herself back as the quetzal's tongue whipped past her parted lips and darted around the inside of her mouth.

She was beyond surprise, terror-locked. Saliva began flowing. The alien flickers of movement inside her cheeks and around her tongue triggered her gag response, turned her stomach.

It seemed an eternity—then the quetzal's whiplike tongue flashed back between the beast's jaws.

Talina's lungs spasmed, drawing breath. Her muscles released and went lax. She barely caught herself before collapsing. Reflexively she spit, clearing her mouth. She made a face as the astringent taste, powerful—like concentrated peppermint extract—filled her mouth. Again she spit. All the while, she stared at the looming quetzal through fearful eyes.

The beast shimmered in white and gray stripes as it exhaled in a purring sound filled with curiosity. The three eyes gleamed as the collar retracted and the beast turned away. She watched it step to the side. Toss its head in the direction she'd been going, as if gesturing her on her way.

Talina, muscles shivering, struggled to keep her feet. She carefully hitched up her shoulder, shrugging the rifle sling back in place.

The quetzal issued a hollow whistling as if in approval.

"My man is back there," she told the beast and pointed back the way she'd come. "He's hurt. You understand? Armed. Leave him alone."

The quetzal tilted its head toward the trail again, as if trying to signal an idiot.

Talina veered wide, then backed her way down the trail. When she started again for Briggs', the quetzal padded along behind her for a ways, then angled off the trail headed west. One minute she could make it out as it passed between the trees. The next it had vanished.

"What the fuck?" she asked herself again and again. "And what's with the tongue in the mouth?"

Knowing.

"Yeah, sure. Knowing."

And then she smelled wood smoke. Periodically turning her head to the side to hawk and spit, she forced herself to a hard trot.

Cap was dying behind her, and a fucking French-kissing quetzal was prowling on the loose. She didn't know if she should be terrified or amazed.

51

The world kept shimmering in Cap's fevered gaze. Capella burned down from a sere and scorching sky. The cracked stone he sat against tortured his back. And damn, did his arm ever ache and throb. He grinned wryly, amused with himself. It could have been worse. He could have been out in the direct sun instead of propped here in the shade of the aquajade tree.

Cap's water bottle was long empty. He shook Talina's. Heard the slight splash of the liquid remaining. How much? A swallow or two?

His mouth had already gone dry, his throat cramped and sticking.

He blinked and squinted out at the too-blue vegetation with its weird leaves that moved in time to the hot breeze. The chime rose and fell, musical. What a curiously odd world this was that he'd come to die on.

"Talina will be coming," he whispered through cracked lips. "Hell of a woman, Talina."

He closed his eyes, floating in blackness. The sensation was so similar. He'd felt it before. In his vacuum suit. Back in Solar System. They left marines out there adrift and weightless in the black for a twenty-four hour stretch. One of the final tests before being certified for space duty. Lots of people couldn't stand it. Went crazy, screaming, pissing themselves in panic at the loneliness, the lack of feeling.

Cap had loved it. Thought it one of the most magical events of his life as he hung there marveling at the distant dot of the sun.

Floating.

He blinked, eyes gritty as he pried them open to stare out at the musk bush and thorncactus. How long had he been out?

He tried to judge Capella's movement, estimate how far the shadows had moved, but couldn't remember their location when he saw them last.

"Not doing well," he whispered. With his good hand he raised Talina's water bottle, glanced around as the chime rose and fell again. Did he dare drink?

His thoughts were muzzy.

How long would Talina be? How far to the Briggs' place?

He chuckled dryly.

Did it even matter?

He lifted the water bottle to his lips and drained the last of the tepid water. God, it felt wondrous as it rolled over his thick tongue.

Cap shifted, trying to ease his back where the stone felt like it was chewing a hole in his hide.

Then he glanced up. Froze.

In the tree across from him, a boy sat in a fork of the lower branches. A brown boy. He wore a dirty brown shirt and ragged pants—all tailored from chamois. Cap would have categorized the kid's skin tones as dark tan, and a shock of thick hair the color of old oak rose from the kid's head. A coiled rope made of what looked like braided leather was draped diagonally across his chest. An oversized knife hung from the boy's belt.

Cap started to smile. Hell, yes, he was fevered. Delusional. Figures that Donovan would kill him slowly and fill his head with hallucinations.

"You real?" he asked, half expecting the apparition to disappear with a pop.

"What happened to you?" the boy asked, his voice filled with accent.

"Skewer."

"You alone?"

"No. Talina. She's going to Briggs'."

The boy cocked his head. Seemed to be thinking. "Quetzal out there."

"She's dealt with quetzals before." That made him smile. Had there ever been a woman like Talina?

"You don't look too good."

Cap chuckled to himself. "No. Probably not."

"Dying?"

"Yeah. I feel like shit."

"I'll see if they are coming."

The boy's eyes seemed to expand, then his image shimmered. Cap's heart had started to hammer in his chest. Nausea tickled at the base of his throat. He took a deep breath, trying to still the floating sensation. Sweat was trickling down his face, his body roasting inside his skin.

He closed his eyes. Panted deep breaths to cool his lungs.

When he got control, he blinked. Stared around.

Yeah, he was still on Donovan. Back propped in the rocks.

Then he remembered the boy. Looked across at the tree opposite him. No boy perched in the fork of the branches.

"Must be losing my mind," he whispered to himself.

He would die here.

It would be all right.

52

Freelander pulsed and hummed, powerful vibrations running through the deck beneath Kalico's feet as she leaned over Zak Chan's shoulder and stared at the holographic display. They were in *Freelander's* engineering control room down near the spindle. Kalico hated the weightless feeling that made her clumsy.

Hated being on *Freelander* even more.

This ship scares the freaking hell out of me.

Chan sat at the control console, his head covered in a translucent interface-helmet that interacted with his implants. It allowed him to virtually think and feel the ship's systems.

At that moment he was projecting a stream of data from *Freelander's* sensors.

"What am I supposed to be seeing?" Kalico asked. "And why did I have to drag myself over here from *Turalon*?"

"That's just the thing, Madam Supervisor. It won't transmit past *Freelander's* hull." Chan turned his head, staring up at her through the transparency. "You have to be here."

"Why? What am I seeing?"

"These mathematics." He pointed to a column of numbers glowing light green in the projected data. Chan blocked them. Bolded the color. And then, to her amazement, pulled a recorder from his pocket and essentially took an old-time photograph of the data block.

"What did you just do?"

Chan took a deep breath, as if to reassure himself. "I'm hoping I can take the image with me. Physically. When I leave *Freelander.*"

Kalico snapped, "I *don't* understand, Zak. Tell me—in simple terms—why I'm back on this godforsaken wreck, and why you're acting so weird."

Zak smiled uneasily as he waved at the streams of data that now scrolled. "Sorry, ma'am. But it's a little complicated. Now watch. Here.

See this sequence? Wait. In about forty-five seconds, you're going to see it start all over again. It's a loop, ma'am. Like the sensor array kept recording the same data over and over as *Freelander* was reversing symmetry."

He made a face, hands palm out to communicate the seriousness of his words. "I *think* that wherever *Freelander* went, it brought some of that universe back with it."

"With it, how?"

"Like a bubble, ma'am. No, scratch that. Like a ghost of a bubble? A sort of shadow. Or a taint. A vestige of that universe, and it's still clinging to the ship."

"That's crazy."

"So is *Freelander* vanishing for one hundred and twenty-nine years during a two-year period in our time-space." He looked up. "And, ma'am. This ship gives people the creepy crawlies. They see things that aren't there. Sometimes people. Phantom movements. I'm still not sure that *Freelander* is completely fixed in our universe."

He waved a hand at the scrolling projection of mathematics. "Like why I can't send these data to *Turalon*. There's no logical explanation, but try as I might, I can't copy them and transmit them to *Turalon*. It's like they don't exist on the other side of this ship's hull."

"There's got to be another explanation."

Chan shrugged. "I'll have a better idea if I can get that photograph to *Turalon*. But, ma'am, I'm not smart enough to solve this. It's going to have to be the brains back in Solar System."

She glanced around at the small room. "Could we space her back?"

Behind the helmet's transparency, Chan's face turned grim. "She might just go back to whatever universe she came from. Maybe she'd make it fine. Maybe she'd pop out in Solar System in another one hundred and twenty years. Maybe she'd go wherever . . . and stay there. Like in the old saying, we're way off the map here. Meanwhile, I'm going to play with some of the energy levels in the reactors and see if I can get a reading."

"All right. Keep me informed." God, she hated every second she was aboard this damned ship.

She turned, palmed the hatch, and mindful of the reduced angular acceleration, left the claustrophobic little room with its consoles and projectors.

Freelander carried a bubble from another universe?

Kalico tried to get her head around it. Most physicists accepted that time—as a thing—didn't exist. That the universe functioned in an eternal now, that what humans perceived of as time was nothing more than changing relationships between particles.

She need only access her implant and the mathematical proofs would run in her head. But what did that mean in the real world? It wasn't the first time that equational gymnastics proved that ultimate reality was different from human perception. It didn't help her solve her dilemma about what to do with *Freelander.*

The ship began to hum louder. Chan playing with the reactors, no doubt.

A queasy sensation ran through her bones, tickled the pit of her stomach. She stopped short, gritted her teeth, and tensed. Either her eyes tricked her, or the light changed, smeared, and slipped sideways.

In that instant, Kalico stepped reflexively to the side, making way for the person who suddenly appeared striding down the corridor. In that instant, the woman brushed through her left arm. A feeling—the same feeling Kalico had experienced the day they broke into astrogation—sent a shiver through her. Like a wind that blew through her body instead of against it.

She caught but a glimpse as the light slipped back into place and solidified. The corridor seemed to dim, reestablishing itself. Kalico staggered sideways into the wall, frantic to feel it solid and cold to the touch beneath her fingers.

She took a deep breath. Heart pounding.

An empty corridor met her panicked gaze as she glanced back toward engineering. The phantom figure had vanished. Gone.

Kalico's heart continued to race. A cold shiver ran down across her skin, lifting her hair.

In that glance, as she had brushed past, she'd recognized the person. Kalico had seen herself as she had been when she strode down this corridor on the way to keep her appointment with Zak Chan.

53

As far as places to live went, Talina had always thought that Chaco and Madison Briggs had one of the most amazing dwellings. The living quarters were built into the canyon's side where Chaco had walled off recesses in the old lava tubes. From the windows the spectacular view was of a four-hundred-foot waterfall cascading down a sheer cliff of uplifted metamorphic bedrock. The geologic layers glistened in pink, white, and black bands of once-plastic strata. Below the cliff house the river churned along its bed in the rocky gorge.

From the main room a chiseled-stone stairway led fifty feet up to the flats above, where gardens of squash, cabbage, corn, beans, peppers, artichokes, peas, and the inevitable prickly pear cactus flourished in the rich volcanic soil. Chaco and the boys had built several storage buildings and equipment sheds, and it was to one of these that they had wheeled Cap.

"Thought I saw a boy," Cap kept repeating in his delirium. "Brown boy."

"Probably Tip," Chaco told him as he and Talina eased Cap from the two-wheeled cart to a makeshift bed they'd set up in the toolshed. It would have been too much trouble to haul Cap down the staircase to the main house.

Chaco had that sturdy back-country look to him: muscular, skin tanned to a hue mindful of age-stained walnut. His black beard glistened beneath a triangular nose and sharp, dark eyes. The man's long hair was what would be called sandy.

Standing back by the door, Madison cradled her newborn daughter in the crook of her arm, lips pinched with concern as she studied Cap's wounded arm and took in his half-focused eyes. The baby had come in the confusion over pickup times, born without issue after a five-hour labor.

Donovan had a sense of humor. Turned out Cap and Talina's trip had all been for nothing.

Talina laid a hand on Cap's forehead. Damn. She didn't like his color, either.

"It will be a bit yet for the sedative to take effect," Madison reminded Talina as she shifted the baby girl to her left breast. "It's best now if he just gets some rest."

Madison stood a little more than six feet, muscular, with ebony skin, medium brown eyes, and long, silky-rich black hair. For someone who just had a baby, the woman moved with a sultry grace. The unusual angles of her face, the high cheeks and slanted eyes, gave her an exotic look. Talina had always thought Madison Briggs was one of the most beautiful women she'd ever seen.

So had others.

One of the reasons the Briggses lived out here stemmed from the time Chaco had killed a man who had been a little too obsessed with Madison.

"A little brown boy," Cap whispered weakly. "Sitting in the tree."

"Tip," Chaco agreed. "I swear. That kid has a sense for things out in the bush." He gestured. "Come on, Mad, let's let the Captain rest."

He led the way past the door where fourteen-year-old Flip—the oldest son—watched. Behind him, Maria, three, stood with large eyes and her finger in her mouth.

Talina leaned down over Cap and took his hand. "Like I told you before, Trish is on the way. You're safe, Cap. We made it."

"Knew you would, Tal," he whispered drowsily.

She bent over and kissed him on the lips, adding, "You sleep now. Help's on the way."

He gave a slight nod.

She let go of his hand and stepped out into the late afternoon sun.

Chaco was seated next to Madison under one of the ramadas that overlooked the garden. Immediately behind, to the north, the land rose precipitously, the slope cracked and rugged with outcrops where the crust had been violently uplifted. In all, it really was a stunning vista.

"Drink?" Chaco called, lifting a glass from a cooler.

Talina walked wearily over, every muscle in her body aching. More than anything, she wanted to curl up next to Cap and sleep for a couple of months. Damn, how long had it been since she'd felt an exhaustion like this?

"You look beat, Tal," Madison told Talina as she stepped into the ramada's shade and seated herself.

Chaco handed her the glass, trickles of water beading on the outsides, foam covering the amber liquid within.

"What is this?"

"Homebrew." He gestured. "Our barley field is just over yonder on the other side of the aircar pad. Not sure about the quality of the hops, though. I don't think we got enough rain last season."

"Beer, huh?" She sipped, lifted an eyebrow in approbation. "I've dreamed of this taste for the last couple of weeks."

"Not sure it will do you any favors," Madison told her as she shifted the little girl to her other breast. "Whipped as you look, it might put you out like a light."

"I'll take my chance," Tal told her. "It'll do my blood sugar good."

Chaco was staring at her, an eerie light in his eyes. "You crossed the forest, huh? Trish kept calling. Telling us to keep an eye out for you. Tip said he'd see if he could find you."

"Cap really see him?"

"Brown boy?" Madison shrugged, her attention on her baby. "That's pretty much him."

"Where is he?"

Chaco turned his weather-lined eyes south. "Out there somewhere. If you hadn't already made it here, he'd have come at a run. Knowing him, he probably checked on Taggart, kept an eye until we got there. Made sure nothing happened to him."

"Why didn't he show?" Talina asked, taking another swallow of nirvana.

"He doesn't like people," Madison told her. "He does his lessons. Usually finishes a week's worth of studies in two or three days. Then he's gone." A tilt of her head indicated the bush. "Out there."

"Chaco told you about my run-in with the quetzal? That worry you? That Tip's out there with it?"

"That quetzal, he hangs around," Chaco said without inflection. "He doesn't bother us. Tip, he seems to get along with it. Freaked the piss out of us the first time we saw them together. That was a couple of years ago. Never had any trouble with it. It shows up when we trap chamois. Helps drive them into the trap. Then, after we butcher, we leave it a couple of carcasses."

"You're kidding?"

Chaco's eyes still had that eerie look. "What about the one inside you?"

"Not sure what it's all about." Tal had told Chaco the whole story as they wheeled the cart out to pick up Cap.

"They're all different," Chaco told her with a dismissive shrug.

"They eat people."

"We eat chamois, bushbok, and crest. So what?"

That he could say it so simply set Talina back a pace. Wild Ones were always a little weird and crazy.

"What do they want?" Tal wondered, her alien vision sharpening as she caught movement out in the trees. From the flickers of color, it was nothing more than flock of scarlet fliers.

"Don't know," Madison told her. "You're still worried about Tip, aren't you? He's got to be who he's going to be, Tal. Flip, well, he's headed back to Port Authority when he's old enough. He's got town in his blood. But Tip? He belongs to Donovan."

"For all we know," Chaco added, "he's the future."

54

Trish sat with one cheek atop the lab table, her leg swinging. She'd tossed her ponytail back and crossed her arms as Raya worked on her patients.

The fan hummed, and the lights buzzed softly overhead as Raya scurried around the examining room.

Okay, a miracle had happened. Talina and Cap Taggart had walked out of the bush after nearly two weeks. More incredible, in the process they'd crossed approximately fifty kilometers of dense forest, river, and uplands.

But at what price? Trish studied her old friend through narrowed eyes. Tal was different. Changed. Something almost feral about her. Not to mention the crazy stuff coming out of her mouth, like the French-kissing quetzal. Or the fact that she'd clearly been screwing Cap Taggart. The guy who had arrested her and was going to stand her up against a wall and shoot her for murder and treason.

Tal's personal life is her business.

Bullshit. It rankled. Seemed like a betrayal. Letting a Skull into her bed? Captain of the marines no less? It was like a saint lowering herself to bedding a pimp.

God, Talina! If you're that desperate for sex, use something with a battery that vibrates.

Trish turned her attention to the big marine. He was a Skull, not even handsome. Definitely not worthy of Talina. Trish wondered if she'd ever hated a man as much as she did him.

The guy's swollen arm was now under Raya's care. She'd drained it, irrigated it, and shot him full of the new antibiotics. Analgesics had brought the captain's fever down. When he spoke now, it was lucid, unlike the muttered ravings she'd listened to as she flew Tal and the marine back to Port Authority from Chaco Briggs' landing pad.

And all that way Tal had sat in the back, holding Taggart's head, talking softly. Call it absolutely infuriating.

What the hell, Tal? Him?

She could hear another of the shuttles as it winged in with another load from *Freelander.* They were running out of room on the shuttle pad. Shit was stacked everywhere around the perimeter. The place was a mess of crates, containers, and pieces of machinery and equipment.

The chemist, Cheng, walked in at that point, his round countenance in an unusual scowl. His too-small nose still looked out of place on the broad spread of his face. The man was nearing fifty, the first gray showing prematurely at his temples.

He gave Trish a wink, then walked over to where Talina reclined on one of the examining tables. She swung her feet to the floor, sitting up and greeting Cheng with an expectant gaze.

"What have you got?" Talina asked.

"Molecules," he told her. "Proteins. Quetzal-specific. Your saliva and blood are loaded with them."

"But not an infection?" Raya asked, looking up from where she monitored Taggart's temperature.

"Maybe you could call it that. It's Donovan," Cheng replied laconically. "What do I tell you? Talina, given what I'm seeing in your serology, it's like you are producing them."

"How?" Raya asked, stepping around.

"Without more tests," Cheng told her, "I haven't a clue. Tal has new, protein-specific molecules in her blood, but her immune system isn't reacting. It's not developing titers. The quetzal-specific proteins aren't causing a reaction among the T cells and antibodies. Never seen anything like it."

"What kind of molecules?" Talina asked, her gaze going absent.

"Like I said: the information-bearing genetic codes. We have DNA, Donovanian life has three molecular chains. To put it in descriptive terms, it's actually an S-twist, tri-molecular thread, but it pretty much works the same way as DNA. Unzips, codes proteins and regulates metabolic processes, and conveys information from one generation to another."

"Conveys information?" Talina seemed to be chewing on something inside. "And you say I'm making it, and it's in my saliva?"

"In your sebaceous glands, too," Cheng added. "I recovered them from a skin swab."

"A quetzal inside you," Trish said. "That's what you told me after we pulled you out of that canyon."

Was that why Tal was screwing Taggart? She was infected? Somehow out of her mind?

Cheng lifted a skeptical eyebrow. He glanced at Raya. "You did bloodwork on her after that?"

"Just the usual screen for metal toxins." Raya's expression pinched. "She was disoriented, slightly fevered, her lymph nodes were swollen as if from an allergic reaction, but I chalked that up to the trauma. Maybe some reaction from the thorn punctures and lacerations."

"She had quetzal blood all over her head," Trish told them. "And when I got on scene, the thing had its head pressed against hers. Forehead to forehead."

"Mouth to mouth?" Tal asked, the vacant look still haunting her gaze.

"Well, sort of. It's tongue was, like, really close to your lips. And then . . . You remember? I shot it? You said you'd been inside the thing's head? That the bullet impact was really rude?"

Talina leaned forward and dropped her head into her hands. "Okay, so I'm infected with quetzal. I mean, the thing talks to me. Tells me things."

Trish glanced uncomfortably at Cheng.

Cheng however, dropped to a knee, staring earnestly at her. "Talks to you how?"

"Hell," Talina muttered, "I just thought I was slightly nuts."

"It's there," Cap added from his bed. "Like a second sense. Time after time, Tal's quetzal kept us from disaster. Each time, she'd say the quetzal warned her. If it hadn't, the mobbers would have gotten us for sure."

"What are mobbers?" Cheng asked.

"Nasty new life-form we found in the deep forest," Talina said, head still down. "Carnivores. Four wings with scimitar-like claws. Fly like maniacs and travel in packs. Even quetzals are terrified of them."

"What else terrifies quetzals?" Trish asked, barely keeping the disbelief from her voice.

"Water," Talina said softly. "The thing was nearly catatonic while we were out on the river. Wouldn't let me get into the canoe."

"Do you know how this sounds, Tal?"

Talina lifted her head, eyes glittering. "Trish, it's real. Inside me."

Cap shifted on his bed. "I'm new here, but from the beginning you've been telling me about the Wild Ones. That they have some sort of truce with the quetzals, with Donovan itself. I was mostly out of it, but I remember when Chaco Briggs showed up with Tal and wheeled me back to his homestead. Tal kept talking about being, uh, kissed by the quetzal. And Chaco, unconcerned, says, 'Yeah, he hangs around.'"

Cheng seemed locked in his head. "If it's true, that would explain some things."

"What things?" Raya demanded.

"Been concerned," Cheng told her. "Thought maybe it was molecules that just passed through the gut wall. But I always get Donovanian proteins in the bloodwork I run on the Wild Ones. The longer they're out there, the higher the frequencies. Thing is, I can't isolate any effect on the people."

"So, what do we do about it?" Raya asked.

"I don't know," Cheng told her. He turned to Talina. "Do you notice any difference? I mean physically? Any decrease in ability? Loss of balance or appetite? Disorientation? Any loss of coordination?"

"Just the opposite. I swear I can see into the ultraviolet and infrared ranges. And my vision is sharper. So is my hearing. I have a lot better sense of balance. And the way I taste things is . . . uh, I guess you'd say richer. And there's almost like a second sense, just a feeling I get."

Raya asked, "What about the dreams? The last time we talked about this, you said they were really vivid."

"Sometimes I dream I'm a quetzal. Like I'm hunting. Just me and the bush, a sort of fantastic in-the-now experience."

"If anything," Cap told them, "she's remarkably fit. I'm in good shape. She walked me into the ground out there. Balance? Coordination? You should have seen some of the things we crossed. And I'll swear to that second sense of hers."

Cheng reached out, took Talina's hands. "You said it talks to you. How?"

"Thoughts. But, Cheng, they're simple. Like when I ask it about Allison's baby. Why it ate it. It just says 'empty.' I don't know what that means."

"If it's not a delusion," Trish made herself say what the others wouldn't. "I mean, how do molecules form words in our language in your brain? That's done by nerves, right? Synapses triggering. RNA and what all."

Cheng nodded. "All those things."

Talina laughed, almost bitterly. "People, what if we're thinking about this all wrong?"

"How's that?" Raya asked.

"We've spent years now busting our asses, trying to understand Donovan and how it works." Talina pressed her palms together. "So, what if the inverse is true?" She looked around, meeting all of their glances. "What if Donovan is trying to understand us?"

Cheng nodded. "I think I have a whole new set of research paradigms."

Trying to understand us? Trish swallowed hard, skeptical gaze on Talina.

"Whoa," Cap said anxiously as he sat up in his bed. "People, keep in mind. I'm a military guy. I think differently."

"How so, Max?" Talina turned to give him her entire attention.

Max? She called him Max? Trish almost made a face. She was really starting to hate the guy.

"In the military we study to understand. Just like you people are doing here. Dr. Cheng, you're trying to work out Donovan's chemistry, right? And you're doing it so that you can exploit it. The mining people are doing the same with the geology, the botanists seeking to understand the plants so that we can use them. In the military we're taught to learn all that we can about the enemy so that we can destroy them."

He paused, then asked, "So, what're the quetzals' goals in all this? Did they infect Talina out of a love for science? Knowledge for the sake of knowledge? Or because we're a threat that they need to deal with? Perhaps defeat and drive off their world?"

"Well, that just sucks methane," Trish whispered. "Tal, are you a spy?"

Talina had gone as pale as the polar snows.

55

Aboard the *Turalon*, Kalico Aguila stared coldly across the table in the captain's lounge. Captain Taggart—freshly returned from the dead and looking the worse for it—sat in his uniform, his left arm immobilized in a sling.

Dr. Tyler had checked him out in the medical bay, pronounced Dr. Turnienko's work satisfactory, and released him for "administrative" duty.

Now the marine sat at full attention, a grim smile playing at his lips, eyes fixed distantly as marines were trained to do when being disciplined.

"Just what the hell were you thinking?" Kalico demanded.

The smile flickered, a break in his expression. To her surprise, he said gently, "Can we go off the record, ma'am?"

She arched an eyebrow, her stomach queasy and dyspeptic as it had been since the discoveries aboard *Freelander*. "Is there any reason I shouldn't have you busted down to private, or even tossed out on your ass and left on this vile ball of rock?"

"How many personnel are you missing?"

She started, wondering how he knew. Who'd told him. She had ordered Abibi to keep the desertions quiet, tell the rest of the crew that the missing individuals had been "reassigned" for at least as long as they could string out the ruse. Hopefully just long enough to space.

"Do you know something about it, Captain? Or"—and her blood ran cold—"is this something you've orchestrated to sabotage me?"

The smile was back, amused. "No, ma'am. So, since we're off the record, let me start at the beginning. I wanted to see Donovan. And I had one tiny window. It should have been a simple trip. Fly out, pick up a pregnant woman, fly back."

"But the aircar crashed."

"Correct. I got more than I bargained for."

"Including Officer Perez, if the rumors are true." She tilted her head suggestively. "Thought she was on your shit list."

"She's more than she seems," Taggart said, wincing as he shifted his arm and relaxed. "The whole planet is."

He paused, then said, "*Freelander* got caught in a time trap? Some weird relativity? More than a hundred years? Officers dead by suicide, a macabre death cult, temples made of bones, shuttles vanishing beyond the inversion? Your crew slipping away in drips and drabs every time a shuttle makes planet? Damn it, Kalico, it's all falling apart."

Kalico? That was way over the line. She felt a crystalline crack in her composure. "Not to mention my captain of marines traipsing off for a nature hike when I needed him the most."

"You didn't need me. Spiro already gave me a full report. So, since we're off the record, I'll give you mine. You're hanging on by a thread. I can see it in you. Brittle, like an overstressed pane of glass. Just the smallest tap, and you're about to shatter into a thousand pieces."

She began to tremble, hated herself for it. "Your life hangs by a thread, Captain."

"I'm not your enemy," he said softly. "Hell, I'd get you out of this mess if I could. You want to space out of here? Count down the seconds until you invert symmetry? And then what? You and the crew living day by day for the next two years as your guts crawl, hounded by nightmares that when the day comes, *Turalon* is not going to pop back into Solar System. Talk about slow torture and psychiatric agony. You might consider yourself a rock, but your crew—what's left of it—is going to disintegrate. Their wildest imaginations are going to have free rein."

She swallowed hard.

"Yeah," he said, reading through the brave front she tried to project. "I'd be scared shitless, too."

"What the fuck is wrong with me?" she whispered hoarsely. "I'm better than this."

The trembling had started in her hands. Images of the bone temple, the broken, desiccated skeleton slumped in the doorway, flickered behind her eyes. Herself, ducking out of the—

"Donovan plays by its own rules," Cap told her. "The saying is that some people come here just to leave, some come to stay, and others come to die."

"Maybe I don't buy the quaint local shit?" *If you leave, you will die.* A shiver played down her spine. She could feel *Freelander* out there beyond the hull and across that short measure of space.

"How's Abibi taking it?"

"Like the officer she is." When he arched his brow in question, she relented. "Okay, she's as scared as I am."

"So, why are you going?"

"Cap, I've got a fucking fortune in metals, clay, and gems in this ship's hold." She stood, pacing, tucking her shaking hands against her sides.

Come on, get it together, damn you.

"This load is everything. A masterstroke. Sure, it doesn't make a blip on The Corporation's annual profit sheet, but think of the symbolic effect it will make: Diamonds, emeralds, rubies, gold, silver, and rare elements. That's treasure. Opulence that speaks to the hearts and souls of men. It's mythic. Jason and the Golden Fleece. Sinbad. King Solomon's mines.

"I can walk into the Board, toss a case on their shining table and crack it open to spill jewels and nuggets like a waterfall. 'There it is, ladies and gentlemen, the wealth of Donovan.'"

"Quite the scene." He cocked his head. "Assuming you get there."

Kalico rubbed her forehead. "Abibi and her people have spent days scouring the *Freelander* logs. They've got nothing. Just crazy hypotheses from people losing their minds. In an attempt to figure it out, Orten's people even tried to break into the computers. Tried using a mining excavator from the cargo. Didn't work so well in freefall."

"So?"

"So, the answer's in the qubit core someplace. Data we can't access here. Don't have the skills or the computational power to analyze if we could." She gestured futility with her now steady hand. "You'd have to get *Freelander* back to Earth. What if it took another hundred and some years? And who'd space in her?"

"Spiro says the crew thinks it's haunted."

"Maybe it is, Cap." She pressed her lids together as if to squeeze out the visions. "I saw things. Heard things. Flitting images at the corners of my eyes. Shadows that seemed to be there, then weren't." She took a breath. "I saw myself emerge from that temple of bones. Passed myself in one of the corridors while Chan was experimenting with the generators."

"Ghosts?"

"Who the hell knows? Maybe afterimages from whatever dimension, universe, or reality she inverted to. What Chan calls a bubble or taint. God help us, we're way beyond our understanding of physics with this thing."

"Kalico, here's my advice: give it a rest."

"Excuse me?"

He waved around. "*Turalon.* Leave it in orbit. Keep the crew on rotation, but learn more about the planet. That wealth you're so proud of will wait, and you might hit on something even more spectacular. Might even be in the biology if Cheng has the right idea about the molecules."

She stared at him, trying to scry out his motives. "Have you lost any sense you might have ever had?"

"Actually, my suspicion is that I've gained some."

"Jesus, Cap. Have you forgotten why you were assigned this duty? What your record looks like? Insubordination? Dereliction of duty? And that fortune you've spent the last two years accruing? Everything hinges on my report to The Corporation." She pointed. "And at the moment—"

"I'm here to tender my resignation."

"—I'm . . . not . . ." She stopped.

"Back on the record: Supervisor Aguila, I hereby tender my resignation from the Corporate Marines. I do, hereby, forfeit any pay, benefits, and privileges which might have been due me. I hereby state and declare that this action is made of my own free will and accord, and that I am not now, nor have I been, under duress. Upon return to Port Authority I will surrender all military equipment to Lieutenant Spiro."

He stood, gave her a respectful nod.

"Cap, if you do this . . . If you walk out of this room . . ." Anger swelled, driven by desperation. "So help me God, Captain, go through with this . . . and, well, by all the powers in the multiverse, I'll break you like a dry twig!"

His expression went from determined to grim, eyes hardening. Snapping to attention, he saluted, palm cutting the air like a blade. Pivoting, as if on an axle, he turned and strode from the room.

Like water draining from a jug she felt her insides empty. Rage dulled into a deep-seated and aching pain. Slumping into the chair, she dropped her head into her hands.

56

The cards fluttered as Dan practiced his false deal. The snap they made was the sweetest music he'd ever heard. The Jewel had exceeded his expectations. As a measure of his success, Tyrell Lawson was over at the machine shop and involved in the process of manufacturing him a new safe. The old one just wasn't big enough.

Around him, the Jewel was bustling. He'd designed a pretty good casino. Folks on Donovan were not only competent, but, by damn—as opposed to back in Solar System—when you hired them to do a job, they actually worked their asses off and got it done. Something about the planet's ethic that if a person didn't, he was likely to end up dead.

A thought which—as Dan remembered Exman's windpipe crushing under his gripping hands—brought a smile to his lips.

That said, with the exception of one local named Art Maniken, the rest of his crew were hired from *Turalon* transportees. People he'd known aboard ship who'd landed and found themselves without a job suitable to their training. Men and women who were thankful for the opportunity to work inside, out of the elements, in a clean environment, and for wages that allowed them to live at a higher standard than their peers.

And unlike Donovanians, they understood authority. Didn't have that independent, screw-you streak to their personalities.

Which meant that Dan didn't have to threaten.

Much.

That was the thing about the soft meat. Unlike the Donovanians, they took orders.

The downside when it came to soft meat? They were a festering lot. He glanced over at the corner table where Fig Paloduro and Abdul Oman had their heads together over a bottle of Inga's brandy. They came here to talk in private, away from the Donovanians, away from lips that might spread rumors.

Dan liked plotters. The fact that they were involved in something they didn't want talked about meant he had a handle on them—an advantage he might be able to exploit someday. And most of the transportees were ripe for the recruiting. Angry, scared, desperate, unhappy, and trapped: it couldn't be a more fertile ground for revolution and revolt.

"Provided they can control it," he whispered under his breath. Control. That was the random variable that left him uneasy. His operation lay squarely astraddle of the two populations: dependent upon the triumvirate's acceptance and the transportees' clientele and cheap labor.

Over the snap of the cards as he shuffled, he could hear male banter; Angelina's more melodic laughter as she worked a mark at the craps table; the click of chips; the slapping of dealt cards onto the tables. Calls for bets rose above the rest, all followed by the occasional curse as luck went against a wager. Rarer—but unfortunately necessary—were the whoops of joy as a long shot came in.

Dan smiled to himself as he dealt out a trey, four, five, six, and seven of hearts. He'd practiced for days to develop the trick of dealing out a straight flush. Even with an implant it took remarkable concentration and practice.

"Sir?" Art Maniken, the big-boned miner and brawler, stepped up to the table. He'd owed Dan more than he could pay. A fact that had landed him a job as bouncer, enforcer, and faro dealer. The guy had really taken to it, delighted to be finished with backbreaking labor on his claim.

Dan looked up, arching an eyebrow.

Art inclined his head toward the door. A knot of spacers, in uniform, were staring around uneasily and blinking in the light after traversing the dark streets.

"They're not supposed to be here," Dan said softly. "Explicit orders from Captain Abibi. And believe me, that woman means it."

He stood, pulled his fancy black vest with embroidered quetzals straight, and set his cuffs. Walking up, he gave his best smile.

He knew one of them, Petre Howe from hydroponics. He'd worked for the guy as part of his punishment after the Nandi episode. Petre had been fair. Required of Dan no more or less than the job had demanded.

Now the man grinned uneasily and shifted awkwardly. "Hey, Dan."

"Petre." Dan gestured broadly toward the tables. "Would you and your party like to come in, maybe away from the door where anyone nosy might report you to the good Captain?"

The worried glances among the others told Dan everything he needed to know. From their uniform patches, they came from all over the ship: a com specialist, kitchen staff, two from engineering, and a slim woman from atmospherics.

Dan shepherded them back past the roulette wheel and craps table, heedless of the stares they drew.

"Now," Dan told them, clapping his hands together. "What can I do for you? You're more than welcome to try your luck, but understand, while I'd dearly love to take them, Corporate credit vouchers can't be redeemed on Donovan. It's cash only at the tables."

"Got a private place we can talk?" Petre asked.

Dan measured the nervous glances the crewmembers were giving each other, the distrust with which they viewed The Jewel's patrons.

"Sure. Right through that door." He shot a wink at Allison where she sat behind the cage clicking chips and led them into the back.

He closed the hallway door behind him, gestured them into Angelina's room, and seated himself on the high stool before her mirror and wardrobe. She'd made the place into a saucy, yet feminine, boudoir.

"Dan," Petre began hesitantly, "we've been hearing about you. That you're the kind of man who can get things done. That you do things for people."

"That depends on what kind of things you need done, Specialist Howe. What the risk is. And it depends on what's in it for me."

The five crewmen looked back and forth.

"You've heard about *Freelander?*" Petre asked.

"Yeah. The ghost ship. People eating each other. Bones made into a temple. Spirit writing on the walls. A century lost in some time dimension beyond the explanation of physics. Not that I believe the stories, but I'm told the spirits of the dead are walking the corridors, all pursued by Captain Orten's howling ghost."

The five were glancing, owl-eyed, back and forth, shifting nervously.

Dan raised an eyebrow. "I take it those aren't exaggerations?"

At their continued silence, he concluded, "Obviously not. So, what brings you to me in search of some service that could get you all spaced?"

"We want out," Petre said, glancing anxiously at Dan. "It's all over the ship. Some of the load specialists and a shuttle pilot stole an aircar. Slipped away. Flew someplace in the interior to some abandoned camp."

"We want to go," the Asian told him.

"Who are you?"

The Asian bowed slightly. "Chan Tzu. This is Rita Valerie. Ngomo Suma. And this is Ashanti Kung." He indicated the petite African woman last. "They've got a marine guard on the aircars. We had to bribe our way past the gate. But we understand that you might help us."

Dan took a deep breath. "Mutiny on the *Turalon*. Oh, Supervisor Aguila, someone, it seems, has dealt a deuce right in the middle of your royal flush."

"What does that mean?" the woman introduced as Rita Valerie asked.

"It means," Dan replied, "that I'm sensing one hell of an opportunity." A beat. "And a whole lot of risk."

"I couldn't think of anyone else to go to," Petre said. "We're ship people."

"What can you pay? And I told you, Corporate credit doesn't cut it."

Again they looked back and forth.

"We have ourselves, Dan." Petre spread his hands wide. "It's like with The Corporation. We'll write you a contract. Our labor. Anything you want us to do if you will get us away from Port Authority. We've been working on *Freelander.* Cleaning, fixing her up, restoring systems. We're not stupid. That ship's worth a fortune to The Corporation. The captain is going to pick someone to space her back to Solar System . . . and we're all junior seniority."

"I hadn't heard they were going to space her back. Just the opposite. I heard they were going to leave her in orbit when *Turalon* spaced."

"No one's said it," Ngomo Suma muttered uneasily. "But why else would they have us fixing systems? Putting atmosphere back to normal, scrubbing filters?"

Ashanti Kung snapped, "It's bad enough to face a spacing on *Turalon*. But I'd rather be flushed out a lock than space on *Freelander*. I'm not going back!"

He met her hot stare with a mild gaze.

"Contract," Petre said. "We're yours if you can keep us from having to go back to either of those damned ships."

"Twenty years?" Dan asked to get an idea of their desperation.

Again they looked back and forth.

Finally Petre said, "Five."

"Ten," Dan countered.

"Seven." Petre shifted uneasily, avoiding the eyes of the others.

"Ten. Period. You understand, I will essentially own you. What used to be called an indenture. You will have no rights. No court. No place of appeal. My word is law."

Again they glanced back and forth. Ngomo and Chan Tzu looked sick, hesitant.

"I don't know," Rita Valerie told him.

"Just like a contract with The Corporation," Dan told her. "The same thing. I provide living space, an allowance for food, and you do what I tell you."

"Works for me," Petre said. "I know you, Dan. I'll trust you to treat me as fairly as I treated you."

The others were still unconvinced.

"All right, here's how it goes," Dan told them, pushing through them to the door. "We're going out front, and I'm going to be loud and adamant. 'Sorry, people! Can't help! That's illegal.'

"You're going to look sad and disappointed. You're going to nod and say, 'We understand.' And then those of you willing to indenture yourselves to me for the next ten years will meet me at the back door in a half hour. By morning I'll have you out of Port Authority. I've got a friend. Owns a mine about twenty klicks out. You'll be fed, have to work as he tells you to, and then after *Turalon* ships out, you'll be brought back here to a more sanitary and comfortable environment."

He glanced around. "Does that suit?"

Petre and Rita nodded, relief behind their eyes. The others were still looking uncertainly back and forth.

"All right, my friends. Let's go. Oh, and make it look good for the crowd."

In a line, he watched them file out of Angelina's room.

"Damn," he muttered under his breath. "If only I had another two or three ghost ships up there in orbit."

He orchestrated their exit, loudly proclaiming, "Nope! Sorry, folks. Can't do it." And watched them vanish into the night.

When he opened The Jewel's back door a half hour later, all five of them were standing there ready to sign.

As he had known they would be.

57

A soft rain fell from low-hanging clouds. While the overcast and precipitation weren't enough to halt operations at the shuttle pad, the moisture that turned the hard pack into sticky clay was. The skid loaders, tires caked with slimy goo, had been idled immediately after the first one got stuck in its own tracks after depositing a sialon crate atop a precarious pile of previously stacked crates. The place was starting to look like a mad child's mess around the perimeter. *Freelander's* cargo was being dumped willy-nilly wherever the field crew could find an open spot.

Talina sniffed at the humid air, her hair frizzed and beaded with rain. The earthy smells of wet clay, spicy vegetation, and the faint tinge of exhaust all mixed with the scents blowing in from the Gulf.

Beside her, Shig, wearing a raincoat, slopped along in the viscous and slippery mud.

The shuttles looked like grounded raptors, their downswept wings glistening and gray as they dripped water. Angled as they were, the forward-facing windows created the impression that the craft were scowling and disgusted with the world, while in the rear their lowered ramps dispelled any illusion created by their sleek lines. People lounged in the shelter of the holds, some reclined, others swinging their feet as they waited out the rain.

"They might be here for a while," Shig noted. Then he glanced up. "This isn't supposed to break any time soon."

Talina took in the marines on guard at the gate, weapons slung, water dripping from their armor. Farther down the fence she could see others standing their posts. The marines' job was supposedly to keep any deserters from *Turalon* from climbing the chain-link and making their way into Port Authority.

Shig stared thoughtfully at the guards. "Word has it that Dan Wirth has set up a regular underground railroad to smuggle crew out of Port Authority."

"Where'd you hear that?"

"From a lost soul who has bound himself to our Mister Wirth. That's the thing about people who sell themselves. They often hawk their wares to more than one buyer at a time. The hope, of course, is that they can serve both masters without conflict." Shig's lips bent into his benign smile. "A hope that I will help my source to achieve."

"You think we should do something about it?" Tal asked.

"Yvette and I have discussed Mr. Wirth to no end. Trish would have the guy suffer a 'healthcare emergency' some night that ended in cardiac arrest."

"I like that plan."

Shig laced his fingers together and pressed them to his midsection. "Trish has suggested several ways in which the cause of Mr. Wirth's cardiac arrest could not be traced back to us."

"Good old Trish. Always pragmatic. Want me to save everyone the time, effort, and skullduggery by just walking in and putting a bullet through his brain?"

"Yvette and I would ask your concurrence that we wait for the time being. We're under no illusions about Wirth. The man is a psychopath. But here is the thing about psychopaths: while they have no empathy, and are in the game only for their own gratification, some can be reasoned with. And in the meantime, he is providing a service."

"What's that? I heard he's turned Allison Chomko into a drugged-out poker shill, that he's bought his way into Betty Able's, and he pretty much runs the underside of Port Authority. He's using people."

"People come to Donovan for various reasons. Some to die. Some to find themselves. And others to leave. But none are unchanged. For the moment, Dan Wirth is expediting that process. But ultimately?" Shig shrugged.

"Trish says he robbed and murdered Thumbs."

"He is the most likely suspect."

"And you and Yvette think we should just let him skate free?"

"What did you make us promise after you killed Clemenceau?"

"That we'd stay out of the way. Let people manage their own affairs and only step in when people's actions threatened the survival of the colony." She made a face as she repeated her own, once hotly held demands.

"Precisely. Does Wirth threaten the survival of the colony, or is he, in his way, adding to its viability by building an organization that accrues wealth and then uses it for the colony's advantage? You've heard? He's building a house. A big thing. He's hired Hofer and his crew to erect his mansion. Close to thirty people are on the payroll to obtain the timber and stone. Lawson is fabricating the metal, piping, and cistern."

"I've heard that half the soft meat are in debt to him. How is that good?"

"You've been out in the bush. Let me get you up to speed." He shot her a sidelong glance from under his hood. "The jobs the Skulls were promised are not here. Port Authority is not what they expected. They've been assigned employment they consider menial, and they see no future. Because of their sense of deprivation, we've had suicides, and homicide is up."

"They can space back on *Turalon*."

"A prospect that terrifies them. Especially with the arrival of *Freelander* after so many lost ships. They feel betrayed, trapped, hopeless, and desperate. An explosive recipe ripe for ignition, don't you think?"

"And how does Wirth play into this?"

"He is becoming a leader. Someone with influence among the Skulls." Shig pointed. "For the time being, the marines act as a reminder that The Corporation still calls the shots. The Skulls are currently in a state of stunned disorganization. Their thinking is in the Corporate paradigm. But as soon as the marines space and *Turalon* is no longer in orbit?"

"It will change."

"And they will lash out. A problem for which we must prepare. There are a lot more of them than there are of us."

"Shit."

Shig tilted his head as he studied the haphazard clutter of crates, tarp-wrapped equipment, pieces of machinery that defied Tal's recognition. "What *is* all this stuff?"

"The bounty of *Freelander*'s hold. The ship's AI was chopped out by the crew, so there is no inventory. I understand that most of the food and drink was sorted through and plundered over the years. But the mining equipment, structural materials, vehicles, and so on, were left untouched. What little of it that still works. The few vehicles that Montoya's crew have had time to work on are iffy. Things like the seals and gaskets are brittle, old, and often deteriorated. The tires on the haulers and trucks are hard and cracked. No telling if they'd last long enough to get across the field, let alone out to the mines. The batteries are dead, of course. But, after nearly thirteen decades, will they ever take a charge, let alone hold it?" He threw his hands wide. "Guess we'll see."

"What's that?" Tal asked, pointing to a huge pile of struts and large folds of what looked like white fabric.

"A huge dome. Though where we'll put it remains a problem, unless we tear down some of the existing structures to make it fit."

"And those things?" Tal tried to figure what the large and irregularly shaped sections of ceramic might be. Large vents or manifolds had been cast into them. Obviously they fit together to create some sort of structure.

"A smelter," Shig told her. "Perhaps the most useful thing they've sent us. Assuming we can figure out how to assemble it, we'll finally be able to smelt our own metals. From there we need only to produce a foundry, and we can take another step on the road to ultimate survival."

"Yeah, but we've got a problem, Shig. The best ore deposits are out there." She waved a hand in the direction of the distant mountains. "How do we get the ore here to smelt? What powers the furnaces?"

"That," Shig assured her, "is our problem to figure out." He smiled in that unassuming way of his. "Assuming the Skulls don't revolt, and we don't all kill ourselves in the meantime."

"Charming, Shig. Really fucking charming."

58

Cap Taggart sat at a back table in Inga's. He had his leg flopped out, half-slumped in the chair, his left hand on the table to ease the healing wound in his arm. In his right hand he grasped a stein half-full of Inga's crystal-malt brew.

The incongruity of his situation wasn't lost upon him. Since the moment he'd been assigned to *Turalon*, the SDRs had been accumulating with each tick of the clock. A small fortune waited in an account with his name on it back in Transluna.

And he'd given it up.

Now, here he sat. The sum total of his assets consisted of overalls and plasticized boots, a quetzal-hide coat, chamois shirt and pants. The latter—local items—had been a gift from Talina. The belt, knife, and pistol, he'd held back from the bundle he'd forwarded to Lieutenant Spiro. When he could, he'd send a nugget or two to pay it off. What the hell, the rest of the Donovanians had paid for Corporate property, why couldn't he?

His parting with Lieutenant Spiro had been anything but pleasant. She'd treated him like dung on her boot, a loathing hatred in her eyes as she'd said, "I ought to shoot you down like the stinking traitor you are. You've betrayed us. As good as spit in our faces."

Nor had the rest of his marines taken it well.

"Figures," Private Talbot had said. "He's as good as his reputation, not worth shit in a toilet."

"Oh, brave new world," Cap quoted, and took a swallow from his beer. But it hadn't all been bad.

Until the day he died, he would remember the expression on Talina's face. He'd been sitting on her step, rain dripping from the awning that sheltered her doorway. He'd had his hands clasped in his lap and looked up at her without so much as a wink or smile.

She'd cocked her head, water dripping from a wide-brimmed hat.

Something he couldn't read had lain behind her eyes, as though unsurprised, but still uncertain.

"You lost?"

"Nope." He'd spread the fingers in his clasped hands. "I know right where I am. I quit. Resigned. Surrendered my commission."

"Aguila let you?"

"I think it happened so quickly I caught her off guard. Nor did I hang around long enough for her to consider the options. So, here I am. What you see is what you get."

She'd just stood there while rain spattered on her hat. Her mouth was pursed—and a thousand thoughts were running behind her large and dark eyes. Cap had waited, his heart beating slowly in his chest.

In the end, she'd nodded to herself, stepped around him, and opened her door. Pausing—as if for a final consideration—she'd said, "Come on in."

He had, waiting as she hung her raincoat and plucked off her muddy boots. Her domed dwelling had looked as he'd remembered it. Then she shook her hair back, no expression on her face as she'd taken his hand, led him to her bedroom, and began frantically ripping his coveralls off.

The miracle was that the bed hadn't collapsed from the impact of their naked and desperate bodies.

"So, what next?" he asked himself as he stared around Inga's. Being midday, the room was mostly empty. He lifted the stein to his lips and took a sip. Across the room, he could see Inga's big board. A new column, labeled "Taggart," now had two beers charged to it.

Great place, Donovan. A man with nothing could have credit for the asking.

He was considering just that fact when two of the transportees came clumping down the steps in muddy boots. Cap couldn't remember their names—he hadn't paid much attention to the transportees—but they were dressed in technician's overalls. Sighting him, they stopped, squinted as if unsure, then put their heads together.

A second later they started his direction, winding around tables, and stopped before his.

The first stood about six feet, looked to be in his early thirties, and had a lanky body that was mostly bones. His blue-eyed face, too, was thin, but dominated by a fierce nose mindful of a knife's edge.

His companion had a narrow skull and face, small mouth, and high brow. Black, piercing eyes gave him intensity, while his well-muscled body appeared used to hard work. The guy looked hard-used and might have been knocking on forty.

"You're Cap Taggart," the blue-eye Skull stated as if making a proclamation.

"That's right."

"Word is you're no longer a marine." The dark-eyed one's pronunciation was more circumspect.

"That's a matter of definition," Cap told him easily. "Once a marine, always a marine. Or so they say. As for my current circumstance, I am officially resigned from the Corps. Let's call it retired."

"Buy you a beer?" blue eyes asked.

"Got one. As you can see."

"Can we ask why you resigned?" Dark Eyes asked.

"You can ask anything you want. Doubt you'll get an answer."

They looked at each other.

Dark Eyes said, "I'm Abdul Oman. This is Fig Paloduro. We came in on the *Turalon*."

"How could I have missed that?" Cap took a sip.

"Hey, don't bust our balls just because you can. We're in the same situation as you are. If you resigned like you say, you're stranded here, too. Probably for the same reasons we are. The contract wasn't what they promised. And anyone with half a brain in his head isn't going to space off to certain death. Not in *Turalon*. And especially not in *Freelander*. You heard what they found on that wreck?"

"Can we sit down?" Paloduro asked.

"It's Donovan. You can do any damn thing you please."

In unison they dropped onto the bench. Oman propped his elbows on the table and leaned forward, an earnest expression on his face. "If we could ask, was your parting with the Supervisor amicable?"

He gave them a grim smile.

Again they looked at each other.

Paloduro asked, "Since you're on your own, what exactly are the nature of your plans? I mean, did the triumvirate offer you a job?"

"Nope. I was just sitting here contemplating what I might do next. Obviously, the two of you have a suggestion. Also obvious is the fact you want a fighting man, which brings you to me. So what particular skills do you want, and what are you willing to pay for them?"

The way they looked at each other was as predictable as gravity.

Oman spoke. "Our concern is the transportees. Abandoned by The Corporation, exploited by the triumvirate. You've heard of the suicides? Our people have no hope. We're trapped in hell. Some of us, we're looking to find a way, somehow, to make things right."

"As it is," Paloduro said, "our people are turning on themselves. Bickering, tearing each other apart. Even murdering each other, and the Donovanians don't care. 'Fair fight' they say, and wash their hands of the matter."

"It can't go on," Oman told him. "We need order, purpose, and to provide a unified front in our negotiations with the triumvirate and the Supervisor."

Cap glanced back and forth between them. "Okay, let's cut to the chase. How do you see this working?"

"The *Turalon* crew is deserting any chance they get." Oman glanced around uneasily. "We say let them."

"Ah, I see. You're wondering if I'm working undercover to catch them?" Cap laughed. "Good ploy, but I could give a rat's ass."

"Why?" Paloduro asked. "That flies in the face of everything you've lived your whole life. You were a marine."

Cap chuckled his self-amusement. "Listen, I've been out there. In the bush. Face-to-face with what Donovan's all about. Talina and I walked out. The locals are calling it a miracle. That's why I don't care. If the spacers want to go, I'm with you. Let them."

They did the clockwork look at each other.

"What about the transportees?" Oman asked.

"Gentlemen, whatever scheme you've got hatched up your sleeves, I'm not going to be your strongman. I've spent my life imposing someone else's will on people who didn't want it. I'm done with it. Over. Finished."

"You don't understand. It's for our people's own good. We need you, not just for the authority you bring, but for your skills and understanding. You've spent a lifetime in command. You know how to make people act in their own best interest. I'm not sure that Fig and I can do this without you."

"Ah, so you're thinking of your own triumvirate?"

Again the look.

"Captain Taggart," Paloduro's voice had a trace of desperation, "building a new society is never easy, never without its regrettable mistakes, but if we don't act now, our people are going to be forever miserable. Second-rate transportees cleaning toilets, washing dishes, digging ditches and mining clay when they are owed so much more."

"All it takes is leadership. Someone for them to look up to." Oman added quickly. "The kind of inspiration you could provide."

Paloduro spread his hands. "Officer Perez will listen to you. And when it comes to negotiations with Supervisor Aguila, she'll know the quality of the man she's sitting across from."

"You have the ability to save lives," Oman immediately followed up. "You can help us avoid those costly and bloody mistakes that people seeking social justice so often make. You can turn a rabble into a potent political force."

"I don't think you boys get it."

"Get what?" Paloduro asked. "We're offering you a seat at the table. Now. At the beginning. What you do with it? Where it takes you?" He thumped the table with a knuckle. "Hey, the future is filled with opportunity."

"Join us," Oman lowered his voice. "Help us build that future. Together, the three of us, with the people behind us, we can do this."

Hot on Oman's heels, Paloduro chimed in: "We can't have our people hanging themselves, slitting their wrists out by the fence. Sure, they're lost and angry, but that anger needs to be redirected into a productive direction. Used to bring this world and the Supervisor into compliance with the will of the people."

"What about *Turalon*'s crew?" Cap asked. "You want them to join this movement?"

"Absolutely," Oman said as if it were essential. "And you're just the person to bring them to us. They'll trust you. We need their expertise with *Turalon*."

Ah, I see. Cap smiled to himself.

"Good luck, gentlemen. I wish you all the best."

Again the shared looks, this time slightly startled.

"You don't have to make up your mind immediately, Captain," Paloduro told him. "Take a few days. Think about it."

"Of course." Cap saluted them with his beer stein. "Have good day, gentlemen. And, as far as the Supervisor is concerned, be assured that this conversation never happened."

"We didn't expect that it would be any other way," Oman said solicitously.

"Then you're nowhere near as good at this game as you think you are. Just be glad I'm no longer on The Corporation's side. So there, you don't need to spend the rest of the day wondering if you'd be better off sticking a knife in my back to keep me silent. Like I said, I don't give a shit. Best of luck to you."

He saw mystification behind their forced smiles.

"Do think about it, Captain." Oman gave him a half-hearted salute as he stood and headed for the door. Paloduro walked doggedly at his heels, head forward, speaking rapidly and softly into his compatriot's ear.

"Social justice," Cap whispered before tossing off the last of his beer. "The will of the people. Going to save them from themselves."

He made a face. "The miracle is that they can spout that shit despite millennia of death, murder, and misery. Worse, they can still tell those lies, and people still fall for them."

He walked over, tossed his cup to Inga, and emerged into the day. He glanced up and down the street, low-hanging rain clouds scudded above the domes and roofs. As he started down the street, he said, "So, Donovan, you're going to see just how bloody foolish human beings really are."

59

"Supervisor?" Astrogation Officer Nandi leaned into Kalico's personal quarters doorway. "I've got a delegation from the planet. Three Donovanians. Rode up on the last shuttle. They say they're here on Corporate business and are invoking the clauses in their contracts."

Kalico leaned back from the desk beside her bed. Her review of fuel stocks had been a distraction. Or perhaps she'd been going over them in the faint hope that the hydrogen tanks might be found to have insufficient fuel to justify risking a return to Solar System. That she had turned to such measures proved nothing more than the extent of her growing desperation.

Had she really seen herself coming out of that temple of bones? The further she got from the moment, the crazier it seemed.

As she studied Nandi, she saw again the woman's deep-seated grief and pain. Ah, yes, it was her fiancée. One of the crew on *Freelander.* An officer. Astrogation. Kenji something. No wonder Nandi was torturing herself. The woman's imagination had to be creating scenario after scenario of the conditions aboard *Freelander*, and in each, the man she loved was either complicit in mass murder, an acquiescent observer on the sidelines as the ghoulish death cult developed, or worse, an active accomplice.

And if the latter, Nandi had to be asking herself if she'd ever really known the man she loved. If the monster had been there all the time, hidden behind his smile, his warm touch, and the supposed love reflected from his eyes.

In the end, however, no matter what his role in the tragedy aboard *Freelander*, Nandi had to know that the femora that once supported him, the skull that had contained his brain and personality, the humeri, tibiae, phalanges, and ribs, all eventually found their place somewhere in that horrible building of bones.

What was that like for her? To look at that intricately assembled mass of wretched osteology and wonder which of the garish bits and pieces were his?

"Thank you, Astrogation Officer," Kalico told the shattered woman. "If you would escort them to the briefing room I will be there shortly."

Three Donovanians? Shit. It surely couldn't be Shig, Yvette, and that vile Perez. Shuttling up to see her? To demand what?

"Should have ordered Spiro to slip in during the night and cut their throats."

Spiro? Just the thought of the woman made her wince. Deb Spiro was no Cap Taggart. She was hell on the execution of an order, but totally lacking in imagination or resourcefulness. Everything had to be spelled out. To the letter. Initiative wasn't in the woman's vocabulary.

Kalico stood, arched her sore back, and paced across her opulent quarters. She was a Supervisor, after all. That exalted rank had earned her an incredible thirty-five square meters of the ship's precious living space.

She took a moment to consider it. *If I order us to space, this could be the extent of my universe for the rest of my life.*

She tried to picture eternity packed into these selfsame quarters. The only image that surfaced as an alternative reeked of bones, cleaned of their flesh, all painstakingly and intricately wired into a hollow dome for the worship of the dead.

She massaged her elbow, feeling the bony protrusions. Those very bones. Now warm and alive. Would they be treated any differently—having belonged to a Supervisor—as they were wired into the whole, interwoven with those of murdered transportees and dead crew?

A second image flashed, of her, scarred, and dressed in quetzal hide, but alive. *"If you go back . . ."*

"God, pus, and damnation, Kalico, get off of it, will you?"

She reached for her official jacket and slung it around her shoulders, sealing it tightly to accent her narrow waist, full bust, and wide shoulders. Then she combed and fluffed her hair, having added shine to it the night before to increase its luster.

She checked her reflection. Definitely not the image she'd adopt for the Boardroom. But impressive enough for Donovanians.

Kalico stepped out, sealed her hatch, and rode down a deck to the conference room.

The Donovanians were standing just inside the door, staring around uncomfortably. Not the triumvirate, but two men and a woman dressed in Donovan's best: quetzal coats and boots, chamois pants. To Kalico's relief, the holsters and scabbards on their belts hung empty. Not all of Nandi's sense had been lost to grief.

The older man had a leather hat in his cracked and callused hands and was gazing at her with gray eyes. A mane of silver-white hair hung to his shoulders, and stubble coarsened his cheeks. He might have been sixty, imposing in a wild sort of rough and tumble way.

The second man was dark, and white threaded his long black hair where it hung in a ponytail. Broad of shoulder, and in late middle age, he had light brown eyes, a scar on his cheek, and an almost feral look.

The woman, too, had to be close to fifty, shorter, with silver-streaked red hair and a complexion of sun-damaged wrinkles.

Kalico paced to the head of the table, turned on her heel, and perched herself behind the chair, hands on the back. "Good day. I am Supervisor Aguila. I am told that you are a delegation come to discuss contract obligations. Would you please state your names and specific concerns under contract?"

The gray-eyed wolf rolled his hat as he said, "I'm Lee Marston. Mining engineer. This feller to my left is Sahlie Shankara."

"And I'm Mollie Meyers," the woman stated firmly. "We're here because we want to go home. There's talk that *Turalon*'s being abandoned. That most of its crew is deserting, and that it's going to stay in orbit forever."

"That's news to me," Kalico said carefully. "As to desertions, we've had a few. They will be dealt with, I assure you. But *Turalon* remains spaceworthy."

What the hell was their agenda?

The men looked at each other, raising eyebrows. The woman, however, remained laser-fixed on Kalico. That trait, so common among Donovanians, still bothered her. Just like their declarations. Throw it out there—a statement of fact rather than a question. And here they were, just common labor, but they dared to address her as an equal. Didn't the damn fools understand the nuances of class and authority?

Marston said, "Well, that's a relief. We're holding you to the contract, Supervisor. We want to go home. We've done our share for The Corporation. Held up our end. More than. The three of us here, we worked long past term. We're owed."

"We've got family we want to take home to meet kin." Shankara stated, the words crisp. "People back there we want to see. I've got children who've grown into adults. I don't know if my parents are alive or dead. Friends I haven't seen since I spaced. I've got a life back there." He indicated his companions. "We all do."

Mollie Meyers had nodded aggressively as Shankara spoke. Now she added, "We need to hear it from your own lips. *Turalon*'s going home, right? She's gonna space for Solar System like the contract says."

Kalico bristled at the tones in their voices. "While I'm not used to being pinned to the wall for an immediate answer, I'll tell you that it remains the operative plan. Yes. That is my intention."

Was it? Or had their insolent tone forced her into it?

"Well, good," Marston almost growled. "There's a lot of stories going around down there. Word was that with the arrival of the ghost ship, you all had lost your nerve."

Kalico dug her fingers into the chair back, oddly curious. "You do know that there have been problems, correct? *Freelander*'s arrival is disturbing. I can imagine the kind of stories you've heard, but I will tell you this: Yes, they were all dead. Something went terribly wrong. The number of missing ships is concerning. There's no guarantee that *Turalon* will make it home. That said, why are you so adamant to make this journey?"

Shankara laughed, actually amused. "Like we said, we all got family back in Solar System. That, and some of us hate Donovan. Look at me. I'm fourth ship. I made it. Lost friends and my wife to that damned planet. More than once it come close to killing me, too. And all that time, I sweat blood and cried tears making The Corporation money. If you leave me on Donovan, it'll get me in the end. Maybe a cave-in, maybe a slug when I'm not looking. Poison water. A sidewinder. There's a thousand ways to die on Donovan."

"You think we're afraid of a little risk?" Mollie Meyers asked. "Life out here? It's all risk. I'm second ship. Got two kids left. Donovan took four others and two husbands. Space on *Turalon*? Sure, maybe she won't make it. Stay on Donovan?" She laughed. "What the hell makes you think I've got any damn chance of dying of old age on that damned rock?"

"There's a hundred and some of us," Shankara told her. "Donovanians and soft meat both. We've had it with Donovan. We want out. We're *demanding* you fulfill your contract obligations."

"Do not use that tone of voice with me."

Marston stuck out a knobby finger. "Word on the street is that you're scared to space out of here. We don't care. We want to go home. Honor your contract, and you'll have no trouble with us."

Word on the street? That I'm scared? She ground her teeth and wondered if the source had been Taggart. She should have never confided in the man.

"We want your word," Mollie Meyers told her. "Don't know that that means much to a Supervisor and Board mucky-muck like you, but it's a bond among us. You promise us that *Turalon* is going home. We're all packed. And since you told us the ship's still able to space, we're ready to go."

Kalico lifted her head, nostrils thinning. A violent rage rose like bile behind her tongue. *How dare they speak to me as if I were some pissant lackey!*

It took all of her control, voice icy, to state, "Right now. At this moment, I cannot make that promise." She raised a hand to still the protest. "I say that only because I have not received the captain's final report on the ship's systems. I cannot give you my word only to find out from her that there's a problem with a generator or the reactors."

Which was the truth. Up to a point.

"Fair enough," Marston warily agreed. "How soon?"

"A couple of days. It's my understanding that the engineers are mostly finished with their inspection."

"Three days," Mollie Meyers said with finality. "And if you don't space, we'll play hell down in Port Authority. You get that?"

"Given my marines, you might want to reconsider—"

"Supervisor." Shankara's eyes narrowed. "Bring 'em on. We got nothing left to lose."

Was the man out of his stark raving mind?

"We'll expect your answer in three days," Mollie Meyers added. "Come on boys, we can find our own way back to the shuttle bay."

Kalico stood as if paralyzed, stunned, as they turned and paraded out of the room. She could have them shot. Could order them arrested, shoved out a lock.

Donovan. Fucking Donovan. What the hell did it do to people?

"Bloody fools," Kalico whispered from between clenched teeth. "You don't know what you're asking."

The panicked laughter caught her by surprise, choked out of her own tight throat. Hot tears began to leak down her face.

60

Soft rain made a hissing sound on the roof of Talina's dome. Through the square of her bedroom window she could see distant strobing bolts of lightning. They illuminated the interiors of clouds—creating great soft-white lanterns that flickered silently. Patterns, torn tufts of cloud, marbled their surfaces as though some mystical artist had begun a composition and left it half-rendered.

The flickers of light strobed to highlight her hung uniform, her vanity, and storage trunk. For brief moments, scattered and crumpled clothing, free-flung boots, and two pistol belts hung from the headboard were illuminated and vanished.

She was looking in Cap's direction when the next white flash bathed his naked body. The thickness of muscled shoulders, his back like a V, the twin curves of his buttocks, backs of his thighs, and calves all ghostly white in an instant.

Then gone.

She reached up, placing her hands over his where it cupped her left breast. She pressed it down, compressing her breast, feeling the hard warmth of him, how the bones lay beneath his strong fingers.

Something about his touch—especially when so intimate—reassured her. Reminded her that she was still a woman—that no matter how the rest of the world saw her, her self-identity as a fully human female remained.

And why do I care?

The quetzal stirred down inside her, as if mildly interested. Mostly the thing was quiet during sex. As though the novelty and intrigue had passed.

So, how do quetzals do it?

"You know."

"If I did, why would I ask?"

Silence.

"Ask what?" Cap murmured.

"Never mind."

He shifted, turned his head on the pillow to look at her. A couple of seconds later, the soft white of distant lightning illuminated his face for an instant as he asked, "You given any thought to Paloduro and Oman? You saw them in the cafeteria. They're drawing a crowd with their speeches. In the business, we call that recruiting followers."

"Shig and Yvette say to leave them alone. People should be free to associate with whom they please. Even if it's not in their ultimate benefit."

"Paloduro and Oman don't share your philosophy. Sometimes I think you people have lost touch with just what kind of self-deluded idiots the rest of humanity can really be."

"So? What do you think they're after?"

"A world of their own making."

"That's nothing new for Donovan. We've been trying that for a generation now."

"The way they were talking about *Turalon*? I'm thinking they're planning to take the ship. They haven't a clue as to how. Yet. But if I know them, and if I remember the backgrounds from most of their followers, they're station people."

"Donovan must be a shock to their systems."

"You ask me, their ultimate goal is to turn *Turalon* into a station. They can live up in the sky, accessing Donovan's resources as needed. Stations aren't free places. Everything's ordered, right down to who lives where, does what, and when. It's a closed system."

"What if *Turalon* spaces first?"

"Then they move on *Freelander.*"

"More power to 'em. From what I've heard, it's a ghost ship. Haunted, and still filthy and unreliable."

"You know that Marston and two of his bunch had a meeting with Kalico? Told her in no uncertain terms that if she didn't space them home, they'd raise hell down here."

Talina rolled onto her side, probing the darkness in an attempt to see his expression. "Seriously? How'd you hear this?"

"Katsuro Miso, one of the marines, still talks to me. Marston and his people didn't want you, Shig, and the rest to drop any obstacles in their way."

"Yeah, they've got all their belongings and plunder stacked in crates by the gate. Got a twenty-four hour guard on them. Just waiting for word that they can load and shuttle up to *Turalon*. Why would they think we'd want to stop them?"

"How do I know how these things get started? Katsuro said he overheard them saying that Kalico would give them her answer in a couple of days."

Talina frowned into the darkness as she considered Marston. Must have been Shankara and Meyers with him if there were only three. Tough people. Honorable people. They didn't give a shit about the odds. They'd wanted to go home for years.

"Why didn't you tell me this?"

"Because you ripped my clothes off when I stepped in the door. Somehow that seemed imminently more important."

She frowned. "Okay, so Marston's folk want to leave. They'll do anything to force Aguila into spacing. You know Paloduro and Oman, what will they do when they hear this?"

"Not that I know them, per se, but I know their type. They're selling themselves to desperate and hopeless people who want to get the hell off Donovan and back to some sense of normalcy. They want to be leaders, form the new order. They promised me a third if I'd join them."

"Might have been a good deal. Maybe you should have taken it."

He shifted onto his elbow and glanced around her bedroom with its curving outer wall. "So, what if they march on Marston's group? Try and dissuade them from leaving. I know Kalico's scared down to her bones about spacing. She'd do anything to put that decision off."

"They march on Marston's people? Marston's bunch will leave their bleeding bodies to pave the streets. They're not the kind of people you want to try and push around. Donovan pushed them, and they're still standing."

"There's always the marines to keep things civil."

"They'll wait for orders before they intervene, right?"

"Of course."

"By then it will be too late." She considered the ramifications. "Shit, if Marston's people kill a bunch of soft meat, it'll split this community right down the center."

Talina took a deep breath, then sat up and threw her hair over her shoulder.

"What are you doing?"

"Getting dressed. I'm going to go stop this idiocy before it gets started."

Cap rolled off his side of the bed and flicked on the lights before reaching for his shirt and pants. "Then you'd better have backup. Your people might take you at your word, but the soft meat won't. They'll mouth off, and you'll shoot one before you think of the consequences."

"And that's bad?" she asked angrily. "Maybe they better figure out who the law is around here. Might keep a bunch of their sorry asses alive for more than a week or two."

"That's my Tal," Cap muttered dryly.

She slapped her belt around her hips, the pistol's weight reassuring. "And what about you, Cap? Showing up at my side? Sort of puts you in the middle, doesn't it?"

"Yep."

"Aren't enough people looking for a piece of your hide? And didn't you tell me that Oman and Paloduro made threats?"

"Yep."

"So, you want to just walk out there and make a target of yourself?"

"Be sure of it. If they're targeting me, and I've got your back, that keeps you safe."

"Why do I need to be safe?"

"Because I want to get you home in one piece again tonight so I can have seconds when it comes to ripping your clothes off." A flash of lightning illuminated his grin. "And then I want to sleep for the rest of the night with you curled safely in my arms."

They had just stepped out into the dark and drizzle when the sound of shouts and a shot carried from the direction of the shuttle landing field.

61

Kalico paced before Margo Abibi as the captain sat at one of the tables in the crew mess. The woman's light brown eyes followed Kalico as she spun and stalked her way back along the rank of chairs pulled neatly under the long table across from Abibi.

"I woke up from a dream this morning," Kalico told the captain. "Everything was so vivid: home. My apartment atop the Transluna skyline. So much space, the elegance, surrounded by art, the soaring columns supporting the transparency that allowed me to look down upon the whole thriving city."

She spread her arms, crying, "And, God, the food! Culinary miracles from every corner of Earth. The tastes, like magic in my mouth. I wore the finest of fabric, gossamer, like a caress to the skin."

She fixed her hard stare on Abibi. "I *ran* the damn Board! They came to *me*." She knotted a fist. "And beyond the splendor, the fawning Boardmembers, I could *feel* Solar System. It's expectant, waiting for my orders. I *am* Solar System.

"And just as I know this for certain, as I am about to order it all to function, to produce, and for all the people and machinery to commence their perfect operation, the door to my apartment smashes open. Everything stops as Shig Mosadek, that Yvette woman, and Perez burst in. In that instant, Solar System begins to shiver."

Kalico flung her arms wide. "And *boom*! The whole pus-sucking Solar System explodes. I pop awake. And where am I? Staring at the ceiling in my personal quarters on *Turalon*."

Abibi shoved her chair back far enough to extend her leg as if to ease a cramp. With her left hand, she rotated a zero-g cup around in circles on the tabletop. "I watched the holo record of the meeting you had with Marston, Shankara, and Meyers. What are you going to do? You've got two days."

"After the way they talked to me? I could send the marines down to kill them. That, or round them up and transport them off to one of those abandoned stations out in the bush and strand them."

"Violate the sacred Corporate contract?"

Kalico placed her hands to her face, pressing on her cheeks as if she could force some kind of sense into her frantic brain. "This is a world full of lunatics, all of them. Mentally disturbed and insisting they're sane."

"Are you going to space us for home?" Abibi asked softly, sympathy in her brown eyes. "It would be so much simpler if we just knew. Part of the desertions? It's the uncertainty. Order us to space, and I'll have the transportees shuttled up and we'll be headed out within six hours."

"Headed to what?" Kalico whispered. "That's the nightmare. As you said, the uncertainty."

Abibi nodded. "You ever read *No Exit*? It's an old play they make people read in university. A Frenchman named Sartre was the author. It's a story about being stuck in a room in Hell. That's what Donovan is. Like *No Exit,* there's a door out. You just don't know where it goes. It could be salvation, or it could just be another, deeper, and more horrible level of Hell."

Kalico raised a suspicious eyebrow. "Tell me the truth, how many have deserted?"

"About a third. I have sixty-seven officers and crew left." Abibi smiled. "And yes, I can space the ship. As soon as I do, those transportees are going to be in training for ship's duty. If they've survived Donovan for this long, they must be smart enough to learn reactor maintenance, electrical, even the finer arts of astrogation and field theory."

Kalico tried to see past the woman's light brown gaze. "What do *you* want to do? Off the record, Margo. Give it to me straight."

Abibi studied her coffee cup for a moment, looked for all the world to be at complete peace with herself. "I'm for spacing, ma'am. That's just who I am. What I've always been. *Turalon*'s my ship. Whatever voodoo mathematics they programmed into the qubit computers, they got us here. Unlike those fools dirtside, I'm staking my future in the stars."

Kalico felt a shiver run through her. *She thinks she can make it.* The effect hit her like the cold hammer of doom. She took a breath, struggling to keep the room from swaying.

When did I convince myself that she was going to urge me to stay?

"Captain, ma'am." A voice caused her to turn. Astrogation Officer Nandi stood uncertainly at the main hatch. "If this is a bad time . . ."

"No, come in, Nandi," Abibi called.

Nandi walked up, saluted, that glass-brittle look still behind her eyes. "Got the final report on *Freelander,* ma'am. Chief engineer Hans says she's stabilized. Reactors are synchronized and running at ten percent. She'll remain in orbit at The Corporation's beck and call for as long as it takes to get a salvage crew on her."

"Thank you, A. O." Abibi hesitated. "Nandi? Chan just found another log. Thought you might want to know that it mentioned Kenji."

Kalico watched Nandi stiffen, panic seeping into her expression.

Abibi seemed not to notice, a wistful smile on her lips as she toyed with her coffee mug. "I'm sorry, Nandi, but he was one of the first ones they eliminated. It's a short reference, just that Kenji, Sampson, and Putchulsky acted in defiance of orders. They were apprehended and killed while on the way to warn the transportees."

Nandi's head had pulled back, as if the muscles in the back of her neck were contracting.

"That's all there was," Abibi said gently. "I'm so sorry."

Nandi swallowed hard, and then as though a cool breeze washed through her, she relaxed, almost smiled. "Thank you, ma'am."

"Dismissed," Abibi told her. "Tell the crew to prepare to space upon orders." She glanced at Kalico. "That is correct, is it not, Supervisor?"

Fear ran cold through Kalico's nerves. "Yes, Captain. Correct."

But the way she said it, it felt like ordering herself to a death by slow torture.

Nandi saluted, spun on a heel, and marched, back straight, to exit the room.

"It's all right to be frightened, isn't it?" Abibi asked after the woman stepped out. "Makes life sweeter, every moment like a tonic."

"Perhaps," Kalico whispered. "Chan really find Kenji's name in the log?"

"No." Abibi gave her a conspiratorial wink. "But Nandi didn't need to know that, did she?"

"No. I suppose not."

"Part of being good at my job, Supervisor, is making sure that people in crisis have a way out that doesn't destroy them and others around them. That's how a good captain saves her ship and crew."

"Well . . . we all need to do what we need to do, Captain."

Kalico turned, nerved her muscles to support her, and walked with as much dignity as she could muster from the mess.

I am in Hell, and there is no way out.

"Damn you, Abibi."

62

Marsten's people had piled their belongings in the narrow gap between the high chain-link fence that separated the shuttle field from the town and the back of one of the warehouses. The piled crates and storage chests created a breastwork that couldn't be flanked. Not the sort of place a mob would want to attack. And it was dark—a shadowy area between the white cones of light where they illuminated the falling drizzle.

For the moment, the attackers had broken off, shouting insults. The people behind the barrier waited silently, dark forms that stood resolutely, their hats gleaming slightly as they shed water.

Cap drove into the melee, shouting, "Break it up! You are in violation of Civil Order 117, violence and inciting disorder! I'll have all of you rounded up and jailed!"

Dark as it was in the crowded space between the dome wall and the high shuttle field fence, the fighting, screaming brawlers had no clue who he was.

The soft meat—trained as they were to obey the voice of authority—broke off immediately. Dark forms shuffled back into the shadowy recesses.

"You assholes, stand down!" Talina bellowed, "or by God I'm going to do some ass-kicking like you maggots have never seen!"

"Tal? That you?" a voice called from behind a stack of duraplast crates.

"You bet your ass it's me, Marston. Want me to come back there and smack you on the side of the head so that you know for sure?"

"We didn't start this," Marston called uneasily. "They came out of the night. Told us to leave."

"That right?" Cap demanded, stalking toward the furtive figures who now backed away and filtered into the dark gap between the domes.

"That you, Taggart?" a voice called from the other side of the fence.

"Yeah. Spiro?" He saw the faint gleam of armor through the chain-link. A flicker of distant lightning left no doubt. "What the hell is going on here?"

"*Mister* Taggart, it's like Marston says. This mob came out of the night, tried to run Marston's group off."

From the dark gap in between the buildings, Paloduro's voice called, "You haven't heard the end of this, Taggart. You said you weren't taking sides."

"I'm not, you three-fingered fool. Get your people out of here, and don't come back."

Someone groaned, and Tal illuminated the form with her flash-light. And then another, and another. All told, seven people lay on the wet clay. Three weren't moving.

Cap bent down, checking the first casualty. Thick blood on his chest was already cooling. In the light of Tal's flash, he touched the man's eyeball. Got no reaction. "One dead."

Talina leaned over another, calling, "Bullet wound in the upper shoulder." She bent her head to her mic, "We need a medevac at the shuttle field fence. Roust Raya out of her bed and anyone else handy. Looks like four wounded."

"What the hell were they doing?" Marston called from behind his barricade of crates. "The way they tried to drive us off? These are our things! Our property and plunder."

"You're getting in someone's way," Talina told him, bending over another still form. "Shot this one through the head. Shit."

Cap walked over to the chain-link. "Lieutenant, what happened here?"

"Just like Marston said, *Mister* Taggart. They came out of the night. The bunch of them. Armed with clubs and kitchen knives. Told the returnees to get the hell away from the fence. Started to climb over the crates to force them out, and bam. The returnees started shooting."

"You were watching all this through night vision? Damn, Deb, why didn't you stop it?"

"Didn't have orders," she told him, a frigid tone in her voice. "Remember orders? Or have you forgotten those along with everything you once knew about responsibility, loyalty, and respect?"

From the darkness, another marine snorted agreement.

"So you let them kill each other?"

Spiro chuckled hollowly. "The Supervisor tasked us with the protection of Corporate assets. The returnees are all out of contract. Legally they are not our people to protect, only to transport. The transportees requesting transportation back to Transluna because their jobs were no longer available here, they are our responsibility. As events unfolded, I monitored the situation. Had the rioters threatened them, we would have taken action."

"Uh-huh, and most of your rioters are still under contract."

"They have been assigned jobs by the triumvirate. Technically they're not working for us. It's a gray area."

"Fucking space lawyer, what the hell happened to you, Deb? Use your head. We've got people dead and wounded. Where's your humanity?" He raised his voice, calling out to the dark figures. "And what about the rest of you? You're all marines. You took an oath."

"Don't lecture us about oaths, *Mister* Taggart. You walked out on all of us," Talbot called from the darkness.

"Sir!" Spiro snapped. "You are a *civilian*. As such, you will not address my personnel. Any conversation will be with me, with my permission. You do not, at this time, have that permission, so turn your ass around and do whatever it is that you civilians do."

"You hate me that much?"

"You walked out on us. I'd as soon cut your throat."

Cap sighed and shook his head, knowing she could see the disgust in his expression with perfect clarity. Worse, what the hell was she doing on the other side of the fence? Did she think her tech was going to give her the edge on the chance quetzal that might be prowling across the shuttle field?

Stepping over, he found Talina was rendering aid to the third casualty.

In her flashlight, a young man was grimacing, sweat popping on his pale face. A bullet had nearly torn his upper arm in two. His blood had pooled on the clay, streaks of it where the arteries had squirted.

"The cart's on the way," she said. "Fortunately Two Spots was on the com. He's drafted the night cleaning crew to help. In fact, that should be them."

Cap glanced up where lights bobbed as they rounded the admin dome.

"Well, something still works around here," Cap said with a sigh. His heart was thumping sullenly in his chest. Damn it, those were his people. His marines. He'd trained them for two straight years. Kept their morale up, built a sense of unit pride. And they treated him like this?

"Gotta see it from their side," Tal told him, as if reading his mind. "But still, orders or no, they could have stopped this before it got started."

"Yeah," Cap whispered, a slow sense of dread building. "But now that Paloduro and Oman's people have taken casualties, what happens next? How do we put the genie back in the bottle?"

"I've never understood that metaphor." Tal's bloody hands kept the tourniquet in place on the young man's arm.

"It's old," Cap told her. "Comes from the deserts back on Earth. Arabic I think."

Two Spots rolled the cart up. The people with him—dressed in coveralls and smelling of bleach—gaped at the dead and wounded displayed in the flashlight's white light.

Two Spots said, "Raya's on the way to the hospital. Whatcha got, Tal?"

"Help me get them lifted. Careful here. Keep this tourniquet tight, or we're going to lose him."

Cap helped load the three living, started along to help, but hesitated when Marston called from the dark crates, "Tal? You need anything from us? We square on this?"

"Yeah, Lee. We're square. I heard it from the lieutenant. They attacked you. It was self-defense. You did what you had to. But do me a favor, keep an eye on the dead. I'll be back for them just as soon as we get the wounded taken care of."

"Yes, ma'am," Marston replied.

"Come on, Cap," she told him. "Something tells me it's going to be a long night."

He started after her, hearing a snicker from one of the shadowy marines on the other side of the fence.

"Hope a quetzal gets him,"Tal muttered under her breath.

"Yeah," Cap whispered, feeling his own sense of cold betrayal deep in his breast.

"I'd cut your throat." The words lingered like a curse.

Spiro had meant it.

63

Dan Wirth nodded to Step Allenovich as he strode saucily down the hall and approached the door to the admin dome conference room. Allenovich—dressed in quetzal chic—stood with a booted leg thrust forward, a large rifle tucked in the crook of his arm. That he'd been posted as a guard for the door, more than anything else, indicated the gravity of the situation.

"Hey, Step."

"Dan. Glad you could make it. They're inside."

In a fit of irreverence, Dan flicked fingers to his forehead in a mock salute.

Inside, the room smelled of freshly boiled coffee. The place was small and shabby, with a scarred duraplast table and seven molded chairs. Maps covered the walls; a single dirty window in the back opened onto the chain-link fence and the shuttle port beyond with its crazily piled containers.

He knew Shig Mosadek and had seen Yvette Dushane often enough to know who she was. Talina Perez needed no introduction, her large, dark eyes almost glistening with dislike. Trish Monagan sat perched on a desk shoved into the room's far corner, her arms crossed under her delightfully shaped breasts. He might have been walking fungus given the way she looked at him.

He grinned at her and winked, which brought fire to her green eyes.

Unexpected, however, was Cap Taggart's presence, dressed as he was in quetzal and chamois. Recently dried bloodstains still spotted his sleeves and pants. Of course it was all over town that he'd either quit or been booted from the marines. His presence in the room this morning? Good lateral move from one seat of power to another.

But then Dan had always thought Taggart was a talented man. Who else could have slipped so quickly into Nandi's bed?

All the more reason why he really hated the guy.

"Very quiet out there on the way over," Dan greeted. "Hardly anyone on the streets. And those you see? Not even a greeting called by old friends. Most tense if you ask me. Must have been quite the set-to last night."

"The town is indeed on edge, Mr. Wirth." Shig opened with his placid smile.

"Have a seat," Yvette offered. "Coffee?"

"That would be very nice." Dan settled himself into the round-bottomed chair and kept his most charming smile in place as he nodded to each of the participants.

Well, well, the high and mighty have come to me. A welling of satisfaction warmed his chest. *Oh, Father, you miserable prick, if you could only see me now.*

Trish set a cup of steaming coffee on the table before him, her gaze as inviting as green frost.

"I heard there were four dead," Dan began.

"Five," Talina told him, her dark eyes hot enough to sear holes in sialon. "A young man whose arm was shot off died on the cart before we could get him to Raya."

"And the shooters?"

"*Turalon* cleared them for transport up to the ship this morning. They'll be gone by midday at the latest," Yvette told him.

"Then things should settle down?" Dan asked mildly.

"That depends," Shig said easily. "Sometimes these events trigger more events, take on a life of their own. Other times agency can mold the direction, intensity, and duration of such squabbles."

"Which agency? I haven't seen a door marked 'Bureau of Public Squabble.'"

Shig's smile irritated the hell out of Dan as the man said, "The agency of human action. Call it the wildcard in your poker game. In times of stress, a single person can often unexpectedly influence the outcome of great events. An entire branch of social science has been devoted to its study."

Dan kept his smile in place. Shig had just neatly, inoffensively put him in his place. A most subtle man, this Shig. Not one to be underestimated.

"And you've asked me here to become this agent?" He spread his hands. "Gentlemen, ladies, I have no part in whatever objective Palduro and Oman are after."

"Of course you do," Cap told him, right eye narrowed in a deadly squint. "See, the thing is, when people are killing each other in the streets, plotting attacks, swearing revenge—not to mention bleeding and dying—they're sure as hell not tossing dice down a craps table." He paused to add, "Income suffers."

"Captain, you do make a point."

He waited, letting them make the next play.

To his surprise, Trish Monagan said, "We know the ringleaders hang out in The Jewel. You're a Skull yourself. Arrived on the *Turalon*. One of theirs. They feel safe there."

"That would be my clients' personal business. Meddling in the affairs of others—as the good captain noted—leads to a reduction in income."

"Which leaves you at something of a disadvantage, doesn't it?" Yvette asked. "If they're rioting, they're not gambling and whoring. And if you were to suggest a different course of action on their part, you're in jeopardy of being accused of meddling and still stand to lose."

"Not to mention," Shig noted, "as your business becomes more and more identified with the disgruntled, fewer and fewer of the rich Donovanians will be willing to patronize your tables. And—as the complaints of the *Turalon* demonstrators so aptly proclaim—the Skulls are . . . how do I put this? Of limited financial means and prospects? It seems you'd want more of the former and fewer of the latter."

Dan chuckled. "Nice try."

They'd expected any answer but that. He leaned forward over his coffee. "See, here's the thing: I've got a brand new safe. Big thing. Tyrell Lawson made it. Clever man, that Lawson. He even figured out a way to bolt it to that huge sialon and steel slab it sits on. It'd take explosives to knock it free now that the adhesives have set."

"And what does a safe have to do with anything?" Yvette asked him.

"It's what's in the safe." Dan smiled. "Sharp lady like you, I'd expect you'd already have figured out why I brought it up. Surely not because I give a particular shit about Lawson's great work, but there it is."

"All right, fart sucker, I'll bite," Trish growled. "What's in the safe?"

"Yuan, SDRs, nuggets, gemstones . . ." He frowned for effect, as if forgetting. "Oh, and a whole folder full of deeds for lots, domes, and businesses." He held up a hand. "Wait! There's more. Seems to me there's a second folder full of notes. Loans that I've made to several of the town's leading figures. Take Inga, for example. Needed a couple hundred SDRs to pay for a truckload of barley. Something about how her creditors were a little late paying up. Seems that cash has been flowing, but most of the money paid out recently from The Corporation has gone to the farmers. Most other folks are in hock up to their asses because they forked over their plunder to pay for town lots, buildings, and pieces of equipment when the Supervisor decided to sell. That cash flow hasn't quite balanced out yet."

"And you get a percentage on these loans that you're making," Yvette filled in.

Dan adopted a pained look. "Kind of causes me a bit of anxiety. Like, what do I call my place? The Jewel Casino and Bank?"

"Your point?" Cap asked.

"A bit slow, aren't you, Captain?" Dan sipped his coffee, meeting the ex-marine's hard gaze. "Let the local politics work out as they will. Any slacking of business because my fellow Skulls are upset, frustrated, and angry, or because the shiny-leather-folk—like you all here—are pissed, is a short-term problem at best, a minor irritation at worst."

He was aware of the violence brewing in Officer Perez's black eyes, the thinning of her mouth.

He lifted a hand in surrender. "Oh, sure. You could apply pressure. Threaten. Maybe do one of those 'raid-in-force' searches of my place. You know, break up the furniture looking for"—he hooked his fingers like quotation marks—"*contraband*." A beat. "Won't do you any good."

"Why not?" Cap asked.

"Because I'd have to repair the damage. That would mean I'd have to call in loans from all over Port Authority. That or seize the businesses, property, or equipment listed as collateral down in the fine print. I have that right in the event of natural disaster or social discord."

"You piece of shit," Perez hissed through gritted teeth.

"Hey, Officer, I'm just a businessman. Don't vent on me. Take it up with Paloduro and Oman. They're the cause of your current difficulties. Me, I'm just a bystander."

Perez started to stand, one hand on her pistol, only to have Shig Mosadek lay gentle fingers on her gun hand. With a feathery touch he guided her back down to her chair.

Still, the glistening and almost alien look in her eyes sent a shiver down into Dan's bones. Fuck, what was it about the woman? She worried him like no other living human being.

In an effort to regain his equilibrium, Dan smiled thinly. "Now, all that said, I'm not unsympathetic."

"Really?" Yvette tried to keep the scorn from her voice.

"Really," Dan said mildly. "Violence in the streets? How ugly. Property can be damaged. Including my own. People killed. That sort of thing can be like a steel splinter, driven deep. It festers, and years later it can burst out again."

Shig, whose mellow expression had never changed, finally let loose of Perez and said, "We have at least one ray of light in all this. The returnees will be off planet within hours. Your festering splinter, as you call it, will be removed from our flesh. What remains is to ensure that another splinter doesn't find its way into the currently exposed and vulnerable hide of our people."

"Good point, Shig. So, tell me. What have you got in mind, and how do I profit from it?"

"You? Profit from—" Perez was cut off as Mosadek's retraining hand shot out with amazing rapidity.

"Glad you can keep her under control, Shig," Dan said solicitously. "We'd never get to the point."

As Perez turned molten and volcanic, Shig said, "We're not without sympathy for the new people. The Corporation brought them out here on a promise, only to find absolute disappointment. They have nothing. Not even a way home, since even their desperation cannot overcome their fear or distaste when it comes to spacing back on *Turalon*."

"Yeah, they've got better odds betting red fifteen on my roulette wheel."

Shig said, "We are willing to work with them. And we have a great deal more latitude to do so now that *Freelander*'s cargo is piled on the shuttle field. We're willing to deal with individuals on a case-by-case basis to meet their needs and minimize the dislocation they are feeling."

"You've had free rein," Yvette added coldly. "It would be a shame if we were to start causing you problems, wouldn't it? Ordinances, laws, asking for protection money, fines, and fees."

God all-fucking-mighty it feels so good to have them on their knees!

Dan kept the delight glowing in his breast from showing on his face. "Listen, we're all in the same ship here. Now that we've got the chest-thumping over with, truly, I'm not unsympathetic. It's my community, right? I need to live in it like all the rest of you. So yeah, I'll help with your little problem."

"How?" Perez snapped.

"Hey, Officer, down. I'm on your side."

He kept his lips from twitching as she, Taggart, and Monagan seethed behind gritted teeth.

Hands raised in mock surrender, he told them, "Let me deal with Paloduro and Oman in my own way. Give me a week to get everything under control. I know these people. Spaced with them for two years."

He paused, looked at Mosadek suggestively. "You got an inventory for *Freelander*'s cargo?"

"Unfortunately, no. The ship's records were destroyed." Yvette told him. "*Turalon*'s crew just unloaded the hold. Piled it all akimbo on the field outside the fence."

"Why would you care if there were an inventory?" Cap Taggart almost spat the question.

"Because there's equipment there that can help the transition for some of the soft meat," Dan told them reasonably. "Take poor old Pete Morgan. He's absolutely terrified to space back on *Turalon*. Figures he's going to be murdered and thrown in the hydroponics like those fools in that bone pile aboard *Freelander.* A core drill—not as good as a rotary bit, I'm told—and seismic equipment were supposed to be on *Freelander.* If it's there, he's suddenly got his job back. The Corporation thinks there's hydrocarbons in the rocks somewhere out in the hinterlands. It's at least hope for them."

"We can work with that," Shig said. "Your help will be deeply appreciated. You will be doing us a huge favor."

"Favor?" Dan gave the man his best and most winning smile. "Let's call it a partnership, shall we? I'm a businessman, after all. Since I'm joining the cabal here, I want a percentage. Nothing big. Just compensation for my time. Oh, and a seat at your council meetings."

The room went coldly silent.

Dan stood, tossed off the last of the coffee. "Good stuff you brewed there, Trish."

He turned, stepped out, and closed the door behind him. As he nodded at Step, Perez was shouting, *"Toilet-sucking son of a bitch! I'm going to shoot that pus-sucking maggot in the back!"*

"Touchy, aren't they?" he asked Allenovich as he started down the hallway, a skip to his stride.

Wonder how long it's going to take them to cave?

And if they didn't, there'd be another riot tonight. Something that would bring them to their senses.

But it would have to be done carefully. No sense in pissing off the other Donovanians.

64

Kalico sat in the observation dome and stared down at Donovan where the planet passed slowly below the orbiting *Turalon.*

Swirls and clots of white cloud contrasted with the green-brown patterns and textures on the surface. Mountain ranges crisscrossed the blue-green verdure. To the north, the world turned tan, accented by glaciers and snowfields as the planet's curvature gave way to the polar region.

She could make out the Gulf—a round bite out of the gently undulating coast of the continent. From a rim of aqua shoreline the water immediately darkened to a deep royal blue that matched the ocean's tones to the east.

The returnees had been boarded for a couple of hours. Their possessions were stored, and they'd been assigned bunk space in the barracks. Abibi had what was left of her crew conducting the last of the checks.

"I can go," Kalico whispered to herself. "Just give the order."

The image of her emerging from the temple of bones seemed to hang in her memory. "If you go back . . ." she whispered in time to the apparition's utterance.

Even as she said it, the cold fear ran through her. The nightmares that woke her—night after night—seemed to loom in the air behind her: An eternity. Locked in these corridors and rooms. Ghosts prowling around her ancient and withered corpse as it rotted in some dark recess.

I don't want to die that way.

How had she come to this? She'd been fearless back in Solar System. Willing to tackle any risk despite the probability of her destruction should she fail. She ground her teeth, knotted her fists. What had Donovan and *Freelander* done to her?

She only needed to give the order. One word to Margo Abibi: "Space."

And she couldn't. If she so much as took a breath in anticipation, the sick curling started in her gut. It might have been the same if a cold pistol muzzle were being pressed against her temple. To have uttered the word would have been to pull the trigger.

"Ma'am?" Abibi's soft voice called from the other side of the pressure hatch.

"Come in," Kalico said softly, refusing to pry her gaze from the planet. They were out over the eastern ocean now, crossing the terminator, the Gulf falling behind toward the sun-bathed horizon.

"Your com's off. Lieutenant Spiro was looking for you. She's got seven of her marines in hack. Three, Garcia, Talbot, and Shintzu, are missing. The eight who stood with her had to force the others onto the shuttle just before the last lift. She told me she's going to have to bring charges for insubordination."

"Shit."

Abibi was giving her that calm, brown-eyed stare, as if seeing into her soul.

Abibi seemed to hesitate, then took a breath. "Something else, ma'am. A delay I'm afraid. Nothing serious. Just a recalibration of reactor six. Figure twelve hours before we can space."

"I see."

"I was wondering, ma'am, if you might want to take those marines. There's the question of *Freelander.* It should probably be decided. Ownership, I mean. We're spacing. You're leaving that ship in orbit. Mighty tempting for the triumvirate, don't you think?"

"Tempting?"

"Yes, ma'am. Floating around in orbit like it is. Mosadek and Dushane might look at it as a prize to be looted. Stripped. You ask me, it wouldn't do to have the next ship to Donovan arrive and find what's left of *Freelander* to be nothing more than orbiting hulk. Questions might be asked. 'Boardmember Aguila, did you or did you not have a written agreement with the Donovanians that *Freelander* was Corporate property, and not to be touched?'"

"How would they get to it? They don't have a shuttle. We berthed them all on *Freelander.*"

"You willing to bet your career on that? That they can't build one? Lot of talent down there."

Kalico stared thoughtfully at the dark ball of planet below. "It's impossible."

"Spiro said that the people who attacked the returnees figured to eventually take *Turalon.* Turn it into a station. Why wouldn't they move on *Freelander* the moment we space?"

A sudden anxiety grew in Kalico's heart. "You're right."

A reprieve? Perhaps a day? Another chance to ask herself if she was making the correct choice?

"Just doing what I have to for my ship and crew, ma'am."

Kalico nodded, forcing herself up from the seat. "Very well, prepare the shuttle. Have Spiro assemble her marines. I'll need all of them to make a statement of force. Even the ones under disciplinary action."

"Yes, ma'am," Abibi told her, a sympathetic smile on her lips.

As the captain followed her out of the dome, she said, "I've taken the liberty of having your possessions packed and stowed on the shuttle." Abibi's gaze sharpened, boring into Kalico's with the full intent of her message: *I'm giving you a way out.*

"Thank you, Captain." The fist that had been tightening around Kalico's heart seemed to loosen, and for the first time in days, she realized she could take a deep breath.

"I've told my people that, pending counterorders from you, we're ready to space in twelve hours. I'll expect to hear from you sometime within the next twelve hours in the event you wish to change those orders. Otherwise, I will proceed at my own discretion." Abibi carefully asked, "Do you understand?"

Again the boring gaze told her: *I'm leaving in twelve hours unless you object.*

"Whatever you think is best." Kalico waved her acceptance.

The walk down to the shuttle bay might have been on legs filled with helium. "*Freelander.* My God, what could I have been thinking?"

"Way too much on your plate, ma'am," Abibi told her in that crisp voice of command. "And then there's the matter of the *Freelander* cargo. It's still technically yours to do with as you see fit."

Kalico nodded, having no idea what might have been in that gaping hold. Her concern had been getting it down-planet.

"Just a thought, ma'am, but those transportees down there are still under contract. Backed by the marines, you could still dictate the conditions of their employment. No one on the planet could prohibit your enforcement of the terms."

In other words: *You've got all the means for success at your disposal down there.*

"That's true," Kalico said, swallowing against the curious pounding in her chest. Twelve hours. She had twelve hours before Abibi spaced. All it would take was a call.

As they walked into the shuttle bay, Lieutenant Spiro was standing at the hatch, dressed again in battle armor, her helmet hanging, a look of curious relief on her normally dour face.

As Kalico approached, the lieutenant snapped off a salute, asking, "Did the captain speak correctly, ma'am? You wanted the mutineers, too? I mean, I've got them in bonds aboard the shuttle, but we packed in their armor and tech."

"That was correct, Lieutenant. You may board."

"Supervisor?" Abibi said at the last instant.

Kalico turned, one foot on the threshold. "Yes?"

"We've noticed some problem with the Port Authority radio. Some of their communications come through garbled. Just wanted that stated for the record, ma'am."

Again, the message was clear: *That's my alibi if you ever come back and accuse me of abandoning your ass down there.*

"Understood, Captain."

Abibi saluted, mouth working, as if she were biting off words. Her almost-tan eyes reflected a conspiratorial wariness as she said, "If there's any change in your plans, I'll hear from you within twelve hours. Good luck, ma'am. As to *Turalon,* we're the best in space. Don't worry about us."

And with that, Abibi spun on her heel and marched—back straight—for the companionway stairs that led up to officer country.

Kalico bit her lip, turned, and stepped into the shuttle.

Her stomach was no longer acid as she strapped in behind the pilot's seat and closed her eyes.

Margo Abibi, bless you for the savior that you are.

65

The tables in The Jewel were filled with Skulls—and that damn Shig had been right. The amounts they were betting was what, in the trade, was called "chickenshit." Mostly chump change, hardly an SDR among them. And what they had left was quickly changing to drink instead of wagers.

Angelina—as proof of the marks' poverty—prowled without purpose among the tables, dropping a word here, patting a shoulder there, but finding no action.

Talk was dark, angry, about the five bodies that had been carted out to the cemetery that morning and dropped into graves that a backhoe had summarily chopped out of the damp red dirt.

And, of course, about the returnees who'd skipped justice and now floated safely above in the heavens.

"My hope"—Paloduro sang out loudly enough for half the room to hear—"is that they space. Vanish. And die like those bastards on *Freelander* did. Slowly. Eating each other until the last one is a fucking half-rotted skeleton."

Fig had paraded himself around *Turalon* for two years, bragging about how he was going to set himself up with a hard-rock mine. His skill—or so he had claimed—was in his abilities to program mucking machines. That with his new programs, the machines could sort good ore from waste, identifying minerals and metal content through a sophisticated laser and sonic scan.

He might still have a chance to prove himself. The mucking machines were supposedly somewhere in the clutter of *Freelander*'s cargo where it lay piled out beyond the fence.

Assuming, that is, that he wanted to give up his newfound status as one of the protest leaders. Somehow, Dan just couldn't see Paloduro surrendering a top spot in the fiery movement that earned him free drinks, accolades, and slaps on the back. What was that compared to the joy of sitting in a dark hole watching a clunking mechanical marvel sort rocks?

Oman—Fig's companion in mayhem—sat across the table, his eyes distant, cards forgotten in his hand. The man had that stunned look on his face. He'd been one of the loudest in calling for the raid on the returnees. That it had gone so badly, that men had died, seemed to have taken something out of him.

"Yeah," Dan whispered, dealing himself four out of the five cards needed for a club flush. How had he managed to screw up and get a diamond in there? "Tough call last night, Oman."

It could be tougher for the both of them if the triumvirate came through.

As if on cue, Cap Taggart stepped through the door, paused, and took in his surroundings as his eyes adjusted from the sunset glare outside.

"Well, well," Dan whispered to himself and slipped the pistol from his belt and into the wire holder he'd rigged to the underside of the table. Smiling, he stood, spreading his hands.

"Welcome to my humble world, Captain. I'm so glad you could wiggle a little time free from your busy schedule. You here for a game? Or by chance have you come bearing word on my proposition?"

Taggart prowled his way across the room, looking side to side, seeming to see everything, one hand on the military-grade pistol at his hip. The quetzal-hide jacket he wore glimmered in rainbow patterns as it passed beneath the lights.

"Have a seat," Dan told him with a smile. "Allison, oh love of my life," he boomed, "bring us a couple of glasses. Oh, and that brandy Inga's so proud of."

Taggart hesitated, his cold, blue-eyed gaze still skipping around the room, as if wary of an ambush. Paloduro and Oman were frozen, expressions hard as they stared icily at Taggart.

Heedless, Dan dropped back into his chair, hands still spread inoffensively wide. "Oh, come, Captain. Even if Shig and Yvette bowed to Security Officer Perez's adamant objections and told you to come spit in my eye, you don't think I'd be foolish enough to take it out on you."

Allison appeared, a saucy sway to her hips, glasses and bottle in her hand. Taggart eased himself down into the chair.

"There," Dan said easily as Allison set the glasses down and poured. "Not so hard, was it?"

Taggart watched Allison's retreat as she headed back to the cage, her walk accented to display the rounded curves of her ass. That was Allison, fully aware that every male eye in the place followed her.

"Who would have thought an angel like that would be waiting on a rock like Donovan?" Dan said with a sigh. He took up his glass. "To opportunity." He raised it in a toast.

Taggart—his stare still glacial—studied him for a couple of heartbeats, then lifted his glass, saying, "Whatever that means." And tossed it off.

Dan drank, smacked the glass down, and sighed. "Not bad, don't you think? Of all the things I was told to expect, fine drink wasn't on the list for Donovan."

"Looks to me like you've found more than brandy on Donovan."

"Hard to believe they sent me here to take care of cows, huh?"

"Yes, who'd have thought? If it hadn't been for that little incident with Nandi, I wouldn't even have known you were aboard. You camouflage better than a quetzal."

Dan's heart skipped. Nandi? The lying slit. Oh, to have savored her throat crushing under his fingers. To have watched the terror in her eyes fade, her pupils widen as her heartbeat slowed.

"You haven't done so badly yourself, Captain. We both know Nandi's charms, but what's it like? Cycle down-planet, slip out of Nandi's bed and into Talina Perez's?"

He raised his hands defenselessly. "Not that I'm complaining! I know firsthand how much of an improvement Allison made in my life. So I sure don't hold it against you for doing the same." He winked. "I like the wilder action myself."

Taggart's jaw muscles bunched, jumped. His eyes narrowing into frigid slits. "After the things Nandi told me about you, I'm surprised you had the courage to try and get it up with another woman."

A chill wave ran through Dan's bones and nerves. He felt the rage—hot and red—stir down in his gut. It burned, went white-hot along his spine. Then that part of him went blank, his heart slowing, a crystalline clarity sharpening his senses. As he twirled the brandy glass with a distracting left hand, his right slipped below the table to the pistol grip.

"Did you have a purpose for coming here today? Or are you simply tired of life? You and I, we teeter on the balance right now."

"Clairvoyant, are you?"

"Captain, I foresee a very short and bitter future for you. Don't push it further. Now, do you have a message for me?"

"You have a deal. That's the message from the triumvirate. God help them. So there it is. You've been told."

Dan's finger slipped along the trigger, tension building, his heartbeat slowed to a steady, emotionless beat.

Not now, you fool! Not here.

Dan smiled, removed his hand, and waved. "I want you out of my establishment."

Taggart stood, a thin smile on his lips, promise in his eyes. "Just so we're clear. Your deal is with Shig, Yvette, and Talina. Me, I'm my own man. So I wouldn't disappoint them, if I were you. Right now, they're all you've got."

Dan had to give the fool credit. He was smart enough to back away from the table, one hand on his pistol. Nor did he take his eyes from Dan's, using peripheral vision to make his way to the door and out into the dying light.

"You're a dead man, Captain Taggart. And more than that, I know where you live." He winced as he imagined the lies that had spun out of Nandi's lips.

Well, *Turalon* hadn't spaced yet. Perhaps there was a way to settle with her, too. After all, one of the first things he'd managed to do was to cultivate the talent necessary to handle the more distasteful projects.

"Art?" he called. "If I could have a word back in the cage?"

He slipped his pistol back through his belt, stood, and met Art Maniken at the cage door.

"What have you got, boss?" Art's normally emotionless eyes quickened as he followed Dan into the office's privacy.

"A job, Art. About as delicate a job as I could ask a man to do. It'll take judgment, finesse. And when you're done, nothing. And I repeat, nothing can be traced back to us. Do you understand?"

Art grinned, exposing a cracked incisor.

Oh, yes. The man lived for assignments like this.

66

The whine of heavy equipment, the hollow bangs of the grapples, and the straining of hydraulics came from the jumbled piles of crates and containers. Skid loaders labored to make sense out of the piled mess that had been haphazardly dropped on the landing field margins. Pamlico Jones and his crew of six had made some semblance of order out of the tangle of equipment, aircars, bundles of struts, beams, tarping, haulers, excavators, and odd-looking rigs whose purpose Talina couldn't guess. In lockstep, she and Trish marched out past the man gate and onto the shuttle field.

They were still days from getting it all sorted, let alone opened and inspected to make a determination of what was salvageable and what was junk. Some of the bigger pieces of equipment had been towed through town to the maintenance sheds. A couple of the excavators and loaders had actually taken a charge and ran on their own power. At least for a ways.

The crates and containers, however, would each have to be opened to figure out what they held, laboriously inventoried, and routed to the proper storage.

Assuming people didn't all kill each other first.

Port Authority might have been a pressure cooker. Bad enough that the Skulls were still stewing. Worse that Shig and Yvette had outvoted her when it came to that slug-in-the-mud Wirth. Now here she was, right at sunset, watching the silver delta of a shuttle winging in from over the Gulf, its shriek as threatening as a quetzal's.

What the hell does the Supervisor want now?

Trouble, no doubt about it.

Talina laced her fingers around her pistol grip. The contours formed to her hand, reassuring, firmly filling her palm.

"Shit in a toilet, I want to shoot someone," she growled. Worse, it had been Cap who'd volunteered to take the one-word answer to Wirth: Deal.

As a result, it had fallen to Talina and Trish to meet Aguila's shuttle as it came in.

"Do you just want her stepping off alone?" Shig had asked when she met him in his office earlier. "Getting into who knows what kind of nonsense?"

"No. But what *does* she want?"

"Two Spots just said she needed to speak to the three of us. Better that Yvette and I prepare ourselves to look at least moderately professional and in control. Especially if this has anything to do with the attack on the returnees. Who knows what they might have told her about last night?"

"We could have used the radio," Trish had growled. "Sent her a message: 'We've got it under control. Now space your ass out of here. And don't come back.'"

Shig's smile had beamed as he said, "Trish, the fine art of diplomacy has never seen the like of your poise, grace, or wit."

"Thank God," Yvette had murmured.

The distant sound of thrusters could be heard as they ripped through the air.

Talina stared out at the bush, wondering where the quetzal had gone—the one seen that first day when The Corporation had roared back into their lives.

The beast in her belly seemed to settle smugly under her heart.

"And I haven't forgotten your game either," she told the creature. "Molecules, huh?"

"What was that?" Trish asked, arms crossed, her pistol grip sticking out suggestively. Wind teased her auburn hair.

"Just talking to my quetzal," Talina quipped.

"You worry me sometimes."

"Here comes the dust."

The shuttle backed air, rotated into the wind, and touched onto the seared clay. As the thrusters spooled down, the struts compressed; the sleek craft rocked like a raptor settling into a nest.

Pamlico's crew had stopped their reshuffling of crates to watch, and now went back to grappling and reorganizing a series of haphazardly stacked containers.

"You sure would have thought the vaunted Corporation would have done a better job unloading that stuff," Trish noted. "It's like they tossed shit wherever they could."

"Ghost ship, remember?" Talina asked. "They wanted it the hell off *Freelander* so they could either desert or scurry back to *Turalon* where the Lords of Xibalba wouldn't get them."

"The Lords of who?"

"Xibalba. The Mayan underworld where the Lords of the Dead and monsters live. It's an old story among my mother's people back in Chiapas."

"But this is Donovan."

"Where everything is different," Talina agreed. "That's why our underworld full of the haunted dead is now up in the sky. A cruel sort of inverted symmetry, don't you think?"

The ramp dropped as the shuttle thrusters' whine thinned into silence.

Talina started forward, hand on her pistol as the apparently requisite marines trotted down to take up position. They'd no more than hit dirt before Supervisor Aguila, dressed in a black, form-fitting one-piece suit, followed.

Apparently she'd learned. This time her thick wealth of black hair had been pulled back and clipped. Her shoes were also eminently more practical.

Talina tried to read the woman's expression as she approached; Aguila's lips were pursed, hands behind her back. This time she was looking around, as if really seeing the planet. The way she walked, the slow swinging of her feet, communicated hesitation, perhaps relief.

Her attention fixed on Pamlico's crew, where they used a forklift to back a crate out of a mess of containers that reminded Talina of jumbled children's blocks. Then the woman fixed on Talina, a smile that spoke of inevitability bending her lips.

"Security Officer Perez," she greeted. "And her loyal sidekick, Trish Monagan. Of course they'd send you."

"Shig thought a band and a parade would be a little over the top. How can we help you, Supervisor?"

"A few last details need to be worked out. Shouldn't take more than a couple of . . ."

"Talina!"

They turned at the frantic shout from across the field.

Pamlico Jones was standing on the forklift seat, waving as he called, "You better come see this. We got trouble. And it ain't good."

"Now what?" Trish grumbled.

"Excuse us," Talina said.

"No, we'll all go. See what sort of trouble you now have." Aguila almost laughed. "I could use the amusement."

Side by side, Talina and Trish led the way, Aguila and her marines followed in formation. And to make the joke complete: Who would have guessed that the Supervisor and her security acted as their own little parade?

Jones had climbed down from the humming forklift; he and his three helpers stood in a knot where they'd just pulled a room-sized sialon container back.

"Whatcha got, Pam?" Talina asked, and stopped to study the recessed area surrounded by the crates.

"Thought this was funny looking," Pamlico said, gesturing. "They'd left a container on top, sort of like a cap, you know? Then we pull this one out of the way, and here's this space all left behind it. And, well, see?"

See she did.

The quetzal inside her hissed its excitement.

Stepping forward, hand on her pistol, Talina took it all in. The containers had been placed to create a sheltered enclosure, bounded on all sides, with narrow gaps that allowed ingress and egress. A tarp had been tied up as a rain fly to shelter bedding where four people had slept. Plates, pans, ration kits, and personal items were strewn around, proof that they'd been there for a while.

She caught the smell at the same time she recognized the mounded excrement; the quetzal shrilled victoriously inside her. What looked like soiled rags told the rest of the story. Scattered about, torn, they were the remnants of coveralls. And there was a boot, another there, and another, and another.

"Trish?" she warned.

"Yeah!" Trish had already pulled her pistol, backing against Talina, eyes scanning the container tops.

"What's going on here?" Aguila asked. "What is all this?"

"Spiro?" Talina shouted. "Weapons at the ready and hot! We got a quetzal."

"Fuck and shit!" Pamlico and his crew scrambled for the rather insubstantial safety of the forklift's cab. "Tal? We're out of here."

"Go, Pam."

Into her com, Talina snapped, "Two Spots? We've got a quetzal kill on the shuttle field." She stepped warily over, flipped a piece of the torn coveralls with a toe, and counted. "Looks like four people."

"*Four?*" Two Spots' voice answered.

"Roger that."

"Damn."

"Tell me what's going on," Aguila ordered, but her voice had taken on a different tone. She was now staring over Lieutenant Spiro's shoulder, an uneasy frown marring her forehead.

Talina carefully stepped into the enclosure, pistol ready, and bent down. She turned over a crumpled wad of coveralls to expose a sleeve and breast patch. "Load specialist. See the *Turalon* patch? You know the uniform as well as I do, Supervisor. Four of them. My guess? They didn't want to take a chance on spacing back on *Turalon*. Instead they figured they could make a nice little shelter here, wait it out until you were all gone. Then they could walk out and make new lives."

"Deserters," Spiro growled from behind her shining helmet. "What happened to them? What is all this?"

"Quetzal," Trish growled. "The damn fools even left a doorway for it." She pointed to the gap in the back, facing away as it did from the landing field.

"Been here for days." Talina noted as she studied the claw-scuffed dirt, the piles of excrement. "It would have killed all four immediately.

Then it ripped the clothing from the bodies and laid them out, eating them bit by bit, piece by piece."

Inside her the quetzal hissed in agreement, the thing irritatingly joyous.

Trish pointed at the heaping mounds of dung. "And there's what's left of your crewmembers, Supervisor." To Talina, she asked, "What next?"

The marines were staring through their visors, faces grim as they fingered their weapons. Aguila's back had stiffened, distaste on her fine features.

She asked, "Is it still around?"

"No," Talina, guessed, feeling the quetzal's agreement. "My guess is that it only stayed long enough to feed. But, my God, four people? Eating them would have taken days. So, why take the chance it might be discovered?"

"One thing's sure," Trish noted warily, "it's energized. Call it supercharged."

Talina backed out of the shelter, turning, running her eyes over the stacks of crates, the parked equipment. "A thousand places to hide."

And then Talina fixed on the Port Authority gate, swung wide. Open. Inviting.

"Oh fuck."

The quetzal under her heart hissed in victory. Talina accessed her com. "Two Spots? We've got a quetzal inside the compound. Sound the alarm. We need lockdown, now!"

"Inside the compound?" Trish cried, spinning around to stare at the gate in horror.

At that moment, the warning siren began to wail, its ugly bellow carrying through the early evening air.

"Let's go, people," Talina called. "Spiro, you tell that shuttle to button up, and no one steps out until this is over. Get Aguila into the admin dome and secure. After that, I need you and your team to help in the hunt."

To Talina's surprise, Kalico Aguila could actually run, and run well.

"What's this thing doing?" Aguila asked as she panted along in the midst of her marines. "It's eaten. Why enter Port Authority? It's got to know we're going to find it. Kill it."

"Got me, Supervisor. But whatever it's planning, it ain't gonna be good."

Talina thought her quetzal was laughing as it slithered around inside.

67

The way Cap felt, he could have used a shower. Something about Dan Wirth just left him feeling unclean. That old sixth sense made him glance back over his shoulder at Wirth's warehouse turned casino.

Not a single soul was in sight; no party of thugs was emerging to follow along in his wake. Still, Cap couldn't shake the feeling that he and Wirth had crossed some unseen line that would destroy one or both of them.

"What is it about that guy?"

He glanced at the sunset as he heard the distant roar of a shuttle approaching. The slanting light illuminated the underside of high clouds: a bank of them that glowed pinkish orange in the light. Their texture and color, given the ripples and lines, reminded him of a thinly sliced fillet of salmon.

Around him, Port Authority was still quiet in the aftermath of the night's violence. People were wary, giving him a nod of the head at best, but none of the usual called greetings as he passed the domes and stone buildings with heavy chabacho-wood doors.

Uncharacteristically, the streets were cluttered with occasional crates and containers. The odd vehicle dragged in from the treasure trove of *Freelander*'s holds lay awaiting attention.

"I tell you, Cap. The guy's a psycho. That night? He didn't have any more feeling in him than a block of ice. I wasn't any more important to him than a fly on the wall." Nandi's voice echoed in his memory.

A psycho? Impossible. Cap had pulled Dan Wirth's profile from the ship's records. The guy had worked for one of the big Corporate farms in the North American Midwest. His entire life history was there. Never a speck of trouble. Not so much as a complaint. Psychopaths always had something in the records. Allegations, charges, some sort of incident report, even if they'd never been convicted.

Besides, Dan Wirth, like all the transportees, had to have passed the psychiatric evaluations and assessment of functioning. Granted, he'd been late, almost missed the last shuttle up to *Turalon*, but nothing else was outstanding.

How could they have missed him?

It wasn't impossible that a clever psychopath could trick the General Assessment of Function test, but it was rare enough that people considered the system solid.

The Dan Wirth he'd just dealt with wasn't any easygoing cattle technician from a Midwest feedlot. This was a stone-cold killer. Nandi had called it right.

"Good thing you had that pistol under your pillow, girl."

So, what did Shig and Yvette have under theirs? Talina wouldn't hesitate. She'd shoot the son of a bitch if he threatened her.

"And don't tell me that Wirth doesn't know that." He stopped, watching as the shuttle swooped in and dropped on the other side of town. When the roar died, he added, "So when it comes to Talina, he'll come at her from the shadows. Never give her a chance."

What are you going to do about it, Cap?

"Kill him before he can kill Tal."

Odd, wasn't it? How easily he could commit himself to taking a man's life? Donovan had gotten into Cap's blood: Dan Wirth was a dead man.

Cap hesitated at Inga's, glanced behind him again to ensure that he wasn't being followed, and then opened the door and stepped inside.

As he looked down into the great room, it was to see Donovanians pretty much on one side, transportees on the other. For the most part, they were ignoring each other. Only the occasional cast glance was spared for either side. Nor was the room particularly loud, but more somber.

He trotted down the steps, nodded as the occasional set of eyes turned his way, and stopped at the bar.

"What'll it be, Cap?" Inga asked as she headed his way.

He leaned on the wood. "How's it been? Any trouble?"

She shrugged. "Not yet. The locals, they're thinking, 'Damn fools. What kind of idiots, carrying clubs, would charge headlong down a narrow alley into a fight with folks totin' guns?' The Skulls, they're thinking, 'What kind of heartless bastards would open fire on people armed only with sticks and stones?'"

"Should Tal and I drop by later?"

"Wouldn't hurt for our people to see her, Cap. Especially later on tonight. I'm pouring light drinks. Cut off a few like Hofer who were getting a bit deep in their cups. And I'll keep cutting. Especially with the troublemakers."

"That sounds like a smart . . ."

The siren—the one he'd only heard in that first day's drill—blared out. The clear tones had an electric effect on the Donovanians. In an instant they were on their feet, cups abandoned, chairs and benches askew, as they pounded up the steps and surged for the door.

Inga slapped a hard hand on the counter, bellowing, "You Skulls! Get the hell home! Lock your damn doors and wait for the all clear! Now, move it!"

Cap, slow to full understanding, was caught in the rush.

It seemed forever before he spilled out into the street as part of the stream of humanity.

He had his pistol, but if this was quetzal trouble, he wanted more. His time in the bush had taught him that. Sure there were rifles in the admin dome armory, but Tal would want her personal weapon. Turning toward the residential domes, he broke into a run. The soft meat stood out, milling, calling questions, a half-dazed look on their faces.

The Donovanians could have been a crack military team as they dropped their bundles and ran. Children, holding hands, called to their fellows, frightened but focused as they hurried toward safety.

Cap charged into Tal's block, surprised to find a big front-end loader blocking most of the street in front of her dome. Atop the engine unit, a man was frantically pitching tools into his toolbox.

"What the hell is this?" Cap bellowed.

"A piece of crap off *Freelander,*" the man bellowed. "Took a charge. Thought we could get it at least as far as the shops. This is where it stopped."

He leaped down, landing with a thud. "Got a solar charger on it! It'll move tomorrow."

"But it's sunset!"

"I know," the man called back over his shoulder. "Get it tomorrow!"

And then he was gone, vanishing into the thinning crowds as people found their domes and bolted inside.

"Toilet-sucking moron," Cap muttered to himself as he made his way around the thing. The tires, despite looking new, showed cracks. If they'd really aged one hundred and some years, it was no wonder.

Cheng was said to be working on a rubberlike compound that could be cooked from mundo tree leaves. Maybe they could make tires from that. Assuming they could figure out how to replace the flat batteries with ones that would allow the big machines to run for long enough to need the tires in the first place.

He stepped around the bucket—a big flat-bottomed scoop that slanted down at an angle from the monstrosity's front like a sharp bulldog jaw.

He pounded up Talina's steps, smiling thinly as he remembered the night she'd found him there in the rain. How she'd looked at him, head tilted. The way they'd made love when she'd taken him in to her bed.

"The perfect woman," he soliloquized. "I just had to cross half the galaxy to find her."

Talk about an ultimate irony.

He threw the door back and grabbed Talina's rifle off the rack. Popping the magazine, he checked it: topped off with explosive rounds. As if Tal would have had it any other way. And yes, it was chambered.

He set the safety and grounded it butt first. Talina had acquired the second rifle—a handmade bolt-action piece made on Donovan. Not military, but for hunting. It would get the job done if he had time to aim. The box magazine held five rounds. He slipped the bolt back to expose the sixth.

Got to count shots.

He slung Talina's rifle over his shoulder, lifted the bolt gun to the crook of his arm.

A soft scuffle of sound behind him was all the warning he got. The blow caught him behind the ear, slamming him forward into the rifle rack.

You piece of shit . . . was the last thought in his head.

68

Kalico Aguila wondered if another person could be squeezed into the conference room. This was what they called the big room, in what they more amusingly called the "ops center." Ask her, and Kalico would have said it was one poor attempt at a CIC. A table—upon which a map had been spread—filled the center of the ten-by-twenty room. The chairs had been shoved back and stacked against the wall to make room for warm bodies.

I've traded terror for horror.

She rubbed the back of her arms as she remembered the deserter's camp, the scattered supplies, the torn shreds of clothing. Had the bits of bloody coveralls been the worst part? Or had it been the mounded excrement that had once been human beings?

And that thing is here? In Port Authority?

"While we can't be one hundred percent sure," Talina had told her, "what we can't be is so much as one percent wrong."

Kalico tried to huddle out of the way, partially protected by Lieutenant Spiro and three of her marines. Decked out as they were in their armor, it was like having an impervious barrier between her and the world. The rest of Spiro's command were lined up out in the hall, waiting for orders.

The suspicious stares she got from the shabbily dressed Donovanians left her oddly off balance and added to the feeling of insecurity.

Shig Mosadek leaned over the map. Talina Perez, Trish Monagan, the big man they called Step, and four others peered down at the way his finger divided Port Authority into districts.

"Trish, you and your team take the residential section. That's our first concern. Especially the children's areas. That's where it's most likely to have headed. Tal, you take the warehouse district. If it rode in on a piece of cargo, that's where it would have gone to ground."

"How long's it been in?" Step asked, his face pinched into crags and lines.

"No idea," Perez told him. "From the scat, not longer than a couple of hours."

"How the hell could it have gotten in?" one of the other men—a round-faced young Asian with a mop of black hair—asked.

"Iji, have you seen how much material we've hauled in?" Pamlico Jones asked. "I've been running loads through the gate all day. It could have flattened itself on top of a container, turned itself gray, and we could have hauled it into the admin dome and never known."

"And the big gates have been wide open," Monagan reminded. "Sure, we've had the usual sentries, but with all the coming and going? Quetzals don't like crowds. And, damn it, it's the middle of the day! They just don't act this way. It's not right."

"Or maybe they do," Yvette said crisply. "Quetzals adapt. And now we're going to have to as well."

"Assuming it's actually in the compound," Shig reminded. "We have to believe it is. Any other course could get more people killed."

"Any questions on areas of responsibility?" Perez asked. "No? All right, people. We know how to do this."

Around the table, heads nodded.

"Unlike the drills," Shig reminded, "you take the safety off before you shoot. You may not get a second chance."

Perez turned, "Madam Supervisor, can you detail us your marines? Their tech, especially their thermal detection gear, could make all the difference. And a quetzal can't slash its way through armor."

Kalico hesitated, staring into the woman's hot eyes. This wasn't her problem. Nothing The Corporation had to . . .

She heard another part of herself saying, "Yes."

I've lost my mind. She slapped a hand to Lieutenant Spiro's armored shoulder. "Detail the squads, Lieutenant. One for each of the search areas."

"Ma'am?" Spiro turned, her face quizzical. Her helmet hung from her web gear, her rifle slung. "Your security at this time is my first and only—"

"Go on, Lieutenant. That's an order. My security will be better served with this *thing* dead, and you and your people have the best chance of finding it. Now, go."

Spiro—still frowning—snapped a salute, ordering into her com, "Finnegan, Miso, Abu Sassi, form squads for search and destroy. Optics and thermal on, people. Weapons hot upon deployment. Let's find this thing and fry it."

A series of "roger thats" could be heard through Spiro's battle com.

Kalico stood mutely as her people trooped out behind the Donovanians. Feeling oddly alone and adrift, she continued to rub the backs of her arms, as if chilled.

Into her com, Yvette said, "Millicent? Can someone bring us a pot of coffee from the cafeteria?" Then she nodded at some response in her earbud.

"I suspect it's going to be a long night," Yvette told Kalico as she dragged a couple of the chairs out. "Have a seat, Supervisor."

"This happens often?" Kalico asked.

Yvette shrugged. "Once every couple of months. Usually it's a false alarm. This probably is, too. But it keeps us on our toes."

Stepping over to seat herself, Kalico stared at the map of Port Authority. To her surprise, it had been hand drawn. The X marks, checks, and areas highlighted in yellow and light blue made no sense.

Shig, apparently reading her mind, stated: "This is what we call the quetzal map. X marks the places we've killed quetzals before. The light blue indicates areas particularly well-suited for them to hide in. Yellow are the slug zones."

"Slugs?"

"Creatures that come out when it's muddy. They grasp onto a person's foot, climb up the shoe or boot until they find cloth or skin. Once they pierce through they burrow into flesh and start eating. Cheng concocted a poison, however, and it seems to be working within the town boundaries. Only two cases this year."

"Abibi was right." Kalico shook her head slowly. "This is hell. There is no exit."

I could still call. Order her to wait.

Across the room, Yvette raised an eyebrow. "We'd argue differently. Sure, Donovan's dangerous and constantly trying to kill you. But you want to talk Sartre? Hell's back in Solar System with its algorithms, rules and laws, and Corporate control. It's all sterile. Everything dictated, running like a perfect machine. And once you've been turned into a part in the mechanism, that's where you'll spend the rest of your life. Like a little gear in the works. Without hope or opportunity."

Were they idiots? Didn't they get it? "It's *safe*. Secure. Ordered. The Corporation takes care of every need. No one starves." *No one gets eaten!*

"You've made humans into ants. Or maybe bees." Shig's enigmatic smile returned for the first time that night. "Supervisor, it is an old argument. Freedom or security."

"Our people *are* free. They have no worries about . . ."

"Section two, deploying," the call came in on the radio. Shig and Yvette immediately bent to the map, all debate forgotten.

"Shig? Tal here. We're starting perimeter check. Everyone's on station. Gates secure. Compound is closed up tight. We've got the drones in the air."

"Roger that. Keep your eyes open, people," Shig replied.

"Now we wait," Yvette said, stepping back as a woman in worn coveralls entered with a steaming kitchen pot.

"Made you a couple of gallons," the cherubic newcomer said, her round face flushed with effort. She flipped a damp strand of hair from her forehead and unhooked a cord strung through the handles of a dozen or so coffee cups. "Didn't know how many cups you'd need. If you want more, just holler."

Shig beamed at the woman. "We appreciate it, Millie. Now, get back to the kitchen and batten down. I'll bring the pot and cups back as soon as we have an all clear."

"Just get the beastie, will you?"

"If it's here," Yvette agreed.

After she'd left, Shig said, "Good woman, Millie." He stepped out into the hall, only to return seconds later with his and Yvette's personal cups. After handing Yvette's cup to her—to Kalico's horror—he dipped his own into the steaming coffee without a thought to sanitation. Unconcerned, he returned his stare to the map.

Yvette followed suit, then to Kalico's amazement, dipped one of the cups Millie had supplied and set it before Kalico. "You get a rare opportunity for a Boardmember. Tonight you get to be one of us. No marines, no privilege, just another scared human being wondering if the monster prowling the streets will come through that door and tear you, me, and Shig apart."

"Oh, come on. This is the admin dome. Surely you've got security. Armed men at the door." Did she dare drink the coffee? Were she to lift that cup, sip, it would be to cross a line she was unwilling to recognize.

"No guards," Shig told her.

"So, that *thing*? There's nothing to keep it from walking in the front door? Into this building? Right now?"

Yvette shot her an inquisitive green-eyed glance, eyebrow lifting. "How's it feel to be as vulnerable as the next person?"

Kalico couldn't help but fix on the door as a quiver ran through her. Yvette smirked.

Shig took another drink of his coffee, eyes on the map, as if willing it to produce the quetzal's location. "Supervisor, she's teasing you, trying to get under your skin. If the quetzal's actually inside the fence, odds are that it won't come here." He shrugged. "And the longer we go without hearing of an attack, the more likely our marauding quetzal's not even inside."

"Then what? It just gets away?"

"We track it. Hunt it down. As long as it's moving, the drones can find it." Yvette narrowed a hostile eye. "It killed four people. Right under our noses. You think we want one as smart as this one to come back?"

"Don't you ever wonder if it's worth it? The fight, I mean. The constant fear and worry." As she spoke her hands had knotted, betrayed by the queasy trembling in her heart. *Turalon* was still an option.

Shig—to her dismay—noticed. The man smiled, his voice oddly kind. "Supervisor, just how do you think the universe was created to function? You know it deep in your heart. You are a walking contradiction of the very things you claim to believe and promote. Safety? Order? Security? Harmony? Yet, here you are, brought to this point by your insatiable need to compete and prove yourself better than the rest."

"As if you had any idea about what brought me here. Save your psychoanalysis for one of the local lunatics."

Shig spread his hands, expression mild. "Why do you fail to recognize in yourself what you condemn in others? You wanted a chance at winning it all. A shot at becoming Chairman of the Board and being the most powerful woman in Solar System. You could no more have turned your back on that, acquiesced to remain a minor functionary in the Corporate system, than one of us could walk away from a chance to kill this quetzal."

"The Corporation keeps the people from destroying themselves," she told him as the Corporate mantra sprang reflexively from her lips.

"Ah, the people. Poor benighted fools. No sense in giving them the same opportunity that you and the tiny percentage of the wealthy and powerful possess."

"If it's so bad, why have we eliminated poverty? Unemployment? Ensured that no one goes hungry? You ask me, we've made a hell of an improvement in everyone's lives. Peace. Prosperity. The quality of human life has never been better."

Shig seemed to beam understanding. "Tell me, would you trade places with a single one of 'the people'? And if so, tell me which one. Name a name, state an occupation. A place of residence. Which one of the worker bees would you become?"

She stared at him, refusing to rise to the bait.

Yvette took a swig of her coffee, and said, "Of course you wouldn't. You're a fart-sucking hypocrite."

"You don't understand." Kalico realized as she said it that it was an admission of defeat.

"It's all right, Supervisor," Shig told her. "You see, the only real difference between yourself and most of us is that in Solar System, you're the tiny minority. Here, on Donovan, you're just one of a majority."

He paused. "When you think about it that way, it would seem that you've come home. Come to a place where you're suddenly surrounded by your own kind."

She grimaced, fuming at the notion that these barbarians in their hide clothes had anything in common with her.

There wasn't a single chance in hell that she'd touch that cup of coffee before her. No matter how wonderful it smelled, or how long the night turned out to be.

Home? In a pig's eye.

69

Patches of cloud left dark spots across the starry sky in the west. Out over the Gulf the clouds had taken on a faint rime of silver where Donovan's moon was about to rise.

If Trish had ever been thankful for tech, this was the night. She followed Katsuro Miso as the marine scanned the dark shadows between two residential domes with his superior gear. He was getting a complete heads-up sensor analysis of combined motion detectors, infrared, thermal, and ultraviolet. Trish and her people only had night-vision drones, the thermal scopes on their rifles, and an occasional IR headset. The rest had to rely on flashlights.

Over the years they'd worked out the methodology for the search. The sweep for each block had been practiced until it was second nature—as was the best way to approach each potential hiding place. Trial and error had taught them where to leave an observer so that a hunted quetzal couldn't double back into a secured area. That knowledge and expertise had been paid for with blood.

Now Trish's team worked through the remaining residential blocks bounded by the curve of the fence. This was mostly filled with transportees, and they kept spilling out into the street as young Benj Martin trotted from door to door to do his head count. Trish continually had to order the Skulls back inside when the curious fools wanted to tag along and watch the hunt.

One thing was sure, it made the head count easier. But the training they'd received—the no-nonsense instruction that when a quetzal was in the compound no one opened a door unless at a search team's knock and call—sure hadn't taken.

"Private," Trish called to Katsuro as they rounded the dome, "You're about to see a storage shed appear on your left. There's an awning and storage area that will be shadowed. The shed's too small for a quetzal, but we killed one that hunkered down back in the shadows under that awning."

"Roger that," Katsuro replied as his gear illuminated the shed. Together they stepped wide around the building, weapons up.

Katsuro called, "It's clear."

Trish instinctively swept the area with her scope, somehow unable to trust Katsuro's sophisticated detectors. People who hunted quetzals wished they had eyes in the back of their heads. Lucky marines. They did.

"Here's Tompzen and Hofer," Katsuro told her with a slight gesture down the alley.

Sure enough, another marine appeared in the narrow confines. Behind him Hofer called, "We're all clear here."

"Next block," Trish called. "Watch your back, Hofer."

"Watch yours!"

Trish led the way back around the dome to where they'd left Smith kneeling in the intersection, his rifle up, eye to his thermal scope as he ensured no quetzal could double around behind them.

Iji's team appeared—right on schedule—the next block down. "*I've got visual on you, Trish.*" Iji's soft voice spoke in her earbud.

"Roger that. Got you, too."

"See you at the next block. Watch your back."

"Watch yours."

They started down the street, warily approached an aircar resting atop a wagon. The inoperative vehicle had been hauled in from the landing field. They carefully cleared it.

"Makes it tougher with all this *Freelander* crap," Trish groused.

"Most of it doesn't work," Katsuro told her. "Wouldn't it be better to pile it in a ditch somewhere?"

"Oh ye of little faith, Private. You're on Donovan now. We reuse everything."

"Even condoms?"

"Okay, so we reuse *almost* everything." She grinned as she stared through her scope at the shadowed angle where an addition had been built onto one of the domes. A produce wagon stacked with empty crates lurked there. No quetzal.

"So, Trish, you're one of the officers, right? You pretty much know everything that goes on."

"Yeah, probably." Trish shifted her rifle, muscles sending the first signals of incipient fatigue.

"You heard about Talbot, Shintzu, and Garcia?"

"Who?"

"Marines. Three of them and their tactical kit. Did your bosses give them sanctuary?"

"Not that I've heard of. And if three marines with armor and kit had deserted, it would have been the talk of the town. Why? You missing three?"

"Yeah," Katsuro sounded depressed as he stepped into a gap between buildings, scanned it, and saw Hofer's team appear on the other side. "They were pretty pissed that Cap resigned. The rest of us, we were just wondering."

"You're not telling me everything."

"Cap leaving? It was like a kick in the teeth. All that talk he used to spout about the Corps and tradition. Of duty and honor and pride in service. And then he vanishes into the bush, and when he comes back, he just walks away. I mean, most of us, we believed in him."

"Maybe he found himself."

"Some say it was Perez's fault. That she took him out there specifically to brainwash him and turn him against us."

Trish burst out laughing. "Not *hardly.* Taggart arrested Talina in her own home. She barely tolerated the guy. The *only* reason she took him that day was because it was supposed to be a quick trip. Wasn't anyone as surprised as the rest of us when they came back holding hands."

And the notion of the two of them still left Trish feeling sour. Things with Talina just hadn't been the same.

Trish ran her thermal scope over the shadows behind the Hang Chow dome. A pile of toys lay where they'd been dropped by the kids when the siren went off.

"So . . . what happened out there?"

"Donovan happened. I guess Cap had more to him than any of us would have thought."

"Spiro hates him."

"Why?"

Trish could halfway wish she had Talina's quetzal sense as she advanced slowly down the street. She could hear the kid in charge of the head count as he knocked on doors behind her.

"He was everything she aspired to as a commander. Kind of a hero worship, because he'd been in the shit so many times. You ask me, she was a bit in love with him. Hit her hard when he left."

He paused, then added, "Cap kept a leash on her. Most of us don't trust her. She plays favorites. And she carries a grudge that turns into pure poison."

"Glad she's your problem and not mine."

"Trish, you sure Talbot, Shintzu, and Garcia didn't desert?"

"Like I said, I'd have heard." Trish sensed his unease. "Why?"

"Something fishy about it. I mean, those guys didn't like Cap to start with. Marines bitch—but they were the ones who griped the most about Cap and his command style. You know, they always found fault, said they could have done it better. Then they vanish? And Spiro says the Supervisor wishes Cap was dead. So, when we get the order to space, we're missing three guys, right? We tell Spiro we're not going. She and her people pull weapons on us, and two guys we think are with us, side with her at the last instant. So we ride up to *Turalon* in cuffs, wishing to hell we'd run when we could. Then we're pulled out of the can and shuttled back down here. So, the question is, what are we really here to do?"

Trish nerved herself. Three of the domes came together here. They'd killed a quetzal in the shadowy recesses beneath the sunshade that had been stretched between them.

"For the moment, hunt a quetzal. And thank God you're here with your tech. You don't know how much faster this is working."

She stepped around the curve of a dome, rifle up, to scan the alley. A second later, Hofer's team appeared at the other end.

"Speculation was that Spiro sent Shintzu, Garcia, and Talbot to kill Cap Taggart. I mean, that's what made us refuse orders. Cap may have let us all down, but he didn't deserve that kind of shit. Especially after that fight with the returnees. Cap broke it up while Spiro just stood there like a stone."

A cold rush went down Trish's back. "You serious?"

"Maybe. Did the Supervisor order it? She hates Cap. No secret there. Did Spiro order it? Was it even an order? That's part of the problem. Me and my mates, we don't know what to think anymore. Since we set foot on Donovan, everything's turned upside down. We don't trust the Supervisor. We don't trust Spiro."

"So . . ." Trish hesitated. "You refused orders?"

"You think we want to space on that bucket? When we could stay here?"

"Then you better bless this quetzal after we kill it, because you've come to the right person. You and your mates get free of Spiro and her backers, we'll get you out of sight until *Turalon* spaces."

Katsuro didn't answer as he scanned the shadows.

In her com, Trish said, "Last block, people. Be double sharp. If we've been driving it, it's gone to ground here."

She and Katsuro waited while Smith closed up. Behind her, Benj knocked on the last door. To her left, she could see Hofer's team where the street met the perimeter fence. On her right, Step Allenovich's team was closing their search grid, having reached the next intersection.

"All right, people," Trish said, "let's finish this."

Heart in throat, she started forward, muscles somehow recharged. If the quetzal was here, they'd have it in the next couple of minutes.

But they didn't.

After searching shadows, scanning rooftops, and looking into recesses, they cleared the last buildings, only to stare at the perimeter fence with its motion detectors beyond.

Talina's voice came through the com, *"All right, people. Good job. Looks like the hunt goes outside tomorrow morning. We'll cut for tracks and run this shit-sucker down. Shig, sound the secondary."*

A short blast of the horn was followed a second later by another.

Everyone in Port Authority would be breathing easier, but still on alert. People knew full well that even as good as the teams were, they still might have missed something.

Benj Martin—a lad in his teens—trotted up with a tablet in his hands. "Hey, Trish. I got the head count. Knocked on every door. Got an answer on everyone but Talina's. So I opened the door and checked. Both of her rifles were missing, so Cap must have gone off to join her."

"Good work. Thanks, Benj." Trish took a deep breath, lowered her rifle and massaged her biceps.

Where the hell is Cap?

Damn it, she really didn't like the guy. Cap's presence made everything different. Especially between her and Talina.

"You serious about making a place for us?" Katsuro asked.

She glanced out beyond the fence. "Damned straight. We'll make a place for you. Starting tomorrow when we try and find the killer's tracks."

"Sounds like fun."

"Promise you one thing, Private. You'll never be bored."

He paused, shifting uneasily. "Before we go back, I need to find Cap. Give him a heads-up about Spiro, Garcia, Shintzu, and Talbot."

"Sure. We'll work our way back to the admin dome. Check and see if he's with Tal. If not, most of the search teams head for Inga's. Probably find him there."

"Hope he's okay."

"Yeah, me, too. 'Cause if you're right and either the Supervisor or Lieutenant Spiro did him harm, Talina will kill them, and then we're really gonna have a bloodbath."

70

Talina led the way, passing from one pool of light to another along Port Authority's main avenue. In retrospect, she wondered if her reliance on the quetzal inside her was a good thing. She'd half depended on it, expecting at any moment that it would warn her if she were about to stumble onto the intruder.

You've got to be damned careful, Tal.

Time to turn to her next problem: Her search team, composed of four locals and three marines, including Lieutenant Spiro, walked with slung weapons. The lieutenant had barely spoken, her presence almost a hindrance in spite of the battle tech that should have enhanced the search.

Talina took a deep breath, exhaling to the night as the first sliver of the half-moon crested the eastern horizon.

"Lieutenant," she asked, "do we have a problem?"

"Excuse me?"

"You don't have to like me, and I don't have to like you, but a modicum of civility might ensure that we can at least cooperate on joint areas of concern."

Tal gifted the woman with a sidelong glance, trying to read her features in the lamplight.

Spiro's blocky face was taut with distaste. "Security Officer, I've got nothing to say to you past what I'm forced to because of duty. So, how about you shut your conniving yap, and your future will be both longer and less painful."

Behind her, Tal's people gasped and responded by unslinging their rifles and swinging them around.

The marines shifted, unslinging their own weapons. Spiro seemed unaware.

"I've never done anything to you."

"Yeah. Right. Now shut the fuck up, bitch."

The quetzal in Talina's gut reacted to the harder beat of her heart, the cold anger under her breast. She forced herself to keep her rifle slung, but her hand dropped to her pistol butt.

Careful, Tal, she told herself. *Something about this isn't right. She's pushing you. Spoiling for a fight.*

With her other hand, she gestured for her people to stand down.

"I don't know why you're pushing, Lieutenant, but no matter what you've heard about me. I'm not playing your game tonight. You got a problem with me, you come tell me when we're not up to our asses in a situation. That suit you?"

"Better than you and that traitorous piece of shit you're screwing can know."

"Ah. I see." She glanced over her shoulder at the marines as they walked under the next light. They looked nervous. "Folks move on with their lives, Lieutenant. Allowing your personal problems to affect your ability to command isn't just unprofessional, it'll get people killed." To the marines, she called, "Keep an eye on her, people."

Spiro halted, hand slapping her rifle as she turned. "I ought to shoot you down right here, right now, you lying slit."

Tal raised her hands. "Like I said, we get the current situation solved and brought to a conclusion, I'm yours. But for the moment, I need you to act like an officer of the marines instead of a jilted schoolgirl. So buck up to the task at hand. Can you do that? As a professional worthy of your people's respect?"

Spiro's lips twitched, her eyes like dark pools in the shadowed light cast by the overhead lamp. "So help me, you and that shitass are—"

"Lieutenant?" the marine called Abu Sassi asked. "Are we still on duty?"

Spiro ground her teeth. "On duty, Private. Just one question for the civilian: Where's Talbot, Shintzu, and Garcia? Did you and *Mister* Taggart add them to your little mutiny plot, or did you take a more severe measure?"

Tal cocked her head, the quetzal bunched in her gut. Her muscles were charged, her vision so fine it read the heat in Spiro's cheeks.

"Never heard of them, but I'm guessing they're some of your marines. I'll tell you straight. I don't have a clue as to where they are. And I give you my word, if they've deserted, they didn't come through Port Authority to my knowledge."

"Your word is as worthless as shit in a toilet, Perez." Spiro turned, stalking off at a fast pace.

"Tal?" Mgumbe asked as he fingered his rifle, eyes slitted.

"Stand down." As she started forward, she asked the marine, Abu Sassi, "What's this all about? Why's she chewing on my ass, trying to get me to kill her?"

The marine glanced at his fellows. "She's ragging on you because it's all falling apart. We're falling apart. Turning on each other. Got to blame someone, and you started it when you ran off with Cap and made him . . ."

"Made him?" she asked when he couldn't finish. "She thinks I stole Cap and seduced him away from his duty?" She laughed aloud and slapped her thigh. "Oh, God, Private. That's about the most ironic joke you could tell. When we went down, my first instinct was to cut his throat rather than have him slow me down in the bush." She laughed again. "Me? Seduce him? The man was going to have me shot, if you'll recall."

Mgumbe and the others were laughing, and he called, "Trust me, Private. Talina Perez isn't the kind to seduce anyone. Crack 'em in the head, maybe."

Abu Sassi glanced at his fellows, then at the lieutenant who was now fifty meters ahead and making distance. "You told the truth about Garcia, Shin, and Talbot?"

"Private, what your people do is their business. Shig, Yvette, me, Mgumbe, and Montoya here, we could care less. But I'd have heard about marines trying to desert, believe me."

Again the marines glanced back and forth before Abu Sassi asked, "So you and Cap didn't hatch any plan to talk us into deserting?"

"Nope. Might not have been a bad idea, but we've had our asses busy trying to keep your people from killing each other. And we're still not sure that's taken care of."

"She fucking lied," Private Anderssoni muttered. "I still think she sent Shin, Talbot, and Garcia after the captain."

"Want to explain that?" Talina asked as they rounded the corner before the admin dome. Spiro had disappeared into the building.

"Nothing we know, just a suspicion," Abu Sassi said, slowing to a stop. "Some of us wonder if the Supervisor might have ordered Spiro to put the captain down. You know, as an example to the rest of us. For Miso and some of us, that cut the cord."

Talina cursed, accessing her com. "Shig, Trish, Step? Anybody seen Cap Taggart? Anyone know where he is?"

She listened as one by one they checked in with negatives.

"I heard he was at Inga's just before the siren went off," Lawson told her. *"Haven't seen him since."*

Talina's lungs seemed starved. "Mgumbe, get everyone back to the dome. Tell the rest I'll be there as soon as I find Cap."

She turned, unslung the rifle, and ran.

At Inga's she slammed through the door, trotted down the steps, and scanned the faces. "Hey, any of you assholes seen Cap?"

"Nope." "Not since the siren." "Figured he was with you." A chorus of rejoinders and shaking heads came in reply.

Turning, she took the stairs two at a time.

Out in the night, she paused, glanced up at the half-moon. "Where would you have gone, Cap?"

He was still a Skull—wouldn't have known the first place she would have gone was to the admin dome.

"Home?" she wondered. Unlike her, he would have thought of the rifles, wouldn't have known that she'd pull one from the armory rack rather than take the time to fetch her own.

Talina took off at a sprint, her heart hammering. That was Trish's section to clear. She'd have had someone dedicated to the head count. Knocking on doors. If Cap was there, he would have answered, asked what the hell was up.

Bullshit. Cap would have come to help. Sitting at home through an emergency wasn't his style.

The quetzal twisted around inside her, agitated, almost electric.

"You piece of shit," she muttered to the beast. "This is Cap we're talking about."

"*Soon now. Both.*"

She ground her jaws, panting as she charged through the night, rounded the corner to her street, and saw the big loader with its tilted bucket in front of her house. If she needed to get the cart in, had to rescue Cap, the thing was going to complicate the hell out it.

She rounded the tire, pounded up her steps, and saw the check-mark on her door. Whoever Trish had assigned had been here. At least knocked on the door.

"Knowing I wasn't home."

She slammed the door open and palmed on the lights. The first thing she noticed was the rifle rack. Empty. Cap had at least made it this far.

"Cap?"

No answer.

She'd turned, headed back out, when the quetzal sent a shock through her, bending her double. She gasped. A blinding pain stunned her. A terrible pain, like something jagged being pulled sideways through her guts. She barely realized when the rifle slipped from her fingers to clatter onto her floor.

Reeling, she staggered for balance. Barely made it to her couch. The pain receded.

"What the fuck was that?" she gasped, struggling to catch her breath.

"*Now.*"

With every last ounce of her strength, she fought her way to her feet. Started toward the door, only to have the quetzal strike again. She heard herself shriek from the pain. Both hands went to her stomach as she bent double and threw up.

"Fuck!" she screamed when she could finally spit and clear her mouth.

"Tal?" the hoarse call barely penetrated her staggered senses. "Run!" the voice rasped.

She glanced at the door to her bedroom. Tried to make sense of the image.

Cap seemed to float in the doorway, feet inches above the floor, legs swaying and flopping. Something big, black, and looming filled the darkness in the room behind him.

The quetzal inside her radiated in hot glee.

Talina pawed for her pistol, gritted her teeth, and drew it from the holster. "Cap?" she gasped, trying to gulp air.

"Run!"

She lifted the pistol, tried to align the sights with whatever held his body to block the doorway.

Agony stabbed through her like a steel spike.

The world spun, and she vaguely felt herself hit the floor. Lost the pistol. Every muscle in her body convulsed.

"Why are you doing this?" she whispered through tears.

She blinked, fingers slipping along the floor. From the corner of her eye, she saw Cap as he was flung across the room to slam into the counter that separated her kitchen from the main room. He hit the counter like a rag doll, the impact loud in the room.

The quetzal that emerged from her bedroom shifted from black to a blaze of white and crimson. The thing was big, a good six meters in length and just shy of two meters at the hips. It carefully closed with her and lowered its head to stare into her eyes.

Paralyzed from within, she stared from eye to eye, the head so close she couldn't focus on all three at once.

Faster than she could react, the quetzal's tongue blurred, striking past her lips and parted teeth.

A squeal tried to form at the bottom of her throat. She jerked her head back as saliva rushed to fill her mouth. The taste was overpowering. Bitter peppermint. The tongue flickered this way and that. Alien, invasive.

Talina stiffened, outraged by the violation, and clamped down with all the power in her jaws. Like biting into a roll of leather, she tried to chew the quetzal's tongue in two.

The quetzal shrilled. Talina's head was whipped sideways, the muscles nearly pulled from the bones in her neck and shoulders.

She hit the wall with a thud, wondering if her teeth had been yanked from their sockets. For a moment the impact freed her from the beast's hold inside her.

She clambered up, supported by the wall.

"*You kill me. We now kill you.*"

"You're related," she realized, the peppermint-extract taste of quetzal cloying in her mouth. "Born together."

"*One for one.*"

"Revenge," she whispered. "That's the word."

The great quetzal was closing. Pulsing in bands of crimson, yellow, and black, the collar flared wide around the beast's scaled head, dazzling in its distracting display.

Talina stared, mesmerized by the brilliant colors. Some part of her howled in terror as the serrated jaws separated. The creature's three eyes glowed from an inner light that sparked with hatred and rage.

The deafening report of a pistol shot broke the spell, and the great quetzal turned in a flash.

Cap had staggered to his feet, somehow managed to lay his hands on Talina's pistol. He wobbled, blinked, took a breath and shot again. To brace himself, he leaned his hip against her couch. Tried to steady his rubbery arms as the pistol wavered in his grip.

The quetzal struck with its tail, taking Cap's legs out from under him as it smashed him into the wall. The couch went with him, crashing through the side of the dome.

In that instant, Talina closed her eyes. Filled her head with images of water. She was drowning, sinking, thrashing for air. She looked up, imagining a bobbing pattern of sunlight through waves. Clawed futilely for the surface as she sank. Then she imagined the sensation of water filling her lungs, the bursting sense of panic.

The beast inside her cowered back. She felt its hold on her loosen.

Talina staggered to the door where it still hung open. She threw herself out, tumbled painfully down the steps. The quetzal in her gut shrilled its rage as it tried to fight its way back into control.

"Quetzal at my house!" she screamed hoarsely into her com.

"What? Where? Your house?"

On all fours, Talina scrambled past the tire on the loader. She huddled back against the front axle as the hunting quetzal leaped onto the street. Clawed feet thumped into the dirt just beyond the bucket.

Talina bent to the com mic. "Fuck you, yes! Get here!"

In triumph the quetzal issued a whistling shriek and ducked its head down to peer at her under the flat-bottomed bucket.

"Talina?" She ignored the rest of Two Spots' frantic questions as the quetzal's gaze met hers.

Talina slipped under the axle as the creature shot its head under the bucket and snapped its jaws within inches of her body. Then, in a lightning move, the huge beast darted around the tire.

Talina barely had time to roll back under the axle as the jaws closed on air where she'd been but a heartbeat before.

She vaguely heard Two Spots chattering in her earbud.

Swallowing hard, heart pumping fear through her veins, she clawed at her belt. Found only her knife.

The quetzal screamed, bounced back to the front, and thrust its head under the bucket.

Talina rolled back under the axle, every muscle trembling. She sucked breath into her shivering lungs. How long could she keep this up?

Again the quetzal shifted, and again her body convulsed in pain. She barely made it back under the axle.

A game of time.

And if the beast in her belly could recover? If it fully unleashed that pain again? Slowed her just a bit more than it already did?

Talina cradled her knife before her, gripping the handle.

You can't kill a quetzal with a knife.

Striking at the scaled head, it would just slip off.

Strike at an eye?

Sure. The only way she'd be able to reach it was if the fucking thing already had hold of her.

She rolled under the axle as the quetzal ducked around the tire, jaws clapping shut like a shot.

Talina glanced up. The gap behind the bucket and load arms was a chance. Could she wiggle up in that space? Could she do it in time?

This time the quetzal tried the other tire. She barely whipped her foot away as she rolled under the axle.

"Nothing to lose." She leaped up, got an arm around a bundle of hydraulic hoses. Hanging, she barely managed to jerk her feet up in time. Quetzal jaws snapped within an inch of her toes.

Talina fought to fill her lungs, to keep her hold in the awkward close quarters. "Come on, someone has to be on the way. Where's the marines when you need them?"

Two Spots was still yammering questions she didn't have time for.

She felt the machine shake as the quetzal tried to squeeze itself under the bucket. Talina pulled herself higher, got her arms over the bundled hydraulic lines.

How long could she keep her legs drawn up? How long before the muscles in her belly and thighs tired? She could already feel them burning.

And then the pain hit her, causing her to scream, "Fuck you!"

Rescue wasn't coming fast enough.

She took a deep breath against the pain. With nothing left to her, she wedged the knife in amongst the hydraulic lines. As hope failed, and the pain lanced through her again, she entrusted all of her weight to the knife.

It would either hold her, or . . .

Everything let loose in a spray of fluid. In that weightless instant she felt herself fall. The quetzal's head was down there. Just below.

71

Trish was in the lead as she and Katsuro rounded the corner onto Tal's dark street. As the marine flashed his shoulder lights to illuminate the scene, it looked like the quetzal was digging its way under a huge front-end loader.

At that instant, the bucket dropped, edge down, to trap the beast. Fantastic colors burst and flared across its hide. Panicked, the quetzal was thrashing, rocking the heavy loader back and forth; the long body whipped this way and that.

Even as Trish pulled up and took aim, the monster gave one last mighty heave. She heard the snap. Then the quetzal stilled, quivering, patterns of crazy color rolling across its hide like waves.

Trish settled the sights forward of the shoulders and triggered the gun. The report split the night, recoil rocked her back.

A second later, Katsuro's rifle boomed.

The quetzal's body jumped under the impacts as the explosive bullets tore it apart inside.

The tail was still shivering reflexively when Trish took a breath, aimed, and put a second round at the junction of the shoulders.

"That should have severed the nerve cord," she told Katsuro.

"Fuck me," the marine said through an awed whisper. "That's what a quetzal looks like?"

"There you go, Private. Welcome to Donovan," Trish said warily as she stepped wide to get a side view of the thing. "Tal?" she called. "You all right?"

Nothing.

Trish sucked a breath into her run-starved lungs. "Oh, God, Tal. Tell me you're not halfway down that thing's throat."

Swallowing hard, she stepped closer, finger hanging in the air above the trigger. Katsuro's light glared on the quetzal where its neck was pinioned to the dirt by the sharp bucket edge.

"Lot of steel pushing down." Katsuro shook his head.

"Yeah, that last thrashing? The way it went still? Probably broke its neck before I could shoot it in two."

Trish took another step. "Tal?"

She'd never seen the like. A quetzal trapped like this. It almost looked like the loader was trying to devour the beast.

"Katsuro? You watch this thing. If it so much as twitches, shoot it again." She set her rifle to the side and eased up to the big tire. Pulling her flashlight, she flicked it on and peered into the gap behind the big bucket.

At first, what she saw didn't make any sense. "Tal? My God! Did that thing just puke you back up? You're all covered with gut juice and spit!"

Talina—gasping and trembling—sat next to the triangular head with its broad jaws agape, the tongue partially extended. The three eyes, set in their triangular pattern atop the skull, were fixed.

Talina looked like a drowned rat. Her entire body was covered in fluid that gleamed in the light. Tal blinked, eyes wide. "Trish? That you?"

"Yeah. It's all right, Tal. You're safe. It's dead."

"So . . . close. Die now. That's what it said."

"Who said? The quetzal?"

Talina nodded, her hair a soaked mass of black that plastered to her head. Her skin shone, wet and dripping.

"It *swallowed* you?"

Tal blinked, absently wiped at the liquid. "So . . . close."

"Hang on. We'll need to get jacks, something to lift this bucket to get you out of there."

Talina snorted, as if amused. "No. I'm all right."

"Tal, you sure? It's like you're dazed . . . not all here. You get hit in the head?"

"What a fucking day."

Through the gap above the tire Trish watched her friend slap the quetzal's head, use her feet to shove it out of the way, and then flatten herself, wiggle under the axle, and crawl wearily out from beneath the loader.

Trish hesitated, then offered her a hand, feeling the slick fluid as it slathered onto her palm and fingers. "What is this stuff?" She pulled a wobbly Talina to her feet. "Gut juice? It's like, not eating your skin off or anything, is it?"

"Relax, Trish. It's hydraulic fluid. And, God, is Montoya gonna be pissed when he learns I cut the lines."

Shig's voice came in through Trish's com. *"What's the status out there, people?"*

Trish accessed her com. "Quetzal's dead. Tal's shaken, but slimy. Final score, loader one, quetzal zero."

"You need a cart? Anyone hurt?"

Talina, her hands and legs still quivering from either fear or exhaustion, said, "Yeah, Cap's in pretty bad shape. Make sure Raya has the surgery ready. Get that cart here ASAP, Shig. Minutes could count."

Talina signed off, staring absently at the colors fading on the quetzal's hide.

"How did it know to pick your house?"

"It's a mate, brother, spouse, whatever, to the one I killed that day in the canyon. It came here for revenge, Trish."

"You know how crazy that sounds?"

Talina nodded, eyes focused on something only she could see. "It knew when it found my house. Call it scent, taste, whatever. It kept Cap alive to use as a human shield. And then it lay in wait."

"No shit?"

"Oh, you have no idea." Talina wiped at a trickle of hydraulic fluid as it ran down her cheek. "The nightmares have just started."

72

The gentle hand on Kalico's shoulder brought her awake. Her back and butt ached, and her legs had gone to sleep. She blinked her eyes open, realized her head rested on an arm, the arm on a table.

She jerked herself upright, staring at the drool spot on her black sleeve. The conference room, the map now rolled up and gone, the table bare, met her disoriented daze.

A cold cup of coffee sat by her elbow, the surface scummy, a ring around the inside of the cup.

"Supervisor?" Yvette Dushane asked. "Come on. I've got a room for you. Maybe not the sort of bed you're used to, but it will beat the hell out of that chair."

"My marines?"

"Over at Tal's looking at the quetzal."

"They got it?"

"Tal did, actually. But that's a story for tomorrow."

Kalico managed to stand, and made a face as the circulation returned to her legs.

"I should get back to the shuttle."

"Gate's locked till morning." Dushane arched an eyebrow. "You're dead on your feet. How long since you've had a good night's sleep?"

"Damned if I remember." She rubbed her face.

"Come on."

I must be out of my mind.

Kalico's first steps were mincing as she followed Dushane down the hall and out into the night. The cool air, the half-moon midway up in the eastern sky, the distant trill of the invertebrates, all seemed to partially rejuvenate her.

The dome Dushane led her to was indeed close, fortunately, because Kalico's thoughts were filled with cobwebs. That vague feeling that she had to do something kept slipping past her memory.

"Who's place is this?"

"Mine," Dushane told her. At Kalico's hesitation, the woman added, "Or what? You figuring to rent one of Inga's beds over the distillery? At least with me you'll have privacy."

"You don't even like me."

"No shit. But we can talk about it in the morning."

Not surprisingly, Dushane's small dome had a homey look with lace curtains, tasteful furniture that had to be of local manufacture, and a library full of antique bound books. The throw rug had a quaint appeal and was made of what looked like strips of braided cloth.

The guest bedroom had been furnished with the barest of necessities: bed, storage chests, wardrobe, and a curtain over the window.

"I should go back," Kalico protested one last time.

"It's the middle of the night, Supervisor. There's nothing that can't wait. And you're dead on your feet."

Kalico settled herself on the bed. Not exactly the high tech, interactive mattress she was used to. Still . . .

She glanced up, eyes feeling hot and gritty. "You know, I was going to execute you."

"Yeah, fancy that." Dushane gave her a smile, flicked off the lights, and closed the door.

"God, they're all lunatics. Every last one."

She swung her feet up, dropped her head on the pillow. "Just a couple of hours," she promised herself. "Get up at dawn and finally make a decision."

She didn't remember drifting off.

That night, the nightmares didn't come.

73

Water spread in a V-shaped wake as the bow of the canoe sliced across the smooth surface. Clouds made patterns in the Minnesota sky overhead. Max's paddle dripped water as he stroked in time with his father. Dad sat behind, in the back of the canoe, and periodically used his paddle to steer as they passed through the narrow channel separating the chain of lakes.

So peaceful.

The next instant Max was floating, hanging in black space, as he gently corrected attitude on his suit to keep him oriented toward the distant sun. Nothing in life had prepared him for the sensations of freefall, the tickle in the gut, the weightless joy. He might not have been part of the universe, disconnected from it, a mote of reality in the infinity of Creation.

Some part of him wanted to float that way forever, convinced that he made his own eternity.

Images tumbled through him. Basic training. He'd thrived on the physical challenges, enjoyed pushing his body because he was better than the others.

And he'd hated advanced training, the classroom sessions, that—despite the implants—had left him feeling challenged and inferior. He'd always been a physical guy. The intricacies of combined weapons synchronization, multiforce tactical operations, and multiple-unit drone coordination and movement hadn't clicked for him.

All of which pretty much limited him to a field commission. Company command. That was as high as he was going to go in the Marines.

In the mirror of his dreams, he saw himself reflected, that "fuck you" smile on his lips. The one he adopted when he didn't give a shit because he knew the "system" had pigeonholed him. That he'd become a cog in the great military machine. That it detailed him and his marines to a specific job. As heedless about employing him to subdue an incipient rebellion as it was to use a core drill to sample the mineral content of an asteroid.

That's who I was.

Until Donovan. Until Talina Perez.

His dreams filled with her high-cheekboned face, the otherworldly glint in her dark eyes. Her delicious lips bent in a smile for him, the flashing of her white teeth. Her hips swayed in that captivating way she walked. Capella's sunlight highlighted blue tints in her raven-black hair.

He could feel her in his arms, substantial, warm, and solid. All woman, that one. Daring and hard, she'd faced him toe-to-toe. Taken him into her own embrace. His soul warmed at the memory of her body against his as they made love, how she'd gasped and trembled at that magic moment.

I love her. With all of my body and soul . . .

A distant pain intruded. A sense of wrongness that clawed at the misty margins of his dream.

Three eyes in a triangular pattern burned in the darkness.

Pain.

Fear.

Helplessness.

His trinity of terror.

Cap gasped as the dream faded and that sense of wrongness slipped up around his consciousness.

"Got to warn Tal," he heard himself whisper. The pain intensified as if someone were twisting a dial.

"He's coming out of it," a voice said from somewhere just above him.

"Cap?" Tal's voice—like an angelic relief—asked softly.

"Quetzal," he croaked. "Got to warn you."

"I got it, Cap. It's dead."

Dead? He shivered, the pain eating through him like acid. The thing was still holding him, its claws fastened in his flesh.

The image replayed: Tal stepping in the door of her house. The claws tightening, ripping deeper into his shoulders and back to stifle his urge to call out.

"Dear God," he whispered, the wetness of tears on his tightly clamped eyelids.

"It's all right, Cap,"Talina told him, her soothing voice next to his ear.

He blinked, vision watery and out of focus.

"Caught me by surprise."

"I know." Talina's face swam into view, and she used a cloth to sponge his eyes. "You did good, Cap. You got my pistol. Those shots you took, that saved us both. Distracted it. Gave me the chance I needed."

Shots? He struggled with vague memories of crawling to where Tal's pistol had been kicked his way in the scuffle. Had he really grasped it? Was that real, or his desperate imagination?

"I shot it?"

"Just before it whacked you with its tail. Raya says it's a wonder you could even stand given the amount of blood you'd lost and as torn up as your back was."

He either imagined or remembered the pistol bucking in his hands, and a losing struggle to hold it steady, to find a sight picture.

And then . . .

"It hit me, didn't it?" He swallowed hard. "After that . . ."

"Hit you with its tail, Cap. Smacked you into the wall, broke you up pretty badly."

He blinked again, struggling to focus on the hazy ceiling overhead. "What's that thing? Up there? Big and round?"

Talina glanced up. "That's a light, Cap. Raya uses it for surgery." She hesitated, glanced questioningly at someone out of sight, then said, "You've been hurt. You're in the hospital. You've got broken bones. Internal injuries. Raya's got the bleeding stopped. I came to tell you to get well."

He heard her voice break as she added, "And . . . that I *love* you and need you to get better."

"I love you, too," he whispered. Light made a halo around her head, shining in her hair and shadowing her face.

"Cap?" Talina told him bravely, "Raya's going to send you back to the dream now. Remember what I told you?"

"You love me. I have to get better."

He felt her lips on his, warm and tender. Tried to respond to them, but things were growing hazy. He was floating again. Down through the gray mist toward his vacuum suit and the freefall. Dropping back to being a mote in the wonder of Creation.

Talina loves me.

All of existence faded in comparison to that.

74

"It's serious." Raya Turnienko sat with her butt hitched up on her desk corner, a cup of coffee in her right hand, the elbow cradled with her left. As she talked, she swung her left foot where it hung free of the floor.

Talina sat in Raya's office chair where it had been pulled out from behind the woman's desk. Outside, a gentle rain spattered on the roof and ran in trickles down the window.

Talina fought an expression of distaste as the quetzal curled inside. Piece of shit.

Raya continued, "The broken legs and pelvis, the liver, spleen, and kidney, those will heal. Same thing with the lacerations. I've managed to suture the worst of the damage. Thank God we've got the antibiotics to kill the infection that was bound to follow. I'll take the drains out in a week or so if there are no complications."

A beat as her dark eyes hardened. "But, Tal, you do understand, there's nothing I can do about the spine. Not here. Not with these facilities."

"The med lab on *Turalon*?" Which meant she'd have to steal the shuttle.

"Best they could do is stabilize him until they made it back to Solar System." Raya took a deep breath. "Talina? When Cap hit that wall his lower thoracic vertebrae were severely . . . well, think of the bones as crushed jelly. And the three fractured cervical vertebrae aren't much better."

Tal leaned forward, dropping her head into her hands. "So, what you're telling me . . ."

"When I dial back the drugs, he's got feeling in his hands, Tal. That's a good sign. I've got him in chemical paralysis. I was able to position and pin the fragments of cervical vertebrae, and I've got the inflammation under control to relieve pressure on the spinal cord in his neck. Whether he'll have use of his upper body? That I won't know until after the cervical fractures begin to form callus and start to knit. Until then I can't risk him moving and screwing it all up."

Talina took a deep breath, trying to soothe the sick feeling in her gut. "This is going to kill him."

"The miracle is that he made it this far. Not only did that thing beat the hell out of him and rip the ever-loving shit out of his back, it bounced him off your counter and nearly threw him through your wall."

"So, what's next?"

"One day at a time, Talina." Raya studied her thoughtfully. "You up for this? It's going to be a long road ahead. If he makes it, it will be because he finds the will to live. That means he's got to have something, someone, to live for."

"I'm in. Raya, the guy saved my life. And had he not bought me the time to kill the thing, who knows how many more it would have taken before we stopped it? This whole fucking town owes him."

Raya nodded, seeming to come to a conclusion. "I just wanted you to know the extent of the damage."

"Yeah. Thanks." Talina stood, winced, and rubbed her neck muscles. "Cap's wasn't the only neck that took a beating. Quetzal tongues are tough as leather, let me tell you."

"In the end, you and Cap were tougher."

"Yeah? You keep believing that, Raya. Fairy tales are good for people. Or so my mama used to say."

She stepped out into the hall, wincing at her own injuries. She might have been a quetzal herself, given how colorful, large, and plentiful her own bruises were turning out to be.

The beast lay like a stone in her belly. Jesus, what came next? The thing had tried to kill her. When would it try again?

"Yeah, well, fuck you," she told it as she headed for the door. She had other trouble just now.

Cap? A paraplegic? She thought back to his smile, the way his blue eyes shone. How he'd taken to the bush, learning, finding himself. She could almost feel his warm and strong hand on her breast. How it had reassured her. The way he'd looked the time she'd come home to find him on her doorstep. He'd given up everything for her.

She stopped, eyes blurring with tears. Leaning against the hallway wall, she fought back the sobs.

75

In the holo, Captain Abibi's tan-brown eyes were level, professional, and unblinking. "Having not heard from you in the allotted twelve hours, I am left with no other conclusion than that the decision to space is mine, and mine alone. As a result of that, I have given the order. *Turalon* is currently accelerating for our inversion point, which we should reach within the week.

"Know that I did not take this step lightly, however. The disposition of my crew, their failing morale, and the contractual requirements and conditions of the returnees necessitated my decision.

"My full report will be placed on file with The Corporation upon our return to Solar System. Should you have an addendum you wish submitted, I will be delighted to attach it herewith.

"I have left you with a heavy-lift, A-Seven series shuttle, serial number 8755089227. Said craft should provide you with access to the entirety of Donovan as well as to the Corporate vessel *Freelander* that we've left in stable orbit around the planet.

"If any of these circumstances or decisions is in contradiction to your express demands, interests, or orders, you must immediately communicate the nature and remedy of that contradiction, and I will do everything in my power to accede to your orders.

"If I do not hear from you in the next twelve hours, I will assume that I have your complete concurrence, and will take all appropriate measures to ensure the success of my mission."

The image flickered out.

Kalico leaned back in her desk chair, rapped her fingers on the scarred duraplast surface, and stared glumly around her office in the admin dome. A sense of despair sucked at her, seeking to pull her down into the depths of depression.

Just a couple of hours until sunrise. That was all she'd promised herself that she'd sleep after the quetzal affair. Instead—and to her horror—she'd awakened and stumbled out to find Dushane's house empty. Worse, when she'd emerged, it was into a rainy night. Checking with the marine standing guard, she found that she'd almost slept around the clock.

"What the hell was wrong with me?" she demanded of herself.

She turned, staring at the dark window behind her. The rain continued. Running nervous fingers through her hair, she stood and paced before the desk, aware of the two marines on guard outside her door.

"Got a minute?" Shig Mosadek asked, appearing in the hallway. His short stature seemed incongruous, though it somehow matched his round face and the pug nose beneath that mop of tangled black hair. A curious gleam lay behind his dark eyes.

"A minute? A week? A couple of years? Hell, I might even have a lifetime, Mister Mosadek."

"Ah, well, then might I invite you to share a drink with me? Inga has decasked, uncasked, decorked . . . Oh, you know, whatever they call it. She's serving a new wine over at the tavern tonight. I wondered if I might buy you a glass while we discuss some of the consequences of your continued presence in Port Authority."

She laughed bitterly. "Yes, I suppose you'd be more than a little concerned about that."

From behind his back, Shig produced a raincoat. "I thought you might benefit from this. I don't know how you might be outfitted for the weather."

She walked over, spreading her arms. "I'm assured that my possessions are aboard that A-Seven out on the shuttle pad. But she's locked up, the crew's somewhere here in town, and more to the point, it's after dark and the gate's locked."

"As it well should be." Shig handed her the raincoat and turned to lead the way. "Have you a place to stay?"

"I . . . No." She made a face as she pulled on the raincoat. "All of this has . . . um, taken me a bit by surprise."

The marines fell in step behind.

"I understand." He led the way out into the night. Misty rain glowed in the cones of the overhead lights. "*Turalon* spacing took us all by surprise. The first we learned about it was when Two Spots reported that Captain Abibi had radioed saying that she was having difficulty receiving any of our transmissions. Two Spots immediately checked the system and radioed her that, to the contrary, our system was working fine."

"And the good captain radioed back that your transmission was breaking up?"

"I would think you were clairvoyant, Supervisor."

She glanced over her shoulder at the two marines. What did they think? Happy to be stranded here, or really pissed off? Half of them had mutinied, wanting to stay. The others, backing Spiro, had voted to return. Or had they? Had it just been a sense of duty? Three of them were still missing. Desertion?

A new unsettling reality now lurked just under her consciousness. The marines had always been her ultimate authority. Had, that, too, gone hollow?

At Inga's, Shig led the way inside and down the stairs. The place assaulted her ears with a low-level roar that dropped a decibel or ten as people recognized her. Shig, however, was smiling and waving to individuals, returning greetings as if they were old friends.

At the bar, Shig led the way to the empty stool at the end that belonged to Perez. With a wave, he dispersed the closest customers and took the chair next to Perez's. "Talina won't mind. She's at the hospital looking after Cap."

Kalico climbed onto Perez's sacred stool and felt a vindictive satisfaction in doing so. "How's he doing?"

"Badly, I'm afraid. The quetzal showed him little mercy. Might have been better if it had killed him." He lifted an eyebrow. "You don't seem sympathetic."

"We didn't part on the best of company."

Shig lifted two fingers as Inga strode down her bar. With a curt nod, she turned back. A big wooden keg rested on blocks in the rear, and from the bung spigot Inga filled one glass full, the other half. She deposited the full one before Kalico; the half she placed on the scarred chabacho at Shig's elbow. As she did the man laid out a coin.

"What's that?" Kalico asked, picking it up. The image of a quetzal head decorated one side, the other sported a crossed pick and shovel. The number two stood out prominently on each side.

"A silver two SDR piece. We've just started to have them struck. I've had Tyrell Lawson working on a master die. Figured we needed our own currency. Me, I've never liked SDRs or yuan. They're made of plastic, you know. Just isn't the same as specie. Oh, we'll keep the plastic and paper currency, of course. The difference being that we'll back them with precious metals and gemstones."

"Starting your own bank?"

"Unfortunately Mr. Wirth forced our hand when he began handing out loans. He might have Port Authority's vices by the balls, but we'd rather not let him get his grip on the rest."

She raised her glass as Shig raised his. "To Donovan," Shig toasted and clinked the rims. She tasted the red liquid, found it only slightly acid. "Not bad."

"We do have certain amenities," Shig told her, replacing his glass. "I like that one."

"A half glass?" She lifted a skeptical eyebrow as she took a bigger swig of her own.

"The better to savor." Shig glanced over his shoulder as a table erupted in laughter behind them. "We need to find you a residence. Several of the domes in the residential section are open."

"I'd rather stay in the shuttle. Though I'll have to figure out a way to get to it."

"Yvette told me that you are welcome to her spare room until you find something more appropriate to your tastes."

"That's kind of her. But I'd rather not."

"She said the bed suited you. But I do understand. If you're not picky, Inga has rooms on the second story of her place. She rents them out to people who come in from the bush."

"I'm picky."

"Then they might not do. You could sleep in Clemenceau's old quarters next to your office, I suppose."

She laughed. "Are we *really* having this conversation? I'm the pus-sucking Supervisor."

"A Corporate personage in a town without a single Corporate

property except an office in the admin dome. A fascinating culmination of events, don't you think?"

She gave him a scathing look. "What do you suggest?"

"I could loan you my study."

"Your study?"

"A small dome behind my garden. I go there to get away, to meditate, to read, and to write my treatises on religion and philosophy. It's clean. Has a small kitchen, a stunning and contemplative view of the perimeter fence, and the bed is most comfortable. I had the sheets—nice chamois ones by the way—changed just on the odd chance you might want to camp there. It's quiet, and you'd have privacy."

She chuckled. "I'm broke. Coinage has been out of style in The Corporation for some time now."

"I'll trade."

"What?"

"Oh, something will come along one of these days. I have faith in you. It won't hold your marines. I'd dicker with Inga over those apartments." He smiled. "She'll extend credit to cover the rentals if I vouch for you."

"You?" She tried to keep the acid out of her voice. "Will vouch for me?"

Shig studied his wine thoughtfully. "You made the right choice, by the way. Letting Abibi and *Turalon* space."

I was a coward. And Abibi knew it. But then, like the time she'd lied to Nandi, Abibi's strength was in letting people believe or do that which worked in the best interest of her ship and crew.

To Shig she said, "Maybe Milton was right. It's better to rule in Hell than to serve in Heaven."

"Which brings me to my question: How do you see this working?"

She considered him through narrowed eyes. "I signed Port Authority over to you. Let you buy the mines, properties, and equipment. That's a done deal. *Freelander,* however—and everything she carried—is still Corporate property. Despite the fact that your people have carted off half of it."

"More like a third."

"Wouldn't matter if it was a quarter. It belongs to The Corporation. We have title. Or is that concept just a sham?"

"Would you prefer if we just left it to sit, rust, and decay on the shuttle field?"

"It would sit, rust, and decay as Corporate property. As Supervisor, it's mine to administer as I see fit. That's Corporate law. Your law, too, if this title and property rights jag of yours is for real."

"How would you enforce it?"

"My marines are Corporate." She glanced around. "And, for the moment, I don't think you've got anyone who could dispute that fact."

Shig gave her that benign smile that curdled her gut. "Then it appears we have a curious impasse. You have the *Freelander* equipment, but no one to run it, and nowhere to employ it. We've got the mines, the know-how, and the people who can fabricate parts and maintain your equipment."

"There's a whole planet out there," she countered. "And I've got more than three hundred people on contract. Something tells me they'll be able to use that equipment just fine."

"And you think you can enforce that contract if they're no longer willing?"

"I have marines."

"You'd have revolution. As we learned the other night, those waters have already been tempestuously churned. They need time to settle out and again grow tranquil."

She arched a challenging eyebrow, her mind clicking through possibilities. "So, tell me, what do you suggest?"

"You have more than marines. You have a heavy lift shuttle."

"And?"

"As you said, it's a big planet, one with better ore deposits and richer diggings than we've been working here. Our people are settled. Making a nice living when something isn't eating them, thank you. Your transportees need direction, a chance to make their own wealth. Your shuttle and equipment—more than your marines—allows them the opportunity to do so."

"What's the triumvirate's angle in all this? What do you get out of it?"

"Survival." He tilted his wine in her direction. "And on Donovan, that's all that matters."

"Status and power?"

He shook his head. "Clemenceau had those alleged advantages. He might not have had marines, but he had Talina Perez and her security force. At least in the beginning."

She said nothing, letting her expression communicate her distaste at the ultimate outcome for Clemenceau.

Shig raised his eyebrows in response. "Supervisor, let me ask: How smart are you?"

Just as she formed an unpleasant retort, he raised a hand. "I care not for what you knew back in Solar System, but how clever, capable, and agile are you when it comes to learning new rules, adapting, and finding innovative ways to solve problems in a totally novel environment."

"That's what it takes, huh?"

"That's what it takes."

"Off the record. Given all that's behind us . . . after all, I wanted you arrested and shot. Surely there's part of you that wants to see me fail. That would revel in my defeat and destruction."

"Actually—and much to my surprise—you've succeeded remarkably well to this point. Your first test was the trial. You were smart enough to back off—though it was a closely run thing. You could have failed again when we asked you to honor the titles. And finally, you've shown promise by staying behind."

"I was left."

"Oh, come. The sham about radio communications makes a satisfying cover story. Abibi's a professional. She gave you an out."

"Don't buy the story that I was afraid." *Damn you, Cap.*

"You'd be a fool if you weren't."

"I overslept."

"Uh huh."

"Are you purposefully trying to enrage me?"

"By no means." Shig smiled peacefully and took a delicate sip of his wine again. "I'm establishing that I think you have a chance here. Oh, to be sure, you're struggling to surmount a lot of cultural debris clogging your mental pathways, but if you can manage to set that aside, look past who you were back on Transluna, ignore who you wanted to be back then, I think you're capable of great things on Donovan."

"You're saying I have potential?" She snapped off the words.

"More so than the vast majority of transportees who come here."

"Transportee? Thanks for your glowing endorsement." She let the acid drip.

Shig, as if oblivious, said, "You're welcome."

"Maybe I should still have you shot."

"The evening is young. And, as you say, you do have marines."

Kalico shook her head. "You're all lunatics."

"Lunacy is catching, Supervisor. It's Donovan. My suspicion is that you'll have caught a dose of it yourself before this is all over."

And with that, he clinked her glass in a toast.

76

"H*ey, handsome man, how are you doing?"* The words had echoed around the inside of Cap's head for hours as he stared at the eternity of his hospital room ceiling. Talina had said it that morning as she breezed in. He'd answered in his croaking voice. Turnienko had dialed back the drugs just enough to let him speak.

For most of the visit, she'd pulled up a chair and sat just out of his field of vision. Her talk had been bright, optimistic. She'd told of how *Turalon* had spaced and was headed for the inversion point. Of how Supervisor Aguila now lived in Shig Mosadek's little work studio as she took an inventory on the *Freelander* cargo. Of how Cap just needed to concentrate on healing and obey Turnienko's orders, and how he'd be out of hospital before he knew it.

He had replied with short pleasantries: "Oh?" "Good." "Really?"

"That's it for now," she'd told him, appearing again in his cone of vision. Holding her hair back, she'd given him a kiss and claimed, "I'll be back in a couple of hours."

And, but for a couple of checks by Turnienko to monitor his IV pack and his urine for blood and volume, he'd had nothing but the eternity of the ceiling.

The doctor had laid it all out: the fractures in his spine and neck, the broken ribs and legs. How he was lucky to be alive.

Cap had taken it, told her he understood, and waited until she'd left the room before he surrendered to the hollow agony that still possessed him.

In the days since, he'd pleaded with Turnienko to let him die. Made her swear not to tell Talina. And the Siberian doctor had given him a knowing smile, her dark eyes like cold stones behind the flat features of her face.

He heard the steps as someone entered the room, and called out,

"Tal? That you?" He could no longer judge time. It could have been a couple of hours since she left. Maybe days for all he knew.

"Sorry."

The face appeared as he shifted his eyes as far to the left as they'd go. "You?"

"Me."

"What are you doing here?"

"You have quite a string of enemies. Now, here you are. Sure, they could fix you up back at Transluna. Tailor a genetic regeneration program and trick your bones into growing back together. Initiate spinal cord growth, nerve renewal, and orchestrate the remodeling of scar tissue." A pause. "But not here. Turnienko doesn't have the technology or the specialized skill."

"Okay, you've really cheered me up. Now, get the hell out."

"Have you heard the saying on Donovan? That people come here to find themselves, to leave, or to die? Which of those applies to you?"

Cap took a breath, one of the few controls he still had over his body. "You'd think it was to die, wouldn't you?" He wet his lips. "But it was to find myself."

"So . . . did you?"

Cap smiled. "You wouldn't understand."

A pause, as if for thought.

Finally the question: "You know why I'm here?"

"I think so. If I'm wrong I'll be disappointed in my judgment of human nature."

"How do you want me to do it?"

"They've got me drugged. I won't feel a bullet . . . or a blade. So, pain's out, if that's what you were looking forward to."

"Still, choose. I'm curious as to what it will be."

Cap flicked his eyes to the right and down. "There, on the IV pack on my arm. See the little wheel? With your thumb, spin it open."

"And what happens?"

"It paralyzes the rest of me. Lungs, heart. I just fade away."

"Why don't I just slit your throat?"

"Couldn't feel it if you did. The dramatic effect will be wasted.

Why horrify whoever walks through that door next? And someone, probably Turnienko's assistant, Felicity, will have to clean up the mess."

"You'd still see your blood blowing through your severed windpipe."

"What did Felicity ever do to you?"

Cap swallowed hard, smiled as his visitor walked around the bed and reached for his right arm.

"Thanks," he whispered.

"Call it an ultimate act of love."

Cap nodded. Closed his eyes, let himself drift. In moments he'd be back, floating in his vacuum suit, forever in the miracle of freefall . . .

77

Talina Perez sat on an angular chunk of sandstone, her gaze fixed on the fresh red mound of earth. At its head a duraplast marker read, "Captain Maxwell Taggart. Corporate Marine. Killed by Quetzal."

Filling her lungs with the morning, she let the gentle breeze coming in from the Gulf play with the few strands of hair that had escaped her braid. Her rifle lay across her knees. A stone's throw away, Capella's slanting sunlight illuminated the eastern side of Donovan's stone monument where it dominated the cemetery.

On the other side of Cap's grave, ferngrass had grown thickly over Mitch's final resting place. Earlier she'd straightened his duraplast marker and given it a pat.

She glanced over her shoulder as Shig came striding up, his hands behind his back, the wind tousling his unruly mop of hair. The morning sun reflected his beatific smile—might have powered it, as a matter of fact. He wore faded brown overalls and quetzal-hide boots that shimmered in rainbow patterns.

"You shouldn't be out here."

Shig found his way to another of the square sandstone rocks. When the backhoe pulled them up, the operators had made a habit of leaving them out rather than have the bereaved watch a big, heavy chunk of stone be dumped atop their beloved dead. As if death weren't enough of an indignity.

Shig seated himself and said, "I think I'm safe. What quetzal in its right mind would brave Talina Perez when she has her rifle across her lap?"

As if it heard, the beast inside shifted.

"Don't be so cavalier. We have to completely rethink quetzals—and probably most of Donovanian life. Molecular communication? Sibling relationships? A willingness to sacrifice themselves for a vendetta? The fact that I was specifically targeted and hunted down with all of Port Authority to choose from? That it figured out how to hide in the cargo so that we carried it in? We're talking abstraction and intelligence here. Because it's alien just means it's going to be harder for us to understand."

"Let alone the fact that you have one inside you."

"And I want it *out*!"

"Cheng's working on that. Haven't seen him this happy in years."

Talina closed her eyes and rubbed her face. "It wants me dead, Shig."

"Yet, it saved you in the bush."

"Because it knew its mate was coming for me. Probably why the one out at Briggs' didn't kill me. It 'read' in my spit that I was targeted by another."

"Despite all of that, how are you doing?"

"I'm sitting beside the grave of another man I loved, Shig. Enraged. Outside of feeling like something's been ripped out of my heart and soul with rusty pliers, I'm a fucking model of beaming joy and happiness."

She ground her teeth as the grief knot pulled tight in her throat and the tears came.

"I *don't* know what to do." She clenched her hands on her rifle. "Raya found the drug dial open. All the way. Max couldn't have done that. Someone else did. Max was murdered."

She wiped the snot from her nose, heart hammering. "Half of me wants to find whoever did it and blow their fucking head off. And half of me wants to kiss whoever did it for . . . for . . ."

She shook her head, finally admitting, "Shig, part of me is so relieved I can't tell you. And that disgusts me."

Had it been revenge or mercy? If the latter, had it been done for his sake? Or hers? And if hers, it just added to her sense of futility.

"Cap made a lot of enemies, Tal. When an individual embarks on the process of authentic self-discovery the people around him or her are left feeling betrayed. The person they thought they knew—and could predict and depend upon for their own needs—necessarily becomes someone different. It causes distress all the way around."

"Then why bother in the first place?"

"Growth and the pursuit of enlightenment are the way of the universe. Cap Taggart took a mighty step from *tamas* toward *sattva.*"

"What if I don't buy your Buddhist crap?"

"That's Hindu."

"Whatever."

"It doesn't matter what we deny or accept. The universe is as it is. Matter and energy transitioning back and forth. Changing relationships between particles. Whether souls are modalities or not, observation creates reality. All of which imperceptivity changes the fabric of the universe itself. So I think I'm on pretty firm ground."

"Charming." A pause. "I'm tired of death, Shig. I'm tired of falling in love and losing them. I'm tired of *hurting*."

"All is *dukkha*. The scars will remain, and they will toughen and turn white with age. But you will heal. You'll go on."

Talina rubbed the tears from her face, the breeze cooling her damp cheeks. "*Turalon* inverted symmetry in the middle of the night. I wonder if she'll make it?"

"Like Schrödinger's cat?" He shrugged. "Perhaps. On the other hand, in a perversity of physics, if a ship appears in orbit five or six years from now, we may discover the cat lived."

"If it happens it'll still be years from now. That's an eternity on Donovan. We'd damned well better be planning on making it on our own."

"The *Freelander* cargo significantly increases our odds. Though the Supervisor claims it as her property. How she maintains her authority and defends her title will be interesting in light of Donovan's realities."

"You might be letting her live in your studio, but you know Aguila's going to be a problem. She's not going to fit in."

"Unless she surprises me with some hidden strength of character, that might indeed be the case." Shig spread his hands, face tilted to the sun, eyes closed as if in worship.

"Want me to just put a bullet in her brain?"

"Not for the time being. Though I may live to regret that decision." He filled his lungs and sighed. "This morning I just needed a walk. Oh, and to remind you that we had a council meeting this afternoon."

"Council?"

"That's what Dan Wirth calls it. He seems to think we're a sort of government, given that we're striking coins and all."

"A government?"

"It's no longer just us old hands who've simply let things work as they may. And, to my absolute distaste, if we don't establish and codify the way we want things to function, either Wirth or Aguila will. Each has his or her own power base, and worse, are willing to use them."

"Aw shit." Talina's gut fell. "Do I have to be there?"

"No. But I can't imagine you'd have been happy to learn that we met with him without your knowledge, or that you wouldn't want to be there on the chance you might discover his hidden motives."

"Damn you, are you always right?"

"Only perceptive."

78

Dan brought his own cup of coffee laced with a shot of whiskey. He nodded at Step Allenovich, who was headed the other way, a use-scarred rifle hanging from his knobby right hand.

Making his way down the hallway, he had to admit, the world was looking up.

Entering into the conference room, it was to find Shig Mosadek and Yvette Dushane already seated across from each other at the far end of the table. Their own coffee cups—apparently the only symbols of office—rested on the scarred wood. In the center, on a hot pad, was a steaming two-liter pot of black coffee.

"Well, good to see the both of you," Dan greeted. "Quite the day, huh? *Turalon*'s spaced for home, her holds packed with plunder. Wonder what the Boardmembers are going to say to that when she docks at Transluna?"

"They'll erupt with a thousand exclamations of glee, no doubt," Yvette told him coldly. "So just what, if I might ask, goaded you to call this meeting?"

Dan seated himself, flipping out a coin as he did so. "A 100 SDR gold piece? Seriously?"

Yvette stared coldly at him, as though it bore no need of response.

Shig picked up the coin and studied it in the light cast by the window. "Excellent detail, don't you think? But then, you wouldn't know, having never seen a mundo tree."

"Where's the gold for all these coins coming from?" Dan asked, as if an afterthought.

"We surely didn't hand everything over to Aguila." Yvette continued her cold stare. "For a time, Brian Malverson was the richest man on Donovan. Took him twenty trips—and that was when the heavy-lift trucks were flying—to haul all of his gold into Port Authority. It's stashed somewhere safe."

"To be credible, a bank must have a reserve." Shig spun the coin around his fingers, and with a flip of the wrist, made it disappear. "You've forced us into a market economy. The old hit-or-miss barter system was strained as it was. The yuan and SDR notes were wearing out. With titles and deeds guaranteed—not to mention used by people such as yourself for collateral—we couldn't very well expect people to trade a stack of chamois hides for a house, could we?"

Dan cocked his head. Even as he formed a reply, Talina Perez entered, walked past him without so much as a look, and propped her rifle against the wall as she took a seat next to Yvette. From her belt pouch she produced a collapsible cup and dipped up coffee.

She wore her old black, patched-up uniform. The knife and pistol at her hip added to the menacing and deadly air she projected. But look at her face, and it was to see a woman tortured with grief.

Good.

He'd wondered if Cap Taggart was just a fling for her. A short-term sack partner. One of the few men she didn't completely intimidate. As threatening as she was, it had to be hard to find a man who could keep it up long enough and vigorously enough to ring her pelvic charms.

Given the red-eyed and haggard look, the tension around her mouth, she'd really cared for the guy. That brought a smile to his lips. *Suffer, bitch. Suffer.*

He pasted a happy smile on his face, saying brightly, "Good. We're all here. I guess we can get started."

"Started with what?" Shig asked, and with a snap of his fingers, the coin appeared as if by magic. Good trick, that.

"We had a potential problem with the transportees. Disgruntled, disillusioned, incipient revolt, blood in the streets, remember?"

"Which I believe you said you were going to handle." Yvette stared at him over her coffee cup.

"Misters Oman and Paloduro demonstrated a change of heart." Dan caught the coin when Shig flipped it his way.

"Haven't seen them around," Shig noted. "My sources tell me that their successors have had a parting of the ways, that many are unsure what to do." He smiled. "And then there's the Supervisor. She's a new piece to the puzzle. She's insisting that as The Corporation's Supervisor, she still has their contracts."

"Yes. A complication, wouldn't you say?"

"The problem isn't the woman," Yvette said in velvet tones overlaying steel. "It's her marines. I can only speak for the three of us, but we're not going to stand in their way if they start combing the streets for transportees. That's their business and hers."

"Which," Shig reminded, "I believe might include you. Or don't I recall a clause allowing The Corporation to reassign a transportee to a related field?"

Dan grinned. "If she had *anything* related to a dead cow, I might consider it. Alas, even if she did, I'd have to decline. So many things on my plate these days. All those minor irritations like Paloduro and Oman. Word is that they've opted to explore distant fields. Doubt they'll be causing any further trouble."

Shig replied amiably. "My sources tell me they disappeared the night the quetzal got in."

"Maybe it ate them." Dan let his smile beam.

At that, Perez swiveled her head and shot him a deadly look. "Not even slightly funny, mister."

"Sorry, Security Officer." He let his eyes narrow in reply to hers. "Perhaps the boys just wandered off. I hear we're still missing three marines, too. And, now that *Turalon* is gone, we've got bits and pieces of her crew showing up by ones and twos."

Dan gestured. "You people putting in a claim for them? Leaving them for Aguila? Or calling them free agents?"

"Free agents," Yvette snapped.

"Okay, fine by me. Let them make their own ways." He cleared his throat. "Some, however, have already entered into agreements. I've got paper on them. Signed of their own free will and accord."

"What kind of paper?" Talina asked darkly.

"A contract, security officer. A *legal* contract. For labor. Nothing else."

A chill eased up his spine on mouse feet as she glared at him. That alien blackness filled her eyes. It was all he could do to keep from raising his hands and backing away.

"A contract is a contract," Shig agreed. "As long as there was no coercion."

"I may be many things, but I'm not stupid. No coercion. And I have witnesses to that fact."

"Good." The way Yvette sighted at him over her coffee cup was eerily similar to how she'd be squinting over pistol sights.

The cold death in Perez's eyes tickled the fear instinct in his gut.

"Excuse me," she said. "I think I need a breath of clean air."

Everyone in the room watched her rise, grab up her rifle, and walk from the room. Nevertheless, she pinned him with her eyes the whole way.

Relieved, Dan took a breath and said, "In summary, I think we're in pretty good shape. With *Turalon* gone, a lot of the uncertainty went with it. I don't see any problem keeping a lid on the remaining transportees. Unless the Supervisor wants them."

Yvette said, "Get between her and them at your own peril. As for us, we're going to declare ourselves neutral."

Shig told him. "There will be enough other problems as the new reality sinks in. Hopefully we can continue to find areas of mutual cooperation."

Wirth got to his feet, gave them a salute with his coffee cup. "Always a delight to do business with you."

He thought of Perez, of the look she'd given him. *You got what you had coming to you, you alien-infested witch.*

As he exited into the hallway, he was already planning. Not a word had been said about the method of Paloduro and Oman's disappearance. He liked how the triumvirate worked. Approved of a "no questions asked" policy. They were all complicit now.

So, they have a cache of gold? They're starting a central bank and minting coins. Aguila is going to enforce contract on the transportees.

"How do I profit from this?"

God, he *loved* opportunity!

79

The whole thing was by chance. Trish had seen Talina as she emerged from the admin dome. She knew that walk. Tal was a woman on a mission. That she cycled the bolt on her rifle as she left, checking to ensure a round was chambered, bespoke the ominous.

Trish chewed her lower lip for a moment, frowned. Putting Cap in the ground had hit Talina hard. But, damn it, Donovan wasn't a forgiving place. It wasn't like Talina Perez hadn't buried a man before, and this one would have ultimately suffocated her.

Shit, she'd really loved him.

Wonder what that's like?

Nevertheless, Trish cut across behind the equipment shed, hurried past the parts depot, and rounded the corner just in time to see Talina climbing the roof access ladder to the assay office. Even as the athletic woman stepped onto the roof, she was unslinging her rifle.

Trish took a deep breath, shook her head, and sprinted to the base of the ladder. Step by step she crept her way up and peered over the stone wall to the sloped roof.

Talina was settling herself behind the meter-high stone false front overlooking the main street. She'd taken a kneeling position, left knee up, right out at an angle, ankle under her butt. She pulled the rifle up to her shoulder, left arm supporting, elbow on her knee as she sighted down the barrel.

On cat feet, Trish topped the roof. The breeze played with her hair, tossing it about. A loose bit of roofing rattled slightly with each gust, covering any sound she might have made.

Taking a position just behind and to the left, she could just see the street and those passing beneath.

"Oh, shut up," Talina said under her breath. "The only thing you and I have left is death. And if I go, you're gone with me, son of a bitch."

Trish made a face. That tone of voice? She was talking to the damn quetzal inside her.

Or was she just insane? A new Donovanian form of mental illness that needed its own definition in the psychiatric diagnostic manuals.

"There he is," Talina told the quetzal. "Thinks I didn't know." She settled her cheek to the stock, eye behind the optics.

Trish took another step forward, the roof squeaking just as she saw Dan Wirth walking happily down the center of the street.

Talina whirled, the rifle, like a thing alive, centering on Trish's chest. The cold quivering of guts and ticking of the nerves at her center was instantaneous, almost debilitating.

"Tal?" her voice wavered. "Don't shoot. It's me, for God's sake!"

Talina exhaled in relief, lowered the rifle. "Trish, what the *hell* are you doing?"

"Came to see who you were going to shoot."

"That fucker, Dan Wirth. Heard from Toby Montoya. Wirth and Cap had words. Almost came to a killing. Not even an hour before the siren went off."

"What if he didn't kill Cap?"

Talina's eyes narrowed. "What do you mean?"

"I've been asking around. Talking to Katsuro."

"Been seeing a lot of him, haven't you?"

"What of it." She held her hands out, hoping to placate the violence in Tal's eyes. "Lots of people wanted Cap dead, starting with Supervisor Aguila. Then there's Lieutenant Spiro and about half of the marines. They're still trying to figure out if the three missing marines were sent to kill Cap, and he got them first."

"That's nuts."

"And Tal, there are other people."

"What other people?"

"About half of Port Authority." Trish felt her gut harden into something that felt like dried leather. "People who knew Cap. Knew you. People who understood that you'd sacrifice yourself to care for an invalid. People who heard Cap beg for death. It wasn't any secret, except from you. Ask Raya."

"Name me some names."

Trish laughed. "Inga, me, Step, Yvette, Iji, Cheng, Mellie, Two Spots, Felicity, hell, probably even Shig. You going to kill us all?"

"So you're saying this was done for me?"

"I . . . I don't know, Tal." Trish spread her arms, dropped to the extending wall, and felt suddenly exhausted. "Hell, go ahead. Shoot the son of a bitch. One of us is going to have to in the end. Might as well be today, but from what I've heard, he may not be the person you're after." Her nervous laughter reeked of bitterness. "For all I know it might even have been Raya herself."

"Pragmatism has never been Raya's weak point." Talina wearily shook her head, resettling herself, back against the wall. "I'm just hurting. Angry. And this fucking thing inside me doesn't give me any rest. It hates me. Wants me dead. And I'm starting to agree with it."

"Don't, Tal. Please. You're not alone in this."

"I loved him." Her head drooped and she picked absently at her rifle.

"So? Living's a dangerous business. You're special, Tal. People *need* you. To be needed like that? Respected and looked up to? That's remarkable. More so than you've ever understood."

"Lucky fucking me."

"I mean it." Trish stood. "Well, shit. We talked so long he's out of sight." She smiled crookedly. "Buy you a beer? Your stool's open."

Talina gave her a half-lidded stare. "Are you insane?"

"Hey, I'm not the one with a quetzal inside me. You coming? Or am I drinking alone?"

Talina's laughter reeked of bitterness and defeat. She shook her head, lines of fatigue darkening beneath her eyes. "Yeah. If you're not bullshitting about buying."

"Got one of these new coins Shig is striking. A gold five-SDR piece. Should set us up for the whole night."

"Well, get your ass down that ladder then. Neither one of us is getting any younger." Talina flipped the safety on and shouldered the rifle.

With a relieved smile, Trish led the way.

80

Three months had passed since *Turalon* had spaced. A soft rain was falling when Pete Morgan stomped the mud off his boots and stepped into The Jewel. He tugged the quetzal-hide hat off of his head and gave it a shake to clear the water off.

As he tramped across the floor, he was feeling pretty good about himself. Thank God he knew how to operate a core drill. He'd signed on with Ollie Throlson when it became apparent that Supervisor Aguila was serious about enforcing contracts. The last place he wanted to be was in town where marines were conscripting people. The Throlson claim lay out west on the other side of the Wind Mountains. Atop a large dome formation, it had originally been recorded as a potential location for hydrocarbons.

Ollie had managed to snare one of the core drills before Supervisor Aguila could get it recorded on her inventory. Lawson had figured out how to power it with a steam-powered electrical generator.

Drilling mud hadn't been a problem given the lubricity of the local clays.

Now Pete was back, a skip in his walk and joy in his heart. He'd survived for three months in the bush. He'd done what no one had ever done before. His father would be so proud.

There, in the back, at a poker game, sat Dan Wirth. The guy looked good. Pete recognized the blonde beauty who stood beside his chair as Allison. Word was that she was running the girls who worked in the back. That, for the right money, she'd take a turn herself. And that, assuming a man could afford it, it was the kind of ride he'd never forget.

Something—a subtle sense of warning—caused Pete to hesitate. An urge filled him to just turn around and walk out.

"Ah, foolishness." He started forward again, calling, "Dan, you old scoundrel, how are you doing?"

Wirth looked up. Took a second. Then smiled. "Pete Morgan. How's life treating you?"

"I've come to celebrate. Ollie Throlson and I have the first producing oil well on Donovan. It's just the start. We've a ways to go. Have to cobble together a refinery. But it's a fuel technology that we don't have to depend on Solar System for."

"Glad to hear it." Dan chuckled, glancing up at Allison. "My dear, this is Pete Morgan. The dire man who swore that Donovan was a disaster. Now look at him. Dressed in quetzal, wearing chamois. And, by damn straight, as they say here, there's a pistol on his hip."

"You don't work in the bush without one," Pete told him. "Can I buy you a drink?"

"Sure." Wirth disengaged himself from the game, slapped Pete on the shoulder, and led him over to the bar along the wall. "This one's on me, Pete."

Wirth cocked his head as the drinks were poured. "How long you been in town?"

"Just got in. Not more than an hour. Figured I'd come see how you're doing."

"You're a good man. Not everyone comes so quickly to pay their debts?"

"Debts?"

"The two thousand you owe me."

Pete sipped at the whiskey. "I don't understand."

"Yeah, lot's happened since then, huh?" Wirth reached in his back pocket. Pulled out a little book and started flipping through the pages.

"Hey, you don't mean . . . Dan, that was a joke."

Wirth's eyes had taken on a deadly glint when he looked up. "I don't joke about a debt, Pete. Two thousand yuan, remember? And, surely it couldn't be my eyes. I'd swear you're dressed just like a Donovanian."

"But I don't have . . ."

"First producing oil well? Ah, but you will, won't you?"

Feeling sick to his stomach, Pete Morgan nodded. Glancing over his shoulder, he could see Art Maniken watching, a cold promise in his eyes.

He'd heard about Maniken. Fear sent its icy little fingers through him. "Yeah, you know I'm good for it."

"You gotta love Donovan, don't you?" Wirth slapped him on the back again. "Of course you're good for it. And we all know that well out there will pay. All I ask is a small part of it."

Morgan could only nod.

EPILOGUE

Kalico Aguila might have been many things. What she was not was stupid. Shig Mosadek's words had sunk in with a passion.

"Oh, to be sure, you're struggling to surmount a lot of cultural debris clogging your mental pathways, but if you can manage to set that aside, look past who you were back on Transluna, ignore who you wanted to be back then, I think you're capable of great things on Donovan."

That agility of thought and action he'd mentioned had taken only a couple of days to figure out after *Turalon* spaced. She had a heavy-lift shuttle. Marines with tech. Equipment from *Freelander*. And a whole world to choose from.

The outcrop on the southern flank of the Wind Mountains lay just inland from the Gulf, nearly five hundred klicks south of Port Authority. A thick forest of chabacho and the occasional mundo tree had covered a rich outcrop of gold, silver, and palladium intermixed with rare-earth elements. The once-deep deposit had been thrust up at an angle. Above it the slope rose ever higher, finally ending in jagged peaks. Kalico had simply ordered Spiro to scorch the ground with high explosives and incendiaries, just like she would if she were establishing a forward operating base in a hostile combat environment.

Next Kalico had traded with a miner: his working bulldozer in exchange for a selection of inoperative haulers from *Freelander*. Within a day her people had bladed away the soil. A week after that they had finished setting up an electrified perimeter fence, materials for which had been found in two sialon containers from *Freelander*'s hold.

The great dome that had been stacked on the landing field had been raised in another two days.

Starting tomorrow, the mining engineers she'd required to fulfill their contracts would begin the first rock fragmentation. Within a week the samples would be flown off to Port Authority for assay.

On the flat below the outcrop, several kilometers to the north, a second clearing beside the river was being hacked out of the forest. The smelter and farm would be established there.

To date—as they'd built the compound—they'd only had to bury four men who'd fallen prey to the wildlife. Not a great record, but acceptable by Donovanian standards. The good news was that no one dared to desert. Not with the bush just meters from the perimeter fence.

That night, an hour before moonrise, she stood beneath the starry sky. Head tilted back, she stared up at the astral patterns and enjoyed the view: a frosting of soft twinkling light laid atop the velvet black.

Turalon had vanished just there, in front of that constellation, hundreds of thousands of kilometers from where she stood.

Thank God I'm not on that ship.

Would there be another? Ever?

Kalico smiled. Perhaps they'd already figured out the navigational problem back in Solar System. Even if they hadn't, human curiosity was what it was. It might be five years, or ten, but eventually that terrible need to know would get the better of them.

It would probably be a small scout and survey ship. Not the sort of thing to waste trillions of SDRs on should it be lost, but eventually it would appear in Donovan's night sky. That was as inevitable as gravity.

"And when it does"—she knotted a hard fist—"it will find me here. And this planet will be mine."